Dear Reader,

Are you like me? Do you have 'reading moods'? Sometimes I like a story with an element of mystery in it, on other occasions I enjoy a sexy read; there are times when I love my romance novels spiced with a little humour and others when I look forward to a warm and involving family-centred story. How about you?

Each month, I work hard to provide a balanced list for you, to ensure that every *Scarlet* reader's taste is catered for. As you can imagine, this is quite a difficult feat, particularly as I may suddenly be offered four similar stories – four tale, all at one time. So fa res, it seems that we're t us know, won't you rly want to see more o ou think is missing fr In the light of the current interest in Jane Austen, would you like *Scarlet* to include some Regency romances?

Keep those letters and questionnaires coming, won't you?

Till next month,

Sally Cooper

SALLY COOPER,
Editor-in-Chief – *Scarlet*

About the Author

Andrea Young started writing because it was a wonderful excuse for not doing housework! She has lived in Cyprus, Abu Dhabi and Oman and has variously been a model, an air stewardess and a teacher of English as a foreign language.

Andrea now lives in Surrey with her husband, two teenage daughters, and, as she says, 'a barmy Spaniel and the fattest cat in the Home Counties!' She's currently hard at work on her second novel for *Scarlet*.

*Other **Scarlet** titles available this month:*

NEVER SAY NEVER – Tina Leonard
COME HOME FOR EVER – Jan McDaniel
WOMAN OF DREAMS – Angela Drake

ANDREA YOUNG

WICKED IN SILK

SCARLET

Enquiries to:
Robinson Publishing Ltd
7 Kensington Church Court
London W8 4SP

First published in the UK by Scarlet, 1996

A copy of the British Library Cataloguing in
Publication data is available from the British Library

ISBN 1-85487-719-4

Printed and bound in the EC

10 9 8 7 6 5 4 3 2 1

For my own 'Category Four', who bore domestic chaos with saintly patience. For my daughters, who kindly told me they'd hate one of those weird mums who actually *iron* things. For my mother, who read out my stars over the phone and kept telling me I'd do it in the end. For Squidgy Boy, who inspired Portly. For Beryl, who saw the sharks. And for Shirley, who was always on the end of the phone when I needed her.

CHAPTER 1

Long before the taxi pulled up outside the restaurant, Claudia was having second thoughts. Third and fourth thoughts too.

By the time it stopped her mouth felt like freeze-dried sawdust. Even now, it would be so easy to run away. One horrified gasp while she was paying the cabbie and a neat little fib about having left the gas on, and he'd have her home again in half an hour.

Don't even think of it, she told herself fiercely. *Since when are you a quitter?*

She tipped the cabbie with reckless generosity and wished she were dead. Three times she walked past that discreet black door. She'd never been there before, but she'd read write-ups in the glossies. Smart, French, with heart-failure prices.

Just do it, Claudia. Take a deep breath and open that door. One, two three . . .

With icy aplomb, she swept in.

She stood erect, clutching her black cashmere coat around her. All the tables were occupied. There was a discreet buzz of conversation and the hum of well-heeled Londoners doing justice to the chef.

She picked him out at once, at a secluded round corner table, bathed in soft candlelight.

Guy Hamilton.

That face had been etched on her memory. Hair the colour of old, polished mahogany, just long enough to show a slight wave. Medium olive skin. The kind of nose and chin that lesser mortals don't mess with. And the kind of looks to make your worst female enemy hate you even more if he happened to have his arm around your waist at a party.

He lifted a bottle from the silver ice-bucket, offered it to an elderly lady on his right. There was an elderly man at his table too, and an exotically attractive girl in her early twenties.

Claudia was rapidly aware of the lessening chat at nearby tables. She knew she presented a dramatic figure: all in black, her coppery hair swept up, her skin creamy pale against the cashmere.

As if sensing her scrutiny, he looked up.

For several seconds, as their eyes locked, Claudia was paralysed with terror.

There was a tactful cough at her elbow. 'Can I be of assistance, *Madame*?'

It was too late to run away. Ignoring the head waiter, she swept across the room.

'How can you do this?' With an impassioned sweep of her hand, she indicated the half-finished rack of lamb, the lobster, the Château Latour. 'What is all this costing? What about us, Guy? Don't you care about me, and the baby?'

There were sharp intakes of breath all round the table. Before anybody recovered enough to utter, she ploughed on, her voice quivering with emotion. 'How can you deny his existence? He needs you, Guy!'

2

Over the restaurant had fallen a deathly hush as the other diners realized there was something far more interesting going on than their own conversation.

She turned to his guests. To the elderly lady, trying to contain her well-bred horror. To the elderly man whose face had gone a nasty shade of purple.

Her voice trembled, but it was dignified, her head held high. 'This man is the father of my son. All I want is for him to acknowledge his existence.'

For several long seconds there was an appalled silence. Not a fork fell, not a glass was lifted.

'Guy, what is going on?' said the elderly lady, aghast. 'Who is this woman?'

'I have no idea.' The Hamilton voice was deep and crisp and ominous. He rose swiftly to his feet, tossing his white linen napkin aside.

Although Claudia stood five feet nine in her heels, she seemed to have shrunk in the wash. The eyes that looked down on her were navy blue, and about as warm as a Scottish loch in winter. 'Have you finished?'

Never had she understood so well that expression about being hanged for a sheep as a lamb. With one swift movement she slipped off her coat to reveal the cream silk teddy, the frothy suspenders – and the red rose pinned at her cleavage. With a flourish, she drew the pin from her hair, letting it cascade about her shoulders. With the other hand she released the rose and offered it to him with a wide, sweet smile.

'Happy birthday, Guy,' she said, with only the tiniest wobble.

The stunned silence was broken by a peal of helpless laughter from the girl.

Nobody else was laughing. The icy disapproval could not have been more marked if she'd stripped at a Buckingham Palace Garden Party. But Claudia was on autopilot to the bitter end.

The next few seconds were a blur; elusive male scent as her lips made an upward dash for his face, the smooth-shaved roughness of his cheek, firm hands on her waist, putting her sharply from him, and firmer fingers on her arm, propelling her to the door.

Once outside, Claudia almost collapsed in her relief that it was over. Only, unfortunately, it wasn't.

'Just for the record,' he said, in tones as chill as the November air, 'how much were you paid to embarrass my guests and interrupt a passable dinner?'

'I haven't been paid anything yet,' she retorted, scrambling back into her coat. 'I did it for a bet.'

Part of a bet might have been more accurate, but it wasn't time for splitting hairs.

'You did this for a *bet*?' His voice rose with sarcastic incredulity. 'Forgive me for asking, but did I wrong you in a previous life?'

'It was just a joke,' she retorted. 'Where's your sense of humour?'

'Believe it or not, I seem to be suffering a major humour failure.'

He stepped off the pavement to hail a passing cab. As it pulled into the kerb the driver leaned over enquiringly. 'Where to, mate?'

Guy Hamilton whipped a wallet from his pocket, thrust a note at him. 'As far as possible.' With that, he took Claudia's arm and steered her cab-wards.

Indignantly she shook him off. 'Do you mind?'

His reply was crisp and unequivocal. 'I want to make quite sure you're gone.'

After all she'd been through, it was a bit much. 'You wretched misery! You deserve to be embarrassed. I hope you get indigestion.'

'Do you, indeed? I'm sorry to disappoint you, but it'll take a damn sight more than you to embarrass me.'

His voice took on a dangerous edge. 'And one last thing, for the record. For a kissogram, it was a pretty dismal failure. Do it properly next time. Like this.'

She was too astonished to protest as he took her in his arms. There was no pussy-footing about with tentative nibbles. It was the firm, compelling possession of a mouth already conveniently open, and gaping like a goldfish.

And it lasted all of five seconds.

'Here endeth the first lesson,' he said, yanking the cab door open. 'Off you go.'

With that, he bundled her into the cab.

Claudia was almost speechless. As the cab pulled away she yanked the window down. 'Why are you taking it out on me?' she yelled. 'It was your girlfriend who ordered it!'

There was no reply. He stood motionless on the pavement till the cab was out of sight.

'Had a bad day, love?' enquired the cabbie tactfully.

Claudia pushed the window up again. 'You could say that,' she muttered.

At the end of a one-way street he stopped at a cross-roads. 'I know he said as far as possible, love, but that's not in my *A to Z*.'

She shook herself. 'Putney,' she said, with a sigh that seemed to come from her toes. Home, to Kate's post-mortem sympathy and a large gin and tonic.

What a nightmare. Even worse than the other night, when she'd done a Tarzan's Jungle Jane at a fortieth birthday party.

From her pocket she drew the photo she'd been given for identification purposes. On the back was written, 'Guy Hamilton. You can't miss him.'

You're right there, she thought.

His face was tanned above a pristine dress shirt and black tie, and half a ball-gowned blonde was visible on his right.

I knew you wouldn't be amused, she told his photographic image silently. *I took one look and just knew it was far too down-market for the likes of you.*

'The kissogram business is a wash-out,' grumbled her cousin Ryan, two days later. 'At this rate you'll be here till Christmas.'

Claudia was praying her ordeal would be over long before that. 'And then I suppose you'll send me out as the naughty fairy from the top of the Christmas tree.'

'That'll be up to the punters, Claud. Personally, I'm praying every night that somebody'll order a naughty nun for the Archbishop of Canterbury.'

Claudia knew her exasperation was wasted, but that didn't stop her. 'Aren't you ever going to grow up?'

Ryan assumed the injured innocence that had always cloaked his wickedness. 'I don't know why you're com-plaining. You're going to get a big fat cheque for a dozen evenings of fun and – '

'*Fun*? It's not my idea of fun, going half-naked into a room of complete strangers and kissing some fat, sweaty – '

'Fun for me, I meant,' he grinned. 'I sit at home with a nice cold beer, imagining every gruesome detail.'

Claudia counted silently to ten. She had not been in the sunniest of moods on entering Ryan's grubby office five minutes earlier, now she was beginning to understand why nice, normal people, the kind you natter to in the queue at the supermarket, suddenly turned into homicidal maniacs.

'*I really don't know what came over me, Officer. One minute he was grinning at me like a monkey, the next I found myself putting bits of mangled corpse through my Speedicook Chopomatic.*'

The nerve-centre of Ryan's dubious empire was located up a scruffy side-street in a scruffy corner of south-west London. The only pristine items in the office were two posters, fresh from the printers.

One read, 'RYAN'S MINI-CABS. AIRPORTS, THEATRES, PARCEL DELIVERIES. COURTEOUS, CAREFUL DRIVERS.'

The other read, 'RYAN'S KISSOGRAMS! FRENCH MAIDS, POLICEMEN, TARZANS, NAUGHTY NUNS, OR YOUR OWN ONE-OFF. TREAT SOMEONE TO A SURPRISE THEY'LL NEVER FORGET!'

'Anyway, I've got to go,' he went on. 'Got a Gatwick run. Mick's sick so we're a driver short and you'll have to use the mobiles because the radio's on the blink.'

She forbore to say that everything in the office was on the blink, including his brain. 'Push off then, you little toad.'

Ryan put on his most irritating smirk. 'May I remind you, Claud, that you are my employee until I've won this bet? I'd like a little respect, please. A little cringing and crawling and yes sir-ing.'

She gave him a contemptuous withering look. 'Until I've won it, you mean.'

'In your dreams.' He grinned and put his tongue out at her as he left, just like the devilish small boy who'd plagued her as a child.

As the door closed behind him Claudia just stopped herself throwing his coffee-mug at it. It was a disgusting mug, well overdue for smashing, but still half-full and she couldn't face the mess.

Still, she had got herself into this. Having heard through her mother that Ryan had come into some money via some ancient great-aunt in Scotland who'd obviously never met him, and naïvely thinking that he might possibly have turned into a reasonable human being, she had called to see him one day, saying brightly, 'Ryan, I'm approaching local businessmen on behalf of a very worthy cause.'

He had listened like an angel and said magnanimously, 'I dare say I could manage a small donation.'

'Er, how much?' she'd enquired, her pen poised to nail him down.

Expecting a mere token, she had nearly fainted at his reply. '*How much?*' she'd squeaked.

Only then had the real Ryan reappeared, with the devilish grin she remembered so well. 'It's real money, Claud. But it's more in the nature of a bet. And I bet you'll never have the nerve to do it.'

With a sigh, she came back to the mess on Ryan's desk, sorted his chaotic paperwork into piles. It was almost a relief when the doorbell announced an imminent customer.

Until she saw who it was.

She'd have been less startled to see Mother Teresa in Ryan's grubby office, and from the way he stopped dead it seemed that he'd had a minor shock too.

Claudia recovered her wits fast. He had come through that door with the grimly purposeful air of a man spoiling for a row, and if that was what he wanted, she was more than happy to oblige. It would liven up a dull morning, at any rate.

She put on her best, tongue-in-cheek smile. 'How nice to see you, Mr Hamilton. Were you so delighted with our service that you want to book a repeat?'

Thrusting his hands into his pockets, he gazed down at her. It was a cool, measured assessment, from the top of her coppery hair, over her crisp white cotton shirt and back to her eyes, where it had started. 'I wasn't expecting you to be running this dubious outfit. I seem to recall something about a bet.'

Claudia was recalling a few things too. Like the way he'd shoved her into that taxi. 'Your memory would seem to be in order, Mr Hamilton. No signs of senile dementia yet.'

Purely for her own satisfaction, she was beginning to wish she'd bothered with more than a smidgeon of lip-gloss. A bit of mascara wouldn't have come amiss either. Although her eyes were wide, vivid green, her lashes needed a bit of help.

He gave her a look that said, *Don't get smart with me*. 'I assumed you meant a one-off.'

'Oh, no. The agreement is a round dozen. And in between my fun nights out, I play office dogsbody. Make the tea, lick my boss's boots, and generally pander to his poor little ego.'

The flicker at the corner of his mouth told her two things. One, that he didn't believe a word of it, and, two, that even if he didn't he was reluctantly amused. 'May I ask what you stand to win?'

It was tempting to say, Money, what d'you think? but she didn't want him thinking she was desperate. Besides, secrecy had been part of this deal. Ryan had been itching to rope in the local press, to capture her in all her glory and plaster it all over the *Echo*. He'd even thought of captions, such as 'LEGGY REDHEAD BARES NEARLY ALL FOR CHARITY'. He'd have revelled in the lurid publicity but she had threatened him with death if he breathed a word. People would think she was some tacky exhibitionist doing the 'warm and caring' bit.

With a flash of inspiration she said, 'A bottle of champagne. Served on board Concorde, halfway to Tahiti.'

'Wonderful. Except that Concorde doesn't go to Tahiti.'

You would be the kind of smart-ass who knows these things, she thought crossly. And as he turned away to scan the posters on the walls she gave him a not-so-subtle once-over.

This was a different customer from the classic-suit model. He was dressed in casual trousers of sludgy olive-green, a lighter shirt and a suede jacket: the kind of smart casual that came with a hefty price-tag.

10

Suddenly she could just hear Kate's voice. Her friend Kate had her own way of grading men. It went like this:

Category One: Not worth shaving your legs for. (Ninety per cent of men fell into this category)

Category Two: Worth shaving your legs for, but only if you're wearing a skirt.

Category Three: Worth shaving your legs for whatever you're wearing.

Category Four: Worth having your legs waxed for, and a cellulite treatment thrown in.

'Definitely a four,' Kate would have said, with more than a hint of yum-yum in her voice.

She had to admit that Kate would be right. If you were into that brand of dark and rather intimidating masculinity, of course.

'You didn't come here to pass the time of day,' she remarked. 'Would you like to state your business?'

'Idle curiosity,' he mused, still scanning the posters. 'I was wondering what kind of primeval lowlife makes a living like this.'

However heartily she agreed with him that Ryan was a superlative example of primeval lowlife, it wouldn't do to admit it now. 'My cousin's main business is the mini-cabs,' she retorted. 'Anyway, some people think kissograms are fun. Normal people, that is.'

He gave her a direct and very penetrating gaze. 'Like you, you mean.'

'Naturally.'

11

'So you'd be tickled pink if some half-naked Tarzan burst in on your civilized dinner?'

She gave an inward shudder. Ryan's current Tarzan had macaroni arms and did the honours in a horrible polyester leopardskin. 'I'd love it. I've always had a thing about Tarzan. And if you've only come to make snide remarks, I've got better things to do.'

'I haven't.' He folded his arms across his chest. 'Exactly how much did my daughter pay for your performance the other night?'

The penny dropped like a meteorite. She very nearly squeaked, *Your daughter?* like a demented budgie. 'Not the dark girl at the restaurant?' she said instead. She could see a vague likeness now, but surely he wasn't old enough to be her father?

She saw the flicker of amusement in his eyes, as if he knew exactly what was going on in her head Those eyes were not quite as chilling as she'd first thought. For some reason she thought of Icelandic pools. Freezing at first glance, but with unexpected warm springs.

'I don't have another daughter that I know of. One like Anoushka is more than enough. And for the record, she's sixteen.'

'*Sixteen?* she echoed. 'I'd have thought – '

'I know. She's looked twenty-three since she was fourteen and a half.'

'She told us she was your girlfriend!'

'Yes, I got the message the other night. You yelled it loud enough for half of central London to hear. I repeat, how much?'

Claudia hesitated. 'Why do you want to know?'

12

'So I can deduct it from her allowance. She's obviously getting too much if she can afford pranks like this.'

Although she had a sneaking sympathy for him, she wasn't going to admit it. 'Aren't we overreacting just a trifle? Besides, I'm afraid I couldn't possibly divulge that kind of information. It's against our ethics.'

'Ethics? *Ethics?*'

The phone cut off his strangled utterings. 'Ryan's minicabs,' she answered. It was a standard airport run, and while she was scribbling the details he was casting a critical eye over her, like some high-tech spying device.

Returning his gaze coolly was getting more difficult by the second. 'If you're going to clutter up the office all morning, I hope you're not expecting me to make polite conversation,' she said. 'I am not at my sunny, sociable best, especially with a man who treated me as if I had the plague the other night.'

'The plague?' he snorted. 'You got off lightly.' As he took a step closer the tantalizing scent he had worn that night wafted within whispering distance of her nostrils. It was very faint, the kind that whispered rather than screamed, and Claudia felt suddenly as if a large and very violent jellyfish had hit her in the stomach.

Like a video on rewind, her brain zoomed back to just how his lips had felt, as he'd shown her how to 'do it properly next time'. She'd been too startled at the time for it to affect her, but delayed reaction was setting in fast.

And as he gazed back at her she sensed a subtle change in the atmosphere. An indefinable oasis of awareness had descended around them: the tingling that surrounded a man and a woman when they had ceased to be just another man and just another woman.

When he spoke again, it vanished like snow in May. 'That bet business was a load of rubbish. You're doing this as a stop-gap but you're ashamed to admit it. Even I can see it's not your style. What are you? A "resting" actress? Your performance the other night had the whole restaurant riveted.'

She wished her old drama teacher could have heard him. The one who'd said, 'You can forget all about acting as a career, Claudia. Your talent is only mediocre.'

'Sorry to disappoint you, but the last acting I did was at school. In a very amateurish production of *Oliver*, if you really want to know.'

She could see it was bothering him, why she was there at all. As his brow furrowed she began to think that perhaps he was older than she'd first thought. Thirty-six, thirty-seven? That would have made him about twenty when his daughter was born.

His eyes flickered over her again. 'What's your name?'

It was the last thing she'd expected. For an aghast moment she had visions of legal action for Malicious Embarrassment Inflicted in a Terminally Swanky Restaurant. 'What's it to you?'

One corner of his mouth flickered. 'Am I making you nervous?'

No, not lawsuits, she thought, with a wash of relief. *He hadn't been quite that angry*. 'For current purposes it's Naughty Natalie,' she said sweetly. 'Or Fetching Fifi when I do the French maid. Satisfied?'

14

'It'll have to do. Just so I know who *not* to ask for if I ever want my worst enemy embarrassed out of his mind. I'd want someone who'd do the thing properly.'

Claudia was stung. 'You just said I had the whole restaurant riveted!'

'I meant by your "abandoned mother" act. The rest of it was as chaste as an old biddy kissing her cat.'

'I'd have done it properly if you'd let me!' Realizing too late that he'd only said it to goad her, she added, 'I'd have held my breath and steeled myself.'

'I'm sure you'd have made a sterling effort,' he said in soothing tones.

She began to realize that she'd have to get up very early to get the better of him in a verbal sparring situation. Trying to sound bored, she said, 'Mr Hamilton, it's half past ten on a Friday morning. Haven't you got a job to go to?' On the other hand, he wasn't exactly dressed for the office. In her current mood, she just couldn't resist it. 'Or perhaps you were on your way to the Job Centre? If so, I should ditch that jacket, if I were you,' she added kindly. 'Looks a tad too up-market. They might think you're fiddling your giro.'

His mouth gave a barely-there twitch. 'Thank you for the advice. I'll leave you to it, Miss whatever-your-name-is.'

Drat. Just when I was beginning to enjoy myself. 'Bye, then.' Ninety per cent certain that it would make him wince, she added, 'Have a nice day.'

He did wince.

What came over her then she would never know. She made no conscious decision to call him back. It just burst out. 'Mr Hamilton!'

15

He turned, one eyebrow raised a fraction. 'Yes?'

Her words tumbled out in an uncharacteristically garbled rush. 'I'm so sorry about the other night – I know you hated it but I hated it even more – the first one was even worse; he had horrendous bad breath and made me feel sick – I never thought it'd be so ghastly – I've got to do ten more to win this bet – my cousin's a complete and utter reptile, right out of the primeval slime just like you said – he offered me a huge cheque – he never, ever thought I'd do it, but he's really enjoying seeing me squirm – I'd tell him to get lost right now, but I simply must have the money – not for me, for Bruin Wood – it's a holiday home in the New Forest for inner-city children – they need new wiring and heaven knows what or they won't be allowed to open next spring – I've been fund-raising like mad but people get sick of being asked for money – I was made redundant, you see, so I'm at a loose end – not that I minded that; the company's going down the drain because of their lousy senior management so I'm well out of it – I've got a much better job lined up for after Christmas but that's beside the point – until I've wiped that grin off Ryan the Reptile's face I've got to grit my teeth and be a kissogram girl.'

With the floodgates closed, she took a huge breath.

For what seemed an eternity, his shrewd, assessing gaze searched her face. 'Exactly how much does this bet involve?'

When she told him, he didn't bat an eyelash. 'Just how badly do you want this money?'

'It's not a question of *wanting*! I've already promised it! Do you realize how many children have never seen a cow

16

in a field, or fed an apple to a pony? Do you realize how many children have never even *seen* the sea?'

He folded his arms and gave her the silent navy treatment. Not just hair to waist, like before, but inside out, back to front, and very possibly upside down as well.

In for a penny, she thought. *In for a few quid, anyway.* 'I suppose you wouldn't care to make a small donation?'

He seemed not to hear her. 'If you really can't face any more kissograms, I might just have an alternative proposition.

She gave a startled frown. 'Sorry?'

'You heard me.' He looked her straight in the eye. 'Have you got a valid passport?'

CHAPTER 2

Her voice dug itself from under her tonsils. 'A *passport*? Of course I have, but . . .'

She began to think this was some elaborate wind-up. Any moment now he was going her offer her vast sums of money to smuggle plutonium to Iraq in her bra, she was going to gape and make choking noises, and that man from the television was going to burst in with a false beard, pretending to be from MI5, and then the beard would come off and a film crew would appear and everybody would crack up.

It had Ryan's handwriting all over it.

She glanced over her shoulder for signs of hidden cameras in the corners, but there were only the usual cobwebs. She had meant to remove them, but felt sorry for the spiders.

'Mr Hamilton, if this is some kind of weird male joke . . .'

With a slight frown, he glanced at his watch again. 'I haven't got time to discuss it now – I was on my way to an appointment. Give me a ring tonight and we'll arrange a talking lunch.'

From his inside pocket he took a pen. On the pad on her desk he scrawled 'Hamilton' and a phone number. 'I'll be in between seven and eight.'

Temporarily deprived of the power of speech, she gaped at him.

He tucked the pen back in his pocket. 'Till tonight, Claudia.'

That was enough to restore her vocal cords. 'I don't recall giving you my name!'

Already halfway to the door, he turned his head just enough for her to see an infuriating flicker at the corner of his mouth. 'I'm psychic.'

The door closed behind him.

It took only five seconds for the mystery to solve itself. Among the half-sorted chaos on the desk was a letter that had arrived that morning from Spain. In her mother's neat handwriting it was addressed to 'Miss Claudia Maitland'.

Devious devil, she thought crossly. *He must have seen it while I was on the phone*. If her father had written it he'd have gone cross-eyed trying to decipher it. Her father's handwriting had been known to reduce postmen to nervous wrecks.

She stared dazedly at the name and number on her pad. At least it was evidence that she hadn't nodded off and dreamt the whole thing.

It was an inner London number – Kensington, if she wasn't mistaken.

A whole forest fire of curiosity was raging inside her, and not even three cups of Ryan's disgusting instant coffee could quench it.

Despite draughty Edwardian windows that let fresh air in whether you wanted it or not, it was passably cosy in Claudia's living room.

Fresh from the bath, Kate was curled in the armchair, digesting the news. 'Sounds decidedly dodgy to me,' she pronounced.

'That's exactly what I was thinking all day. Only . . .'

'Only what?'

'Only he doesn't *look* dodgy.'

'They never do.' Kate unwound the towel from her head and shook her hair into a damp curly halo. 'Think of those Mafioso godfathers! Perfect pillars of the community until they get found out.'

'Maybe he's a drug baron.' Claudia was absently stroking Portly the cat. Slumbering fatly beside her, he was taking up the other half of the sofa. 'Maybe he's going to ask me to take a kilo of heroin to Bangkok, disguised as prime Stilton for the Ambassador.'

'For heaven's sake, anybody can see you're not stupid enough to fall for that. It could be drug *money*, though. Wodges of readies that he wants laundering. You'll have to buy a yacht or something. They buy huge great yachts for cash and sail them to Florida then sell them and stick the money in fourteen different false bank accounts.'

'But he doesn't *look* like a drug baron.'

'How do you know what drug barons look like? Have you ever met one?'

Claudia thought back to the classic-suited Guy Hamilton in the restaurant and tried not to think like her mother. Margaret Maitland would sum people up in an instant, and her verdict on Guy Hamilton would have been, 'Good family. You can always tell. Look at his shoes.'

Margaret Maitland was one of those people who never could believe that anybody of 'good family', who was also

English, could possibly be dodgy. Dodginess was for foreigners, and Englishmen who wore loud shirts. Why her mother had gone to live in Spain, Claudia could never quite fathom.

'They all wear expensive suits and drive flash cars and live in whacking great houses,' Kate went on. 'People always think they're stockbrokers or something until they get nicked.'

'How do you know? You've never met one either.'

'No, but I've watched that chap on the telly who exposes posh crooks. They all sound like old Etonians and keep racehorses and stuff and their kids belong to the Pony Club.'

Claudia barely heard her. 'Mmm.'

'Where's that photo?' Kate demanded. 'I'll be able to tell if he's dodgy. I can spot dodgy men at fifty paces with my eyes closed.'

'I keep telling you, he doesn't *look* dodgy.'

'Show me anyway. I'm dying to see what he looks like.'

'I must have left it in the taxi. Can't find it anywhere.' This was a big fat lie. The photo was safely tucked in the zip pocket of her bag, along with might-have-to-take-it-back receipts and dry-cleaning tickets. She had not shown it to Kate for the simple reason that Kate's eyes would spark instantly like a faulty fuse-box. She'd say things like, 'Wow! I wouldn't mind playing sardines-in-the-dark with him,' and the fluttery feelings Claudia had felt in the office would return, redoubled. And Kate would know, and then there would be no peace.

'You're hopeless,' Kate sighed. 'Give me all the details. What category, for a start?'

21

Unable to lie completely, Claudia shrugged and lied in moderation. 'Two and a bit. Fortyish. Darkish. Six-foot-two-ish. Good-looking in a stuffy, poker-up-his backside sort of way. No sense of humour.'

'I suppose not,' Kate sighed, 'if he went berserk just at a kissogram.'

'He didn't quite go *berserk*. Chillingly unamused was more like it.'

'Boring, in other words.'

Portly stirred, yawned, stretched himself and began a vigorous claw-sharpening on the loose covers. They were by no means new, but would last a good bit longer if Portly would just manicure his weapons elsewhere. Detaching his claws, Claudia lifted him on to her lap.

Portly gave a mildly indignant squeak, decided it was too much effort to argue, and curled into a squidgy marmalade ball.

'If he's boring, it won't be drugs,' Kate pronounced. 'Criminals aren't boring.' Her face brightened. 'Maybe he's a politician. All respectable family values on the outside but a real sleaze-bag underneath. Maybe he thought there was a photographer waiting to catch you draped all over him and plaster it all over the Sunday papers. With a headline like "JUNIOR MINISTER SNOGS LOVE-CHILD STRIPPER".'

'Don't be daft. If he'd thought that, he wouldn't have come out on the street with me. Never mind kissing me in public!'

'Ah, yes. He can't be that stuffy, then. Was he a good kisser?'

Claudia's internal video went into rewind once more and her stomach gave a tiny, involuntary lurch. 'For heaven's sake, I was too shell-shocked to be giving scores!'

'Oh, come on. *Roughly*. Slobbery and disgusting?'

'Well, no. I suppose not.'

'Not disgusting but no shivers either? Or a real, woozy toe-curler?'

'Kate, for heaven's sake! It was over in about two seconds!'

'OK, OK,' Kate soothed, but an instant later her mouth did its she-devil curve again. 'Tongues?'

'Shut *up*!' Half laughing, Claudia chucked a cushion at her, but even that didn't stop Kate's idle speculations.

'Probably just getting his money's worth,' she mused. 'Maybe he really *has* got a love-child. That would account for him not seeing the joke. I bet he's a family values sleaze-bag anyway. Probably wants you to go and "entertain" foreign businessmen on a private island somewhere.'

'*What?*'

'Only kidding,' Kate giggled. 'But there's only one way to find out.'

Claudia glanced at her watch. It was twenty to eight. 'I'm not ringing yet. I'll wait a bit longer. Let him think I'm not going to.'

'In that case, I'll ring for a pizza. There's nothing in the fridge, in case you didn't know.'

Claudia knew. She had meant to go to the shops on her way home, but salad and cold meat from the deli had been the last things on her mind.

While Kate was ordering a medium pizza f m hell, with jalapeño peppers and garlic bread, she had a stern and silent conversation with herself.

Why are you even contemplating ringing a man you don't know from Fred Flintstone, who has just offered you a lot of money to perform some unknown and possibly dodgy service?

I don't know.

Liar.

All right, then. Because he's dishy.

Go on.

And for a second or two he made me go all fluttery and I haven't felt fluttery in ages.

What else?

And if I don't ring him, I'll –

'Twenty minutes,' said Kate, replacing the receiver. 'I'll go and open some vino plonko.'

While she was gone Claudia stroked Portly mechanically. A 'talking lunch'. Talking of what, pray?

Three-quarters of her brain was on Guy Hamilton and what he was going to say; the rest was on draught-exclusion measures. The curtains were billowing like ocean-going spinnakers, just to let you know there was a gale blowing outside. The rain sounded like vandals throwing gravel at the windows.

The house had started life in the 1890s, probably as home to the kind of family that employed a live-in servant and a nursemaid to push the perambulator along tree-lined streets.

The area had since come down in the world; the houses had been converted to flats and bedsits. It was now coming up again. Several had been converted back into spacious, elegant homes, with swagged curtains at every window.

Claudia's flat was on the ground floor. The plumbing was erratic, the floorboards creaky, but it was her own – or would be when she was about ninety-three and had paid the mortgage off. She'd had two tenants before Kate. One had been silent and odd, the other had done a flit owing two months' rent.

It had been a colossal relief to bump into her old college friend at a party. Kate had spent a full twenty minutes relating horror stories of her landlord; a hybrid of Scrooge and Peeping Tom. She had moved in three days later.

Kate reappeared with two glasses of special offer Chablis, and handed her the phone. A certain wickedness gleamed in her round brown eyes. 'Maybe he's playing games. Maybe it was just a tortured way of getting you on a lunch-date.'

'Then why didn't he just ask me?'

'How could he, when you'd just been shooting verbal arrows at him? You know what you're like when you're snappy. Maybe he thought you'd bite his head off.'

Claudia pushed back the growing-out fringe that constantly drove her mad and shook her head emphatically. 'Believe me, if he'd just wanted a date, he'd have asked.'

The torn-off sheet with his number lay on the little gateleg table beside her. She glanced at it and pushed buttons rapidly.

'Hamilton residence.' The voice was female, elderly, and a mite sniffy.

Suddenly, Kate's game-playing remark didn't seem quite so ludicrous after all. But if he *was* playing elaborate games, what was the reason?

Elementary, my dear Kate.

'May I speak to Mrs Hamilton, please?' she asked.

'I beg your pardon?'

25

'I said, may I speak to Mrs Hamilton?'

There was a brief silence, then, 'There is no Mrs Hamilton.'

That was one suspicion out of the way. 'Then I'll speak to Mr Hamilton, please.'

During the pause that followed, Claudia could almost hear the pursing of lips. 'I hope you're not selling double-glazing or fancy kitchens, because I can assure you we're not interested.'

'I'm not selling anything. Is he there?'

'May I ask who is calling?'

'Claudia Maitland.'

'I'll see if he's free to speak to you.' Her tone said, *I can't imagine he'll want to.*

With her hand over the mouthpiece, Claudia looked up. 'Sounds like a housekeeper,' she whispered to Kate. 'Of the snobby, old-school variety.'

Kate giggled. 'Maybe he's got a Jeeves as well, to tidy his sock suspenders and – '

'Shh!' Kate's giggles were infectious, and she didn't want to be erupting like Volcano Bimbo when he finally came to the phone.

When he did, his voice held an edge of very dry amusement. 'Claudia, you have a nasty, suspicious mind.'

She was unrepentant. 'I had to check. I know absolutely nothing about you.'

'If I were married, which I'm not, and up to no good, which I'm not, I'd hardly give you my home number.'

'I don't see why not. She might have been away.'

'And the big bad mouse playing in her absence?'

'You said it.'

26

On the other end of the line there was a sigh of very controlled, very patient exasperation. 'Claudia, even if the whole of married male London is writhing on the kitchen table right this minute with his kids' au pair, it's irrelevant. This is a business proposition, nothing more.'

'Well, hallelujah. So now we've sorted that out, can you tell me what sort of business proposition?'

'If you'd phoned earlier I could have. As it's now three minutes to eight, and I have a dinner-date, I can't. Can you meet me tomorrow, around one o'clock?'

She hesitated. It wasn't so much alarm bells ringing in her head, as *Crimewatch* reconstructions.

'Claudia has not been seen since lunchtime on the seventeenth of November, when she set off to meet a man calling himself Guy Hamilton, who had offered her a large sum of money for some unspecified service.'

Cut to a tearful Kate. *'I told her, but she wouldn't listen. She said he didn't look dodgy.'*

'Maybe,' she said, trying to sound as if she were nonchalantly examining her nails. 'Where?'

'Paolo's. Do you know it?'

Phew. 'Vaguely. Near Covent Garden?'

'That's it. Till tomorrow, then.'

She was just about to hang up when he added, 'It's nothing illegal, in case you're wondering.'

Her relief was only partial. ' "Legal" covers all manner of unsavoury activities. I might as well warn you that if it's anything remotely unsavoury – more unsavoury than kissograms, anyway – you'll be wasting your time.'

The amusement in his voice was more marked. 'What exactly had you in mind?'

'Nothing to do with kitchen tables, I can assure you. Sounds most unhygienic to me. Besides, I'd rather not say. I was a convent girl and old Sister Immaculata would be whizzing in her grave.'

'She can save her energies for pushing up daisies. I'll see you tomorrow.'

Infuriated and intrigued in roughly equal proportions, she replaced the receiver. 'He's playing games, all right!. How am I ever going to contain myself till tomorrow?'

Kate's face was a picture of agogness. 'Whatever was that about kitchen tables?'

Claudia was already wishing she hadn't referred to kitchen tables, and wondering at the same time whether he was speaking from personal experience. She recounted the conversation word for word until the pizza arrived.

'Paolo's is Italian, isn't it?' Kate asked, cutting it into wedges. 'You like Italian. Be sure to order the most expensive things on the menu.'

Claudia picked up a wedge of pizza, its gooey strings of cheese sticking like warm elastic to the rest of it. 'Oh, I intend to. Pity I can't charge him a taxi fare too. If the weather's like this tomorrow, I'll be arriving with mud splashes all up my tights.'

She felt unaccountably miffed with Guy Hamilton, and nearly said as much to Kate. But then Kate would want to know why, and she'd have to confess that Guy Hamilton was a wildly fanciable Category Four. And when a wildly fanciable Category Four invited you out to lunch you didn't want him saying, 'This is a business proposition, nothing more.' And Kate's eyes would gleam and she'd say, 'I knew it!'

'Whatever he's offering, I'm not going to do it,' she said carelessly. 'I can't possibly deprive myself of the pleasure of seeing Ryan's face when he writes that cheque. I'm only going for the free lunch. And if I smile nicely enough, he might even throw in a cheque with the coffee.'

Having told herself firmly that she was *not* going to dither over what to wear, Claudia proceeded to dither for England.

A dozen discarded garments lay on the bed: too sexy, too unsexy, too short, too girly, too boring. Eventually she opted for a mid-grey suit of soft wool that had cost only half a bomb in last year's January sales.

With it she opted for a thin lambswool sweater of palest dusty rose, pearl studs, and cream tights.

Passable, she thought, finishing her make-up. *Nice green eyes, pity about the lashes, but one can't have everything*. Why ever had she hated her nose so much in her teens? From the right angle it was really quite aristocratic. She applied a layer of Smoky Rose to her lips. The teenage Claudia had hated them too. Too wide, the bottom lip too fat in the middle. She liked them now; people paid thousands to have their lips plumped up like that.

Her face done, she gave the rest a critical going-over. *Suitably restrained*, she thought. *Neither too much leg, nor the 36Bs begging for attention*.

Next she inspected her back view. The jacket was long enough to conceal the fact that her bottom was also 36B, not 34A as she would wish. Finally she dithered over the final touch. Amarige or Cabotine? Maybe the former was a bit too warm and come-into-my-boudoirish for business lunches. She misted her hair with fresh green Cabotine, grabbed an umbrella and ran. It was still raining like the wrath of God, but Kate was giving her a lift to the tube.

She was six minutes late, but he had evidently been at least five minutes early. With a *Financial Times* and what looked like a Bloody Mary for company, he was seated at a corner table.

Her mother's voice was at it again. 'Lovely manners, dear,' it said approvingly as he rose to his feet the instant he saw her coming.

How often had her mother said that? And how often had Claudia replied, 'Mum, you'd be a gift to any con-man with lovely manners and "good family" shoes.'

'Sorry I'm a bit late,' she said, taking the seat opposite. 'The underground was murder. A heaving mass of humanity off to do its Christmas shopping.'

He put his FT on a spare chair. 'You should have taken a cab.'

She nearly said, I'm trying to save money, not squander it, but desisted. 'The traffic's even more murderous than the tube. Last time I took a cab on a wet Saturday morning, the driver cursed all the way. He possessed the most colourful repertoire of curses, but since they were mostly muttered, I couldn't quite catch them all. It was maddening.'

One corner of his mouth lifted in the half-smile she was beginning to associate with him. Did he ever smile properly? she wondered. Or was the other side of his mouth permanently fixed in world-weary mode?

'Have a drink,' he said.

30

There was no classic suit this time, and no suede jacket either. He was wearing what fashion editors call 'city casual' at its understated best: a jacket of charcoal-grey with a black polo shirt underneath.

She ordered a gin and tonic, which appeared with miraculous speed. As she sipped, Claudia studied both menu and ambience.

Paolo's managed to combine city-chic with easy informality, quite unlike the hallowed-shrine atmosphere of the French place. Here you didn't feel the chef would quiver with outrage if anybody asked for salt.

Her lips quivered as she remembered an incident in a similar hallowed-shrine place.

It did not escape him. 'Something funny?' he murmured, glancing up from his menu.

Should I tell him? she wondered. *Oh, what the hell.* 'I was thinking of that French place. A few months ago I was taken to a place very much like that by a very down-to-earth Aussie on my birthday.'

He raised his eyebrows in a 'go on' fashion.

Claudia's quivers were rapidly turning into barely suppressed laughter. 'The service was rather sniffy, and since he was paying an arm and a leg he was a mite put out. He ordered some incredibly elaborate dish, with a sauce that had probably taken fourteen hours to prepare, and then he called the head waiter over and said, 'Where's the ketchup, mate?'

The mere memory of Adam's wicked expression and the shock-horror on the head waiter's face was enough to bring her giggles to the surface. 'I nearly choked to death, trying not to laugh. I had to go to the ladies' and collapse.'

31

Guy Hamilton wasn't laughing. He wasn't exactly sniffily disapproving either, but the hint of amusement that flickered at his eyes and mouth was as dry as James Bond's martini.

'At least it didn't spoil your evening. Behaviour like that would have had some people cringing with embarrassment.'

Her laughter died as if it had never been. Suddenly she was back on the pavement after that kissogram, his voice echoing in her ears. 'How much were you paid to embarrass my guests and interrupt a passable dinner?'

'Were they your parents, the other night?' she asked. 'I do hope it didn't spoil their appetites.'

'They were an aunt and uncle who live very quietly in Suffolk. My aunt is the kind of person who would rather have all her teeth pulled out than cause a scene.'

He said it crisply enough, but that didn't stop her feeling awful. Especially when he went on, 'She was too distressed to finish her meal. We left about fifteen minutes after you did.'

She swallowed hard. 'I'm terribly sorry.'

'I don't hold you entirely responsible. You didn't order it.' He nodded towards her menu. 'If we don't order soon we'll be here all afternoon.'

Suitably chastened, she cast her eye over lists of assorted diet-busters. *The only trouble with Italian restaurants*, she thought, *is all the veal on the menu*. If Guy Hamilton ordered baby veal, she would go off him instantly. Which might be no bad thing, in the circumstances.

'*Insalata di calamares*, please,' she said to the patient waiter. 'Followed by *petti di pollo* Alla Fiorentine.' It was chicken breasts in lovely, yummy, to-hell-with-the-diet butter. She and Kate never bought butter, as they'd instantly gorge themselves on baked potatoes swimming in it. Low-fat marge wasn't nearly so tempting. 'And a green salad.'

Once he had ordered his *gnocchi verdi* and *fritto misto di mare* – no veal, thank heaven – she sat up straight and went into crisp and businesslike mode. 'So shoot. What do you want me to do?'

He finished the Bloody Mary. 'If you don't mind, I'll get some food down first. I negotiate better on a full tank.'

She stared at him, curiosity turning to exasperation. 'Mr Hamilton, will you please stop these delaying tactics? You stalled in the office; you stalled on the phone. I'm beginning to think . . .'

She hadn't been thinking anything until then, but a ghastly thought had just plopped into her head – a thought so ghastly it momentarily paralyzed her. She'd had a similar sensation once before at a beachside taverna in Greece, when a cockroach had plopped from the overhead vines into her retsina.

He raised an enquiring eyebrow. 'What?'

The cockroach had been a whopper, wiggling its beastly upside down legs and waving its feelers. Claudia glanced over her shoulder towards the door. Any minute now . . .

'Expecting someone?' he murmured.

His faint amusement only fuelled her suspicions. 'Are you playing games with me?'

'No.'

'Can I have that in writing?'

'No.'

33

You have my word as a gentleman? Well, we've all heard that before. A swirl of fresh air told her the door had just opened. She glanced over her shoulder again, but it was only a young couple with an umbrella. *Don't be ridiculous,* she told herself. *He wouldn't.*

Would he?

She scanned his face sharply for signs of malicious relish, but there was only a one-inch chasm appearing between his brows.

'Claudia, if you've got a jealous swain who's liable to charge in with a meat-axe and apply it to my head, would you kindly say so now?'

'How could I ever have contemplated kissograms if I had a jealous swain?'

'Then he's not going to get the wrong idea if I ask you to pack a suitcase and come to the Arabian Gulf?'

She quite forgot to say there was no swain, jealous or otherwise. 'The Arabian *Gulf*?'

'Muscat, to be precise. The Sultanate of Oman.'

A breathing space arrived with their starters, and she needed it. Once the waiter had gone, he said, 'Now I've started, you might as well hear the rest. I have a business trip which I can't postpone. My daughter, who has just been suspended from school, is counting the days till I go. She's looking forward to a spell of unfettered freedom: sleeping all day, clubbing till breakfast-time, and hanging out with the kind of people who think it's fun to do eighty miles an hour over Chelsea Bridge at four in the morning.'

At least I was wrong about the other thing, she thought, spearing a ring of squid. 'Go on.'

'I am not going to leave her unsupervised in London. Given her record, none of her schoolfriends' parents will have her. Therefore I have to take her with me. And I have a very hectic schedule. I won't have time to keep an eye on her.'

Her fork had frozen halfway to her mouth. 'And you want a minder? You want *me* to tag along as glorified nanny?'

'That's the general idea.'

She stared at him. 'You must be off your head.'

He speared a plump green *gnocchi* pillow, dripping with melted Parmesan. 'Merely desperate.'

She was beginning to sense a fireworks situation. There had been more than a touch of mischief in the kissogram – something a group of employees might inflict on a well-loathed boss.

He devoured more spinach pillows and went on, 'As you may have gathered the other night, Anoushka gets a kick out of shocking people. In Muscat, she would revel in proving an embarrassment. Knowing I have highly placed connections, she'd get a grade A kick out of, say, causing a scene by sunbathing topless at the pool. Or getting herself arrested for wandering the streets in jeans cut off to her backside.'

Claudia took a sip of Soave, and then another. She could have done with the whole bottle, but gulping any kind of booze gave her hiccups. 'What about that aunt and uncle at the restaurant the other night? Surely they could –?'

'It's out of the question. My uncle has high blood pressure.'

Nuff said. 'Friends, then. Your friends, I mean.'

He shook his head. 'Either can't, or couldn't cope if they did.'

She didn't bother asking about other relatives, or the girl's mother. If these were options he wouldn't be asking a stranger. Maybe he *had* to ask a stranger because anybody who knew his daughter would have a nervous breakdown at the very idea of being responsible for her.

'I couldn't possibly undertake to keep her out of trouble. You'd need some bomb-proof old battleaxe from an agency. With handcuffs. In any case, she'd recognize me. How on earth would you expect her to pay any attention to a kissogram girl?'

'That's precisely why she might relate to you. She can't relate to middle-aged women in tweed skirts who look as if they've never done anything remotely indiscreet in their lives.'

You've got a point there, she thought. But one correct point was hardly sufficient. 'I can see you're worried about leaving her, but lots of girls go through a wild phase. I know I did – out all night and taking lifts with boy-racer idiots and drinking too much and throwing up. My parents used to have pink fits with monotonous regularity, but I survived. We nearly all do, you know.'

A hint of half-amused impatience came into his voice. 'Claudia, I am not what Anoushka would call a "prehistoric old fart". I know all about misspent youth. I enjoyed one myself.'

I bet you did, she thought, suddenly seeing him at nineteen or twenty, before that world-weariness had etched itself around his mouth. *I bet you had a spark and a half. And you still have, come to that, and not that far under the surface either. If only . . .*

'I don't expect her to live like some earnest social reject,' he went on. 'If she never wanted to go out I'd think there was something wrong with her. But she's overstepped the limit too often and I have to make a stand. She was furious at being suspended from school. She was hoping to be expelled.'

Claudia almost choked on her last morsel of squid. Hoping he wouldn't realize it was laughter rather than shock, she forced her lips into a pained expression and took another sip of Soave. 'Excuse me.'

She was conscious of a sneaking admiration for Anoushka. How often she had longed to be expelled from the convent! How often she had daydreamed during boring geography lessons, thinking up outrageous escapades that would get her banished instantly! 'Why was she suspended, or shouldn't I ask?'

'Not over lunch.'

Spoilsport.

They ate in silence for a little while, and she spent the time wondering a good many things about him. Divorced or widowed, and for how long? If divorced, whose fault had it been? Had he been playing around, or had his wife left him for another man? Or had she just been fed up because he was a workaholic? If he *was* divorced, why hadn't the girl gone with her mother? Maybe he'd got custody because she'd run off with some wild and hairy rock singer? Or was he a widower? He wore no wedding ring, not that that meant anything.

Rings led her to hands. Hands were one of the first things she noticed in a man, and they could put her right off. Dirty nails, flashy rings, fat, podgy fingers, thin, white, bony ones, damp, clammy-looking, crawly ones . . .

His were quite worthy of a Category Four rating. Firm and capable, the nails short and clean, they looked strong, but sensitive too. Equal to anything from chopping logs to activities requiring much more gentle artistry.

The main course arrived, and just as well. Her imagination had drifted into lazy, delicious speculation about just how sensitively those fingers would ease a bra-strap from a . . .

Claudia, for crying out loud, behave yourself.

'This looks lovely,' she said brightly, just as if food had been the only thing on her mind. What if he was one of those wretched men who *knew*? She'd met such a man once – someone she'd long fancied from afar, but had tried not to show it because he'd loved himself so much.

On their first and only date he'd said smugly, 'I knew you fancied me. I can always tell when a woman fancies me because of the way her pupils dilate when I talk to her.'

For half a minute she concentrated on the least erotic things she could think of: the state of the oven, and half an undigested mouse that Portly had sicked up on her bed. Its tiny, pathetic paws and minute kidneys had been perfectly visible on the duvet, making her feel quite ill.

This worked brilliantly. Feeling faintly queasy all over again, she toyed with her chicken, wishing the chef had not been quite so heavy-handed with the butter after all.

After a mouthful or two of assorted seafood, Guy Hamilton said, 'You've gone very quiet. I hope that's a good sign.'

Although she had more or less made up her mind that his offer was out of the question, something stopped her saying so at once. Playing for time, she said, 'You know nothing about me. If you don't mind my saying so, it's not generally the done thing to ask total strangers to look after one's child.'

He looked her straight in the eye. 'She's not exactly a child, and I'm a very good judge of character.'

'You mean you can't find anybody else.'

'That too.'

The restaurant was nearly full, the cheerful buzz of conversation and clinking glasses all around them. 'Just out of interest,' she said, 'how exactly would you expect me to keep her from embarrassing you? I mean, suppose she decided to go into town in shorts? How would I stop her?'

'She won't be able to go anywhere. I've booked an out-of-town hotel – only a few miles out, but I won't give her any money for taxis.'

'So what's she supposed to do all day?'

'What do you think?' He topped up her glass. 'History. Maths. Biology. She thinks she's won this round. She thinks I'm going to give in and leave her to hang around clubs for a fortnight. But she's got another think coming. She's coming with me, and she's going to do her school-work. If she plays ball, she can have time off for the beach, the water ski-ing and so on. If she doesn't, she'll be bored out of her mind. And, believe me, the one thing Anoushka cannot tolerate is boredom.'

He raised his glass to his lips. 'Cheers.'

Determination glinted in his eye like polished steel. *Sooner you than me*, Claudia thought, wondering what his not so hapless daughter would say when he told her she was getting on that plane. She was rapidly getting the impression of two brick walls, engaged in a fight to the death.

'Cheers,' she said, with no conviction whatsoever.

'Is that a yes?'

'I'm afraid not. I have every sympathy for you,' she went on quickly, 'but I just couldn't play the bossy, big-sisterish, have-you-done-your-history-type figure. It would go right against the grain.'

'That's only one aspect. Even if she were as earnest and studious as her headmistress would wish, she'd be fed up on her own all day. I'm not entirely unfeeling.'

She was not convinced. 'She'd hate me on principle.'

'She would at first, but she'll have a sneaking respect for anyone with the nerve to strip off in a top-notch eatery.'

'I did not *strip off*!' Much to her annoyance, she coloured faintly at the mere ghastly memory. She might as well have stripped right off, the way they'd all reacted. The silk teddy had felt like a G-string.

'You know what I mean.' He leaned back, scanning her face so minutely she felt he could see right into her head. 'By your own admission, you loathed it. Can you really face doing that again? Can you face being groped and squeezed and slobbered over by beery yobs at stag nights?'

His graphic description made her wince, as the devious man had obviously intended. 'I don't suppose it'll kill me. It'll be something to tell my grandchildren.'

'On the other hand,' he went on, just as if she hadn't spoken, 'you could be soaking up the sun by the pool in a hotel that's generally considered one of the most luxurious

40

in the Middle East. The weather's very pleasant at this time of year. Mid-eighties, probably. The hotel's on a little bay and there are all manner of water sports, as well as the usual tennis and gym and all the rest. And it's a fascinating country. Mountains and oases full of date palms, old forts and camel races and friendly people who never tell you to have a nice day.'

She stared at him helplessly. 'This is blackmail!'

'Rubbish. I'm just filling you in, so you can make an informed decision.'

For the first time she wavered. It sounded too good to be true.

And probably was.

'Put it on hold till we've finished eating,' he advised. 'And let's change the subject.'

But Claudia could not finish her food. What with Portly's mouse and indecision squirming like a bucket of earthworms in her stomach, she'd gone off it. 'Fair enough. You start.'

He nodded towards her plate. 'What's wrong with that chicken?'

'Nothing. I've just gone off it.'

'Then get something else.'

'I'm not really hungry any more.'

'Then stop playing with it.'

She gaped at him. He had said it as if she were a six-year-old making islands with her mashed potatoes and gravy. 'Next you'll be telling me to eat up or I won't get any pudding!'

Rather to her surprise, his mouth lifted in half a wry smile. 'Sorry. Force of habit.'

'Like the female company director who found herself cutting up some poor chap's food at a business lunch?'

'More or less.' He added an almost proper smile, revealing lovely white teeth that would never make any dentist rich.

Please don't smile like that. It was difficult enough to look at his offer in a cool and detached manner without him employing such unfair tactics.

Maybe that's why he's doing it. You can bet your sweet life he knows the effect he's having. He's trying to get round you. Get you eating out of his Category Four hand.

His next words bashed that theory right on the head. 'Just who were you expecting to come through that door a while back? You looked like a cornered ginger rabbit.'

CHAPTER 3

Ginger? How dared he? Copper-gold was the term she'd have used, if asked.

For a moment she was tempted to invent a psychopathic weightlifter who'd already been done three times for GBH. Any second he might burst in with an '*Oi! What d'you think you're doing with my bird, you toffee-nosed git?*'

But somehow she didn't think he'd buy it. 'If you must know, I was expecting some sort of tit-for-tat for the kissogram.'

One dark eyebrow lifted sardonically. 'Like what?'

'Like some disgusting Tarzan, asking me to peel his banana.'

For an instant she could have sworn she saw the unmistakable twitch of a man struggling not to laugh.

He fought it manfully, however. 'For crying out loud, do you really think I'd go to all this trouble for such puerile idiocy?'

'You might. After telling me how horribly embarrassed your aunt was, I thought you might be taking revenge on her behalf. Besides . . .' If he was too much on his dignity to laugh, she might have some fun winding him up. 'Men can be very puerile when they're made to look ridiculous in public. You weren't at all a happy bunny the other night.'

He fixed her with a very level gaze. 'The only person who looked ridiculous was you.'

'If you say so, Mr Hamilton.' She added a sweet smile intended to madden him.

It didn't seem to work. With an air of noble male patience stretched to its limit, he put his knife and fork down. 'If you thought I was planning a tit-for-tat, why did you come?'

'Tit-for-tats hadn't even occurred to me till I was actually here. Tarzans hadn't so much as crossed my mind. Let alone bananas.' She paused just long enough for dramatic effect. 'If you really want to know, I thought you might be a drug baron.'

To her chagrin, he seemed not in the least put out. 'I thought you might. That's why I said it was nothing illegal.'

She raised her eyes to the ceiling. 'Oh, *please*. In the immortal words of whoever it was, "You would say that, wouldn't you?"'

His only reply was a pair of shrewdish, drily amused eyes across the table.

'My friend Kate,' she went on, 'thought you might be a family values sleaze-bag politician with a love-child tucked in the closet.'

'Well, thank you,' he said drily. 'If she based her verdict on your information, you must have painted me in a very flattering colours.'

She could hardly say, Actually, I gave Kate a rather false impression, because if I'd told her the truth she'd have realized I find you rather fanciable and given me no peace.

'I hardly "painted" you at all,' she shrugged. 'Kate's just got an over-vivid imagination. Not to mention too much television and the more lurid kind of Sunday paper.' *Sorry, Kate, blaming it all on you.*

He raised an expectant eyebrow. 'Go on.'

'Go on with what?'

'With your imaginative friend's conjecture. I'm all agog to hear what sleazy proposition the politician would have had in mind.'

He was turning the tables now, winding *her* up. 'I couldn't possibly say,' she said, in mock-shocked tones. 'I'll have you know I was very carefully brung up.

His mouth twitched again. It was beginning to twitch so often she began to wonder whether she was mistaking it for a nervous tic. For a minute he ate in silence, watching her with microscopic attention whenever his eyes weren't actually on his lunch. 'So if you thought I was a) a drug baron, or b) something that crawled from under a Parliamentary rock, why did you come?'

She could hardly say, To tell the truth, I haven't met a Category Four in ages. A girl has to grab what excitement she can, you know.

'For a free lunch,' she confessed. 'I'd never been to Paolo's.'

'Who said anything about free?' he said drily.

She knew he was only winding her up, but she still felt vaguely awkward. 'It wasn't just that.'

'I think it was.'

He said it crisply enough, with no overt accusation, and maybe that was why her conscience was suddenly playing up. Added to that, the alcohol was working on her carefully constructed business-mode.

Suddenly he was far too close for comfort. Her antennae were going like mad, sending minute electric messages to every nerve-ending she possessed. *Do you realize*, they were screaming, *that there's about fourteen stone of dynamite within crackling distance?*

She sat back, hoping her antennae would settle down. 'I didn't come with the express purpose of getting a free lunch and telling you to stuff whatever your deal was. I was curious, naturally enough. Only I didn't think it'd be anything I could possibly accept. And to tell the truth . . .' She sighed. 'It's my cousin. If I let him win, the little toad'll crow for ever more. I just can't give him that satisfaction. He never thought I'd accept that bet. When I said "You're on," I practically had to retrieve his jaw from the floor.'

'Well, naturally. An ex-convent girl would be far too demure to contemplate it.'

There was no missing the sardonic glint in his eye. With a bored expression she said, 'Can we get the clichéd old jokes over with? Just for the record, I've heard about a million variations on "Phwoor, convent girls! Always the worst when they're let out!" '

Twitch or tic, it was at it again. 'No such thought ever crossed my brain cells.'

Liar.

'If you really want to know, we'd had a massive argument about kissograms at a family do last year. He was telling me he was going into kissograms as a sideline, and I ranted on about it being degrading to women and all the rest of it. So when I asked him for money, he couldn't resist it. Seeing me eat my principles, so to speak. And it suited him. His regular girl, who did the kissograms and played office dogsbody, had just taken off for India for a couple of months, and his back-up girl is . . .' She winced. '"*A bit rough*", to use his own charming expression.'

She put her fork down. 'It's turned into a deadly battle of wills. He's convinced I won't be able to stand mass male piggery and drunken idiots yelling "Get your kit off", and I'm equally determined to rub his nose in it as he writes that cheque. So there you go.'

His eyebrows lifted sardonically. 'Are you sure it won't bounce? That outfit he's running didn't strike me as a thriving concern. Will he have that kind of cash available?'

She had almost known he'd ask that. 'I'd never have asked him in the first place if I hadn't known he'd got it. He came into some money from some misguided old aunt. She'd have done better to leave it to the cats' home,' she added, with feeling.

He was regarding her intently, one elbow on the table, fingering his chin thoughtfully. 'Why not just tell him you've had a better offer? That should irk him enough to give you some satisfaction.'

She'd already thought of that. 'He would be irked, but then he'd be pleased about saving his cash. Whatever I do, the little toad'll make it look as if he's won.'

The earthworms of indecision had multiplied tenfold. She put her knife and fork together, a third of the food uneaten.

The waiter came to take it away. 'It wasn't nice, *signorina?*'

Wasting food always made her feel horribly guilty. 'It was lovely, only I'm afraid I haven't got much of an appetite today.'

He wiped away the crumbs and cleared unnecessary cutlery. 'Dessert, *signorina?* We have a very delicious strawberry granita – very light, very good for the little appetites.'

A strawberry water ice would be lovely, and hardly any calories either, but she still felt bad after leaving so much chicken. She half thought of asking for a Portly bag, but the chef might be offended. 'Next time, perhaps,' she smiled.

Guy Hamilton declined also, and they ordered coffee only.

'I get the impression,' he said, as she sipped proper cappucino, 'that you're going to say, Thanks, but no thanks. And I can't say I blame you.'

It was as if someone was hovering round the table with a box of matches, saying, '*Will you stop dithering and burn that boat?*'

Not just yet, but keep them handy.

'When do you leave?'

'Friday.'

'For how long?'

'At least ten days. Maybe a fortnight.'

Oh, Lord, the agony of decisions. Apart from anything else, a glance out of the window at dismal November rain was affecting her judgement. Ten days to a fortnight of expenses-paid sun in a good cause! Could any teenage

48

rebel really put her off that? Her mind strayed briefly to last summer's bikinis and half a bottle of Suntan Lotion in the bathroom cupboard. It might have gone off by next year.

'I'd need to talk to her. Find out whether there's any possible rapport between us.'

His eyes were very shrewd. 'She'll do her damnedest to put you off.'

'I dare say, but I have to make my own judgement.'

He tossed a gold credit card on top of the bill. 'No time like the present. Why don't you come home with me now?'

'Will she be in?'

'She'd better be.' His mouth gave a grim twist. 'She's grounded.'

Oh, Lord. In that case, she'll hardly be in a sunshine and smiles mood. This proposition is beginning to look about as inviting as a fortnight banged up in Holloway.

With this in mind, the sight of his credit card on the bill made her feel vaguely awkward.

Why? You can bet it's nothing to him.

That's not the point.

Before he could stop her, she whipped the bill away, glanced at it, put it back, and took her purse from her bag. Extracting roughly the right amount, she pushed it across to him.

'Put it away,' he said.

'It's my half.'

'I'm not going to argue the toss about it.'

The waiter took the saucer away, and still her money lay there. By the time the bill was signed and they were ready to go it was still there, unloved.

'It's up to you,' he said shortly, rising to his feet. 'Either you take it, or that waiter's going to think it's Christmas already.'

She knew he wasn't going to give in. Leaving a small extra tip, she returned the rest to her purse. 'Are you always so pigheaded?'

'Yes,' he said, opening the door. 'Are you?'

'That was nothing, I can tell you.'

'I'll take your word for it.'

She'd expected expensive wheels parked not far away, but they had to stand in the street trying to spot a vacant cab before somebody else did. *Of course, only an idiot drives if he's going to drink,* she thought.

It was still raining, though not as hard, and since he had no umbrella they shared hers. As they crowded together under such inadequate shelter she tried to pretend he was just another man. An ugly one with bad breath and dandruff on his collar. Or just an idiot, like Ryan.

'Thank God,' he muttered as an orange 'For Hire' sign hove into view. 'Hop in.'

He said little as the taxi stopped and started through the pre-Christmas traffic, past the shops with their Christmas lights winking merrily.

'Thank heaven for Christmas,' she remarked, for something to say. 'Imagine how depressing November and December would be without Christmas!'

'I'm afraid it leaves me cold,' he said. 'Grossly over-commercialized.'

Well, that puts me in my place. Why did everybody say they hated Christmas? Did they really, or was it just the fashion to be cynically bored with it all?

'I love it,' she retorted. 'I love the crowds and the last-minute panics and Carols from King's on Chrismas Eve. I love wrapping presents and real Christmas trees and even grotty plastic things in crackers.'

His mouth twitched minutely as he gave her a sideways glance. 'So there.'

So nothing, she thought wanly. There were no proper Christmases any more, not since her parents had gone to live in Spain. It was all very nice sitting in the sun on Christmas Day, but it wasn't the same.

It wasn't long before they turned off the main road, into the leafy backwoods of Kensington. The quiet streets were lined with the kind of elegant period houses in which dwelt discreet but very comfortable money.

'Here,' he said, halfway down.

A minute later he was leading her up four steps to an imposing, panelled front door. Her first impression was of space and warmth, of high period ceilings in a large square hall and ornate original covings.

He closed the door behind them. 'Mrs Pierce!' he called, in a voice that wouldn't have to try much harder to be a shout.

Almost immediately a door opened at the end of the hall and a plump, fifty-five-ish woman in a blue dress bustled out.

'Where's Anoushka?' he asked.

The woman had pursed-up lips, to match the pursed-up voice Claudia recognized from the phone.

'She went out, Mr Hamilton. I told her you'd be angry, but she just said, "So what's new?"'

'Might have known,' he muttered.

The woman gave Claudia a look as if to say, *Well, it's none of my business who he brings home.*

'This is Claudia,' he added.

Claudia smiled politely. 'Hello.'

'How do you do?' There was a vinegary *If I must* smile. 'Will you be requiring anything, Mr Hamilton?'

'Maybe some coffee, thank you.'

With a barely audible sniff, Mrs Pursed-up disappeared whence she came.

Claudia wavered. Was this fate sticking its oar in? Telling her to run a mile while she still could? 'Maybe I'd better go.'

'Give her half an hour.' Through double Georgian doors he ushered her into what estate agents would describe as 'an elegant drawing room'.

The first thing she noticed was a real fire, flickering in a real, period fireplace. There were three cream sofas, of the unashamedly squashy, luxurious kind. The carpet was soft green, and the other furniture was a curiously happy mix of the modern and the beeswaxed antique. Several lamps glowed on side-tables: the kind that cost a fortune even when they were half-price in Harrods' sale.

'Take a seat,' he said.

The sofa was even squashier than it looked, making her long to kick her shoes off and tuck her feet underneath her.

She expected him to sit opposite, on the other side of a square coffee-table, but he said, 'If you'll excuse me, I have to make a couple of phone calls.'

'Feel free.'

He picked up a mobile phone from a side-table and took it with him. Thank heaven he hadn't taken it with him to the restaurant. Nothing irritated her more than people whose beastly phones rang in restaurants. Another thought struck her. That number he'd given her evidently wasn't his mobile number, or Mrs Pursed-up wouldn't have answered.

So what does that tell me? That he doesn't dish out his personal number on a casual basis? That he doesn't dish out his personal number to women *on a casual basis? Now why is that, my dear? Obviously in case they start pestering. And what does that tell me? That he's been pestered in the past?*

More than likely.

Once the double doors had closed behind him, her attention was taken by something else: a magazine on the coffee-table. There were others in a neat pile, but this was open at a double-page spread entitled, 'HOW TO HAVE THE BEST SEX EVER'.

It was a young women's glossy that Claudia sometimes bought herself. The article didn't interest her much; despite the title, there wouldn't be anything she hadn't read fifty times before. Leave your knickers off when you go out and tell him over dinner; smother him with maple syrup and lick it all off, etc., etc. What interested her was why his daughter – it had to be her – had left it open like that. Not to shock him, surely? Unless Claudia was very much mistaken, it would take an awful lot more that that. He wouldn't play into her hands with so much as a wince.

If not him, who? Mrs Pursed-up, no doubt. She looked exactly the type to be endlessly wittering on about 'smut and filth' on the television.

Closing the magazine, she picked up *Newsweek* instead, and was still flicking though it when he returned.

He parked himself opposite. 'Sorry about that.'

'No need to apologize.' *Polite conversation time,* she thought, putting the magazine back. 'Now lunch is out of the way, are you going to tell me why Anoushka was suspended?'

He sat back, crossing one leg over the other, his ankle on his knee. 'Why don't you ask her? She'll give you all the graphic details I'd leave out. It'll be a nice little ice-breaker.'

She was about to say, If she comes back before midnight, when the doors opened. It was Mrs Pierce, with a tray. Depositing it on the table, she said stiffly, 'Mr Hamilton, I'd like a word before I go out. In private.'

He rose to his feet and followed her out, but did not quite shut the doors. Claudia wasn't exactly listening; she just couldn't help hearing the conversation in the hall.

'I really cannot be responsible for her when you go away, Mr Hamilton. Not after last time.'

'I wouldn't expect you to be, Mrs Pierce. I'm making alternative arrangements.'

'And another thing. I really will *not* be told by a sixteen-year-old to get back to my Fairy Liquid and – '

'Mrs Pierce, we'll discuss it in the study, if you don't mind.'

There was the sound of another door opening and closing firmly. *Just when it was getting really interesting,* thought Claudia. *Typical.* She picked up *Newsweek* again and flicked through it, before realizing she'd flicked through it before, at the dentist's. For want of anything else to do, she wandered over to the fire. How long was it since she'd seen a real one, not a log-effect gas thing?

Over the mantelpiece was a painting of a sailing ship in a heavy sea, but something else was claiming her attention.

Feeling guiltily nosy, she picked up a silver-framed photo from a polished side-table. It showed a baby girl of maybe fifteen months, her whole face lit in an enchanting baby smile.

Anoushka, she thought, looking at the liquid dark eyes and recalling that exotic girl in the restaurant. *She was gorgeous even then.*

There were two other photos, including one of an older Anoushka with a gap-toothed smile, but it was the third that made her heart suddenly constrict.

It showed a much younger Guy Hamilton, with longer hair. He was smiling. Really smiling. His arm was round a woman, a dark woman whose beauty resembled Anoushka's, but with a much more fragile quality. In her arms was a squashy little bundle in a white shawl.

The proud new father with his little family.

All thoughts of divorce or estrangement vanished instantly. Somehow, she just knew that frail-looking mother was dead. Her throat constricted painfully, but the sound of voices made her replace the photo with a guilty start. When he returned, she was back in her seat, apparently intent on *Newsweek*.

'Sorry about that.' He began pouring the coffee, but then paused. 'I should have asked. Maybe you'd have preferred tea.'

'Coffee's fine. No sugar.' She smiled brightly, praying he would not notice that her eyes were fractionally brighter than they should be.

Claudia, control yourself. But the harder she tried, the worse it got, until she was forced to rummage in her bag for a tissue.

Piddle and bum; there wasn't one. Before a tear actually made it on to her cheek, she rubbed her eye with the back of her hand. 'Wretched mascara.' Blinking hard, she tried to sound merely irritated. 'I think I've got a filament in my eye. Have you got a tissue?'

'I've got a handkerchief.' Leaning across the table, he handed her something clean and white.

'Thanks.' She dabbed her eye briskly, and felt her weepiness retreat. She was just thanking heaven when she realized her dabbing had been overdone. Now there really *was* something in her eye.

Double piddle and bum. Why do I buy mascara with bits in it?

She dabbed again, blinked hard, but it was still there, like a lump of gravel on her cornea.

With a faint 'tut', he rose to his feet.

'Let me.' He sat beside her, taking her chin firmly. 'Hold still and look up.'

As if he'd done it a million times, he pulled her eyelid down and took the handkerchief from her hand. 'I can see it', he muttered. 'Keep still.'

In an instant, it was out.

'Gosh, thanks.' Her voice was just a touch unsteady, partly from her recent weepy fit, but partly because he was close enough for her to see the tiny gold flecks in his eyes.

Her antennae were at it again, as if their lives depended on it. They were prickling the tiny hairs on her arms, prodding dark, sleepy corners of her stomach. 'I can see you've done that before,' she said, with a forced, bright smile.

'Not since Anoushka was small and used to get sand in her eyes on the beach.'

Whether it was two glasses of wine on top of a gin and tonic, or whether it was that poignant photo, her defences were disintegrating like wet tissues. Suddenly she saw only a single parent with a great worry on his mind and nobody to help him.

Oh, what the hell? Moistening her lips, she began, 'Mr Hamilton, I – '

'Make it Guy.' He gave a tiny, wry smile that had a most unfortunate effect on her nerve-endings.

'Guy, then.' She tried to sound brisk, but it wasn't easy with those navy eyes and all the rest of that Category Four within crackling distance. 'I've been thinking about it, and in the circumstances – '

She got no further.

The double doors had opened, on nearly silent hinges. On the threshold stood a girl she barely recognized from the restaurant version. Her hair was stuffed into a baseball cap, she wore jeans, a leather biker jacket, and an expression of pert disdain that matched her voice exactly.

'At it again, Dad? Having a final fling before the male menopause gets you?'

He was already on his feet. 'Where have you been?'

Claudia winced at the gritty ice in his tone.

'Out. Where d'you think?'

Guy moved towards the door, and as he did so the girl's expression altered sharply. 'My God, the mother of your little love-child. What are you doing? Sorting out maintenance?'

'Anoushka!'

An indignant flush washed the girl's face. 'So that's why you forced the address out of me! You pretended you wanted to have a go at the morons who make a living out of other people's embarrassment, and all the while you just wanted to see *her*!'

'It was nothing of the kind!'

'Do you think I'm stupid? You're nothing but a flaming hypocrite!' She turned and almost ran from the room.

He was after her at once. 'Anoushka!'

'Get lost!' There was the sound of a pair of feet making themselves scarce up the stairs.

For several seconds it was very quiet, like the aftermath of a hurricane. Eventually he returned, sinking to the sofa opposite and running a weary hand through his hair.

Feeling she'd only made matters worse, Claudia rose to her feet. 'I'll go home,' she said awkwardly. 'You go up to her and explain.'

A cynical snort escaped him. 'Her door'll be locked for hours. And then it'll be fun and games, telling her why you were here.'

Reality hit her like a cold shower. *Heaven help me. What was I about to do, just before she opened that door? Was I quite mad?*

'Guy, I'm terribly sorry,' she said unsteadily, 'but this minder business just isn't on. I can't see her even condescending to talk to me, let alone listening to anything I say. It'd be an utter waste of your money.'

'She's not so stroppy with everybody, you know. It's generally directed at me.'

Why? she wanted to ask. But what was the point? Adolescent dramas were common enough. 'It wouldn't work. I might make matters worse, and I couldn't have that on my conscience when I think what it would all cost.'

58

Not just what he was going to pay her, but the air fare, the hotel bill . . .

She was half expecting him to say, I can afford it, but he was not so crass. 'I guess it was a lousy idea. I'll call you a cab.' Suddenly straightening his shoulders, he picked up a phone off a side table.

'It's really not necessary. I'll walk to the main road and get one there.'

'For crying out loud, you'll never get a cab at this time in the rain.' His voice was much crisper now. 'Hamilton,' he said, to whoever was on the other end. 'I need a cab to . . .' He shot her a questioning glance.

'Putney,' she said.

'Putney. As quick as you can. Thanks.'

As he replaced the aerial, she gaped at him. 'You didn't give your address!'

'I didn't need to. I have an account with them. Anoushka uses them all the time. They'll be here in five minutes,' he added, glancing at his watch.

She felt deflated, as if she were being dismissed now she no longer served any purpose.

Well, you don't. What on earth do you expect him to do? Ask you to stay to tea?

Reseating herself on the sofa, she said, 'I'm so sorry I've wasted your time.'

'I've wasted yours too.'

'It was a lovely lunch, though.'

The ghost of a smile hovered on his lips. 'Maybe I should have ordered that Tarzan after all.'

Even that glimmer was better than none. 'At least you'd have got a good laugh.'

A question that had been lurking at the back of her mind pushed its way to the front. 'Why did she want to get expelled? Just so she could be on the loose while you're away?'

He shook his head. 'She's been wanting to leave school ever since her sixteenth birthday.'

'And do what?'

'Nothing. Unless you count hanging round clubs and picking up boyfriends with Ferraris.'

Ah. Life in the fast lane, versus the tedium of geography lessons and teachers who seemed to think 'fun' was a dirty word.

'I know the feeling,' she confessed. 'Although at that age I'd have settled for a Mini.'

'But you didn't get yourself kicked out of school.' His eyes narrowed a fraction. 'Did you?'

'Only in my dreams.'

'It's – not – funny!'

His tone made her instantly contrite. Feeling distinctly awkward, she got up. 'I know. I'm sorry. I'll wait outside for the cab. Please don't get up.'

But he followed her out, as she'd almost known he would. At the door he paused. 'I shouldn't have snapped.'

'It was my fault. It was a stupid thing to say.'

Thrusting his hands in his pockets, he gazed down at her. 'It would have been poetic justice for that kissogram to backfire on her.'

'Is that why you asked me? Just to serve her right?'

'I'm not that twisted. I just had a feeling you'd hit it off. A wild delusion, obviously.'

'What will you do now?'

He shrugged. 'I'll sort something out.'

The bell made them both start. He opened the door and a wind straight from Siberia hit them.

'You ordered a cab?' said the man on the step.

'Twenty seconds.' Guy closed the door again.

For a wild moment, as his eyes flickered over her face, she thought he was going to say, Why don't we do dinner some time? Or even –

'You know something?' His voice was subtly different: rough and soft at once, like an old Shetland sweater.

She swallowed hard. 'What?'

'You were a bloody hopeless kissogram girl.'

Her voice came out just a trifle unsteady. 'I'd be an even more hopeless minder for your daughter.'

A ghost of a smile flickered at the corners of his mouth. 'I'll take your word for it.' He opened the door again. 'All the best.'

'Bye.' With a bright smile she took the hand he offered. 'She'll be fine. 'It's just a phase.'

The sardonic twist to his mouth said, *I've heard that before*.

Before he knew what had hit him she stood on tiptoe, brushed her lips against his cheek. 'She'll be fine. You'll see.'

She ran down the steps to the waiting cab and waved brightly.

Once the door had closed behind him her smile vanished like snow in May. *You idiot*, she thought miserably. *One gin and a couple of glasses of wine and you're fluttering like a bimbo butterfly. Couldn't you see he was just waiting for you to get the hell out?*

61

CHAPTER 4

'And the miserable devil didn't even give you a donation?'

'Not a sausage.'

'Then he deserves his daughter from hell. You're well
out of it.'

Two cups of coffee and a long post-mortem with Kate
had made her feel better – except that she'd left any
fluttery bits right out. That way they'd fade all the
faster. 'I didn't even think about donations at the time.
And, to be quite fair to him, he had other things on his
mind.'

'That's no excuse.'

The more she thought about it, the more Claudia was
inclined to agree. While she and Kate were knocking
together a stir-fry she said, 'It's almost obscene, the
amount of money he was prepared to spend. When I
think what Bruin Wood could do with that cash . . .'

Kate was chopping spring onions. 'I expect she's spoilt
absolutely rotten.'

'Of course she is. She was only wearing jeans and a
leather jacket, but they had that designer look. And the

dress she was wearing the other night – not that I remember exactly; I was too wound up – but it wasn't from one of those fall-to-bits tat shops where most girls that age buy their clothes. She had the look of an expensively maintained woman.'

'Probably got a Harrods chargecard.'

'It wouldn't surprise me. When I was that age I was scouring charity shops.'

'I still am,' Kate grinned.

Claudia laughed, reaching a jar of sauce from the cupboard. She'd lashed out on limed oak units in the July sales and her father had fitted them during a summer visit. It hadn't taken long in a kitchen where even two cooks tripped over each other.

Portly's antennae could pick up pork fillet at fifty paces. He strolled in and rubbed ingratiatingly against her legs. 'No,' she said firmly. 'You've had your dinner.'

He sat and gazed at her, one paw raised pathetically, and uttered his best, orphaned kitten mew.

'No way,' she said. 'The vet says you're obese and I have to harden my heart.'

Portly went on to Plan B: to pretend he didn't care one way or the other about pork fillet and kid them he'd just come in to have a nap on the kitchen floor. Then, with a bit of luck, they'd both turn their backs at the same moment and he'd leap up on to the worktop and grab a smackerel of whatever was going.

He stretched out accordingly, and pretended to be asleep.

'I know what you're up to,' said Claudia severely. 'So push off before somebody treads on your tail.'

Portly gave it up as a bad job and strolled out, his tail quivering with disdain.

'He's spoilt rotten too,' she admitted. 'I over-compensated because he'd been mistreated before the shelter found him.' Her brain rapidly connected this to something else. 'I dare say Daddy Hamilton's been over-compensating because the girl has no mother.'

'You don't know that.'

Claudia tipped the pork into a wok. 'No, but I'd put money on it. Even if they were divorced, he'd still over-compensate. Especially if it was his fault.'

'Oodles of pocket money, I bet. Anything she wants.'

Claudia added peppers and onions and stirred mechanically. 'I expect so. But probably no time. He's obviously got a very demanding job. She takes taxis all the time too. On his account.'

'Lucky little brat.' Kate was straining Chinese noodles. 'So it's back to Naughty Natalie,' she grinned. 'With any luck, it'll soon be over. Christmas is almost upon us, and you know what that means.'

'Parties,' Claudia groaned. 'Offices full of idiots wondering how to spice up their Accounts Department party. Ryan wants me in the office tomorrow and I'm dreading it. I just know there'll be a booking and the little toad'll be grinning his face off.'

She couldn't actually see his face when she walked in next morning, since it was hidden behind the latest boy-racer car magazine. His feet were on the desk, next to a carton of fast-food fries.

'You're late,' he said.

'And you're talking with your mouth full.'

He munched and slurped even louder, just to annoy her. 'Found a great car in here. Porsche Carrera, only two careful lady owners.'

She slung her coat on the back of a chair. 'Ryan, who on earth would insure you for a Porsche after you've written off three cars?'

'Got a friend who knows a dodgy insurance bloke.' Through a mouthful of food he added, 'Knew there was something wrong with this burger. Not enough gherkin. You wouldn't like to nip down the road and –?'

'Don't push your luck.'

'Suit yourself. I'll need you to man the office in a minute, anyway. I'm off home for a kip.'

'But that only leaves two drivers!'

'Tough. I had a heavy night.' He added a wink just calculated to make her cringe. 'With Belinda-the-Boobs.'

She raised her eyes to heaven. 'Ryan, I am not in the least interested in your sordid sex-life. How do you expect to build up a solid client base if you're sleeping when people want cabs?'

He put on his best injured expression. 'I can't drive safely if I'm knackered. I don't suppose you appreciate just how knackering a really wild night can be. For your information, an hour of rampant nookie burns as many calories as running the London Marathon. Never mind several hours of mind-blowing – '

'Ryan, shall I tell you something?' She stood with folded arms and a pitying expression. 'A psychologist once told me that men who brag about their sex-lives are either impotent or lousy lovers.'

'Cobblers. Who's bragging, anyway? I was merely stating facts.'

She hadn't really expected her inspired fib to wipe that grin off his face, but it was always worth a try.

'You're just jealous,' he went on. 'Going to bed on your tod every night. I could fix you up, if you want. I've got this friend who won the Mr Wet Boxer Shorts last year. Hung like an elephant.'

She filled the kettle. *He's just winding you up. Ignore him.*

'He's got a couple of birds on the go, but I dare say he could fit you in,' he went on, stuffing the last of the burger into his mouth. 'Specially if I tell him you're desperate. He's good like that. Kind-hearted to the lonely and deprived.'

Just do that saintly smile that really gets up his nose. 'That's terribly sweet of him, Ryan. When I'm desperate for a really elephantine seeing-to, I'll bear him in mind. And what makes you think I'm going to bed on my tod every night, anyway?'

'Jungle telegraph,' he said, aiming his burger paper at the bin and missing. 'Also known as your mum ringing my mum and my mum ringing me.' He put on a passable imitation of her own mother's voice. ' "And I'm so terribly worried about *Claudia*. What a pity she broke up with Matthew – such a *lovely* boy and a very nice *family*. His father was a wine merchant, you know." '

It wasn't much use retaliating, since she could imagine her mother saying exactly that. She had never stopped going on about Matthew and what a 'lovely boy' he was, even though they'd broken up over two years back. Still, if Ryan was stirring, she might as well stir in return.

'Next time your mother rings, tell her I'm right off men,' she said, filling the kettle. 'And I'll see how long it takes for my mother to hear I've become a rampant lezzie. I'd hazard a guess at ten minutes, knowing your mother's gossip potential.'

She put the kettle on, wincing at the spilt coffee and dirty mugs he'd left on the tray. 'Why are you such a *slob*?'

'I was thinking of you, my dear Claud. Something to keep those idle little mitts out of mischief while I'm gone. Besides, I never clear up if there's a woman to do it.'

She repressed the urge to strangle him with the lurid tie he was wearing. Rising to his bait was exactly what he wanted.

Leaving the fries carton on the desk, he got up and put his jacket on. 'Tatty-bye, then, sweet cousin. Be good.'

For the thousandth time, she marvelled that to the untrained eye Ryan actually resembled a normal human being, even in a bright pink jacket and that dreadful tie. About five feet eleven and on the lanky side, he still had the mischievous, curly-haired choirboy look that had let him get away with murder as a child.

He still had the curls, rather longer now. And he still had the look. And he knew it.

'D'you know why old Auntie Flora from Killiekrankie left me all that dough?' he'd remarked the other day. 'Because she came to stay one Christmas when I was six. Ma and Pa carted her off to school to see me be a shepherd in the Nativity Play and the poor old dear was moved to tears.'

He had actually got up and demonstrated, putting on a piping little voice. 'We must haste at once to Bethlehem! Come, let us follow the bright star!'

67

He'd sat down again, chuckling. 'She used to send me a postal order every birthday after that, and I used to write her a little letter in my best joined-up writing, saying, "Dear Great-Auntie Flora, thank you very much *indeed* for the money. I have put half in my savings bank and I have sent the rest to the poor children in Africa who don't have any food. I hope you are well, love from Ryan."'

Claudia had gazed at him with withering contempt. 'You unutterable little creep.'

He had only grinned the more. 'You haven't heard the best bit. I was in Scotland a couple of years ago so I dropped in. Ma had said she was on the way out, so I thought, Well, no harm in reminding the old girl of her saintly great-nephew, just in case she hasn't finalized her will.'

Remembering it all made her want to kick him, but since he was on his way out it would only delay him.

'Oh, by the way,' he said casually, his hand on the door, 'if you check the diary, you'll see there are a couple of bookings. One's for Wednesday night; a French maid for some old bugger's seventieth. The other's much more fun. A rugby club bash on Saturday night. They want a Little Red Riding Hood, would you believe, as their captain's name is Bill Wolfson. And, you've guessed it, they call him Big Bad Wolf.'

Her heart was plummeting to her ankles.

'Should be a good laugh,' he grinned. 'Especially for me. I've told them you'll need a minder at a do like that. They want you to trip up to Big Bad Wolf and say, "Goodneth me, Mithter Wolf, what big eyeth you have!"'

She feigned indifference.

Ryan was grinning fit to split. 'And then you'll do the ears bit, and the teeth bit, and then you'll say, "Goodneth me, Mithter Wolf, ith there one thingle thing about you that ithn't abtholutely whopping?" And then Big Bad Wolf'll – '

'I get the message.' Acting harder than she ever had in her life, Claudia flopped into her chair with a yawn. 'Sounds a bit tame for a rugby club, if you ask me.'

It was no comfort to see the grin wiped off his face as he left. He had deflated, just as if somebody had stuck a pin in him.

Kate was out when she got home. She had left a note.

Paul's dragging me off to some do in darkest Hampshire. Will stay the night as will probably be far too ratso to drive back.

See you tomorrow, luv K. XXXX.

Paul was Kate's latest and had already lasted four months, which was a record, for Kate.

Typical, she thought. *Just when I need a shoulder to moan on.*

After a long, soaky bath she donned the tartan flannelette pyjamas her mother had bestowed as an extra present last Christmas, because 'That bedroom of yours is horribly draughty, dear.'

Too dispirited to cook, she pinched Kate's boil-in-the-bag cod in butter sauce from the freezer and slung a baked potato in the microwave. She ate on her lap in front of the television and Portly drove her mad, trying to scoop the

69

fish off the plate with his paw when he thought she wasn't looking.

'*No!*' Firmly she picked him up and dumped him on the floor. As always, when offended, Portly sat with a huffy back to her for thirty seconds before stalking off. To her bedroom, probably, to sleep in the basket of nice clean ironing. If he was especially miffed, he might even be sick on it.

She finished her supper and tried not to think about rugby club dinners. She tried even harder not to think how Ryan would crow if she jacked it in now. The television jabbered to itself, unnoticed, as she thought about rocks and hard places and Big Bad Wolves. Most of all, she thought about Ryan in the background with a pint of lager, grinning his face off as he egged them all on.

There comes a point where a girl just has to draw the line. She picked up the phone, her heart beating rather faster than usual.

It was Pursed-up Pierce who answered.

Claudia moistened her lips. 'May I speak to Mr Hamilton, please?'

'I'm afraid he's not at home. Who is calling?'

Her mother's voice was at it again. 'If it's not meant to be, dear . . .'

'It wasn't anything important.' After replacing the receiver, she tried to distract herself with a documentary about tigers. She might even have enjoyed it, but a poor little tiger cub died and the wretched camera crew didn't lift a finger to save it.

At twenty past ten she decided to draw a line under an unsatisfactory day and head for bed. She was just straightening the cushions when the doorbell rang.

70

Oh, hell. Given the kind of day she'd had, it just had to be Peter the Pain. Peter the Pain had moved into the upstairs flat a few months back. A wimpy type, with clammy-looking hands, he nonetheless fancied himself like mad, as such creeps are wont to do. He had obviously got it into his head that life was like a spiced-up instant coffee commercial. All you had to do was constantly run out of coffee, teabags or washing powder, and sooner or later one of those girls downstairs would realize you were the best thing since Mel Gibson and turn into a raging nympho.

Bracing herself for a, Yes, but you're not coming in, she opened the door.

Her first reaction, apart from the shock of seeing Guy Hamilton on the step, was to curse those sensible pyjamas. Why wasn't she wearing ivory silk ones, like you were supposed to when a Category Four that you fancied like mad came to the door? Why did she not even *possess* ivory silk ones?

He was wearing jeans and a rough-textured grey sweater, and he smelt of wool and cold night mist. He looked somehow different: younger, but more rugged too. More earthy, as if his city skin had been stripped away.

'Was it you who phoned?' he asked.

She nodded. 'How did you know?'

'Mrs Pierce recognized your voice.'

'But how did you find out my address?' Her brain answered this almost before she'd asked it. 'I suppose you asked the cab company.'

He shook his head. 'I have a photographic memory.' He added a smile; a trifle wry and lopsided, but it did something funny to her heart, as if it were being kicked hard and kissed better both at once.

'That letter on the desk?'

'I'm afraid so.' With a glance at her pyjamas, he added, 'I'm sorry. It's a bit late for dropping in.'

She collected her scattered wits. 'I wasn't going to bed yet. Please, come in. It costs a bomb to heat this flat, and it's all whooshing out the door.'

Once she'd shut the door there was a faintly awkward pause. The hall was more like a cupboard, and had been horribly dark when she'd bought the flat, but a lick of white paint had worked wonders. There was a huge aspidistra there too, called Veg, who didn't seem to mind icy blasts. And what with three-foot-odd of Veg and six-foot-odd of Hamilton, the cupboard was more like a shoebox.

'You seem to have shrunk,' he observed.

She was just thinking the same thing, but then she'd been wearing high heels on both previous occasions when facing him vertically. 'I always shrink in the bath,' she said lightly. 'But I'm usually back to normal by morning.'

His mouth quivered in the half-smile that was becoming heart-stoppingly familiar. 'Why did you phone? Second thoughts?'

Taking a deep, steadying breath, she nodded. 'Why don't you come through?'

Thank heaven the living room was tidy. When it was tidy it looked quite nice, despite the horrible brown carpet she hadn't got round to replacing. She had diluted it with dhurries instead. The bookshelves on either side of the fireplace were newly painted in cream, against a dramatic dark green wall. She'd done that too, and had been delighted with the *Homes and Gardens* effect.

He barely glanced at anything.

'Do sit down,' she said, indicating the sofa. 'Can I get you a coffee or something? And no, it's not instant,' she added, seeing his give-away hesitation.

'Coffee's fine. Dark brown, no sugar.'

Only when she reached the sanctuary of the kitchen did she realize how erratically her heart was racing. Not just because he was there, but because those boat-burning matches were lost for ever.

You're going to regret this, said a severe little voice in her head as she spooned Blue Mountain into the filter. *And don't say I didn't warn you.*

Oh, shut up.

Having got the coffee on, she made a dive for her bedroom and stripped off the pyjamas. No matter what, she wasn't entertaining a Category Four in those. She pulled on a pair of grey leggings and added a soft pink sweater that covered her hips. She gave her hair a frantic brushing, so that it fell in a silky tumble to her shoulders. Changing her mind, she tied it back. And then she changed her mind again and let it loose once more.

No make-up, though. Not a smidgeon of lip-gloss, not a whisper of perfume. Heaven forbid that he should think she'd done it for him.

What about the sweater, though? A bit low-cut? Don't want him thinking I'm flashing my assets.

After a check in the mirror she decided there was no obvious cleavage unless he was actually gaping right down her front.

73

Unlikely, Claudia.

A toasty-brown smell was already wafting from the kitchen. *Good cups, Claudia, not manky old mugs. Where the hell's the milk jug?*

He looked reasonably relaxed, one ankle resting on his knee. 'Thank you,' he murmured. 'Smells good.'

He made no comment on her quick change, but his eyes said he'd noticed. Feeling she had to say something, she made a joke of it. 'I couldn't entertain a practically strange man in my pyjamas. Poor old Sister Immaculata would have a pink fit.'

This time he did not try to conceal the glint of amusement in his eyes. 'For the benefit of Sister Immaculata . . .' He raised his eyes to the ceiling. 'I'm not strange. I'm completely normal.'

'That's precisely why she'd have a pink fit.'

The glint glinted once more and died. It was as if he'd said, Let's get the funnies over and down to business. 'Are you serious about this trip?'

He didn't add, Because if you're just wasting my time, I might as well leave now, but his crisp tone said it for him.

She tried not to notice the sudden, poignant ache in some unnamed organ. She'd have given anything to hear him say, Look, I've made other arrangements for Anoushka. That's not the reason I came.

Fat chance. She nodded. 'As you said, second thoughts.'

His eyes were very shrewd. 'Any particular reason?'

'Two more bookings that I couldn't face.'

'I thought as much.' His eyes scanned her briefly. 'I'll need your passport, to get you a visa.'

74

She went back to her room and retrieved it from a bedside drawer.

As she'd almost known he would, he opened it. And for more than a second or two he gazed at the first page. 'It's a good photo,' he said at last.

'Thank you.' She knew he didn't mean in the technical sense. Anyone looking at that photo, taken four years back in a Woolies cubicle, would have thought that glow, that smile and sparkle in her eyes, could only denote a twenty-five-year-old wildly in love.

In fact she had just enjoyed a very alcoholic lunch with two girlfriends who'd just spent a week on a nudist beach. Descriptions of the gruesome wobbly flab, never mind the amazing range and variety of male dangly bits, had kept her in fits throughout the meal.

Still, he wasn't to know that.

Tucking her bare feet under her, she changed the subject. 'Did you tell Anoushka why I was there?'

'Of course.'

'Did she believe you?'

'Eventually. Even she realized I wouldn't make up a thing like that.'

'What did she say?'

'Nothing, at first. Dumb fury would sum it up. When I added that you'd turned the offer down, it turned to glee. Her precise words were, "Told you to get stuffed, did she? Serve you right."'

'I told her you were doing the kissograms for a bet,' he went on. 'You instantly shot up fifty points in her estimation. I should have stopped there, instead of telling her why you wanted the money. That instantly pigeon-holed you as some noble, earnest type.'

'Maybe you should have told her it was for a holiday in the Caribbean.'

'It's too late now.'

'What will she say when you tell her I've changed my mind?'

'She'll sulk ferociously and probably lock herself in her room. She'll spend hours on the phone to her friends, telling them I'm a sadistic control-freak and that she'd rather be dead than be dragged off to "some Arabian hellhole".'

More or less what I expected.

Portly chose that moment to stroll back in. He yawned, stretched, and uttered an 'Anything to eat?' mew.

Guy Hamilton eyed him dispassionately. 'My God. What do you feed it on? Anabolic steroids?'

'He's not an "it"! He's a he! Or he was, till he had the operation. Food's his only pleasure in life, apart from sleeping.'

'You don't say.'

Hurt on Portly's behalf, she picked him up and kissed his ginger head. Portly, however, was still miffed about the cod in butter sauce. Wriggling from her arms, he wandered over to inspect her guest. He sat like an overweight doorstop, scrutinizing him with a steady, unblinking gaze.

Guy Hamilton returned the compliment. 'You could do with starvation rations for a bit,' he told him, raising his cup to his lips.

Portly was not in the least offended. On the contrary, he decided that this stranger was wearing just the kind of woolly jumper he liked kneading his claws into. He made a surprisingly athletic leap on to the Hamilton lap, knocking his coffee all over him.

Claudia's hands flew to her face. 'Oh, heavens. I'll get a cloth.'

She dashed to the kitchen, grabbed the wiping-round cloth, decided it was too grubby, grabbed a clean one from the drawer, rinsed and wrung it out and dashed back. He was on his feet, cursing only mildly as coffee dripped from the large brown stain on his sweater over his jeans.

'I'm terribly sorry. That cat just has no brains at all.' She began a frantic mopping of his sweater. 'I hope it won't stain.'

'That's fine,' he said, after ten seconds.

'Don't be silly. Coffee's the worst possible – '

'Claudia, leave it.' His tone was as firm as his grip as he took her mopping hands by the wrists.

She stopped and looked up at him. Her hair had tumbled over her face and the soft pink lambswool over her breasts was rising and falling, and not just from sudden exertion.

The jellyfish hit her again, but this time it was a whopper. It seemed to disintegrate on contact, ooze into her bones and make them buckle.

He was so close she could see tiny gold flecks in his eyes, and the individual blackness of his eyelashes. She could see minute, shaved-off pinpoints under his skin, and smell soap and elusive male scents mingling with damp wool.

'I was only trying to help,' she said unsteadily.

'And I appreciate it, but it's fine now.'

77

Cutting both eye and wrist contact, he let her go. 'There are things we have to run through.'

Somehow, she made her voice come out normally. 'In a tick. I'll just mop the rug.' She knelt and scrubbed furiously at a couple of coffee-drips on the cotton dhurry.

When she reseated herself, the jellyfish was still oozing into her legs regardless. She could still feel his hands encircling her wrists, and it made her feel like woozy eggshells.

'The flight's around ten on Friday morning,' he said crisply. 'Have you got suitable clothes? It'll be in the eighties or nineties, but the kind of things you'd wear in the Med are right out, except on the beach. You need to keep your knees and shoulders covered, and anything tight around your . . . hips is right out too.' His eyes flickered to the V of her sweater. 'Ditto anything low-cut.'

Something weird suddenly lurched in her stomach. *Christmas! He must have got a right old eyeful while I was mopping his sweater! Never mind the carpet!*

This reaction startled her a good deal. So what if he had? Why in heaven's name was she fluttering like something out of a daft Victorian novel?

'Oh, Lud, fetch the smelling salts!'

'Why, dearest Claudia, what is amiss?'

'Oh, sister, I fear Lord Filthyrich just glimpsed my . . . my bosoms!'

'And obviously no tight jeans,' he was saying.

'No tight jeans,' she repeated obediently. In the circumstances, it was difficult to sit up straight and look intelligently interested. Something very odd was going on and it wasn't just the jellyfish. She had hardly thought of Sister Immaculata in years, but mentioning her so flippantly seemed to have produced a ouija-board effect. Suddenly she could hear the tetchy old nun's voice as if she were right there:

'*If you accept this offer, Claudia, it should be for the right reasons. Firstly, because you want to raise money for Bruin Wood without degrading yourself, and secondly, because you want to help this man cope with what must be a very difficult situation. You should not accept just because he arouses – ahem – certain **feelings** in you . . .*'

'Claudia, are you still with me?'

She came back with a jolt, to find him frowning at her as if she were not quite all there. 'Absolutely. One hundred per cent.'

The frown disappeared. 'Will you need to buy anything? Not that you'll find much in November.'

'I think I'll have enough.'

'Then I'll be off.' He rose to his feet, flexing his knees in the way long-legged men do. 'I'll need your phone number.'

If only you wanted it for something else. She scribbled it on the pad by the phone and tore the sheet off.

He put it in his pocket. 'I'll be in touch in the next day or two.'

'Fine.' Her voice came out so bright it sounded fake even to her own ears. 'Do you want me to meet Anoushka properly before we go?'

'I can't see much point. She'll only try to put you off.'

He followed her to the front door. Just before she opened it he paused, car keys in his hand. 'You didn't leave a message when you phoned. Did you have second thoughts about the second thoughts?'

She pushed back the growing-out fringe. 'I suppose I did.'

He scrutinized her face. 'If I've steam-rollered you into this, say so. I won't throw a fit if you back out now. Nobody knows better than me that coping with Anoushka is no picnic.'

It wasn't exactly weariness in his voice, nor was it resignation. It was a statement of fact from a man with a problem that had no obvious solution.

And it was exasperating to a man accustomed to handling anything. She could see that all too well. She could see him handling cut-throat boardroom politics, ocean-going yachts in a storm, almost any sort of crisis with deadly unflappability. But he could not handle a sixteen-year-old daughter.

So often it had given her satisfaction to see a man who thought he could handle anything shown that he was not God after all. Why not now?

'I'm not going to back out.' He voice was just a trifle unsteady, so she smiled, shrugged, and lightened it. 'I won't tell you what Ryan had in store for me, but it'll be a colossal relief to tell him to stick it.'

One corner of his mouth twitched almost imperceptibly. 'Something else to make old Sister Whatsit whizz in her grave?'

'Enough to cause a minor earthquake. Mind you, she always did think I was beyond redemption.'

'Then you and Anoushka should have something – '

The doorbell cut him off. And this time it *was* Peter the Pain, complete with ingratiating smirk.

It vanished pretty fast.

'Yes?' she said, trying to conceal her impatience.

With a glance from Guy to her and back again, Peter the Pain pinned on something between a nervous grin and a leer. 'Hope I'm not interrupting anything.' He shot a ghastly, conspiratorial 'nudge, nudge, us lads' look at Guy.

She almost felt him bristle. 'What is it, Peter? Teabags again?'

'Er . . .' He seemed to have mislaid his usual perkiness, possibly because Guy was standing three feet away, doing a passable imitation of an unamused concrete wall. 'You wouldn't have a slice or two of bread, would you? Only I've run out.'

Anything to get rid of him. On the other hand, she had a feeling there was only just enough for breakfast. 'I'll have a look, but I can't – '

'It's a bit late to be on the scrounge.' With a good deal of asperity, Guy cut in. 'This is not Much Twittering-on-the-Marsh. There's a twenty-four-hour petrol station not half a mile down the road, complete with all-night shop.'

Peter the Pain bared his teeth in a nervous grin. 'Is there? Must be new.'

Just to show his machismo was not entirely quashed, he shot a glance at Claudia that somehow managed to say, *'Don't feel bad. I know you'd have just loved to see me if this interfering thug hadn't stuck his oar in.'*

'Sweet dreams, petal.'

It was Guy who shut the door behind him, his face a picture of appalled incredulity. *'Petal?'*

She was torn between laughter and ridiculous guilt. 'He's a terrible nuisance, but now and then I get the feeling he's just lonely.'

'Lonely my backside.'

Kate's Paul had put it more graphically. 'That nerd fancies the pants off the pair of you, and if you keep encouraging him he's going to think he's in with a chance. One of these days he's going to give one of you a sweaty-handed grope, and don't come running to me when you throw up.'

All this she read in Guy's eyes as clearly as if he had said it himself. 'He's harmless,' she shrugged.

'How often does he come round on the scrounge?'

Half of her was tempted to tell him it was none of his business if she dished out groceries to all the nerds in Putney on a daily basis. The other half was only relieved he had dispatched the nuisance so easily. 'Once or twice a week. I can't just tell him to get lost.'

'Why the hell not? It's the only way to deal with people like that.' His voice was still crisp as an iceberg lettuce, but his eyes had softened a fraction. 'You're too soft.' With a wry half-smile, he gave her shoulder the most casual pat in the world. 'Goodnight.'

It was not a good night at all.

Claudia lay under her duvet, wishing to heaven she had never mentioned Sister Immaculata. The old nun was hovering about just as if the whole of south-west London had been ouija-boarding all night. There was no swishing habit or ghostly face at the end of the bed, but she was there just the same.

Serves me right for taking her name in vain, she thought crossly. But it wasn't just Sister Immaculata robbing her of rest. For the first hour after going to bed, Guy

Hamilton had dominated her thoughts. And slowly, dreamily, those thoughts had turned into the kind of daft fantasy she'd enjoyed in her teens, especially during boring geography lessons.

She would just happen to be walking down the street at home when her favourite pop star would just happen to be driving past. A dog would just happen to run into the road and he would swerve and nearly hit her, and she would fall gracefully to the pavement. The gorgeous hunk would leap from his Maserati, scoop her up and carry her to her house, from which her parents would just happen to be conveniently absent for the entire weekend.

There he would tend her bruises and she would smile in a faint but fetching manner and beg him not to delay his journey. He would declare that he could not possibly leave her in case she had concussion. By Monday morning he would have fallen hopelessly in love with her, and Emma Cartwright, who had pinched her very first boyfriend, would be absolutely sick with envy.

She was having similar fantasies now, with someone else in the starring role.

Only the fantasy had grown up a bit.

CHAPTER 5

And that was where Sister Immaculata would appear.

'*Claudia Maitland, you're thinking impure thoughts. Say fifty thousand Hail Marys at once.*'

They'd called her Old Immac at school, partly because of her impressive moustache. Old Immac's favourite subject – after not wasting food – had always been impurity and the avoidance thereof. Some of her warnings had gone down as never-to-be-forgotten classics. 'Girls, you must never sit on a man's lap unless you're engaged to him.'

They had all fallen about for hours, wondering whether the poor old thing thought this was how you 'did it'. How you 'did it' and what it would be like had been a favourite topic among the fifteen-year-old convent girls. One or two had soon found out, aided and abetted by the boys from Monkswood High down the road.

It had been a little longer till Claudia had found out, and it had been something of a let-down. The earth hadn't budged one centimetre, any fireworks had fizzled out pretty fast, and she'd been terrified the whole time that his mum and dad would come back and catch them.

Later there had been Matthew, who'd been past the fumbling adolescent stage and had known roughly what buttons to press. It had been a long and happy enough relationship, until they'd both realized it was just a comfortable habit.

Much later there had been Adam, who'd been anything but a comfortable habit. He'd disappeared from her life five months back.

So, if Sister Immaculata was so bent on popping back with lectures on impurity, why in heaven's name had she waited till now, when Claudia was merely indulging in a harmless and not particularly X-rated fantasy?

'Oh, go and polish your harp or something,' she told her crossly. 'I was just getting to the good bit.'

As she'd expected, Ryan was triumphant. 'I knew you'd give in. I knew you couldn't hack it.'

'I've had a better offer, Ryan. Something infinitely more congenial.'

'Oh, yeah?'

She had decided against seeing him in person. The phone would do. 'Yeah, as a matter of fact. All expenses paid in the sun. I'll think of you when I'm sitting by the pool. With a nice long drink with a straw and a hibiscus flower in it.'

'Sitting in front of the telly, more like, with a Cup-a-Soup and a Marmite sandwich.'

She could just see the smirk on his face. It was going to be fun wiping it off. 'I'll send you a postcard.'

'Where from? Bognor?'

She was dying to tell him, but perhaps not. In bare detail it still sounded potentially dodgy. Given Ryan's mischief-making potential, he was quite capable of ringing his mother with some wildly exaggerated story, and then *his* mother would ring *her* mother and all hell would be let loose. With Interpol and the Vice Squad thrown in, if her mother had anything to do with it.

'Wait and see,' was all she said.

He was instantly triumphant. 'I knew it was cobblers. You're just too chicken for Big Bad Wolf, and you're too chicken to admit it.'

Let him think that, if it gladdened his toadish little heart. That would make it all the sweeter when she popped in with a tan and waved the Hamilton cheque under his nose. 'I thought Belinda-the-Boobs would do it so much better.'

'You must be joking. I wouldn't let her within a mile of that shower.'

'She can do the French maid, then. For the old boy's seventieth.'

'Are you kidding? He'd have a heart attack with all the excitement. Anyway, she'd probably throw up.'

'What about me? Did you think I'd *enjoy* it?'

'Of course not, Claud. That was the whole point. Tell you what, though, if you'll just do the rugby club I'll give you a bonus. No old buggers there, just a load of heaving muscle and testosterone, all panting for your phone number.'

'You do it, then. In drag.'

'Very funny, ha ha. I've promised them a sultry redhead with legs that go right up to her bum.'

'Your legs go right up to your bum, so shave them and buy a wig. I'm sure Big Bad Wolf'll be far too ratso to know the difference. And I want my money. It was part of the deal, remember? The going rate for those two kissograms. And the days in the office.'

'I don't remember anything about that,' he said, feigning puzzlement. 'As far as I recall, the bet was it. No bet, no dough.'

She had been half expecting it. 'I want my money, you ghastly little toad, and if I don't get it there'll be trouble.'

'OK, OK, don't blow a gasket. If you pop in in the next day or two, I'll dig out my chequebook.'

'Pop *in*? Ryan, there's this thing called the Post Office. You stick things in envelopes and put them in letterboxes. They're the big red things in the street, with large openings about the size of your mouth.'

It was dark when they landed at Seeb International Airport, but even so the heat felt like a warm blanket.

Instantly Claudia felt that tingle that comes from first setting foot in the unknown. Everything not only looked different, it smelt and sounded different. The signs were in Arabic and English. Arabic was being spoken all around her. It felt odd to hear a language of which she understood absolutely nothing. Even in Greece she understood bits and pieces.

The policewomen in the airport wore ankle-length skirts; the policemen wore guns.

If they weren't in uniform, the other local men wore long white robes with little caps on their heads, or turban-style head-dresses.

The airport was much more modern than she'd expected, but it was packed as a huge planeload headed for

Immigration. An enormous queue formed at once, and Claudia braced herself for a long wait.

Anoushka stood sulkily, pushing her hand baggage with her foot as the queue inched forward.

'Tired?' Guy asked her.

'Of course I'm tired. We were eight hours on that plane!'

'How about you?' he asked Claudia.

'Not too bad,' she fibbed. It was eleven hours since she'd left home, and she hadn't even got to bed till two-thirty, after going out for a meal with Kate and Paul and another couple of friends when she should have been packing. She had ended up ironing frantically at two o'clock and hunting through drawers for things she absolutely knew she'd had last summer but that seemed to have walked.

It was always a colossal relief, she felt, to actually get on the plane. By then it was too late to worry about anything you'd forgotten.

The Immigration queue was moving as slowly as a centipede with corns. Guy was frowning, glancing towards the exit. 'There should be somebody to meet us,' he muttered. 'Otherwise we'll be here all night.'

'We'll be here all night anyway,' Anoushka said. 'Unless you happen to know God, who will kindly make everybody ahead of us drop dead.'

Guy made no reply. He was already moving from the queue towards a man in a beige safari suit who was heading their way.

They shook hands warmly. 'I'm very sorry, Mr Hamilton,' said the man. 'The plane was a few minutes early and – '

'It doesn't matter.' Guy turned to Claudia. 'Joseph'll need your passport and immigration card.'

She handed them over, and he gave up his own and Anoushka's. Joseph, who wore an airport identity badge on his jacket, headed straight for the front of the queue.

'What's he doing?' Claudia asked, nonplussed.

Guy winked at her. 'That's our Mr Fixit.'

Before many minutes had elapsed, Mr Fixit waved them to the front and they were out.

'It's not fair on the other people,' Anoushka complained as they waited at Customs. 'Swanning through like Princess Di . . .'

'Would you rather have waited half an hour?' he demanded.

'No, but – '

'Then stop moaning. In a place like this everybody uses a Mr Fixit if they can. If they can't, tough.'

Customs opened everything but objected to nothing, and minutes later they were outside.

There were scores of people waiting, mainly local. As they waited for the car Claudia's eye was caught by a very regal-looking figure. Over a pristine white dishdasha he wore a black robe, trimmed with gold braid, and a curved silver dagger in his belt.

'I hope that's just for decoration,' she said to Guy.

'It's ceremonial dress. Like a Scot wearing a dagger in his sock with a dress kilt.'

Their Mr Fixit brought round a sleek white limo with smoked windows that whisked them off from the crush.

'It's about a forty-minute drive to the hotel,' Guy said as she got in. 'We go through the capital area and out the other side. You won't be able to see much in the dark, but I'll point out anything as we go.'

He sat in the front, talking to Joseph. Anoushka sat next to her in the back and said not a word.

There was a lot more to see than Claudia had expected: an exotic eastern fairyland of graceful Islamic architecture and mosques brightly lit against the night sky.

'This is Muttrah Corniche,' Guy said, as they turned right on to a road that hugged the sea. Brightly lit shops were still open on the other side, and the world and his wife wandered by the water.

Further on, he turned to her again. 'We're coming to the Old City Of Muscat. You'll see the Sultan's palace and the old Portuguese forts either side.'

When they passed them, the sight took her breath away. The forts were perched high on rocks, with the palace in between and the sea beyond. 'It looks almost like a Hollywood film set,' she remarked to Anoushka, before realising that she was asleep. Or pretending to be.

The road wound through deep cuttings in to the rocks, finally bringing them to another palace that called itself a hotel.

The following morning she was gazing through the window of her hotel room at the gardens that stretched down to the beach. There were frangipani trees and bougainvillaea, and a man in overalls tending the grass. Beyond the gardens, the intense blue of the Arabian Sea lay placid under a sky that looked as if it had never even heard of clouds.

On an impulse, she picked up the phone. The connection took only seconds. 'Hi, ratbag,' she said when Kate answered.

'*Claudia!* How's it going?'

'Fine, except for a touch of culture-shock. It's beautiful. Brilliant blue sky and flowers everywhere.'

'Oh, shut up. It's peeing down here. Seen any camels yet?'

'Give me a chance! Kate, listen a minute. I forgot to say that if my folks should phone, don't for heaven's sake tell them I've gone swanning off to the Middle East with a strange man. Mum will think he's a white-slave trader.'

'So what shall I say?'

'Anything you like. A de-stressing health farm with no phones might do. If, heaven forbid, it's an emergency, give me a ring.' She dictated the number.

Kate repeated it. 'Okey-doke. How are you getting on with Superbrat?'

'So-so. She virtually ignored me all the way, but no real cheek. I got the feeling he'd threatened her with death if she misbehaved. She didn't come down to breakfast this morning so it was just me and him.'

'The flight must have been a killer.'

'Not as bad as I'd expected, but I was pretty shattered by the time we arrived. There were a couple of messages for him already, and he had to go and see someone. Anoushka said she was going straight to bed, so I just had room service and crashed out. Hold on, there's someone at the door.'

It was Guy. 'Come in a minute,' she said hurriedly. 'I won't be a tick.'

Grabbing the phone, she said, 'Kate, I've got to go. Be good and lots of love – how's Portly, by the way?'

'Not pining for you, I'm afraid. He slept on my bed last night.'

'Typical faithless male. He'll sleep with anyone. Give him a kiss anyway. I'll ring again soon. Bye.' She replaced the receiver hurriedly.

'That was Kate, who shares my flat,' she told Guy. 'I'll tell Reception to make a separate bill for my phone calls.'

A faint amusement flickered over his lips. 'You're allowed a few phone calls.'

'I might be phoning Australia every night for all you know.'

'In that case, *I'll* tell Reception to make a separate bill.'

An hour ago, at breakfast time, he'd been wearing the bottom half of a navy tracksuit and a white T-shirt, his hair still wet from the pool. He'd looked more like a lifeguard than anything else – the kind who makes a certain kind of woman wiggle her hips and remember to hold her stomach in as she walks round the pool. It had been a bit much to cope with first thing in the morning.

He had now changed – into the bottom half of a light grey suit, a short-sleeved shirt of white with navy stripes and a silk tie. His hair was wet from the shower and he looked like the kind of businessman who makes a certain kind of woman wiggle her hips and remember to hold her stomach in as she walks past the photocopier.

It was still too much to cope with. 'Did you see Anoushka?' she asked brightly.

His expression turned to grim satisfaction. 'She's having the purple sulks. The school's been remarkably co-operative in setting her work. I'll fax it back for marking, and if anything comes back with a C minus, heaven help her.'

He glanced at his watch. 'If you come to my room, I'll give you some local money.'

'I've got some sterling. The front desk can change it if I need any.'

'Don't be silly, Claudia. Never spend your own money if you can charge it to expenses.'

Well, if you insist. She followed him a few yards down the plushly carpeted corridor. His room was furnished with exactly the same understated luxury as her own. The bathroom door was open and the faintest of masculine scents wafted out.

The phone rang just as they entered and he answered with a crisp, 'Hamilton.'

There were twin beds, one still pristine, the other bearing the signs of a very restless sleeper. On the end of the bed was tossed a large, used towel. A jacket was tossed over a chair and an open newspaper on a little table.

But there were no tossed pyjamas, waiting for the maid to pick them up. *Of course not, you dope. Men like him don't wear pyjamas. They sleep* au naturel.

For a moment she gazed at that bed and imagined the tossings of an *au naturel* Guy Hamilton.

For heaven's sake, you've got it on the brain. Think about something else.

She moved to the window. It showed the same view as her own, and on that placid sea somebody was now waterski-ing. It wasn't one of those experts who made you sick. He went twenty wobbly yards and fell off.

The phone call finished, he came to stand beside her. 'How do you like the hotel?' He was so close that the dark

93

fuzz on his arm just brushed the almost invisible down on her own.

'Oh, not bad,' she chirped. 'Not quite what I'm used to, but I don't mind slumming it for a bit.'

His little chuckle told her that her ploy had worked. He had no idea that that fleeting, hair-to-hair contact had felt like a thousand minute electric shocks. She thought about moving fractionally away, but why waste thrills? She hadn't had any for a bit.

He, on the other hand, was obviously unshivered.

'That sea looks good,' he mused, thrusting his hand in his pocket. 'I must make time for some sailing. And an early-morning ski or two.'

I bet you're one of those experts who make me sick. 'I thought I might have a go. I tried ages ago in Spain. An ex-boyfriend tried to teach me.'

He gave her a sideways glance. 'Unsuccessfully?'

'Let's just say if we'd been married, we'd probably have got divorced.'

The skier was down again, floundering helplessly in the water. 'I hope there aren't any sharks in the vicinity,' she said, thinking suddenly of *Jaws*. 'If there are, I hope they've already had a five-course breakfast.'

He chuckled. 'There is the odd beastie with teeth, but you're not likely to see any. You're much more likely to see turtles or dolphins. Even a whale, if you're very lucky.'

'Really?' She turned to him, astonished.

He smiled, the little half-smile that was beginning to have drastic effects every time he produced it. 'You'd have to be very lucky, I'm afraid.' His eyes dropped from her face and scanned her arms. 'Watch the sun. You've got the kind of skin that's better under wraps.'

She glanced defensively at her winter-cream skin. 'I do tan, eventually. Not exactly mahogany, but enough to take the pallor off.'

'Take it easy, that's all. Or you'll end up like an over-boiled pink shrimp and I'll have to pickle you in after-sun.'

Both the words and his tone made her look him sharply in the eye. For a second she thought she saw the unmistakably lazy flicker of a man who knew precisely the effect he was having on a woman and was thinking, *Mmm. Wouldn't say no.* But before she could be sure, it was gone.

'Money,' he said crisply. From a briefcase on the desk he took a wodge of notes and peeled a few off. 'Just in case you need anything from the shop. You can sign for all your meals and drinks. Just don't give any to Anoushka. If she spins you a line about needing shampoo or whatever, buy it for her.'

Her forebodings about this assignment were rapidly boding even worse. Especially when he went on, 'She's to work till one. After lunch she can have an hour at the pool, and then it's back to the grind till five. I'd like you to check on her now and then, but not at predictable intervals. Otherwise she'll be channel-hopping the in-house movies.'

'I hate spying on her. She's going to hate me.'

'She knows you're under orders. She'll hate me instead.' His tone relaxed. 'What are you planning to do while she's working?'

She hesitated. 'Would it be dereliction of duty if I went for a walk along the beach?'

'Of course not. I don't expect you to be breathing down her neck.' He cast appraising eyes over her olive skirt of thin Indian cotton and the short-sleeved shirt of cream linen, and his expression seemed to say, *Suitable. Even attractive.*

With a glance at his watch, he added, 'My God, is that the time?' He ushered her to the door, where he paused. 'I really do appreciate this, Claudia. I know it's a tall order.'

His eyes had thawed at the edges, his voice doing its Shetland-sweater bit again.

It was getting worse, every time he was within shivering distance. 'Off you go,' she said brightly. 'They chop your head off here if you're late for a business meeting.'

'Don't make jokes like that, for crying out loud. Not in public anyway.' He smiled as he said it, though, and gave her shoulder a little pat. 'I'll be back around six.'

She watched him walk to the lift and returned to her room. Catching sight of her reflection in the mirror, she suddenly felt like throwing something at it. Ghastly, English, just-off-the-plane white. And before she went even a pale gold she'd go pink. Ghastly, unsexy, boiled-shrimp pink.

Don't knock it, taunted an infuriating little voice in her head. *You'd just love to be an overboiled shrimp if he'd pickle you in after-sun.*

In her fantasies, maybe. In practice, hot pink flesh was not the way to turn a Category Four on. She made up her mind then and there that for once in her life she was going to time herself religiously and slap on factor fifteen every twenty minutes. Not even a clothed walk on the beach was going to be left to chance. She applied sunblock to every exposed centimetre, grabbed a hat and departed.

For half an hour she wandered the gardens, picking up the odd frangipani flower and inhaling its delicate scent. The sun was pleasantly warm, making her realize that by midday it would be blistering.

She wandered down to the beach. At this time, there was hardly anybody there. She took her sandals off and enjoyed the feel of soft sand under her feet. There weren't many shells, but there were one or two odd, disc-shaped things, with a curious petal design on the front, like a child's drawing of a flower. On the wet sand she found more. They looked quite lifeless, but when she turned them over, some had masses of minute legs, wiggling pathetically on their undersides.

Sorting the quick from the dead and throwing the still wiggling into the sea kept her occupied for a while. Keeping a couple of the obviously dead and desiccated, she strolled on. *What a setting*, she thought.

Behind the multi-sided 'palace' and its gardens rose stark, mini-mountains of rock. The bay was bounded by rocks too, and at one end a fisherman was busy with his nets. He wore a long checked sarong, an untidy turban and a long grey beard. And when she walked past, he gave her a wide, one-toothed smile.

'Good morning,' she smiled.

His answer was unintelligible, but obviously kindly meant, making her ashamed at knowing not one word of the language. She walked back and headed for the shop in the foyer for a phrasebook. There were guide books too, which she browsed through for ages. It was a shock when she glanced at her watch and saw the time. For a while she had felt she was on holiday in a new and fascinating country, but that mood was vanishing fast. It was time to check on Anoushka.

The man at the desk was very friendly, helping her with the unaccustomed *rials* and *baizas*, and then, bracing herself, she headed for the lift.

'It's like being in prison. A flaming five-star prison with hard labour.'

'It's not that bad. You'd be doing exactly the same at school, but you wouldn't have that lovely pool to fall into after lunch.'

The only answer was a grunt.

'It's time you had a break anyway,' Claudia pointed out. 'Have a Pepsi from the mini-bar.'

'I've already had two. And all the nuts.'

Trying a different tack, Claudia showed her the flower-discs from the beach.

Anoushka gave them barely a glance. 'I've seen millions of those, in America or somewhere. They're called sand dollars.'

Claudia gave up and put them back in her bag. 'How's the work going?'

'How d'you think? I'm bored out of my mind.' Throwing her pen down, she sat back in her chair, rocking it at a perilous angle. She was wearing a baggy white T-shirt and grey cycling shorts, her hair an unbrushed mess. 'I still can't get over Dad carting you along. I suppose he thought it was poetic justice, after that kissogram. And while we're on that particular subject,' she went on, 'you were a great disappointment to me, by the way. I nearly asked for my money back.'

'It wasn't much of a kiss,' Claudia confessed.

Anoushka stared at her contemptuously. 'I didn't mean the *kiss*. I knew he'd never stand for necking in public. I meant the other bit. I wanted somebody really slaggy, with whopping great double Ds hanging out. You were far too ladylike.'

'Sorry,' Claudia said sheepishly. 'Was he really mad with you afterwards?'

'Not as mad as I'd expected. I don't think he wanted to give me that satisfaction. But he made me tell him where I'd booked it. Said he was going to go round and give the whole bunch of morons some choice and original abuse.'

Claudia drew her chair fractionally closer. 'Will you tell me something?'

'Depends what it is.'

'Whatever did you do to get yourself suspended?'

Anoushka swivelled on her chair. 'Do you mean he hasn't told you?'

'Only dark hints.'

She shrugged. 'I tried bunking off a lot, but that didn't work. Even they managed to work out that getting slung out was exactly what I wanted. I had to resort to infantile, second-year shock tactics.'

Even if she'd tried, Claudia could not possibly have managed to tut and look disapproving. Aeons ago St Trinian's films had been her favourites, and she had a feeling Anoushka would have been a fitting Head Girl at St Trinian's. 'What did you do?'

'Nothing very original. It was my friend's birthday so I took a litre of vodka to school to make a change from the usual boring Coke. I dished it out to half the class at lunch, and one of the really sad girls was sick during a biology practical.'

'And then you got hauled into the office and ranted at, I suppose?'

Anoushka gave her a pitying glance. 'Our head hag doesn't *rant*. She droned reproachfully and told me how "bitterly disappointed" she was and how "bitterly disappointed" my poor father was going to be, then gave a little lecture on the effects of "strong drink" on our livers and said all the staff were "frankly worried" about my attitude problem and sincerely hoped I was going to start "maximising my potential". The usual crap, in other words.'

Claudia was nonplussed. 'Was that it?'

'Yep. This is the modern, psychological approach, you see. They appeal to your better nature. They try to make you think that *they* think there's really a wonderful human being inside that attitude problem, and wouldn't it be wonderful to let her out?'

Her cynical tone amused Claudia rather than shocking her, and this reaction instantly made her feel guilty. She ought to be shocked, or at least distressed, in an earnest, caring sort of way.

Instead she was only perplexed as to why an obviously intelligent girl with everything going for her should be so anxious to get slung out of school.

'But the vodka didn't get you suspended?'

'No such luck. I had to resort to even more infantile tactics – planting a few veggies in a window box outside the deputy head's office.'

'*Vegetables?* What on earth for?'

Anoushka gave her a pitying look. 'They were cucumbers. Six big fat phallic ones from the supermarket. And then I dressed them up in dear little coloured condoms. I thought it looked quite decorative, especially since the window box is right on the street.'

Claudia was choking back her appalled laughter. 'That must have gone down like a lead balloon.'

'They'd have made less fuss if I'd slit the old hag's throat.' She stopped rocking her chair, picked up her pen, and sucked the tip thoughtfully. Then she picked up a sheet of maths and studied it. 'Do you know how to do quadratic equations?'

'I'm afraid I can't remember.'

'Neither can I, so stuff it.' Calmly she tore the sheet in half and tossed it in the bin. Then she picked up the rest and gave them the same treatment. With a satisfied smile she sat back again. 'There. That's cleared the decks nicely.'

Although she was appalled, Claudia knew the last thing she must do was show it. The girl was taking her for a gullible idiot. Quite deliberately she had lulled her into thinking they were getting on fine before launching her offensive. 'That was a bit daft. He'll only get the school to fax some more.'

'Let him. I'll tear those up too.' She pushed her chair back, flopped on her bed and picked up the TV remote control. 'I know why he brought you along. He thinks I'm going to like you just because you're not a sad social reject in a tweed skirt. He thinks you're going to be an iron hand in a velvet glove to make me "be a good girl". Well, I'm not, so you might as well give up now.'

Rapidly deciding that boredom was the best policy, Claudia shrugged. 'Well, enjoy your morning. I'm going back to the beach for a bit. See you later.'

She was halfway out when Anoushka spoke again.

'You fancy him, don't you?'

CHAPTER 6

The pert, knowing tones hit her like a kick in the stomach.

With what she prayed was mild amusement, Claudia turned. 'What on earth makes you say that?'

Anoushka shrugged. 'The law of probability. All my friends' divorced, neurotic mothers fancy him. And half my teachers too. That's why they haven't expelled me. He went and charmed the thermal knickers off the head hag.'

Thank God it wasn't telepathy. Still, tread carefully. 'I can see he's very attractive, but he's really not my type.'

Anoushka looked her over with dark, liquid eyes. 'What is your type, then?'

Claudia gave what she hoped was a dreamy sigh. 'The sun-streaked Australian surfer. Longish blond hair. Laid-back. Good fun. You know.'

This was no off-the-cuff fib, since it described Adam exactly.

It seemed to convince Anoushka. 'Just as well, because he doesn't fancy you.' She clicked the television on to Arabic cartoons. Little figures were leaping about the screen, squeaking, 'Sindeebad' Sindeebad!' and a hideous, one-eyed ogre was busily stuffing one of them into his hideous mouth.

'If he did, he wouldn't have brought you here. Whenever he's got a rampant thing about somebody, he always keeps the lust object right away from me, in case I put the kybosh on it.'

At ten to four, Claudia was sitting on the side of the pool. It was still very hot, so the splashes that hit her were more than welcome. And there were plenty of them, from children who frolicked like baby dolphins.

It was easy to tell the mothers, from the way they continually glanced at the pool for a quick head-count. There seemed to be hardly any tourists, and hardly any locals either. From a little judicious eavesdropping and general observation, she'd soon worked out that many of the women stretched out by the pool were expatriate wives, enjoying an afternoon out with the kids.

But not all. A little more eavesdropping – not that she was listening on purpose – told her that some were aircrew, on a stop-over.

At the end of her ten lengths Claudia had collided with a man doing much the same. He was now sitting beside her. They were chatting, idly kicking their feet in the water, when a dark head surfaced about three feet away. It looked her straight in the eye and said, 'Hello, Claudia.'

With a cool nod at her companion, the head ducked, swam twenty yards underwater, covered the rest with an effortless crawl, and heaved itself out at the other end.

'Who was that?' asked the man beside her.

'My sort-of boss. Would you excuse me?'

With an apologetic smile, she slithered back into the water and swam back to the other end. She could have walked, but displaying her winter whiteness among all those bronzed bodies was not a tempting option.

Guy was standing by a sunbed not far from her own, towelling himself. Grabbing her own towel, she wrapped it round herself, sarong-style. While she was fastening it he strolled up.

'I thought you weren't due back till later,' she said.

'Life is full of little surprises.' With a nod at the far end of the pool, he added, 'Who was that?'

'A 747 pilot. He was telling me what a boring job it is and how he hates being away from his family.'

'Oh, yes.' His tone said, *Been spinning you that old line, has he?*

However subtly done, it was irritating to hear him hint that she didn't know a corny chat-up-line when she heard it. The man hadn't been chatting her up, and even if he had, was it any of his business?

Well, maybe it was, since she was supposed to be on duty. 'I hate to tell you this, but – '

'Anoushka's torn up all her work.'

What a relief I didn't have to break the news.

'She was my first port of call.' He sat on the end of the sunbed next to her own, facing the pool with an air of grim tension.

She winced, imagining the scene.

Father: 'Let me see what you've done.'

Daughter: 'Help yourself. It's in the bin.'

105

Discarding the towel, she sat on the end of her own sunbed, arms around her knees. 'I didn't make a fuss. I thought it would only encourage her.'

'I'm glad you've sussed that much out.'

'I suppose you read her the riot act.'

He gave a cynical snort. 'I'd been half expecting it. I'd taken the precaution of making photocopies of everything, so I just presented her with another lot and told her to get on with it.'

'What did she say?'

'I didn't give her a chance to say anything. I walked out and left her to stew.'

And to rip that lot up, no doubt. Claudia's impression of two brick walls had perhaps been understating the situation. Reinforced concrete might be nearer the mark.

He, at any rate, would make a very passable concrete wall. No physical defects had been revealed with the shedding of his clothes – no incipient gut or skinny, hairless legs, both of which would have made her go off him instantly.

With Anoushka's words barely cold in her ears, she almost wished she *could* go off him instantly. 'Whenever he's got a rampant thing about somebody . . .'

Still, a good erotic fantasy passed the time nicely, especially when you were sitting in the sun with the object of your fantasies within crackling distance.

He was wearing a pair of navy shorts-type trunks, not the skimpy, male-knicker type she particularly hated. Firm, interlocking muscles moved under his skin like a mobile jigsaw. There was enough dark brown hair on his chest and legs to indicate abundant male hormones without making him a gorilla. If there was an ounce of surplus fat anywhere, she couldn't see it.

He called to a passing waiter. 'Bring me a beer, please.' Turning to Claudia, he added, 'Anything for you?'

'I could do with something long and cool.'

'They do a good Pimms.'

'That would be lovely.' She touched a hand to her shoulders, where the sun was making its presence felt.

'I hope you haven't been sitting here all afternoon,' he said, giving her exposed bits more than a passing glance.

'Does it look like it?' Glumly she eyed the long, ghastly excrescences that connected bikini bottoms to feet. OK, so they weren't blue or mottled or wobbling with cellulite, but they were nearly as pale as the double-cream bikini, which had looked so wonderful last year with a Greek-honey tan.

'If I had, I'd look like something out of *The Revenge of the Killer Tomatoes*, instead of like something that's crawled out from under a rock.'

His lips twitched. 'Is that my cue to say, Of course you don't, Claudia. You look like a rhapsody in cream?'

Will you please engage brain before opening mouth? she told herself fiercely. 'I wasn't fishing,' she said aloud.

He gave her a sideways glance. 'If you had been "fishing", you might have caught a tiddler.'

His evident amusement only made her crosser. 'Well, I wasn't.'

Just to emphasize her wretched pallor, two girls so sickeningly tanned that she hated them were shimmering past, one saying to the other, 'That girl is a complete *pain*. I did a Nairobi with her last month and the lazy cow spent the entire flight painting her nails in the first class loo.'

Clandia badly wanted to torture herself with a quick glance at the Hamilton face to see whether he was ogling them, and, if so, whether subtly or unashamedly. But since he was now lying back, she couldn't see without being obvious.

She glanced at her watch. According to her schedule, it was time for twenty minutes on her front, which meant slathering factor fifteen all over her back view from neck to ankles.

And this presented her with one of the tiny dilemmas that spice up the daily round. If she began this slathering exercise and Guy really *was* one of those wretched men who 'knew', he'd instantly think she was hoping he'd offer to do the honours. After all, she'd be the first to admit that getting the sun cream out when you'd just met a Category Four by the pool was a perfect way of breaking large amounts of ice.

She had done it often enough when she was younger; it had been part of the ritual. You sat there nattering about nothing in particular and wondering why you only ever meet a Category Four two days before going home, and then you delved in your bag for the sun cream and started oh-so-casually smoothing it into your shoulders.

And then he said, 'Let me,' and you demurred for a second or two, pretending such an idea had never occurred to you, before handing the bottle over and enjoying the subsequent shivers.

But since this was not a normal flirt ritual situation, she was still dithering over her options.

One: she could go inside. *Two*: she could carry on sitting here unslathered, and end up pink. *Three*: she could anoint herself, let him think what he liked, and stop agonizing over something so stupid.

She took the bottle from her bag and began smoothing cream into the backs of her legs.

Even when she started on the other bits he seemed to be paying not the slightest attention. Without looking directly, she could see from the corner of her eye that he was still facing the pool, apparently lost in thought.

What the hell was I agonizing about?

Wishful thinking, you dope. Wishing he'd offer, and trying to kid yourself you'd –

'You're making a pig's breakfast of that.'

'Sorry?'

'You're missing bits.' He rose swiftly to his feet and his crisp, 'Move up,' fazed her completely.

Too startled to argue, she shifted forwards.

He was *supposed* to say, 'Here, let me,' or 'I'm a dab hand with that stuff,' in which case she might have managed a careless, 'So am I.' The wretched man just hadn't read the rule book.

Still, she wasn't exactly complaining.

He sat right behind her, took the bottle from her hand. 'I don't suppose you want a patchwork effect,' he said, squeezing a cool drizzle of cream on to her skin. 'You can't do your own back unless you've got arms like an orangoutang and eyes in your backside.'

The next minute was like one of her own fantasies, only fourteen times better. And fourteen times worse, because she had to sit there looking nonchalant as firm, obviously practised fingers smoothed factor fifteen into her shoulders.

'Get that hair out of the way,' he said.

Well, what now? Do I pour foul, feminist scorn on such crisply masterful orderings and finish the job myself?

Not on your life.

Obediently she lifted the wet mass out of the way.

Oh, God, the gorgeous shivers as he just missed the little erogenous bit at the back of her neck.

It was over all too soon. 'I'll leave the rest to you,' he said, meaning the relatively accessible area from strap to bikini bottoms, where his fingers had not strayed, dammit.

Somehow she managed a nonchalant, 'Thanks.'

'No problem.'

Oh, Lord, was there just a smidgeon of amusement in those two words? Did he sense my inner flutterings through his fingertips?

Don't be ridiculous, Claudia.

'That waiter's taking his time,' he mused. 'I'll work up a thirst with a few more lengths.'

You do that. Push off for five minutes while I get myself under control. She watched him dive in and move in a stylish crawl to the far end. He could obviously not go as fast as he wanted because of the other swimmers, but he kept a good rhythm, coming up for air every four strokes like a wet, dark seal.

Face-down on her towel, she turned her face from the pool so she wouldn't be able to watch him. Like this, her flutterings calmed down, and her thoughts turned to his daughter.

Why do I feel guilty? She's a spoilt brat and it's not my fault if she wants to sulk in her room all day.

110

Why is she being so difficult? Is he a hateful, overbearing father?

Unlikely. Probably over-indulgent. Putting his foot down too late.

And what about the kyboshing? Does she put the kybosh on his relationships on purpose?

I wouldn't put it past her.

But perhaps it was to be expected. No child liked another woman taking her mother's place. What *had* happened to his wife? She was dying to ask, but it wasn't the kind of thing you chuck in over breakfast.

While she was thinking all this Guy returned, just as the waiter appeared with the drinks.

Still in her back-tanning position, Claudia sipped through a straw. The Pimms was laced with mint and cucumber, perfect in the heat.

He drained half his beer in one go. '*El hamdulillah*. I needed that.'

'Is that cheers in Arabic?'

'It means thanks be to God, and you'll hear it a lot.' Sitting down, he added, 'The other thing you'll hear a lot is *Insha'allah*.'

'Which means?'

'God willing. So, *insha'allah*, my daughter will even now be applying herself to her English course-work. Though I may be forgiven for doubting it.'

Lying face-down was getting uncomfortable, as if her 36Bs were clamped to an ironing board. Raising herself on her elbows, she said, 'I'm afraid it'll take more than a few God willings. She's made up her mind to be awkward. She wouldn't even come down for lunch. She ordered room service.'

111

'She'll soon get fed up with that.'

Clandia wasn't so sure. 'What will you do if she won't play ball?'

With an impatient shrug he put his glass down. 'I'll think of something.'

'Like what? Cutting off her allowance?'

'I've already done that. Not that it makes much difference when we're at home. She has friends with money coming out of their ears.'

'And grounding her obviously doesn't work.'

'As you saw. I can't physically lock her in her room.'

Claudia glanced at her watch. The twenty minutes were almost up and she had an uncomfortable feeling that twenty was pushing it. She sat up, and draped a filmy black pareo around her hair and shoulders and then around her knees, encasing herself completely.

He raised a dark eyebrow. 'Going native?'

'Just being careful.' After a moment she went on, 'I feel dreadfully guilty, sitting here in the sun. I feel I'm not earning my money. She thinks you've brought me to exert a not-so-subtle influence, and she's made up her mind she's not having it.'

'Fairly typical behaviour for Anoushka.'

She was beginning to be exasperated. 'Then why did you bring me? Doesn't it occur to you that I might be making matters worse?'

He turned to her. 'Doesn't it occur to you that if you weren't here she'd be down here, or on the beach, flirting with anything available and just looking for trouble? I prefer her sulking in her room any day.'

112

'Trouble?' With a sweep of her arm, Claudia indicated the sunny terrace, the placid gardens and the beach beyond. 'Just what could she get up to here?'

'Take it from one who knows. Anoushka could get up to trouble anywhere.' He drained his beer and added, 'I've got things to do. What time do you want to eat?'

She had not expected him to charge off so soon. 'Any time before nine.' She hesitated. 'But don't feel you have to eat with me. I don't mind sitting in a restaurant on my own.'

'You might not; I loathe it. I'll knock on your door around seven-thirty.'

He stood up, stretched, and picked up his towel. 'See you later.' For an instant he paused, scanning her black tented body. 'You don't look bad in a yashmak.' As he turned to go she just caught an infuriating flicker at the corner of his mouth.

Thanks a bunch, she thought, eyeing his departing back. *What's that supposed to mean? That I look better swathed in black like some hairy-legged bedouin woman than poured into two scraps of Lycra? Well, maybe you do*, she answered herself gloomily, as a before-and-after roast chicken analogy sprang to mind. Nothing but imminent death from starvation would induce you to nibble the raw version, but once it was all hot and golden you couldn't wait to get stuck in.

Putting raw flesh out of her mind, she delved in her bag for the blockbuster she'd grabbed at the airport bookshop. She'd been trying to get into it earlier, but little had gone in, and now she'd lost her place too.

'Bonkbuster' would describe it more accurately, she thought, flicking the pages for clues. As she recalled,

113

Dominic somebody had been raking hot, hungry eyes over Cara. And here he was on page forty-three, doing exactly the same with Natalya! Boy, this chap got about a bit.

His hypnotic, dangerous drawl made her legs buckle. 'Show me your breasts, Natalya. Undo your blouse.'

Don't you dare! The bastard's just been bonking your stepsister! And very possibly your stepmother and your voluptuous Puerto Rican nanny too.

But Natalya didn't listen, of course. Before you could say 'monogrammed designer bra' she was doing his dastardly bidding and Dominic was doing all sorts of naughty things to her full, swelling, etc. etc.

In the kitchen too. While she had a dozen VIP dinner guests in the next room and her *moules marinière* and goat's cheese *soufflés* to see to. And any minute, her husband was surely going to pop in with a, 'Have you seen the cork-screw, darling?'

Asking for trouble.

As she read on, Claudia tutted to herself. Why did these women always have nipples like full, bursting plums? Weren't plum-sized nipples just a bit on the big side? Mind you, the book was American. Maybe they had nipple implants as well as everything else. And why did they always have to have small, firm buttocks? Small, firm buttocks just did not go with full-to-bursting bosoms. It was against all the laws of nature.

All this perfection depressed her. Why ever had she spent nearly eight pounds on depressing tripe?

Because you like the naughty bits, you hypocrite. You were flicking through it for naughty bits in the shop but then Guy

114

came and said the flight was boarding and you grabbed a
Daily Telegraph *to stick on top of it in case he thought you
were a complete airhead.*

In the event, he hadn't cast so much as a glance at what
she'd paid for at the checkout. He'd been too busy paying
for half a dozen magazines for his daughter.

Not that she could cope with any naughty bits just now.
Her imagination had quite enough real live raw material to
be going on with. And, talking of real live raw material,
what about dinner tonight?

Presumably Anoushka would not be joining them, and
she didn't know whether to be glad or sorry. A sulky
teenage girl would be sure to dampen any flutters. On the
other hand . . .

*Think about something else. Write a postcard to Kate.
Learn some Arabic. Go and order a nice cup of tea from room
service.*

Slinging everything in her bag, she went inside, wondering whether to call on Superbrat on her way up. Superbrat
wouldn't *want* to see her, but that was beside the point.

Anoushka answered the door with a mutinous expression. 'Now what?'

'May I come in?'

'If you must.'

She flopped back on the bed and picked up one of the
magazines that littered it.

Claudia sat on the other bed. 'Was your father spitting
nails?'

'I don't know why you're asking. You've obviously seen
him and had an earnest discussion about the *enfant
terrible.*'

'We hardly spoke about you at all.' She wondered instantly whether she'd said the wrong thing. Superbrats generally liked to think they were the centre of everyone's universe. 'Look, I know you don't want me here, but – '

'I couldn't care less whether you're here or not. If Dad wants to shell out on a babysitter I don't need, that's his problem.'

'He thought you'd be fed up on your own all day.'

Still Anoushka did not look up. 'If you believe that, you're even dumber than I thought. He thought I'd do something to embarrass him.'

'I'm sure you wouldn't.'

'How do you know what I'd do?' At last the girl looked up, her face a picture of terminal boredom. 'Can we just get a few things straight? I don't want you coming in here like some flaming family counsellor. I don't want you patronizingly trying to "understand" me. I just want the pair of you to leave me alone till I can get out of this gold-plated hell-hole and back to civilization. OK?'

Oh, suit yourself. 'I wasn't trying to patronize you.' Claudia left, feeling cross and upset, and cross with herself for feeling upset. Why the hell should she care if a brat like that didn't like her?

Guy knocked on her door at twenty to eight.

'I take it Anoushka isn't coming,' she said, seeing him alone.

'What do you think? She's already had room service.'

'But you did ask her?'

'Of course I asked her!' His tone thawed a fraction. 'I didn't meant to snap. Are you ready?'

116

'Absolutely.'

'Then let's go. I could eat a fair-sized camel.'

His eyes had done a quick scan of her appearance, but he made no comment. She hadn't been expecting compliments, but a mild, You look very nice, would have been gratifying, even if uttered in the tone he might use to an elderly aunt in her best hat.

While kidding herself she wasn't, Claudia had taken a fair amount of trouble. Unsure whether they were heading for the coffee-shop or restaurant proper, she'd played safe for either with beige linen trousers and a severely plain cream silk shirt. Her only jewellery was pearl studs in her ears.

Thinking a flirty tumble of waves might be inappropriate, she had swept her hair back in a tortoiseshell clasp. The growing-out fringe was playing up, though, continually flopping over her right eye.

It was obvious as soon as they were in the lift that he was not in the mood for a relaxed dinner. An air of preoccupied tension clung to him like mist.

The foyer was like a vast, marble cathedral. Or maybe more like a mosque, with vast blue and gold Islamic arches leading off it. Fountains filled the air with musical waterfalls.

Guy did not take her arm or touch her as they approached the restaurant, but he walked close enough for some faint male scent to waft past her nostrils. He was wearing grey chinos with a casual jacket of what looked like dark blue linen and an open-necked shirt of a lighter blue.

There was no camel on the menu, but just about everything else. The restaurant was not busy. It was

117

quiet, discreet and candlelit. And after ordering she had to sit and face him in that gentle flicker.

Since Anoushka was probably the source of his tension, she opened another topic. 'I'm surprised they serve alcohol here,' she said, sipping a glass of white wine. 'I thought it'd be dry.'

'You're thinking of Saudi Arabia. This country's a bit more tolerant, although the locals can't buy liquor in the shops. Foreigners can get a liquor licence, as long as they're not Muslim.'

End of that conversation. 'What is it you do?'

'I work for an oil company.'

Ah. She was dying to ask, In what capacity? But he obviously wasn't the office boy. On the other hand, it was refreshing not to have to listen to a ten-minute monologue on what a frightfully high-powered job he had. Not so long ago she'd had a dinner date with a man who'd spent an entire course telling her how virtually the whole nation would collapse without him, about his five-trillion litre turbo-whatsit company car; exactly how many dozens of complete idiots worked for him, how many times he flew Concorde on expenses each month, and even how many air miles he clocked up.

She had stifled endless yawns.

'How about you?' Guy added.

Since the thought of her old job rather depressed her, she told him about the new one. 'The company I'm going to is still relatively small, but growing like weeds in fertilizer. The MD started in her own living room, making up-market children's clothes. It's really taken off, and now she's exporting all over Europe – even the

118

States and Japan. And since I speak passable French and German she's taken me on for overseas sales. I'm really looking forward to it. The person I'm taking over from is expecting twins, so we'll have a couple of weeks' overlap before she leaves.'

'Will you be travelling?'

'Most definitely.'

'Sounds good,' he said. 'What were you doing before?'

Now that really *was* boring. To save him stifling any yawns, she lowered her voice and said, 'Don't tell anybody, but I was a gangster's moll, only he's out of circulation, as they delicately put it.'

A minute flicker crossed his lips. 'Banged up, as they delicately put it?'

'Of course not!' She pretended to be shocked. 'He's done a runner with three suitcases of dosh and once the Old Bill stop tailing me I'm going to join him. That's partly why I came here. To confuse them utterly and put them off the scent. They're probably watching me right this minute.' She lowered her voice to a hissy whisper. 'Better watch what I say. The table's probably bugged.'

In the candlelight she could see that whatever had been on his mind was now pushed to one side, at least. The ghost of a spark flickered at the back of his eyes, and his mouth bore that trying-not-to-laugh twitch again. Somehow, it gave her an odd ache to see it. *Why can't you loosen up a bit*? she thought. *Before we get back on that plane, I'm going to make you laugh properly if it kills me.*

'Actually, it was much the same kind of thing, but with a much less go-ahead company and no overseas travel,' she went on. 'They were losing their market share and "streamlining" as they put it. I'd probably have left anyway. They were too rigid and hidebound and unwilling to innovate.'

'Companies that stay static go under in the end. Take your talents where they're appreciated.'

'You said it.' Her spicy tiger prawns arrived, distracting her for a while.

After a minute or two he said, 'Why has that cousin of yours got it in for you?'

The toad was the last thing she wanted to talk about, but if she didn't he'd think there was something to hide. 'It dates back years, to when we used to spend our summer holidays together. We're both only children and our misguided parents thought we'd be company for each other. His parents ran a hotel on the coast so I always went to him, and since they were always terribly busy and I was two years older, I was a sort of unofficial babysitter.'

She made a face. 'He was an absolute little devil, always up to something stupid or dangerous, and I was always the one who had to stop him killing himself. So, naturally, he resented me bitterly. And my Auntie Barbara just used to smile fondly at the little beast and say, "Boys will be boys, dear." I swear she was proud of him, even when they had to get the coastguard out because he was trying to sail his dinghy to Cape Horn.'

The smile on the Hamilton face was almost a proper one, which was an achievement. 'Now it's your turn,' she went on. 'Tell me all about that misspent youth you were bragging about.'

'Oh, no. Entertaining me over dinner is part of your job description.'

120

'My mother always says it's terribly bad manners to talk about yourself and bore people to death.'

'I'll tell you when I'm bored.'

Since he obviously wasn't going to open up, it wasn't much use arguing. 'So what do you want to hear? All about my detention-ridden convent days?'

He winced. 'A bit close to home.' With a medium-to-dry smile he sat back, one arm resting on the table. 'Tell me about that other kissogram. I could do with a laugh.'

At my expense, naturally. Still, if it made him crack his face . . . 'It was ghastly,' she confessed. 'In the more raucous kind of packed-to-bursting pub. I had to change in the ladies' and emerge in three square inches of itchy polyester leopardskin and a fake tan that made me look like an orange. He was very appreciative, though.'

'I bet he was. Did he sit you on his knee and give you a good old squeeze?'

He had, but it had been good-humoured rather than lecherous. If it hadn't been for his horrendous halitosis problem it mightn't have been a complete nightmare. 'At least he didn't look at me as if I were something growing fur at the back of the fridge,' she retorted. 'At least he didn't shove me in a taxi and tell the driver to take me as far as possible. He kissed me goodnight and said, "Ta ta, darling."'

That faint flicker did its stuff again. 'I kissed you goodnight, as I recall.'

Don't remind me. And I was too shell-shocked to enjoy it. 'That wasn't a kiss,' she retorted, hoping she sounded suitably unimpressed by the memory. 'It was shock tactics.'

121

'Oh, dear.' His chastened murmur didn't fool her, not when coupled with that glint of laughter in his eyes. 'I must be losing my grip.'

Suddenly she was almost miffed enough to walk out. Entertaining him was one thing; watching him amuse himself at her expense was quite another. Without consciously thinking, she said, 'What happened to your wife?'

As soon as it was out she'd have given anything to take it back. As if someone had flicked a switch, the pre-spark Guy returned.

'She died when Anoushka was seven.'

She swallowed hard. 'I'm terribly sorry.'

'It was one of those things.'

The main course arrived. She had chosen local fish in a cream sauce with fragrant rice. He had barely looked at the menu, had just asked for grilled lamb chops with a baked potato and green salad.

Although they talked during the rest of the meal, it wasn't the same. With that one remark she had shattered his lighter mood.

Was he still in love with his wife's memory, after nearly ten years? Or was it just because, by association, she had reminded him of his problems?

If Anoushka's 'rampant thing' remarks were anything to go by, he wasn't languishing over a dead love. Or was he? Rampant things were not the same as love, and few men lived like monks unless they had to, because nobody would have rampant things with them. And she would stake her mortgage payments for the next ten years that Guy Hamilton would never be short of rampant thing material.

It was barely nine o'clock when they finished their

coffee. 'I'm afraid I have work to do,' he said as they left the restaurant.

'That's OK. I know you're not on holiday and I wasn't expecting to go clubbing.'

Halfway to the lift he said, 'But I could do with some fresh air. Do you fancy a quick walk on the beach? Just fifteen minutes or so.'

Having expected to go back to her room, watch a film and go to bed vaguely bored, she was totally unprepared. 'My shoes aren't exactly beach material,' she said, eyeing the expensive brown leather.

'So take them off.'

Oh, what the hell.

'I need to clear my head,' he said as the lift whisked them down to beach level. 'Get out of the air-conditioning for a bit before I hit the computer.'

Outside, warm air brushed her like a caress. 'It was a bit chilly in that restaurant,' she said as they strolled through the gardens. 'The air-conditioning's a trifle overdone.'

'You wouldn't say that in the summer. It goes up to a hundred and twenty-five – even a hundred and thirty.'

She took her shoes off as they stepped on to the soft sand. The sea was very calm, quicksilvered with moonlight. They walked in silence for a while, not far from the little breaking waves. His hands were thrust in his pockets and she could sense his brooding preoccupation.

After a minute or two she said, 'Guy, you can tell me to mind my own business if you like, but don't you think it'd be better to spend some time with Anoushka, rather than have this cold-war situation? Couldn't you find time to take her sailing, or sightseeing?'

'Sightseeing?' It was almost a snort. 'I've taken her sightseeing everywhere from Brussels to Bangkok. She drags around with an air of determined boredom.'

'I can remember being a bit the same myself,' she confessed. 'My parents once took me on a tour of Wales and I hated it. I sat in the back of the car reading magazines and determinedly hating all the lovely scenery. I just wanted my friends and a really noisy disco.'

'Enough said, I think.'

On the horizon she saw the lights of a vast ship. 'Is that an oil tanker?'

He nodded. 'This stretch of water's littered with them.' He paused and pointed left. 'That way are Dubai, Abu Dhabi and Bahrain, and straight ahead is Iran. This bit of water's the Arabian Sea, but if you carry on round the corner, you come to – '

'The Indian Ocean. I did check the atlas before I came, Guy. I'm not completely clueless.'

'I never thought you were clueless.' His voice softened at the edges, like bitter chocolate in the sun. 'Stroppy, perhaps, but not clueless.'

Oh, Lord. That lethal half-smile was decorating his lips again, and, what with the lap of waves on the sand and the moonlight, she was beginning to wonder whether this was such a good idea, after all.

'I'm not usually stroppy,' she said unsteadily. 'Only when under extreme – '

Her voice broke off in a strangled shudder and she jumped several feet.

'What the – '

'Something just ran over my foot!' Standing on tiptoe, she scanned the sand at her feet. 'Ugh! A cockroach or something!'

'There it is.' On the white sand, it wasn't too difficult to see. He indicated a point about eighteen inches from her panicky toes.

She dated sideways and rammed her shoes back on, still shuddering. 'Horrible thing!'

'It's not so horrible.' He picked the scuttling thing up. 'And it's not a cockroach either. Look.'

Holding back her fluttering fringe, she took a wary step forwards. 'It's just a shell!'

'Wait.' She could hear the amusement in his voice. He came closer, stood right beside her, The Thing on his outstretched palm.

For about twenty seconds the shell stayed still. And then it tilted a little and some little legs poked hesitantly out. 'It's just a hermit crab,' he said. 'Just going about its crabby little business.'

Her frown vanished. She watched as it crept hesitantly across his palm and stopped again. 'I do apologize for insulting you,' she told it, 'but you really did feel like a cockroach.'

He put it back on the sand. When he straightened up there was more than a half-smile on his face. It was more like three-quarters.

'Go on, then,' she said half defensively. 'Have a good laugh.'

Paradoxically, his smile faded. 'I wasn't laughing at you.'

As he gazed down at her, her heart and stomach lurched together like two drunks.

When he spoke, it was that old Shetland-sweater again. 'Can't you do something about that hair? It's falling in your face all the time.'

'It's the remains of my fringe,' she faltered, pushing the errant locks back. 'I'm growing it out.'

Almost at once, the breeze fluttered them back.

'It's driving me insane,' he said, in that rough-soft voice.

For the second time that day, Claudia thought she was in one of her own fantasies. Was he actually doing this? Brushing her wayward fringe back with those delicious, Category Four fingers? He seemed to do it in slow motion, his fingers brushing her hair as softly as the breeze. And all the while his eyes were dark and unfathomable as the sea.

She saw it coming like you see the car that's about to hit you. She could have moved, made some bright, daft remark and broken the magic.

And kicked herself for ever more.

CHAPTER 7

It was just a tantalizing brushing of lips, but it electrified her. It electrified her so much that when he drew back she wanted to scream, *Is that it?*

But that was before he came back for more.

Have I died and gone to heaven?

She knew she wasn't dreaming. In her dreams the man she was kissing turned out to be Peter the Pain and she woke up in a cold sweat.

The man knew what he was about. On a Richter Scale of kissing, this would score a ten. Tremblings and shiverings and warm, liquid rushes were playing havoc with her insides. Things stirred, shifted, rearranged themselves as he probed and possessed.

Stop the world, somebody. I could do this all night.

Even when they came up for air, the tremors didn't stop. As his lips brushed her hair, his fingers brushed the sensitive skin at the side of her neck.

Oh, Lord. How did he know the precise spot, the precise delicacy of touch that got her erogenous zones tingling like nothing else? Had he been her lover in a previous life?

If so, she must have died happy.

127

The seconds were even better than the starters. Standing on tiptoe, she reached her arms up around his neck. In all her best fantasies, this was the beginning of the next, tremblingly delicious bit. With her breasts thus raised invitingly, his hands would move in tormenting slow motion over the thin silk of her shirt and come to rest within a shivering millimetre of their lower curves.

The tremors would go right off the scale. She'd want to scream, *Go on!*'

And that was exactly what happened. A heart-stopping almost-touch that made unnamed organs lurch violently.

And, as always when she'd got exactly what she wanted, suddenly she wasn't sure she wanted it after all.

Detaching herself without making a thing of it wasn't easy. For a moment or two after he felt her try to ease herself away, his grip increased. And even before he let her go she was wondering how to play the next bit. There'd be a tense silence and then he'd say something like, What did I do?

With the sea only yards away, the perfect, daft remark came into her head at once 'Doesn't it just remind you of *Jaws?*' she said brightly. 'You know, that bit right at the beginning when the girl goes skinny-dipping and the music's going boom-*boom*, boom-*boom*, and giving you heart failure?'

Her heart was going boom-*boom* too, but he wasn't to know that. She had shattered the atmosphere perfectly, just as if someone had squirted them both with Thrill-Kill spray.

'I can't say it does,' he said, with the controlled, frustrated patience men reserve for such occasions.

She glanced at her watch. 'Don't you think it's time to be getting back?'

In the short, tense silence before he spoke, she knew exactly what was going through his head.

But all he said was, 'What's the rush?'

'You did say fifteen minutes.' Painfully aware of his questioning eyes, she began a quick, light walk back.

As they approached the hotel gardens, he said, 'Spit it out, Claudia.'

'If you must know, I need the loo.' She knew he didn't believe her, but he could hardly argue.

'I know what you were thinking,' he said

She had a fair idea of what *he* thought she was thinking. Something about job descriptions and what else might be in them apart from entertaining him over dinner. 'I don't think so, Guy.'

'Then perhaps you'll tell me.' He stopped suddenly. 'It was just a kiss. I don't know why you're charging along as if half a dozen muggers were after you.'

All right, it was just a kiss. But there are kisses that are just kisses, and kisses that hint at an awful lot more, given half a chance. But that's not the point just now.

Now the Richter Scale havoc was subsiding, she knew exactly what had felt wrong. 'You should be with your daughter, not me. She's all alone in her room. She's been alone nearly all day!'

'So what do you suggest I do? Tuck her up in bed? Read her a bedtime story?'

He could not have found a better spark for her fuse. 'You could talk to her, at least!'

'She won't talk. Except to tell me she's not listening.'

'I'm not surprised, if this is how you – ' She stopped dead on the path, as some helpless frustration erupted within her. 'You know what I think? I think you just can't be bothered. I think you'd rather amuse yourself with me than make an effort with your own daughter. And you know what else I think?' She carried on, throwing words at his impassive face.

'I think you've given her too much of everything. Too much of everything money can buy, that is. And not enough of the things money can't buy. Like time and attention. She's crying out for attention. Can't you see it?'

For a moment she though he was going to react with sarcasm, even anger. She could see him fighting whatever was inside him.

'Fine.' It was all he said, in a voice that stung like lemon juice on a cut. 'I appreciate your advice. Now shall we go in?'

She felt almost as if he'd slapped her face. 'I'd rather stay here for a bit.'

'I'd rather you came now.'

'And I'd rather not.'

Controlling himself with obvious difficulty, he said, 'I'm not going to argue the toss about it. You're not at home now.'

She glanced around her, at the quiet, deserted gardens, just a few insects buzzing round the lights in the trees. 'There's nobody here!'

'That is not the point. The point is that this is a Muslim country where a woman wandering around on her own at night is open to misinterpretation.'

OK, so you're right. I don't want any nosy hotel staff telling the management there's a loose foreigner soliciting in the gardens.

They walked in tense silence back to the hotel and into the lift. They stood in tense silence as the red light went G,1,2,3, then walked in tense silence down the corridor.

They reached his door first. 'Just for the record,' he said crisply, 'I have had it up to here with pious advice from earnest amateur psychologists telling me where I'm going wrong. And if I misunderstood your body language, I apologize. Maybe I need a new dictionary. Goodnight.'

A 'goodnight' in return was more than she could manage. Once in her room, she threw herself on the bed. She wasn't quite in tears, but they weren't far off. First kiss and first row, all in the space of ten minutes. And last of both, no doubt.

My God, the sarcasm in his voice! 'If I misunderstood your body language . . .'

A painful flush washed her entire body. It took no imagination to know what a less subtle man would have said. 'You were standing there like an asking-for-it bimbo and I gave it to you. So what the hell are you bitching about?'

What was I bitching about? Was I really being so ridiculous?

If they'd been colleagues on a business trip she wouldn't have given two hoots. Not that she'd ever have got into such a situation with a colleague on a business trip. They invariably had a wife and three kids in Richmond, and if they hadn't they were first cousins of Peter the Pain who thought a friendly chat over dinner constituted an invitation to wild sex till breakfast-time. Like that sleazy junior manager she'd once been sent on a course with.

But at least he hadn't had a problem daughter on the premises.

Probably Guy had only been telling the truth when he'd said it was no use trying to interest Anoushka in anything, but that was not the point. They weren't even on a *date*, for crying out loud. He was paying her to look after his daughter. The daughter he had led her to believe he was worried sick about.

Realizing exactly how she felt was rather a shock. She felt disappointed in him. Cheated, even. She could not call it low or despicable behaviour, exactly, it was just that she'd never have thought he'd do it.

Do what? Kiss you?

It wasn't just a kiss. That's the whole point. If I hadn't slammed the brakes on, it would have gone on to rather more.

But he hadn't planned it. Of that she was certain. All evening he had not done or said one single thing to make her think he was about to make a move.

He hadn't told her she looked gorgeous or smelt gorgeous, or accidentally-on-purpose brushed her thigh under the table. He hadn't put a totally unnecessary hand on her arm or waist as they'd entered the lift or the restaurant.

There had been no lingering looks over dinner. He'd looked her in the eye often enough, but not like that. His voice had not taken on the husky, I-hope-I-sound-sexy note men assumed when they thought they were in with a chance. He had not so much as patted her bottom, and that was one of the first things a man did when he thought a woman fancied him and wanted to encourage her.

Adam had been a great bottom-patter. From his usual horizontal position on the sofa he'd say in his quaint Aussie way, 'Jeez, what a bum,' and give it a friendly whack as she went past. After one too many beers at the Newt and Ferret he'd once told a riveted audience that he'd been a tit man until Claudia's bum had made a new bloke of him.

But it had been impossible to be offended or get cross with him. Everybody had liked Adam. He had come into her life like a warm, seductive ray of Aussie sunshine. He had made her laugh and sponged off her shamelessly, but she hadn't cared. She'd lived for the moment, knowing he would leave in the end.

One day he had packed his backpack, taken the last cold tinnie from the fridge, said, 'Cheers, luv. Come and see me in Adelaide,' and departed for the next leg of his round-the-world trip.

For ages it had seemed as if the sun would never come out again, and yet now she thought of him only with warm, nostalgic affection. And she knew who she had to thank for that.

The more she thought about it, the more she was certain Guy had acted on impulse. He knew how she felt. Such men always knew, and that little remark over dinner had given him away. Never mind that amused glint in his eyes.

Yes, he knew all right. But what had he thought? *Mmm, not bad*, probably. Coupled with, *But I'm not taken enough to start anything that might get complicated.*

She'd been standing there like something dished up on a plate with parsley on top and he'd thought, *Oh, what the hell. Might as well make her day with a minor thrill.*

So he'd kissed her and she'd loved it, so he'd kissed her some more. And, being only human, he'd thought he'd test the water with some subtle will-she, won't-she tactics.

They'd been subtle, all right. Just a shivering almost-touch that had whispered, *'There's more, if you want it . . .'*

Just the memory of it made that something in her stomach stir and shift itself again. What *was* that wretched thing? Why didn't they tell you such things in O level Biology? Even old Immac would have dealt with it in her own inimitable way.

'This, girls, is the Lurch organ, which nice girls need know nothing about till they're married. Turn to page sixty-four, please, and look at the kidney.'

It was still early, but since her body-clock was still on UK time, she went to sleep almost at once. And woke in the small hours in a cold sweat.

Oh, God, the relief of waking up. It was a bit much, having a sleeping nightmare when she'd only just had a waking one. And, as if that weren't enough, it was doing an action-replay in her head and she couldn't find the stop button . . .

Dressed as she'd been that evening, she was on the beach with Guy, but it was broad daylight, with other people all around.

He was standing a few feet away, in the dark suit he'd worn in the French restaurant, and his arctic navy eyes were doing things to her insides. In a crisply masterful voice he was saying, 'Get that shirt off, Claudia. How can I do naughty things to your naughty bits if you won't take your shirt off?'

'I can't!' she whispered. 'People are looking!'

'Don't give me that. I know you want to. I'm one of those men who know.'

Slowly her fingers moved to the buttons of her silk shirt.

Just yards away Anoushka was saying triumphantly, 'See? I told you she fancied him.'

Adam was sprawled in the sand at Anoushka's feet, a tinnie in his hand and a splitting grin on his face.

'If you think those beauties are cool, mate, just wait till you get a load of her bum!'

That wretched bonkbuster was going straight in the bin.

Unable to sleep, she lay tossing things around in her head. *You're pointing the finger at him, but what about you? You'd never have come if you hadn't fancied him like mad. And now you're wishing his daughter a million miles away, so you can fancy him with a clear conscience. You wouldn't even be here, if not for her. You'd never even have met him, if not for her. You're a self-righteous cow and if you're miserable, it serves you right.*

At seven-thirty, just as she was out of the shower, there was a sharp tap at the door.

'Who is it?' she called, fastening a towelling robe around her.

'Guy.'

Oh, help. 'I'm not dressed.'

135

'Then put something on.' His voice was tense and impatient.

She wound a towel round her wet hair, belted the robe, and gave her face an automatic check in the mirror. She had not slept well, and it showed.

Keep cool, Claudia. Cool, polite and distant, like you should have been last night if you'd had any sense.

He was wearing grey shorts, a white T-shirt and running shoes. The T-shirt was damp with sweat, his hair was tousled, his face suffused with the blood heat of exercise.

'There's no need to look like that,' he said, seeing her stiff expression. 'I don't want to come in.'

Thank God for that.

In cool-to-chilled tones he went on, 'I came to tell you I'm leaving in half an hour. I'm going further afield today, and won't be back till ten o'clock at least.'

Well, hallelujah. Eating with him tonight would not exactly have been a warm, cosy experience. 'Fine,' she said coolly. 'Will you see Anoushka before you go?'

'Of course. Contrary to what you obviously think, I do not deliberately neglect my daughter.' He paused. 'You'll be pleased to know that I'm taking your very wise and excellent advice. On Friday I'm going to take her into the Interior.'

His tone almost made her flush. 'There's no need to be sarcastic. I'm sure she'll enjoy it.' She wasn't sure of any such thing, but at least he'd be making an effort.

His mouth gave a sardonic twist. 'Why don't you come too? Then you could see at first hand just how much she enjoys it.'

'How do you expect her to enjoy it if you're starting off with that attitude?'

'I do not have an "attitude", Claudia. I have experience, which is more than you had when you dished out your pious advice.'

This was rapidly turning into another nightmare. Obviously she had hit a very raw nerve last night.

Just as she thought he was about to go, he spoke again. 'Just for the record, whatever happened on the beach last night it was not a prelude to horizontal gymnastics. Right now I have more than enough to occupy my energies. I need my sleep. And if I want to work up a sweat . . .' He glanced down at his damp T-shirt. 'As you see, there are more straightforward methods. I'll see you tomorrow.'

She felt as if he'd dealt her a stinging slap in the face. 'Have a nice day,' she said, like broken icicles, and shut the door behind him.

Oh, for Kate. She longed with painful desperation to talk to her, but it was Sunday morning and she'd probably be in bed. With Paul.

In any case, explaining it all would take for ever; telling her she'd fibbed like mad and that actually he'd made her flutter like crazy practically since she'd first laid eyes on him . . .

Besides which, it'd cost a fortune. If the hotel added its own massive mark-up the way most of them did, it'd cost enough to feed a family for a fortnight.

On her way down to breakfast she tapped at Anoushka's door, but there was no reply. On her way back up she tapped again, and this time the door opened a crack.

'What do you want?' said Anoushka grumpily. 'I'm fed up with being woken up.'

Feeling rather more sympathy for her than she had the day before, Claudia had made up her mind to make a fresh start. 'Are you coming to the pool later? I got a bit fed up all on my own yesterday.'

Widening the crack, Anoushka surveyed her through grumpy, half-asleep eyes. 'I've got to do some work. Dad's just been having a massive go at me.'

'But you haven't got to work all day, have you?'

'I've got to do an English essay about some crap book I've hardly even read. It'll take me years.'

Claudia wondered just what he had said to make his daughter decide to work. 'What book is it?'

'*Hangover Abbey* or something.'

'Not *Northanger Abbey*? Jane Austen?'

She nodded. 'About some stupid girl who thinks somebody's murdered somebody or something and makes a complete prat of herself.'

Bells were ringing like mad in Claudia's head. 'I had to do that at school too.'

Anoushka folded her arms. 'And I suppose you're going to tell me you *liked* it.'

Claudia felt a pang of sympathy for poor old Sister Bernadette, who'd tried so hard to make them all enthusiastic about literature – 'It's really terribly amusing, girls, if you can just get over these silly prejudices about nineteenth-century language.'

'Not at first,' she admitted. 'I thought it was the most boring thing since watching eggs boiling.'

'But you liked it in the end.' *I knew you would*, her tone said. *Because you're on the other side of the great divide between Still-at-School and Escaped.*

Claudia could still remember when she'd actually started to enjoy the book. The villainess of the piece had suddenly reminded her vividly of that cow Emma Cartwright who'd pinched her boyfriend.

'Well, not exactly,' she fibbed. 'But I remember the story pretty well. Maybe I could help you.'

She saw exactly what went through Anoushka's mind next: *I know she's only trying to get round me, but nobody else in this dump is going to help me.*

She opened the door wider. 'Come in a minute.'

'Thanks.' Claudia followed her inside. Anoushka was wearing only an oversized, faded black T-shirt that bore the legend 'WINDSURFERS DO IT STANDING UP'. Underneath it said, 'ANTIGUA, WEST INDIES'.

Seeing Claudia's eyes on it, she said, 'Yes, I know it's tacky. I only bought it to brown Dad off when I was thirteen and not supposed to get the joke.'

Anoushka's room would have done justice to Ryan in his best slob-mode, and it wasn't just the clothes on the floor. The remains of at least four meals were littered all over the place: trays, dirty plates, cups, glasses.

With startling efficiency, Anoushka gathered them all up, stacked the trays and put the whole lot outside the door.

Having done that, she picked up the phone. 'Room service, please.' After a few seconds she went on, 'Yes, please, I'd like some breakfast. No, not off the room service menu. I'd like some Rice Krispies . . . and two apples . . . and a Diet Pepsi . . . and some hot chocolate with double whipped cream. Have you got all that? *Shukran.*'

Claudia was duly impressed. 'Where did you learn that?'

'There's a Lebanese girl at school.' She surveyed Claudia with still-sleepy eyes. 'You can do my history essay too, if you're really that bored.'

Perching on the end of the other bed, Claudia made a face. 'You'd get a D minus. What's it about?'

'The rise of Fascism.'

'I'll pass, thanks.'

Anoushka rolled on to her back and propped herself up on the pillows. 'Actually, it'll be dead easy to write about Fascists. I just had one in here, goose-stepping up and down the room and ranting like Adolf Hitler on a bad day.'

Twenty-four hours previously, Claudia would choked back a laugh. Today, still smarting from Guy's caustic 'advice', she only raised an eyebrow.

Anoushka was evidently a lot more awake than she appeared. 'Have you and him had a barney?'

Oh, help. 'What makes you say that?'

'Your face. And the foul mood he was in this morning.'

Tread carefully, Claudia. 'We had a minor disagreement.'

'What about?' There was no mistaking the glee in her tone.

Think, Claudia. What do people disagree about? 'Politics,' she said.

The glee faded into disappointment. 'How boring.' After a moment she added, 'I thought he'd have you eating out of his hand till we left. He's very good at charming people. When it suits him.'

140

The barbed undertones were so obvious, Claudia gave her a sharp glance. But Anoushka missed it. Somebody had just tapped at the door and she was on her way to answer it.

'Clean the room, please?' asked a hesitant voice.

'No, thanks. I like it messy.' Before shutting the door she hung the 'DO NOT DISTURB' sign outside.

'If you hang that up now, room service might not like to knock,' Claudia pointed out.

'Oh, yeah. Better wait till they've been.'

As she took it down again, Claudia rose to her feet. 'I'm going for a walk on the beach. If you like, I'll come back in about an hour and see if I can help you with that essay.'

'OK.'

'Not that I'm any English Lit genius,' she added hurriedly, 'but I can try.'

'OK.'

Don't overdo the enthusiasm, will you?

But during her walk on the beach, she was glad she would have something to do, even if it was only helping with a school essay. Sitting round the pool on your own was boring, especially when you had to watch the clock and keep running for shade. If Kate had been with her, they'd have had such a laugh.

They'd have talked about every single person within eye-shot, making outrageous speculations about their private lives. Kate would say something like, '*See that man over there? Don't you think he looks like the kind of chap who dresses up as Superman and ties his wife to the bed and jumps on her from the top of the wardrobe?*' Claudia would look up and see some rather timid-looking middle-aged man – the kind who worries if he's not 'regular' – and crack up.

Vaguely restless, she went to the pool and did twenty hard-and-fast lengths. Feeling better, she returned to Anoushka's room.

She was dressed, at least, in another oversized T-shirt and cycling shorts. Her hair was still wet from the shower, but it was combed.

'This is going to do my head in,' she grumbled, flopping back to the desk where books and bits of paper lay. 'What's the *point?*'

Claudia picked up the assignment sheet. ' "Contrast the characters of Catherine and Isabella and show how they affect the story." '

'I don't know where to *start*,' Anoushka moaned. 'I haven't got a clue about their stupid characters.'

Claudia drew up a chair. 'You've probably got girls just like Catherine and Isabella at school.'

Anoushka gave her a look that said, *Oh, please.*

'I bet you have. If you met them today, you'd say Catherine was sad and Isabella was a complete bitch.'

From then on, it got easier. Half an hour later, while they were jointly scribbling notes, Anoushka glanced at her sideways and said, 'Go on, then. Ask me.'

'Ask you what?'

'What you've been dying to ask ever since you came in.'

There were a good many things Claudia would have liked to ask her, such as how often her father had rampant things, and who with. She had even conjured a rampant thing out of her imagination: a willowy blonde with a company BMW, exotic cheekbones and an accent to match. She had christened her Svetlana, and hated her instantly.

'I'm afraid you've lost me,' she said.

Anoushka put her pencil down. 'You're dying to know why I'm working after I tore everything up yesterday.'

Oh, that. 'I *was* wondering. Has he threatened you with death?'

'Worse.'

Claudia wondered briefly what could be worse. 'Packing you off to some boarding school in the wilds of Scotland? The kind that believes in porridge for breakfast and lots of good healthy exercise?'

'I'd run away.'

Yes, of course you would. 'What, then?'

'No ski-ing at Christmas.'

You poor child. Claudia thought of the pale little faces at Bruin Wood, who thought a few days in the New Forest akin to heaven. Still, it wasn't Anoushka's fault she was spoilt rotten.

'And you think he means it?'

'Yep.' Her face was bent over an A4 pad, hidden by her hair.

'Has he made threats before?'

'Hardly ever, but I could tell he meant this one. Going to Switzerland at Christmas is the thing I love best in the world, and he knows it.'

'You mean you go every Christmas?'

She nodded. 'And every Easter. Ever since I came to live with him.'

It took a second for this to sink in. 'What do you mean? Haven't you always lived with him?'

143

With a quick glance at her, Anoushka shrugged. 'He hasn't told you, then?'

'No! He told me your mother died when you were little, but I'd assumed – '

'You would. I bet there's a whole load of stuff he hasn't told you.'

I'm beginning to think there is. 'How long *have* you been living with him?'

'Three and a half years. Three and a half years of playing sweet little happy families in sunny South Kensington. The ever-loving father and his dear little daughter. Not forgetting Frau Iron-Knickers Pierce, of course, the trusty Kamp Kommandant.'

There had been few occasions in her life when Claudia had been lost for words, but this was very nearly one of them. 'Where were you living before?'

'Why don't you ask him?'

When Anoushka finally looked up, the mask that had been steadily slipping for the past hour was doggedly back in place. 'Thanks for helping me, but I'd like to get on with this poxy essay now, if you don't mind. On my own.'

CHAPTER 8

For the rest of the day, Claudia's head was buzzing like a hive full of bees. She wasn't in the least surprised at Anoushka clamming up like that; it was predictable awkwardness. *I know you're dying to know, so therefore I'm not going to tell you.*

The situation was obviously more complicated than she'd realized. *No wonder he had a go at you about 'pious advice'*, said an irritating, big-sisterish voice in her head. *You didn't know the circumstances. And therefore you had no right to make sanctimonious accusations.*

OK, maybe. But he still shouldn't have been on the beach like that, getting me all worked up with his masterly snogging techniques. He should have had other things on his mind.

It wasn't his mind you were on, if you ask me. It was another bit of his anatomy altogether.

Don't be so coarse.

Well, pardon me for breathing! Look who's talking anyway!

This internal argument went on until she bought an expensive paperback to take her mind off it; a whodunnit with no bonking whatsoever.

After a solitary supper in the coffee-shop and a bath, she wrote a postcard to Kate and took it to Reception to post.

And who should be there, collecting his key?

Oh, Lord.

She would have turned back, but since he'd already seen her she walked casually to the counter, said hello very casually, handed her postcard over to the receptionist and turned away again.

'Claudia!'

It was peremptory enough to stop her short. 'Yes?'

'Will you just wait a minute?' He was picking up messages as well as his key.

With a firm hand just above her elbow, he led her just out of earshot of the desk. 'I am paying you a good deal of money to supervise my daughter, and I do not appreciate your behaving like some sulky temporary secretary who imagines herself "put upon".'

That not-mincing-words expression came instantly to mind. Guy Hamilton was no mincer. He dished his words up in king-size mouthfuls.

'I am not sulking,' she said evenly, trying to ignore her furiously reddening cheeks. 'But after this morning, I was not exactly in the mood for big smiles and cosy chats.'

'I do not want big smiles and cosy chats. I would just appreciate a one-minute debriefing on how my daughter spent her day.'

Just as she was realizing that this was not an unreasonable expectation, he startled her by running an exasperated hand through his hair. 'Look, I'm sorry. It's been a long day.'

It showed. The short-sleeved shirt was creased, his tie wrenched loose, and up-to-here tension came off him in waves. He put her in mind of a tightly-coiled spring.

'Come and sit down,' he said, less curtly.

There were groups of armchairs in the foyer; they took the first unoccupied one.

Claudia was split down the middle. Half of her was miffed enough to walk off, but a little river of sympathy was trickling through her miffedness. She'd almost have liked to get him a nice cold beer and massage the tension out of his shoulders.

In theory, of course. In practice, no way. Not after last night.

Casually she said, 'I'm sorry – I shouldn't have charged off like that, but I didn't want any more . . . well . . .'

'What?'

'Any more of what we had this morning.' Before he could reply, she went on rapidly, 'Today was fine. Anoushka started her English this morning, came to the pool for lunch and went back to her room around two.' She made it sound as if they'd got on fine, whereas Anoushka had gone back into the grunt-mode which bordered on downright rudeness.

'I saw her again about seven to see if she was coming for supper but she'd already had a burger and chips sent up. In other words, everything was hunky-dory.' With her best bright-and-businesslike smile, she stood up. 'End of debriefing. Goodnight.'

With that, she walked rapidly to the lift.

Hurry up, she urged silently, as it dithered several floors up. *Otherwise he's going to* –

147

He did. But he said nothing as the little light went 3, 2, 1, and dithered again.

Keeping her eyes on that light, Claudia wondered what on earth people did while getting in and out of lifts that took so long. She had experienced similar irritation over those people who spent forever in aeroplane loos while there was a queue like a caterpillar with all its legs crossed practically up to Club Class. You'd wonder whether they were suffering from unmentionable embarrassing disorders or merely trying to have a bath and hairwash in the titchy basin.

When the lift finally opened its doors, two fiftyish men got out, speaking German.

Guy pressed the button and stood sideways, watching her. Even though she wasn't looking, she felt it.

As the lift took off he said, 'I suppose you've eaten?'

'Of course. Haven't you?'

'No.'

She had to look at him then. 'Then why don't you go straight to the restaurant?'

'I want to shower and change first. And see Anoushka.'

The doors opened, and as she stepped out he said, 'I don't suppose you'd like to keep me company while I eat?'

'I don't think so, thanks.'

'No, I thought not.'

They walked down the corridor and outside Anoushka's room he paused. The 'DO NOT DISTURB' sign was on her door.

'She's had that on nearly all day,' she said. 'To keep the dreaded cleaners out.' With a casual goodnight, she carried on.

She heard him knocking, and glanced back as she put her key in the door. Anoushka was evidently either asleep or just not answering. Glancing at his watch, looking wearily fed-up, he gave up and headed for his own room.

She shut her door and lay on the bed with the who-dunnit, but realized after several pages that it might as well have been an ancient Egyptian shopping list. Tossing it aside, she lay back, her arms folded behind her head.

Heaven help me, I'm feeling sorry for him now. He's had a long, hard day, his daughter doesn't even want to speak to him, and now he's going to have to eat all on his own. I feel like a complete cow for refusing to keep him company.

You would.

Should I ring him and say I've changed my mind?

If you've got the nerve to pick up the phone.

End of that idea.

She glanced at her watch. At least twenty minutes had elapsed since coming back to her room. He'd have gone now, if he was going. Or maybe he'd decided on room service. In which case she'd look a prize twit if she phoned to say she'd changed her mind and *he* said, Too late, thanks.

After dithering a bit longer, she wrote another postcard, gave her hair a quick brushing and inspected her face. The faintest hint of honey was now perking it up. She added a whisper of apricot lip-gloss but nothing else. The navy linen jeans were only slightly creased from her lying on the bed, not that she'd have changed anyway. She pulled the white cotton sweater down further over her hips and grabbed her key.

In the lift her stomach felt as if she'd swallowed a whole rain forest of butterflies. Since the restaurant would probably be closed by now, she headed for the coffee-shop, telling herself he probably wouldn't even be there.

It was a lot busier than the restaurant had been last night, humming with talk and laughter and clinking plates. She stood on the threshold, looking for a solitary male figure.

She couldn't see one anywhere. And then, just as she was about to go, she saw him.

And he saw her.

She was back in the lift in seconds, feeling sick. Sick, and furious with herself.

He hadn't been lonely after all. He hadn't been miserable either. He'd been lively and animated, and no wonder. Sitting right opposite him had been one of those shimmeringly tanned stewardesses, giggling her stupid face off.

In her room Claudia furiously tore her clothes off and got into an old Snoopy nightshirt. Furiously she cleansed her face and brushed her hair and teeth.

How could I have been so stupid?

Because you are stupid, you silly cow. When you fancy someone the way you fancy him, your brain only fires on one cylinder. Why on earth did you charge off like that, just because he happened to be sitting with another woman? After last night he's bound to think about dogs in mangers. Or bitches in mangers, come to that.

I know. And I feel like a pile of poo.

On an impulse she picked up the phone, dialled an outside line and her home number. *Please, Kate, be in. Please, Kate, be in.*

She let it ring for over a minute. When she finally hung up she felt so bereft she'd almost have welcomed Ryan

150

with open arms.

In her jangled state of nerves, the sharp tap on the door made her literally jump. 'Who is it?'

'Guy.'

Oh, my God. Trying to sound merely irritated, as if he'd interrupted a riveting whodunnit session, she called, 'Just a minute.'

Quick, a dressing gown. That nightshirt barely covers anything and you've got no knickers on.

Having donned and belted, she opened the door.

He looked as casual as you like, one hand on the doorframe, one leg crossed over the the other at the ankle. The only non-casual bit about him was a faint air of exasperation. 'That's the second time you've charged off tonight. Am I using the wrong soap?'

Straightening her shoulders, Claudia discovered a hitherto unwritten fact of life. Viz: when confronting a man who arouses assorted violent emotions it is preferable *not* to carry out said confrontation in bare feet and no knickers. For some perverse reason, this will make you feel fifty times more vulnerable than necessary.

She gave what she hoped was a really good shrug. 'I'd just been to post another card and I thought maybe I'd come and keep you company after all. But since you already had company, there was no point.'

His eyes said, *I wasn't born yesterday.* 'The place was busy and I had to share a table.'

OK, but did you have to look so flaming pleased about it?

'You could have come and joined us,' he went on.

It had been rather a good shrug, so she repeated it. 'I might have, but I'm in the middle of rather a good book.'

She nodded towards the bed, where it still lay. 'A toy boy is accused of murdering three wealthy women, but if you ask me it was their plastic surgeon. His mother used to lock him in a cupboard and put him in frilly dresses, and I strongly suspect that his bungled silicone implants were on purpose.'

Gosh, what a brilliant fib. Maybe I should have been a politician.

She wasn't at all sure it had convinced him, however. His expression didn't exactly say *Who are you trying to kid?* but there was a hint of it.

'Then I won't keep you.' Just as he was turning away, he seemed to change his mind. 'I'm going to grab a water ski tomorrow, before breakfast. Maybe you'd like to join me. Give it another go.'

This knocked her sideways. Her first instinct, recalling the frustrations of trying to learn the gentle art of water ski-ing with Matthew yelling orders, was to say, No way. On the other hand . . .

'I'll think about it. What time?'

'Eight-ish.'

She hesitated. 'If I feel energetic enough in the morning, I'll see you on the beach.'

'Fine.' For a moment she thought he was going to say something else. His eyes reminded her of Scottish lochs again, with the odd ray of sun playing on the surface, and his mouth seemed about to speak.

He evidently thought better of it. Back in crisp-and-businesslike mode he said, 'Check the sea before you come down. If it's not flat calm, it's not worth going.'

'I will.' *What had he been going to say?*

His C and B mode cracked just enough for half a lop-sided smile to escape. 'Goodnight, then.'

If only he wouldn't smile like that! The voice she managed to dig up sounded like her best dizzy-bimbo impression. 'Nighty-night. Sweet dreams.'

She shut the door behind him.

What in heaven's name was he going to say?

Lord knows.

Probably something he couldn't say without being offensive. Something on the lines of, Look, I got a bit carried away last night. I thought you were giving out 'available' signals but if you weren't . . .

He's not going to try it on again, is he? I think we got that little message loud and clear.

No, dammit.

I think he's got a little message loud and clear too. That you're not in the market for a quick, no strings, stress-busting bonk.

He said he wasn't after a quick, no-strings bonk! He said he wasn't after horizontal gymnastics anyway.

Claudia, get real. What man isn't after horizontal gymnastics if he thinks he can get them? Do you really think he'd have slammed the red light on last night if you hadn't? You were miles away from the hotel, and not a soul to be seen. It could have been one of your most X-rated fantasies come true. A delicious, urgent, illicit . . .

Just the thought sent her Lurch organ wild. *Oh, God. Just imagine it.*

The sand would get absolutely everywhere.

Who cares?

And imagine it afterwards. You'd have felt awful, won-dering if he was thinking you enjoyed quick, no-strings bonks on a regular basis.

But when she finally got to bed, Claudia couldn't help wishing she was the sort of person who could enjoy a quick, no-strings bonk. She had a feeling that memories of even a quick bonk with Guy Hamilton would keep her wonderfully warm during those long winter nights.

In theory. In practise, the side-effects would make her wretched. There would be the leaping-to-the-phone-every-time-it-rings side effect, plus the I-wonder-what-disgust-ingly-slim/sexy/hateful-bitch-he's-with now? side effect.

The trouble with you, she told herself, just before drifting off to sleep, is that you can't fancy someone like mad without falling for them. And the male animal, as we know full well, operates on a different basis. The male animal is led not by his heart, but by his dangly bits. 'Tis the nature of the beast, alas'.

The sea was flat calm next morning, but she still dithered until it was nearly too late.

With the black pareo over her bikini, she found him already selecting a ski and a jacket while the driver sorted the boat out.

He looked mildly surprised to see her. 'I'd given you up. We're just about to go.'

Any reservations about coming down vanished at once. He was firmly back in C and B mode. She could see that from the crisp way he buckled his jacket and pulled on a horribly professional looking pair of gloves.

'Shall I get in the boat?'

'Unless you prefer to stay on the beach while I go.'

She did not prefer. Sitting in a speedboat with the wind in your hair beat sitting in the sand any day. The boat was bobbing close to the shore, the driver sorting out boaty things. Hitching her pareo up, she waded out. The water was deeper than it looked, and by the time she reached the boat, she was up to her waist.

In such circumstances Matthew would invariably have been right behind her, doing his Big Strong Man bit, lifting her in as if she were six.

She had half expected Guy to do the same. She'd expected a pair of hands suddenly to appear on her waist and pop her up like a cork. She had even prepared a cool 'I'm perfectly capable, thanks' for that very purpose.

It was wasted. She had to haul herself up and clamber over the side. Once in, she glanced back at Guy, wondering whether he'd witnessed this inelegant performance. It seemed not. He was adjusting the binding on a horribly professional-looking mono-ski.

She was perversely miffed. He *should* have offered to help her into the boat, just so she could turn him down. It would have given her a certain satisfaction.

And that's probably precisely why he didn't, you dope. In case you haven't already sussed it out, he's no amateur when it comes to these little games.

He was obviously no amateur at water ski-ing either. Instead of wading into the water and starting off there, he was standing in three inches of water, his ski just clearing the tiny waves.

Having watched Matthew try to do 'beach starts' many times, fail nine times out of ten and curse very colourfully, she watched the next bit with interest.

155

The driver threw him the line and straightened the boat up. Guy caught the line, lifted his ski and yelled, 'Hit it!'

The force with which the boat took off jolted her right back in her seat. Alas, he was not floundering in the shallows, practising his Anglo-Saxon. He was not only up, but sending up a cloud of spray worthy of Niagara Falls.

Matthew would have been sick as a pig.

She watched for a while as he cut back and forth across the wash. The so-and-so made it look so easy, even with only one hand and a shoulder practically skimming the water.

Whether to keep watching or not was a difficult decision. She didn't want him thinking she was over-impressed; on the other hand, if she *did* keep watching he might be tempted to do some really clever stuff and fall off.

It was her hair that decided her. When she faced backwards it flew all over her face; when she faced the front it was at least blowing in the right direction.

After three circuits of the bay, the driver zoomed back and cut the engine.

Guy passed his ski in and hauled himself back into the boat. She tried not to look as he unbuckled his jacket. He was too close for comfort. The way his muscles moved under his skin was far too close for comfort, especially with all those sunlit droplets clinging to it.

'Your turn,' he said.

Oh Lord, is this really such a good idea? All too vividly she was recalling those sessions with Matthew; the endless trying-again, swallowing half the Med as she fell on every imaginable bit of her anatomy. Never mind their friends cracking up on the beach, asking whether she'd given herself an enema.

'I think I'll leave it,' she said, casually smoothing her tangled hair. 'I need some breakfast first.'

'Rubbish. You won't get a sea like this again in ages. It's like glass.'

It wasn't exactly like glass, more like a smooth blue jelly giving the odd little ripple. Conditions could not have been more perfect, and she knew it would probably roughen up later, but still . . .

'Give her the jacket,' he said to the driver.

Make your mind up, Claudia. Chicken out, or do it and be damned.

Put like that, there was no contest. 'I suppose it'll give me an appetite for breakfast.'

The driver handed her a thick yellow belt.

'Aren't you wearing a jacket?' Guy frowned.

'This is fine,' she told him. 'I wore one just like this in Spain. It kept me up perfectly well.'

He actually took it from her hand and replaced it with a jacket much like the one he'd just taken off. 'You'll be better off with one of these.'

It looked bulky and restrictive. 'I'd prefer the belt, thank you very much.'

'Suit yourself.' She had taken the pareo off and his eyes swept over the curves that her bikini top didn't even try to cover. 'But I can tell you now that if and when you manage to get up, the force will have that top round your waist. If you want to flash your assets, that's fine with me.'

'That never happened in Spain!'

'Maybe because you never made it to the vertical. Or maybe you were wearing a more suitable swimsuit.'

157

She made a rapid memory search. Blast him, he was right. She'd been feeling fat that summer, and had stuck to sleek one-pieces. 'I'll take the jacket.'

By the time she was actually in the water, trying to get the wretched skis on, her stomach was in a terrible state.

I just know I'm going to screw it up and he's going to laugh.

Don't be so defeatist! You're going to do it first time and stick two fingers up at the pair of them.

Unlike Matthew, who'd loved playing instructor, Guy let the driver tell her what to do. Knees bent, arms straight. *Yes, yes, yes. I know what you're supposed to do.*

The problem was *doing* it, especially with Guy watching her every move from the back of the boat.

After the first two disasters, ending in a tangle of legs and skis and feeling her bikini top come adrift under the jacket, Guy began sticking his oar in.

Leaning over the side, he said with infuriating male patience, 'Claudia, you're trying too hard. All you've got to do is stand up.'

'What d'you think I'm bloody *trying* to do?' she snapped, struggling to get her other ski back on.

'Cursing isn't going to achieve anything.'

'You call that cursing? Just wait till I really get going.'

Third time lucky, she told herself, and tried not to try too hard. That didn't work either, and while she was trying to sort out the next inelegant tangle, he leaned over the side again. 'You're trying to stand up too quickly.'

'Bugger off,' she muttered under her breath.

'I didn't quite catch that.'

'I said . . .' For fear of shocking the driver, she mouthed it silently, but emphatically. 'Got that, did you?'

He reached over and held the tip of the ski she was trying to get back on. 'If you want to pack it in, say so.'

'I – do – not – want – to – pack – it – in!'

'Then calm down.'

What is it about a man telling you to 'calm down' that makes you want to hit him?

If he'd been close enough, and she hadn't been so busy adjusting her twisted bikini bottoms, she might have.

'Stand up *slowly*,' he said, tossing her the line. 'Watch me, and don't try to get up till I tell you.'

That did it. 'The reason I'm having difficulty, Mr Flaming Hamilton, is because I'm strung up. And the reason I'm strung up is because you're watching me like a hyper-critical hawk. Will you please do me a colossal favour and watch something else instead?'

At last his noble patience cracked. 'The reason you're having difficulty, Miss Stroppy Maitland, is because you're not doing what you're bloody well told.'

Still mindful of the driver, she lowered her voice to a hissy whisper. 'Why don't you go and find the prickly end of a pineapple and shove it up your bum?'

Much to her surprise, this had the desired effect. With an air of up-to-here exasperation, he took himself to the prow and sat beside the driver.

El hamdulillah.

The patient driver called, 'Ready?'

'You bet.'

She popped out of the water like a champagne cork. Oh rapture and bliss! How easy-peasy it was once you were up! Any fool could do it.

Seeing Guy look at her, she wished she dared take a hand off and stick two fingers up, but it wasn't worth falling off for.

After one circuit of the bay, she felt quite amazingly confident. Even turning corners was a doddle. It was only when she realized that they were not going in circles any more that she began to get uneasy. Heaven help her, they were heading straight out to sea!

Immediately she began to think of deep waters and the beasts that lurk therein. 'Turn round!' she yelled, but they couldn't hear her over the noise of the engine. Letting go and falling in on purpose was a possible option, but she didn't fancy it. Who knew what might be down there, licking its lips?

Her arms were getting tired from the unaccustomed strain, and just as she was beginning to think she couldn't hold on any longer she really panicked. About fifty yards away she saw several dark fins breaking the glassy surface. 'Go back!' she screamed.

The driver stopped instead, and as she sank into the water the boat came round like a boomerang to pick her up. 'Are you trying to get me killed?' she gasped, as Guy grabbed her arm. 'The water's crawling with – '

'They're dolphins, Claudia. The driver thought we'd like a closer look.'

'I don't care what they are, just get me out!'

'Turn around.' With his hands under her arms, he lifted her in.

'No need to scare, madam,' smiled the driver. 'Dolphins very nice, very friendly.'

Oh, God the relief. She could see they were dolphins now, the way they broke the surface in a graceful curve.

There seemed to be dozens of them, and as they watched some of them began jumping, twisting in spirals in the air, as if they knew they had an appreciative audience.

But the show was short-lived. Within minutes, the school had moved on.

As they headed back, Claudia sat in the seat behind Guy. 'I nearly had heart failure,' she said crossly 'If I were American, I'd probably sue the pair of you for post-traumatic stress disorder. All I could see were fins! Shark fins!'

'You're obsessed with sharks.'

'I am not!'

'For somebody non-obsessed, you seem to bring them up with monotonous regularity.'

She knew exactly what he meant by that. 'I did it, anyway. Once you stopped watching.'

'You made the most almighty heavy weather of it.' He turned right round, a dangerous glint in his eye. 'You are without doubt the stroppiest woman I have ever had the misfortune to encounter.'

'Thank you,' she said sweetly. 'That's the best compliment I've had all year.'

'Don't mention it.'

As they neared the beach, he turned round again. 'Just out of interest, how long after that ex tried to teach you to water ski did the relationship last?'

She thought back. 'About three months.'

'I wouldn't have given it three minutes. I'd have strangled you. Or at least turned you over and tanned your backside.'

'That is a very typically prehistoric utterance from an older man,' she said kindly. 'I suppose it must be difficult, dragging your attitudes into the late twentieth century. But I hadn't quite realized you belonged to the sub-species *homo chauvinisticus piggicus.*'

'I always had a fair idea what sub-species you belong to. *Femalicus bloody awkwardicus.* With the accent on the *cus.*'

'I think you'll find that should be femalic*a*, being feminine,' she said helpfully.

His eyes said, *Don't push your luck.*

The boat slid almost on to the sand. Feeling rather pleased with what she had accomplished even before breakfast, Claudia stood up and unbuckled her jacket. And just too late she remembered what all that exertion had done to her bikini top.

Guy was already out, steadying the boat, and did not miss the fleeting display before she hitched her top back into place. 'Claudia, do behave yourself,' he said mildly. 'You can get ten years for flashing your assets here.'

If he'd pretended he hadn't noticed, she might have behaved with her usual 'so what?' aplomb. As it was . . .

Just to be really perverse, he took her arm as she jumped down. 'And you call me prehistoric,' he murmured. 'I thought blushing went out with hula-hoops.'

OK, fifty points to you. And time to even up the score. 'I really don't know what you were gawping at. If you haven't seen a pair of 36Bs before, your education must be sadly lacking.'

She walked up the beach very fast. She would have bet her last *baiza* that there was an infuriating little twitch on his lips. And if there was, she didn't want to see it.

162

CHAPTER 9

Strenuous exercise before breakfast was all very virtuous, but it would seem to defeat the object if it gave you the appetite of a carthorse. As she showered, Claudia realized she was ravenous. Too ravenous to bother blow-drying her hair properly. Slicking it back into a clasp, she pulled on a pair of white cotton jeans and a baggy pale pink shirt, and went down.

Oh, yum, such lots of lovely food. Cereal, fruit, juice, cheese, yoghurt – and that was without all the cooked stuff. Helping herself liberally, she found a table and got stuck in.

Until a shadow loomed. 'May I join you?' Guy enquired sardonically. 'Or are you going to make more colourful suggestions about where to stick pineapples?'

Now the drama was over, she began to think perhaps she'd been a bit over the top. 'I won't mention pineapples. Except perhaps in the context of eating them,' she added, indicating her two fresh, fat slices.

'Very gracious of you.' Although he was doing his best, he could not quite hide the minute spasm at the corner of his mouth.

Well, that was a relief. If not actually kicking, his sense of humour was at least alive and twitching. On the other hand, if he'd been behaving like what she and Kate called a BHP – for boring, humourless prat – she would begin to go off him, which might be no bad thing. A man could be rolling in dosh and dishy as you like, kind to old ladies and even a ten on the Richter Scale kisser, but without a sense of humour he was about as much use to Claudia as a 32A bra.

In the circumstances, perhaps a little penitence was in order. 'I'm sorry I swore at you,' she said.

'I've heard worse.' He added with half a resigned and lopsided smile.

She'd almost have preferred the BHP. The BHP would not have got all her internal flutterings going again. 'It was nothing to what I said to Matthew, I can tell you.'

'I'll take your word for it.' He raised his eyes from a well-heaped plate. 'Believe it or not, I was only trying to help.'

Oh, Lord, now she felt dreadful, as well as fluttery. 'I know, but I was trying so hard, and it felt like pressure. I couldn't relax.'

A waiter came to pour his coffee and refill her cup. She carried on with her breakfast and tried not to watch him. The flutterings he had aroused were refusing to go back to sleep and they didn't need much to keep them awake. They didn't need skin-to-skin brushings or even a few seconds' eye contact. The faint scent of his aftershave was quite enough, and the arms that looked so lovely and hunky against the snow-white short-sleeved shirt.

'You've caught the sun,' he said. 'It suits you.'

'Thanks.' She had to smile and look him in the eye now, or it'd be obvious that she was trying not to. He had caught the sun too, although he obviously hadn't been working at it. The olive of his face and arms had deepened into a tan, making his eyes bluer by comparison. Instead of arctic northern waters, they were now beginning to remind her of Greek Island blue.

Why isn't there one single thing about you that really turns me off? she thought despairingly. It wouldn't take much. Just watching a man shovelling food into his mouth like a pig and eating with his mouth open had worked wonders in such situations.

'But that hair's flopping in your face again.'

Did he have to bring that up? If it hadn't been for that flopping hair . . .

It was drying fast, the errant fringe escaping.

'It's really getting on my nerves,' she muttered, pushing it back. 'I've got a good mind to go and have the whole lot cut off.'

'The hairdresser in the lobby's supposed to be very good,' he said mildly.

Well, what did you expect? For him to say, Cut off all that beautiful hair? Don't you dare!

It would have been nice.

And that's precisely why he didn't say it. Remember what we said about little games?

After they'd both put food away for a minute he said, 'I'm sorry if you thought you were suddenly stuck in the middle of a *Jaws* movie. It was the driver who spotted the dolphins. He thought if we stopped and messed about getting you back in the boat, they'd have gone.'

Having wondered whether he'd engineered it on purpose, just to wipe that grin off her face, she felt double guilty.

'If I hadn't been in such a state, I might have got in and had a swim with them.' Thinking back to all the dear little Flippers, she wished she'd been in a better frame of mind to enjoy them. 'What a shame Anoushka wasn't there to see them.'

A fleeting regret crossed his face. 'Yes, I think I can safely say that wild dolphins would not come under her "terminally boring" heading.'

'Did you ask her if she wanted to come?'

'I put a note under her door last night and I phoned her this morning, but all I got was a half-asleep mouthful for waking her up.'

It seemed an appropriate moment to bring burning questions up without seeming offensively nosy. 'She told me she's only been living with you for three and a half years.'

'She has. Before that she was living with her grandmother in Geneva.'

Just as she was trying to frame another question with suitable delicacy, he saved her the bother.

'Her grandmother became ill,' he went on. 'She had a stroke and obviously couldn't cope any more. So Anoushka came to me.'

She kept a tactful silence. If he wanted to tell her more, he would. If he didn't, no amount of intrusive questioning would get it out of him.

When he finally looked her in the eye, there was no particular expression there. 'Her mother and I split up when she was a baby, so coming to me was the last thing she wanted. And as you've probably gathered, she's been making that perfectly plain ever since.'

For a moment Claudia just did not know what to say.

What did I tell you about sanctimonious accusations? Now you feel like a pile of poo, and serve you right.

She moistened her lips. 'Guy, I'm really sorry for all those things I said the other night. I had no idea.'

'You weren't to know.'

Such forbearance only made her feel worse. 'I wish you'd told me.'

His eyebrows rose and fell in a 'too late now' manner. 'Like your mother says, it's not the done thing to bore people to death with all your problems.'

She was about to say, I wouldn't have been bored, but didn't get a chance. 'As I mentioned I'm going to take Anoushka into the Interior on Friday,' he said. 'Friday's the local Sunday. She won't want to come, but I'm going to show her there's more to this country than four hotel-room walls and a pool.'

He paused. 'I know what you said about spending time alone with her and you're probably right, but the atmosphere'll be less fraught with a third party to dilute it. So if you'd like to join us . . .'

She didn't hesitate long. She had done atmosphere diluting before, on the odd occasion when her mother had had words with her own mother – 'If I don't go she'll be even more put out, dear, but it'll be so much easier if you're there too.'

'Thank you. I'd love to.'

'Good.' He said it crisply, as if another item from his 'In' tray was now in the 'Out'.

Draining his coffee-cup, he added, 'I'd better hit the road. I'll probably be late again so don't wait for me to eat.'

'I won't. Will you see her before you go?'

'I most certainly will. Whatever work she's done needs faxing back to the school.'

As he stood up she said, 'Are you surprised she started working after all?'

'Not really. She's bored. Anoushka's very bright, you know. If she weren't I wouldn't be taking a stand. I'm not going to see her jack everything in and turn into one of those waste-of-space girls whose only ambition in life is to get a mention in the gossip columns.' He dropped the lightest of pats on her shoulder. 'I'll see you.'

'Bye.'

She watched him go and thought, *I wish he hadn't done that.*

It was just a friendly pat.

Friendly pats do not feel like friendly pats when you're all of a dither over the patter. If our relationship is supposed henceforth to be on a strictly no-thrills basis, he ought to stick by the rules. Which means no touching. How am I supposed to keep a lid on my flutterings if he keeps touching me?

What are you complaining about? You know you love it.

I'd love it a lot more if it was leading somewhere. I'd love it a lot more if he said, Look, while we're here, our relationship should be on a purely professional basis. But when we get home . . .

Will you stop it? Finish your breakfast and think about something else.

Easier said than done. While stirring her third cup of coffee, idle thoughts were stirring too.

I wonder how long it is since he's had a rampant thing? They say men think about sex every two seconds, and if he hasn't had a rampant thing for a bit . . .

Neither have you, come to that. And, not to put too fine a point upon it, sex has hardly been the last thing on your mind lately. It's not just him, if you ask me. It's good, old-fashioned frustration, considerably intensified by close contact with a Category Four. Maybe you should buy a vibrator.

Oh, please.

At least you won't suffer agonies afterwards, waiting for it to ring you.

I'd rather have the agonies.

Thinking about vibrators took her mind off Guy Hamilton quite nicely. She and Kate had once been invited to a naughty variant on the Tupperware party, where the emphasis was definitely not on keeping your left-overs crispy-fresh. Kate had ordered a ten-inch black item, and when it had finally arrived they had nearly wet themselves laughing. Thinking it might be rather good for unblocking the sink, they had christened it Dyno-Rod.

Remembering Dyno-Rod set her shoulders shaking, and the two Germans who had got out of the lift while they'd been waiting last night and were sitting now at a nearby table, started giving her very funny looks.

Around ten, she called to see Anoushka. 'How's it going?'

'If you're really interested, I'm probably going to die of boredom in this dump. There's not even any decent radio. At home I always have music blasting out.'

169

She gave Claudia an up-and-down glance. 'You went water ski-ing with my Dad this morning, didn't you?'

There was just a touch of hostility in her tone, as if Claudia had been sleeping with the enemy.

'Yes, I did. Did he tell you about the dolphins?'

The hostility increased a fraction. 'What dolphins?'

'We saw a whole school of them, all leaping about like Flipper.'

'He didn't tell me anything. I was looking out of the window and I saw you both coming back.'

It was obvious that she'd have loved to see them, even if she was never going to admit it. 'They didn't stay long, so you didn't miss much.'

Anoushka was back at the desk, giving her a sideways glance. 'I suppose he was showing off like mad and trying to impress you.'

This gave her food for thought. Men frequently show off, of course – particularly the sub-species *homo Ryanicus* – but Guy hadn't struck her in that light. There had been none of the overtly macho body language you normally got on such occasions.

'He was trying to help me,' she said. 'I'd tried to do it before and failed miserably.'

Anoushka gave her another sideways glance. 'And I suppose his brilliant expertise got you going in no time.'

'No, as a matter of fact. He tried to help, but the more he tried, the more I couldn't do it. I got very cross and said some very rude things, I'm afraid.'

As she'd fully expected, this produced a modicum of interest. 'Like what?'

'I couldn't repeat them.'

170

'Go on.'

Well, if it'll cheer her up . . . 'Among other things, I suggested he find the prickly end of a pineapple and shove it up his bum.'

For the first time since that night in the French restaurant, there was a look of mischievous delight on Anoushka's face. 'God, I wish I'd been there. What did he say?'

'He ignored it.'

'He would.' She sat back and added, 'I bet he got a shock when you weren't giggling and playing up to him. It makes me sick the way women play up to him.'

Now why does that surprise me not at all? She's only going to tolerate me as long as she thinks I'm not 'playing up' to him. Was I quite mad to wish he'd make 'when we get home' noises?

On the other hand, she could not help feeling for a girl who had not only lost her mother, but had been transplanted at a difficult age to what must have felt like a strange country.

She would have liked to steer the conversation delicately to this topic, but that would imply to Anoushka that she and Guy had been having cosy heart-to-hearts about her. 'Anything I can help you with?' she asked.

'Not unless you want to do my maths.'

She made a face. 'No, thanks. Will you come to the pool at lunchtime?'

'I might.'

'See you later, then.'

Claudia went back to her room, sorted out a few things for the laundry and wrote a long letter to a friend now

171

living in Canada. After that she went to the pool, did twenty lengths and then sat in the shade with the whodunnit, feeling vaguely bored and restless.

Over a toasted sandwich lunch with Anoushka at the pool, she turned the conversation after all. 'I never had all that trouble with snow ski-ing. With snow ski-ing at least you start upright.'

Anoushka was sitting beside her in a black swimsuit that screamed '*expensive*'. The cut was very simple: just one shoulder-strap, high-cut legs and a very low back. She looked much older than sixteen, but that was also due to a figure that owed absolutely nothing to stick-insect supermodels.

'I never had trouble with either of them.' Anoushka shrugged. 'I can't even remember when I started snow ski-ing. I suppose I was about three.'

'Lucky old you. It must be lovely to learn these things when you're too young to be self-conscious about making a fool of yourself.' Claudia paused. 'But I suppose ski-ing was on your doorstep if you were living in Switzerland when you were little.'

'I suppose Dad's been telling you?'

'He mentioned it.'

'Well, I was. When they split up my mother went to live with her parents in Geneva. I was only a baby then. And when my mother died, I stayed with Granny.'

Claudia hesitated. 'Was your mother Swiss?'

'Her Mum was English, her Dad was Brazilian, but her Dad had worked in Europe for ages and they'd settled in Switzerland.'

At last it was making sense. The Brazilian element certainly accounted for Anoushka's smouldering looks.

172

She'd had a friend with similar looks once, a girl of Italian descent who'd looked like a woman at thirteen, when the rest of them were still children. She had once overheard her grandmother saying sniffily to her mother, 'I wouldn't encourage Claudia to be friends with her, if I were you. Girls that age have no business looking like that. She'll get herself into trouble, you mark my words.'

Her mother had been quite cross and told her not to be so silly, and it was only later that Claudia had properly understood. Sara had projected a magnetic, inborn sensuality that the likes of her exceedingly prim grandmother mistrusted on sight.

Anoushka had the look too. A parent's nightmare, no doubt. Especially a father's. Especially a father who, maybe, not so long ago, had been a bit of a lad himself.

'It must have been very difficult for you, moving to England,' she said.

'I hated it. I thought London was a complete hell-hole.'

'But surely you'd visited before? You must have seen your father over the years?'

'Now and then.' She shrugged, and picked up her magazine with an end-of-conversation finality.

Claudia saw little of Guy for the next couple of days. He was out early and back late and their conversations were brief and businesslike. It was on the Thursday afternoon that he sought her out by the pool.

'Anoushka's not in her room,' he said.

She'd been lying back, half-dozing in the sun, and since it was only four-thirty she had not been expecting to see him.

Sitting up, she put her sunglasses back on. 'She's gone for a walk on the beach.'

'A *walk*? Is she sickening for something?'

'Just fed up, I think. Suffering from radio withdrawal.'

'That figures.' He lifted the magazine that Anoushka had left on her sunbed and sat himself down. 'Why does she read this stuff?' he muttered, giving the cover a cursory withering loose.

In large letters it screamed, TEACH YOUR MAN TO FIND YOUR G-SPOT!'

Just as well he hadn't come twenty minutes earlier and found her reading that very article – after her stars, which had been disappointingly irrelevant. 'What do you expect her to read at sixteen? *Good Housekeeping? The Economist?*'

'I guess not.'

He was wearing the navy shorts again, with a casual, short-sleeved blue chambray shirt. It was completely unbuttoned and fell open as he sat back.

She tried not to notice the way the hair on his chest tapered down over his stomach and disappeared into those shorts. 'Why don't you go and find her?'

'Because I wanted to see you first.' He gave her a sideways glance. 'Sort out a couple of evident misconceptions about the nature of your job description.'

Oh, my God. 'Like what?'

'Like, I am not paying you to do Anoushka's school-work for her. More specifically, I am not paying you to write her English essays.'

'*What?*' Relief was instantly followed by indignation. 'I did not *write* it for her!'

'But you helped her.'

'A bit! So what if I did?'

'It was more than a bit, according to her.'

She made a mental note to have words with Anoushka. Stirring with a king-size wooden spoon was the phrase that sprang to mind.

'OK, so I helped her!. She hadn't a clue where to start and I just happen to have had that particular Austen rammed down my own throat at school!'

'All right, keep your prickly red hair on. I can see you're no great fan of the classics.'

Oh, damn. His eyes had fallen on the bonkbuster that lay between the sunbeds. He picked it up. And with her aircraft boarding pass making the perfect bookmark, it fell open at the point where she had left off. Right in the middle of the imaginative contortions of Dominic, Natalya, & co.

She was fully expecting him to give it one glance, and put it down with a caustic remark about trash, at which she would mutter something equally caustic about literary snobs.

Instead he scanned it for perhaps twenty seconds.

It was ridiculous to feel embarrassed, but she did. Not because he was reading about the imaginative contortions of Dominic and Natalya, but because he was probably imagining *her* reading them and getting all hot and erogenous in the process.

In fact, she had not. As scenes of rampant nookie went, it had been disappointingly unerotic – more like a DIY plumbing manual than anything else.

'Jesus,' he muttered at last. 'This is anatomically impossible.'

She recovered a modicum of composure. 'Not necessarily.'

He shot her a sardonic glance. 'Are you speaking from personal experience?'

Thank heaven for sunglasses – not that she was actually looking him in the eye. 'I refuse to answer that on the grounds that it might incriminate me. But if you really want to know, Natalya is an ex-Olympic gymnast.'

He snorted. 'She'd need to be.'

This conversation was getting way out of hand. 'I think you should go and find your daughter. I'm going for a swim.'

She half ran to the pool and dived in. It was more like a warm bath than a cold shower, but better than nothing. Dammit, she almost *was* hot and erogenous, just from thinking of Guy thinking of *her* getting hot and erogenous.

Three fast lengths cooled her off nicely, and while she was getting her breath back at the deep end she saw him strolling towards the beach.

Good luck, sunshine. She could just imagine the forthcoming scene, and it wasn't exactly a happy, smiley daughter running up with a Hi, Dad! Had a nice day?

Still, he was making an effort. After a couple more lengths, weaving in and out of splashing children, she took another breather at the deep end.

While she was there, her arms stretched out along the bar behind her, doing some thigh-firming leg lifts, he came back. Anoushka was beside him, with a sulky expression.

When they arrived back at the sunbeds she picked up her bits and pieces and he said something to her. Anoushka barely looked at him as she replied, and he said something else. With another very short reply, Anoushka walked back towards the hotel.

She could not tell what Guy had said, but from his expression it didn't look as if he'd been having a go at her. Suddenly, Claudia felt like running after Anoushka and shaking her. Couldn't she ever be pleasant? What was the matter with her?

She's a brat, that's what.

Guy watched his daughter's back for a moment, and then turned towards the pool. He stripped off his shirt and dived in.

She almost knew he was coming up to her, and he did. He swam most of the way underwater, and surfaced a few feet away. Shaking the water from his head, he came and held the rail beside her.

'She wasn't in the sunniest of moods, then,' she said.

'Is she ever?' Wiping the water from his face, he turned around. Now they were facing in different directions, but since he was only about a foot away she could see his face well enough. Exasperation was written all over it.

'All I get is monosyllabic grunts. Would she like to go for a ski? No. Would she like a drink? No. Is she coming for a swim? No.' In the pause that followed, he gave a tense, exasperated sigh. 'I've had it up to here with her.'

Before she could utter, he went on, 'I'm going to be out again tonight, I'm afraid. I've been invited for dinner with a guy from one of the ministries and I haven't told him I'm accompanied. You don't tend to tell such people you've had to bring your daughter because she's been suspended from school.'

'No, you wouldn't.'

With the ghost of a smile, he glanced at her. 'I hope you're not getting bored, hanging round the hotel all day.'

'Oh, no,' she lied. 'Anyway, we're going out tomorrow. I'm really looking forward to it.'

'I'm glad somebody is. The way Anoushka reacted when I told her, you'd think I'd suggested a trip to a public beheading.'

Oh, Lord. 'They don't have those here, do they?'

'You're thinking of Saudi again. Friday mornings in Chop Square.'

She shuddered. 'What time will we be leaving tomorrow?'

'Around half-nine to ten. To allow time for her ladyship to wake up and get her best happy face on.'

Several small children were playing 'bombs' not far away, jumping in a scrunched-up position to see who could make the biggest splash. As the next hit the water Claudia half turned, to miss the worst of the blast.

'At least somebody's having fun,' he said drily, as delighted shrieks echoed round the pool. 'Anoushka was like that once, believe it or not.'

'She'll grow out of it,' she said, with an assurance she was far from feeling. 'It's just her age.'

'People have been telling me that ever since she came. It's her age. Her hormones. Normal, adolescent bolshiness.' His mouth gave a wry twist. 'I suppose you can't tell me how long it takes for a girl to grow out of hormones and bolshiness?'

'I'm not sure I ever have.'

His mouth gave a wry little twist that played havoc with her already fragile composure. 'OK, point taken. But in theory?'

Well, if it is theory you want instead of the unpalatable truth . . . 'Give her a year or two,' she said. 'By the time she's eighteen I'm sure she'll be a perfectly charming, rational adult.'

'You reckon?' A water-bombing child landed barely three feet from his shoulder, and he moved closer. 'Sometimes I think it's more than just hormones and bolshiness.'

'Like what?'

He was almost touching her under the water, and just as she was wondering whether to move or make the most of it a child on an inflatable crocodile bashed into her from behind.

She hit Guy from chest to thigh. For about a second, the heat of his body burned her. 'Sorry,' she said unsteadily, moving away.

Keeping her eyes firmly ahead, she watched the child paddle away on the crocodile. 'So what do you think it is, if not hormones and bolshiness?'

'I think it's me.'

She had to look at him then. 'What do you mean?'

For just an instant, before he looked away, she saw a fleeting bleakness in his eyes. 'If you really want to know . . .' He paused. 'Sometimes I think she hates me.'

Whatever it was that normally lurched inside her, it felt as if someone had stuck a rusty knife in it. 'Why?'

'I don't know.'

Suddenly she wanted to put her arms around him and tell him not to be so daft. If they hadn't been in the deep end of a swimming pool, she might have. It would be a bit difficult treading water and cuddling someone at the same time.

But even before this impulse had died, something else came into her head. That mischievous kissogram.

Trying to keep her voice steady she said, 'Guy, can I ask you something?'

'You can. I might not answer it.'

She nearly changed her mind. If he did answer, she might well wish she'd never asked. 'When you and Anoushka's mother split up, did *you* leave *her*?'

In the seconds before he answered, she knew she should have kept her mouth shut.

'Oh, I get it,' he said sardonically. 'I begin to follow your logic. The reason my daughter hates me is because I walked out on her mother?'

Swallowing painfully, she looked straight at him. 'Well, did you?'

'As a matter of fact, *she* left *me*.'

Why ever did I say it? 'I wasn't meaning to imply that you had.'

'But you thought it.' As she was about to reply he went on curtly, 'Not that it matters a toss one way or the other. Excuse me, I've got work to do.'

That evening was one of the most miserable she'd spent in months, even though Anoushka condescended to join her for supper and even condescended to talk just a bit.

The thought of tomorrow's trip didn't cheer her at all. With her father there, Anoushka would be sulky and uncommunicative, and after this afternoon Guy would doubtless be tense and impatient, and she would be stuck between the pair of them, trying desperately to dilute the atmosphere.

A barrel of laughs, in other words.

She went to bed very early and very bored, and couldn't sleep.

Why did I ever come? Ryan and his wretched kissograms would almost be better than this. At least I know that particular devil.

And talking of devils, why had Guy's wife left him? Why did wives leave their husbands?

Was he knocking her about?

Highly unlikely.

Playing around?

Possible.

Down the pub with his mates every night?

Not the type.

Maybe he had a horrendously possessive mother who drove her round the bend.

Not the type to stand for it. He hasn't mentioned a mother, anyway. Or a father, come to that.

What, then?

While she was trying to answer this, the phone rang. *Oh, help.* What if it was Guy, saying he was sorry for being ratty and suggesting another walk on the beach?

'Hello?' she said unsteadily.

'Claudia? Did I wake you up?'

'*Kate*! Thank heaven, I've been dying to talk to you! You didn't wake me up at all. I can't sleep.'

'I wouldn't have phoned so late, but . . .'

Just as it dawned on her that Kate was far from her bright and bouncy self, she heard Paul's voice in the background. 'Just tell her, Kate.'

The line went muffled, and she heard Kate's tearful voice saying, 'I can't. You tell her.'

Claudia went cold. 'Parents', 'accident' and 'fatal' were the first words to flash through her head, but before she could get a word out Paul cut in.

'Kate's a bit upset. It's Portly, I'm afraid. He got hit by a car and – '

'Oh, give it to me!' Kate's voice was full of wobbly gulps and sniffs. 'He's not dead, but he's not too good. It was only about an hour ago. He hadn't been in for his dinner and I was getting worried and then somebody rang the bell and said they'd just found him in their front garden. Paul was here and we took him straight to the vet's and they're operating right now but they're not too hopeful.' Her voice cracked badly. 'I'm so sorry, Claudia. I feel so bad.'

'Don't feel bad, Kate.' Claudia's voice was unsteady too. 'It wasn't your fault.'

'I can't help it. Poor Portly.' Her voice was wobbling again. 'Paul said not to worry you until we knew one way or the other, but I thought you'd want to know, so you could send him thought messages or something. About the lovely dinners he'll get if he gets better.'

It was a job to put a smile in her voice. 'You bet. Chopped chicken livers and double cream.'

'I knew you'd want to know.' Her tone altered considerably as she spoke to Paul instead. 'What did I tell you, fart-face? I said she'd want to know!'

'Yes, dear. Of course, dear. Whatever you say, dear.'

In spite of poor Portly, Claudia had to smile. Every time Kate laid into him, the placid Paul reacted with his henpecked-little-man voice.

'I'll ring you tomorrow, as soon as we know how he is,' Kate went on.

Damn – that wretched trip. 'No, I'll ring you. We're supposed to be going out tomorrow, and I don't really think I can wriggle out of it. If they let you see him, give him a big kiss for me.'

She went to sleep still sending messages to Portly. *You can have a cod in butter sauce all to yourself, and I'll forget what the vet said about not giving you milk, but don't you dare die.*

CHAPTER 10

Even before they started, the trip did not augur well. Over breakfast Guy said sardonically, 'I'd expected to have to cart one wet weekend up to Nizwa, but not a brace of them.'

Claudia forbore to say that he had not exactly been a joyous little sunbeam himself for the past twenty minutes. The three of them had been eating more or less in silence: Guy tense, Anoushka predictably sulky, herself miserable from thinking about Portly. She had kept quiet, however. Talking would very likely make her tearful, and for all she knew Guy might be the sort of person who considered tearfulness over a mere cat tiresomely sentimental.

'What do you expect?' Anoushka said, in between noisily sucking cola through a straw. 'I don't suppose she wants to be dragged into some poxy desert any more than I do.'

Guy's tense frown deepened. 'Will you stop *slurping*? And do you have to drink that stuff for breakfast?'

'I don't like tea or coffee.'

'Then have orange juice!'

'I – don't – like – orange juice!'

184

Claudia was not in the mood for atmosphere-diluting. 'Are the pair of you are going keep this up all day? If so, say so now and I'll stay here. I do not want to be piggy-in-the-middle of World War III all day!'

Her abrasive tone seemed to startle them both.

'Sorry,' Guy muttered, with a pointed glance at his daughter.

Anoushka said nothing, but still looked as if the straight talk had come as something of a shock.

Maybe they both need a bit of straight talk, she thought. *Maybe I should bang their wretched heads together.*

A blue Range Rover was waiting outside, and that sparked the next argument. 'You sit in the front,' Claudia said, as both she and Anoushka moved towards the rear passenger door.

'I want to sit in the back.'

Since Guy was already in, he couldn't hear. 'For heaven's sake, go and sit next to your father!' she hissed.

'You sit with him! How can I crash out in the front seat?'

Oh, please yourself.

After they'd been going a few minutes she was increasingly aware of Guy giving her sideways glances. *Wondering why I'm in a foul mood, I suppose. Well, let him. I'm sick of the pair of them.*

Poor Portly. Please don't die.

He might be dead by now, and then they'll chuck him in the the dead-cat bin for the council to dispose of according to hygiene regulations.

'Claudia, you're not sick are you?'

His voice brought her back. 'No.'

He glanced at her again. 'Then what is it?'

'Nothing!' She hadn't meant to sound so irritable. 'I'm fine,' she said, in forced, bright tones. 'It's lovely to get out and see something of the country.'

'Speak for yourself.' From the back came Anoushka's wet-weekend voice. 'It's like the surface of the moon.'

Depends on how you look at it, Claudia thought. If you were the sort of person who only liked soft, pretty landscapes, you might be disappointed.

The capital, with its expensively watered grass and flowers, was many kilometres behind them. The rocky wilderness they were now passing through was dotted with scrubby trees that looked as if they hadn't had a drink in years.

'There's not a blade of grass anywhere,' Anoushka went on.

Well, no. But the scenery possessed a harsh, dramatic beauty. In the distance, mountains of dark, purply-grey rose against a brilliant blue sky.

'It's the most horrible place I've ever seen in my entire life,' Anoushka went on.

'If you keep on moaning at this rate,' Guy said tersely, 'I'll take you straight to Nizwa souk and swop you for half a dozen goats.'

'I wouldn't put it past you.'

An exasperated 'tut' escaped Claudia's lips. 'Will you two please cut it out? I'm trying to enjoy myself!'

'Consider it cut.' Guy removed his sunglasses and handed them to her. 'Give those a clean, would you? I can't see a damn thing.'

She polished them with a tissue. As she handed them back and he tried to take them without taking his eyes off the road, their fingers brushed.

What with Portly, the flutter this produced was practically non-existent.

Maybe it's nothing to do with Portly. Maybe the buzz is simply wearing off and you're going off him.

If only. She knew it was only thoughts of dead-cat bins keeping the buzz at bay. Yesterday she'd have had one eye on the scenery and the other on his hunkily tanned arm, his hand on the gear lever, or his reinforced-concrete thigh under the beige cotton trousers. She'd have wished for nice deep potholes that would lurch her into his lap. But since there weren't any potholes, and she was wearing a seatbelt, she'd have had hard luck.

Today, she was keeping both eyes firmly on the scenery, and for ages nobody spoke. Eventually, as they rounded a bend in the climbing road, he said, 'That's Izki, over there.'

In the distance, a broad green swathe stood out of the arid wilderness like a candle in the dark.

'Heavens, it's an oasis!' she exclaimed. 'I'd always imagined a few palm trees in the sand.'

'There are some pretty big oases here. The water comes from the Hajar Mountains.' He pointed towards the rows of craggy peaks that seemed more forbidding the closer they came. 'Nizwa's not too far now.'

Claudia was perking up considerably. Over her shoulder she said, 'Don't you think it's exciting, Anoushka, to see a real live oasis?'

There was no reply. After a glance behind her she said ruefully, 'She's asleep.'

He shot her an equally rueful glance. 'At least she's not moaning.'

187

Nizwa was a still bigger oasis, looking from a distance like a forest of palm trees set in an arid brown sea. 'This fort's about three hundred years old,' said Guy, as they drove past a massive mud-brick construction with a huge round tower. 'The locals were busy fighting off the Portuguese colonists.'

Anoushka had evidently woken up. 'The Portuguese must have been off their heads. Who on earth'd want this dump?'

'And in another fort not too far from here,' Guy went on, 'there's a cosy little dungeon labelled "Female Reformatory", where they used to sling all the bolshie sixteen-year-olds until they'd sorted out their attitude problems.'

'Very funny.'

'You think I'm kidding?' He gave her an ominous glance in the rear view mirror. 'Maybe I'll call on the local *wali* and ask if I can rent it out for six months.'

'The *wally*?'

'W – A – L – I. The headman. A sort of mayor.'

'Go and see him, then. I'm sure he'll be over the moon. Probably give you a nice cup of rancid goat's milk and a few sheep's-eye biscuits.'

He ignored this and parked in what seemed to be the town square. In the shade of a large tree sat several bearded men, clearly discussing the merits of the various goats that bleated nearby. Traffic consisted of everything from dusty, goat-laden Toyota pick-ups to pristine Mercedes, to a man on a donkey.

After the air-conditioning, the heat hit Claudia like a wave. 'We'll head for the souk,' Guy said, leading them

188

towards a large, mud-brick building with heavy, carved wooden doors. Inside it was cooler, almost dark after the brilliant light outside.

She took her sunglasses off and blinked. They were in a narrow alleyway lined with tiny, open-fronted shops crammed with everything from aluminium cooking pots to brilliant cottons.

'God, it stinks,' Anoushka said, wrinkling her nose.

'It's the spices. I think it's rather nice.' Claudia paused by a tiny shop where an old man with a long grey beard sat behind open sacks. 'Look, these are black peppercorns.'

The old man gave her a gap-toothed grin and said something she did not recognize from her phrase book. 'What was that?' she asked Guy, in an aside.

'How are you doing? more or less. Just say, *Tayyib, shukran.*'

Her efforts were rewarded with a torrent of Arabic, most of which was directed at Guy, however.

Anoushka gave a bored 'tut'. 'I suppose he's asking if we're your second-best wives.'

'Anoushka, that'll do!' After replying to the old man, he scooped a handful of what looked like larger than usual lumps of brown coffee sugar from an open sack and held it to Claudia's nose. 'Can you guess what it is?'

It smelt warm, aromatic. 'Something they put in perfume?'

'Nice try.' He held it to his daughter instead. 'Take a wild guess, Anou.'

With an expression of disgust, she twisted her face away. 'For heaven's sake. It's probably dried camel pee or something.'

Obviously steeling himself, he turned back to Claudia. 'It's frankincense.'

'*Frankincense*? A whole sack of it?'

'They produce it here. It's the resin of a tree that grows in the south.'

'Then I absolutely must have some for Christmas.' She scooped a couple of tablespoons into her palm. 'Can you ask him how much?'

After a short exchange with the vendor Guy said, 'He says it's *baksheesh*. A present. Because you're a guest.'

'But isn't it terribly expensive?'

'Not really. They usually sell it by the kilo.'

'But I must give him something! I'll feel really bad otherwise!'

'You might offend him.'

'Then I'll buy something else. Half a kilo of black peppercorns. Those silly little tubs you get in the supermarket don't last five minutes and I bet these are much fresher.'

They wandered on, pausing to admire everything from camel sticks to battery operated toys to copper pots. The narrow alleys were crowded and bustling, plaintive Arabic song echoing from scores of radios.

More than once, Guy shot an exasperated glance over his shoulder. 'Anoushka, keep up!' Despite his efforts to amuse her, she was dragging behind, refusing to take an interest in anything.

'I do see what you meant,' Claudia said wryly. 'If you want me to grovel, I will.'

His mouth twitched. 'Not here, perhaps, but I appreciate the thought.'

As they turned left in the maze of alleys, he touched her arm. 'Look at these. They dry them by the ton on the beaches.' He was pointing at a sack of tiny dried fish. 'They use them in a dish with onions and limes but I can't say I fancy it.'

As she gazed down at the dead, fishy little eyes, Claudia's eyes misted. They were exactly like the pussy-treats she occasionally bought for Portly. He'd go mad for them, even try to open the kitchen cupboard. With no sunglasses, it wasn't easy to hide the state of her eyes. She turned away, but not quite quickly enough.

'What's the matter?' he frowned.

'Nothing.' With her back to him, she dabbed her eye with a fingertip.

'I see. You've just sprung a spontaneous leak.' He didn't try to turn her round, but he was so close behind her she could feel his breath on her hair. 'Should I call a plumber?'

'I wouldn't bother. I think it's under control.' Turning back to him, she tried to smile. 'I'm sorry. It's my cat. He got run over last night and the prognosis wasn't too good, as they say. The fish reminded me.'

'Why didn't you say?'

With a little sniff, she shrugged. 'I don't know. I suppose I thought you'd think it was daft, getting worked up over a fat cat.'

Very drily, his eyebrows rose and fell. 'Well, thank you. It's nice to know my more human qualities haven't gone unnoticed.'

Now I've upset him. 'It wasn't just that. I didn't want to be a miserable wet blanket.'

191

'We already had one miserable wet blanket, so one more wouldn't have made much difference. Come on.' He gave her waist a little pat. 'Let's go and find something more cheerful than desiccated fish. Like the silver souk.'

Just as well he didn't overdo the sympathy, she thought, as they strolled on. *Then I'd really have sprung a leak. What if he'd been like that ex of Kate's who only lasted three weeks? Whatever was his name? Aidan. Oh, yes.*

Aidan had been to evening classes in 'Getting in Touch with Your Emotions'. He'd liked to look soulfully into your eyes and say things like, 'I want you to know I'm here for you. I share your pain'.

She'd have thrown up if they had been like that. On the other hand, an arm around her waist would have been nice, with a comforting little squeeze or two.

That would only have got your flutters going again. You wanted him to play by the rules.

Yes, but I didn't mean it.

'Where the hell's Anoushka?' he frowned, looking back down the alley.

She followed his gaze. Among the assorted dishdashas there was no sign of a girl in a red T-shirt.

'Typical,' he muttered. 'She made up her mind to be awkward from the word go.'

Claudia felt a pang of dreadful guilt. All that time they were by the sack of fishlets she had not given a thought to Anoushka. And neither had he, she was almost certain. 'Maybe she went back to the car.'

'What for? She can't get in without the keys.'

They retraced their steps, past the copper pots and battery toys, until they were back at the first spice seller.

'She must have got lost,' Claudia said. 'She wouldn't remember which way we'd come, since she wasn't looking at anything.'

'Lost, my backside. This is her "brown Dad off" strategy. We'll have to go back,' he added in a mutter, as they threaded their way back into the bustle.

Now and then he paused to ask. Sometimes there were shaken heads, sometimes an arm pointed further on. They had been searching for some ten minutes when Claudia caught a glimpse of red in the distance. She grabbed Guy's arm. 'Down there!'

They half ran down the alley. 'Anoushka!' he yelled.

When the T-shirt whirled around, Claudia got an odd little jolt. Instead of the bored, 'so what?' expression she'd expected, she saw only the terrified face of a lost child.

'Where have you been?' Anoushka burst out in a trembling rush. 'I've been looking for you everywhere, and . . .'

'It's all right, Anou.' Guy's change of demeanour startled her even more than his daughter's. His voice was mild and soothing as he slid an arm around her shoulders.

As if by magic, the child disappeared. She shook him off with a petulant, 'I could have been dragged off and murdered for all you care! I suppose you were so busy nattering to Mary flaming Poppins that you didn't even notice I wasn't there! And some horrible man just tried to –' Her voice broke off. 'That's him!' She pointed at a thirtyish man in a pristine white dishdasha who was approaching with an apologetic expression.

'My name is Sayeed,' he said, in heavily accented English, offering a hand to Guy. 'I maybe 'fraid your

193

daughter. I see her look lost so I say her maybe wait by my uncle shop with maybe cold drink until you come. I think maybe better than walk and walk and maybe not find.'

'Guy Hamilton.' He returned the man's handshake warmly. 'That was very kind, but we come from London, and I'm afraid we have many bad people in London. She didn't understand.'

'Sorry,' Anoushka mumbled.

The man smiled. 'I am understand. Too much bad peoples everywhere. But not too much in Nizwa, I am think. Sorry for trouble.'

'No, it was very good of you,' Guy said. '*Shukran.*'

'*Afwan.* Please, enjoy visit to Nizwa. *Salaam alaykum.*'

'Well, how was I to know?' Anoushka said defensively, once he was out of earshot.

'You weren't,' Guy said patiently. 'But, for the record, you're probably safer here than in any city in England.'

'If I was in England, I wouldn't give a stuff how lost I was. I wouldn't give a flying f – '

'That's *enough*!'

They made for the silver souk, where the shops were larger and more elaborate; Aladdin's caves of anklets, bracelets and heavy necklaces, curved daggers, silver dhows, perfume bottles and things for which Claudia could not imagine a use.

For the first time, Anoushka showed an interest. While she was looking at belts of twisted silver threads, Claudia fingered a tiny box, cunningly fashioned from Edward the Seventh Indian rupees. Beside her, Guy was examining a curved dagger, the sheath covered with intricate silver threadwork.

194

'Are you going to buy it?' she asked.

'No. You need an export licence for these old *khanjas*.' He put it back, thrust his hands in his pockets and gazed across the shop at his daughter.

'Sometimes I forget she's still just a kid. God knows what she thought that poor guy was up to. I suppose she thought he was going to slip her a spiked lemonade.'

'You can't blame her,' Claudia pointed out. 'I heard about a woman who accepted a cup of coffee in a bazaar while looking at rugs or something. Her boyfriend got fed up and wandered on. When he came back, the shopkeeper said she'd gone and he looked everywhere. Eventually he found her unconscious in the back of the shop.'

'All right, it happens. But I'd be very surprised if it happened here.'

Claudia glanced at Anoushka, who was trying belts around her waist. 'She looked like a little girl I found in Selfridges once. All alone in a heaving sea of strangers. Panic-stricken.'

'But you see what happens if I try to comfort her? I get ice. Or lip. Usually both.'

It was all she could do not to put her arm round his waist, give him a little squeeze and say, Come on, she doesn't really hate you. 'I expect she just felt a bit silly, getting scared for nothing.'

'You reckon?' His eyes searched her own, as if checking that she wasn't fobbing him off with soothing flannel.

From a flutter point of view, it was lethal. A direct attack with twin megawatts of Greek-island blue that made her wilt.

'Dad, can I have this?'

They turned an instant too late. Anoushka's face, momentarily animated, walled up again as she caught the tail-end of their eye-to-eye contact.

Guy strolled over with a cheerful, 'Let's have a look, then.' Claudia stayed put, pretending to examine the little silver box once more.

Why did she have to catch me gazing up at him like an idiot? Now she'll think I'm playing up to him.

So what if she does? She's his daughter, not his wife.

She's jealous. It was written all over her face.

Jealous of what? She apparently rejects every overture he makes. She didn't even want to come.

She glanced across at them. Guy was haggling the price down, as was obviously expected. Anoushka was looking at something else, and she couldn't see her face.

'Thank God we're out of that dump,' Anoushka said as they finally left the souk.

'You'll be pleased to know it probably won't be here much longer,' Guy said, with barely controlled irritation. 'They're going to build a new one. So if you ever come back you'll be able to shop in something more resembling the local High Street. Infinitely more satisfactory when you're far away from home and want to find everything just like it is in London.'

'Sarcasm is generally considered to be the lowest form of wit,' returned his daughter. 'Anyway, the High Street's full of chainstores and I never shop in chainstores! I wouldn't be seen dead in a chainstore! Only people's mothers buy things in boring old high streets!'

Time for a bit of atmosphere-diluting, Claudia thought. Or maybe not. 'Do you know something?' she said brightly.

'Until now, I thought my cousin Ryan was the person I'd most hate being stuck on a desert island with. But now I think I have to hand that coveted award to you two. I'd hang myself from the nearest palm tree.'

'If I was stuck on a desert island I'd hang myself anyway,' said Anoushka. 'I'd have hung myself here if I could have been fagged to find a piece of rope.'

'Just get in the car,' Guy said tersely as they arrived back at the Range Rover. 'And the word is "hanged".'

'I know. I only said it the other way to give you the little pleasure of correcting me.'

I'm going to scream, Claudia thought. The sun was beating down on her head and she was suddenly dying for both a drink and the loo.

While Guy was round the other side, getting in, Anoushka said, 'I think it's my turn to sit in the front this time.'

'Go ahead,' Claudia said shortly.

'But I wouldn't dream of depriving you,' the girl went on, lowering her voice to mock sweetness. 'I could see from that touching little scene in the silver shop that you fancy the pants off him, after all.'

Oh, God. 'I was telling him about my cat, if you really want to know. He got run over last night, but don't let it spoil your day.'

A wash of defensive guilt came over Anoushka's face. 'I'm sorry. I didn't know. Is he OK?'

'Of course he's not OK. He had a major operation last night. I won't know whether he's survived till we get back. Now, will you get in the front with your father?'

Anoushka got in without another word.

At least she has some feelings, Claudia thought, but it was no comfort. How could she have used poor Portly in such a lie? Now he really would die, and serve her right.

Feeling utterly wretched, she gazed out of the window as he started the engine. Her head was beginning to ache and she was dying of thirst, but before she had anything else to drink she needed the little girls' room.

'Where are we going now?' Anoushka demanded. 'Because before we do anything else, I need a large freezing drink and the loo. Not that I suppose there are any proper loos for hundreds of miles.'

'Of course not,' Guy said tersely. 'But don't fret, I shall find you a nice prickly bush, with only half a dozen goatherds for an audience.'

'*What?*'

'Stop fussing. You have to learn to rough it a bit now and then.'

Oh, God, not bushes, Claudia thought. *Why wasn't I born a man?*

Sliding his arm across the front seat, he turned to reverse out of his space. 'Claudia doesn't mind roughing it, do you?'

Her face was a mask of dismay. Until he gave her a tiny, conspiratorial wink.

He drove to the Nizwa Motel, where the cons were as mod as anybody could wish. While Claudia was giving her hair a brushing in the mirror, Anoushka came to wash her hands.

'Dad's such a bastard,' she muttered. 'I really thought he meant it.'

The way you were moaning, I don't blame him. 'It was just a male idea of a joke.'

'Pathetic, in other words.'

Claudia swallowed a remark about pathetic childishness. 'Shall we go? I'm starving.'

In spite of all the morning's aggro, lunch was a little more cheerful than breakfast. Halfway through Guy said, 'You can ring home from here, if you want a progress report on your cat.'

Claudia shook her head. 'If he's shuffled off his little mortal thingy, I'd rather not know till I have to.'

After putting away more chicken curry, Guy said, 'Anoushka had two kittens a year or two back. Kit and Kat.'

'And the poor little things both got run over within six months,' Anoushka said.

Claudia felt a pang of empathy. 'How awful.'

'They had no road sense whatsoever,' said Guy. 'Engaging little beasts, but brainless as they come.'

'Mrs Pierce didn't think they were engaging,' Anoushka said sulkily. 'If you ask me, she got that horrible son of hers to come and run them over on purpose.'

'You know that's ridiculous,' Guy said patiently.

'I don't know any such thing. She's an evil old cow and I hate her. I wouldn't be at all surprised to find she's sleeping in a coffin up in her room. One day I'm going to hold up a crucifix in front of her and see if she screams.'

Across the table, he closed his eyes with a 'Give me strength' look.

Anoushka barely spoke for the rest of the meal, and still less during their hour-long wander through the groves of date palms afterwards. She kept apart, refusing to be 'with' them.

And if his daughter was sulking for England, Guy wasn't much better. He spoke now and then as they wandered the baked-earth paths between the trees, pointing out growing bunches of dates or a green parrot flying overhead, but gently seething tension came off him in waves. Not that she blamed him. That girl was enough to have even Sister Immaculata practising her Anglo-Saxon.

And all the time he stuck rigidly to the rules. Even when the paths narrowed, there was no arm-to-arm brushing, or even a 'you go first' touch on her waist. It was almost as if he'd put a no-go zone between them.

Well, isn't that what you wanted?

Not now. The air was warm and hazy, the buzz of crickets all around them, and after a larger than normal lunch and two glasses of wine, her thoughts were drifting off down Fantasy Lane . . .

A warm, lazy summer's afternoon, a field of warm, daisy-filled grass with no cow-pats, the remains of a picnic and you-know-who. They'd just be starting the second bottle of Moet et Chandon – pink, for preference – and she'd be lying on her back in the grass. He'd be lying beside her, propped on one elbow, tickling her chin with a buttercup and feeding her strawberries. They'd be laughing lazily, and then slowly, in a soft-focus haze, there'd be a bit more than strawberries being eaten in the grass . . .

Getting hot and erogenous just from thinking about it, she gave a delicious little shudder.

'What's the matter?' he frowned.

'Nothing.'

'You just shuddered!'

Strewth, was he watching her behind those dark glasses after all? 'I was just thinking.'

'What about?'

You're obviously not telepathic, or you wouldn't ask. 'Scorpions,' she said, with a flash of inspiration. 'I once found a scorpion sharing my shower in Greece. There aren't any here, are there?'

'Of course there are. Scorpions, snakes, camel spiders . . . Camel spiders are about the size of saucers. They come out at night, crawl over their prey, inject an anaesthetic and chew a lump out of it. But you're not likely to find any of them sharing your shower in a five-star hotel.'

'Thank heaven for that,' she said, with a rather different shudder.

On the other hand, finding some massive wiggly in your shower was the perfect excuse for playing the helpless bimbo. She had resorted to such tactics once; rushing in a barely covering towel to some Category Four two doors away and pretending to be in hysterics. Only he hadn't been there, of course, only his Category Two mate, who'd explained that Chas was getting paralytic in the bar but he'd be only too happy to do the honours.

Story of my life, she thought glumly. *Here I am, with the Category Four to end them all, and he's behaving as if I'm using the wrong deodorant.*

What the hell do you expect? You warned him off!

I was suffering from temporary insanity.

But, since the scorpion remark, he seemed to have reduced the no-go zone. It was now about eighteen inches, close enough for wafts of warm male body and subtle aftershave to have her flutters going wild.

201

It was a terrible temptation to pretend to feel faint or accidentally-on-purpose trip over a stone and force some really delicious body contact.

Don't even think of it. He'd know exactly what you were up to. And so would his daughter. You won't fool her again.

Why should I care what she thinks? She's a pain in the neck, mooching along in a non-stop sulk.

Anoushka was well ahead, and if she was looking at anything it was the ground beneath her feet. Her whole bearing said, 'I'm bored stiff! When can we go?

'I should never have brought her,' Guy muttered, as if reading her thoughts. 'I should have left her to fester at the hotel.'

'You don't mean that.'

'Don't I?'

'I thought the whole point of the exercise was to show her something of the country.'

A piece of grit had lodged itself between her foot and her sandal. She stopped to take it off, standing on one foot to shake it.

And that was when he breached the no-go zone. As she hopped and shook, he put a totally unnecessary steadying hand on her arm. 'Maybe the whole point of the exercise should have been something else altogether.'

There was a rough catch to his voice, and if she hadn't needed steadying before she did now. Like a hot avalanche, it hit her. His simmering tension was not just due to his daughter.

'Would you have come?' he said, very quietly. 'If it had been just you and me?'

My God, did I leave all my brains behind at Heathrow?

202

It was just as if two tightly lidded pans had been simmering for ages and somebody had just lifted the lids. The steam knocked her for six and she wasn't prepared. Not now, and certainly not here, with his daughter liable to turn round at any second. 'Guy, for heaven's sake,' she said unsteadily.

'For heaven's sake what?'

For heaven's sake let me go before I wooze completely. 'For heaven's sake, I can stand on one foot without a support system.'

She shook him off and replaced her sandal with trembling fingers.

Why the hell did you do that? Haven't you been dying for some shiveringly delicious contact this past half-hour?

Yes, but I never thought I'd get it. Not here . . .

She shot a guilty glance at the red T-shirt, twenty yards ahead.

The catch in his voice got rougher. 'Well, would you?'

Oh, strewth. What do I do? Look into his eyes and whisper, Yes, oh yes! like something out of a corny old film?

'I don't think it would have been very nice to leave her all on her own,' she said, in a barely wobbly voice.

'She didn't even want to come.'

That's not the point. The girl might be a pain, but she was a mixed-up, unhappy sort of pain, and leaving her behind would never have been an option. 'She'd have thought we didn't want her.'

The instant it was out, she wished she hadn't said it. She didn't want her illusions shattered with some callous reply like, I couldn't give a toss what she thinks.

So she forestalled him with one of her best daft remarks. 'Fancy a Polo?' she said brightly, delving in her bag. 'I did have some Opal Fruits, but I've eaten them all.'

For a moment it was just like that night on the beach, after she'd made that daft remark about *Jaws*. Waves of *Why are you doing this?* came off him like, well, like steam off a pan.

She peeled back the foil before offering him the packet of mints, but she hadn't peeled it enough, and then there was fumbling and finger-brushing as they tried to do it together. *Heaven help me*, she thought. *It's coming to something when I can't even give him a Polo without fluttering.*

He took it with agonizing slowness, and she thanked God for sunglasses. Curtains for the windows of the soul. For dilated pupils, anyway.

Before he could resume any kind of conversation, she carried on walking, rather faster.

The path veered left beside a mud-brick wall, and as she rounded the bend Claudia got another shock. Anoushka was mooching no longer. For once, she looked like any normal girl, taking pleasure in something simple.

As she stood watching, Guy came up behind her. '*El hamdulillah*,' he murmured drily. 'That's two things she's taken an interest in today. Silver belts and donkeys.' A sleepy old Eeyore was tethered to a tree, and Anoushka was stroking his furry head.

'Maybe she'd have more time for me if I had four legs and a tail,' he went on.

Under his sardonic tone she heard an echo of the stark words he'd used at the pool, and a poignant twist caught

204

her heart. At least, she supposed it was her heart. Whatever it was, it seemed to affect her Lurch organ too. Were the two somehow connected?

'Most girls that age like animals,' she said, trying to sound casually reassuring. 'And, by the same token, most of them treat everyone over twenty-five like an alien species. What a pity she hasn't got a carrot. I wonder if he'd like a Polo?'

She walked on and offered the packet to Anoushka. 'Try him with one of these. I never knew a horse that didn't go mad for Polos, and I don't suppose donkeys are much different.'

The donkey appreciated the Polos immensely. He crunched and slurped and nosed greedily into Anoushka's hand for more. Within a couple of minutes they were all gone.

Quite deliberately, Claudia stayed closer to Anoushka as they strolled on. She even managed the odd scrap of conversation about donkeys, and a sanctuary where she'd paid to adopt one.

Guy was gradually catching them up. 'There's not much more to see here. Shall we head for the fort?'

'I'd love to,' Claudia said, casting a glance at Anoushka. 'How about you?'

Daft question. She gave only a bored 'if I must' shrug.

They walked on, past mud-brick houses where little children grinned and waved. The boys were dressed like their fathers, in mini, dusty dishdashas, the girls like their mothers, in bright-coloured dresses with pantaloons underneath, dark, smudgy kohl round their eyes.

Water ran in narrow stone channels, disappearing underground now and then. In shaded areas, plants sprouted from the stone sides. 'It's maidenhair!' Claudia exclaimed, bending down to take a closer look. 'Whenever I buy a maidenhair, it shrivels up inside a week.'

Seeing something dart in the clear, rushing water, she peered further. 'Look, Anoushka, there are masses of little fish!'

'They're *falaj* fish,' Guy said. 'These waterways are called *falajes*. They were first built by Persians, about a thousand years ago.'

Even before he'd said it, Anoushka had wandered off. 'See that?' he said sardonically, watching her go. 'Mention the dreaded H word and she disappears. History,' he added, seeing Claudia frown.

He put his hands to his mouth and yelled, 'Anoushka! This way! We're going to the fort.'

She wandered back up with a long-suffering expression. 'I hope we're not going to be *hours* and *hours*, because I'm really – '

'OK, fine.' Something inside him suddenly seemed to snap. 'We'll forget it.'

She put on an injured expression. 'There's no need to get ratty! I didn't say – '

'I said, we'll forget it. I don't want you traipsing along like a martyr, moaning that it's boring and a dump, as you undoubtedly will.'

Anoushka's face walled up as if a mask had come over it. Without a word, she turned and walked off.

Claudia looked despairingly from one to the other. 'Guy, did you have to say that?'

'Why not?' he said tersely. 'It is true. She's wrecked the day.'

'She hasn't wrecked it for me.'

'Please don't be polite about it.'

They walked back to the car in silence.

Anoushka was already waiting by the rear passenger door, but she said not a word.

In the circumstances, Claudia was not going to encourage her into the front seat.

Once they were in, Guy turned to his daughter. 'Put your seatbelt on.'

'I can't lie down with my seatbelt on.'

'Then – sit – up!'

'All right, keep your wig on. Stress is very bad for middle-aged men, you know.'

He said nothing, but he didn't have to. He didn't quite slam his door, but he shut it with rather more force than necessary. He didn't quite reverse out of his space like a road-rage maniac, but he did it aggressively enough to leave Claudia in no doubt as to his state of mind.

Simmering pans weren't in it. He was more like a volcano about to blow.

CHAPTER 11

And, in the circumstances, she wasn't altogether surprised.

There are two sources of tension cooped up in this car with him, she thought. *One's right behind him, and he'd like to strangle her. As for the other . . .*

'What's your cat called?'

The shock of a normal question from Anoushka gave her a jolt. 'He started off as Little Puss and when he got bigger it was just Puss. Then he had the operation and started getting fat, so it was Portly Puss. And now he's just Portly.'

'I hope he's OK,' said Anoushka.

'Thanks.' She glanced over her shoulder and smiled. 'So do I.' Suddenly she couldn't wait for the dusty miles to pass so she could ring Kate.

Before long another glance over her shoulder told her that Anoushka was asleep, and for ages neither she nor Guy spoke.

Gradually, the silence became as pregnant as an overdue mother of twins. And, equally gradually, she began to wonder whether he was just miffed, because she hadn't woozed all over him the minute he turned on his flutter techniques.

Eventually he shot her a sideways glance. 'Your hair hasn't flopped once today. What have you done? Superglued it?'

His short tone provoked an equally short reply. 'More or less. Half a can of hairspray.'

'I think I prefer the flop.'

Such typical male perversity got all her latent prickles going. 'I didn't do it for you. I did it to stop it driving me mad. Anyway, I thought it was driving you insane.'

'It was. You kept flicking at it like one of those idiot women in a shampoo commercial.'

Dear me, the gloves are really coming off now. 'Then you should be pleased it's superglued,' she said tartly. 'To stop you going any more insane than you already are. The way you were driving back there I wondered whether we were going to arrive in body bags.'

'There was nothing remotely dangerous about my driving, and if I was driven temporarily insane today, you know perfectly well why.'

'Of course I do, and she's asleep. And can you turn the air-conditioning down a bit? I'm getting cold.'

He touched a switch and the blast lessened considerably. 'I didn't just mean her. And if you start shoving Polos at me again,' he added, as she looked deliberately out of the side window, 'I won't be responsible for my actions.'

'I haven't got any more Polos. The donkey ate them all.'

She could almost hear the rumble of impending eruptions. 'Are you actually *trying* to wind me up?'

She knew it was a dangerous game, this verbal cut-and-thrust. If they hadn't been in the car, he'd have called her bluff. He'd have shown her very firmly that there were better things for her mouth to do than make smart remarks. The fact that he couldn't only added an edge to it. And at least it took her mind off poor Portly. 'If I were really trying to wind you up, you'd know all about it.'

'I wouldn't try, if I were you. You might get more than you bargained for.'

'Is that a threat or a promise?'

Watch it, Claudia. Don't get too carried away.

He gave her a sideways glance. 'Maybe I should have left you to the tender mercies of your cousin and the kissograms.'

'I'm beginning to wish you had. It would have been a doddle, compared to this. And keep your eyes on the road, please.'

He gave a sardonic snort. 'You'd never have lasted the distance.'

'That's what you think.'

'You didn't look remotely like a kissogram girl. You looked like an ex-convent girl dressed up in a silk whatsit and suspenders, pretending to be wicked.'

If he was trying to wind *her* up, it'd be a shame to disappoint him. 'Excuse *me*,' she said, affecting her best, highly miffed voice. 'I got that outfit checked out by Kate's boyfriend before I went out. *And* his friend. They both said I looked quite wicked enough for a classy French joint like that. Any wickeder and I'd probably have got myself arrested.'

'Who else did you display yourself to?' he asked sardonically. 'That scrounging idiot who lives upstairs?'

'Not on that particular occasion. I did for the one before. He'd just popped in to borrow some washing powder so I asked him what he thought of my Wild Jungle Jane.'

She knew he didn't believe a word, but she couldn't resist it. 'And for your information that silk teddy and suspenders I wore for your little birthday treat cost a bomb.'

'Then you wasted your money. I'd have preferred black.'

'I didn't waste my money. They were Kate's. And you'd have preferred me not to do it at all. You were embarrassed.'

'I – was – not – embarrassed!'

As he changed down hard, to overtake a goat-laden pick-up, she thought maybe she'd wound him up quite enough for now.

She gazed out of the window instead. The late afternoon sun was casting purply shadows over brown rocks; it looked quite different from the morning. Here and there goats wandered, standing on their hind legs to reach the leaves of the few, bare-looking trees.

'What on earth do they find to eat?' she wondered.

'They eat anything. Cement bags. Discarded tea bags. Fag packets. Anything.'

Anoushka stirred and yawned loudly. 'How much further? I'm starving.'

'Twenty minutes,' he said.

It passed more or less in silence. While they were picking up their keys from reception he said shortly, 'Is anybody going to eat with me tonight?'

211

'I'm having room service,' Anoushka said.

'Well, what a surprise. I don't know what they'll do with themselves when you go home.' To Claudia, he raised a sardonic eyebrow. 'Don't tell me. You're going to keep room service busy too.' *And chicken out*, his eyes said. *You're all very smart and sassy when my hands are safely occupied, but once it's down to you, me and a dinner for two . . .*

Since she'd been more or less expecting it, she was prepared. 'I don't much like eating in hotel rooms. I'll join you, if you like.'

The barest flicker crossed his face. 'I'll give you a ring in an hour or so.'

'Fine.'

He paused 'I hope it's good news. About your cat.'

It was no time for tart rejoinders. 'Thank you.'

As he strode purposefully towards the lift she followed more slowly, with his daughter.

'As if I'd want to eat with him,' Anoushka grumbled as they waited for the lift. 'He's in a foul mood.'

'You've hardly eaten with him since we've been here. And if he's in a foul mood it's not surprising, the way you were behaving all day.'

'You can't blame me! I didn't even want to go! I *told* him I didn't want to go!'

Save your breath, Claudia. 'Well, we're back now, so you can slob all you like.'

They got in the lift and she pushed the button viciously. Heaven help her, Guy was right. He should have left her to fester. Her sulks and miseries had cast a blight over everything. Without her they'd have enjoyed the day so much more. Without her they'd have –.

212

'It must be you, making him in a foul mood,' Anoushka went on. 'He's not usually as bad as this. Were you having a go at him?'

'What would I be having a go at him about?'

She shrugged defensively. 'About me. The only time he gets in a really foul mood is when Mrs Pierce has a go at him about me.'

'I suppose you brown Mrs Pierce off on purpose?'

'Of course I do. She hates me. She thinks I'm a spoilt brat.'

Heaven save us. Don't say anything. It'll come out like broken icicles and she'll have it in for you for the duration.

The doors opened and they walked down the corridor. 'See you tomorrow,' she said, as they reached Anoushka's room.

'Bye.'

My God, what a day. And now I've got to ring home about Portly. After delaying the dreaded moment with a much-needed shower and a cup of tea from room service, she steeled herself. 'Kate, it's me.'

'Oh, thank heaven. He's OK, Well, not exactly OK, but still with us. The nurse did tell me all the gruesome details, but I rather switched off. He's going to have to stay quite a few more days so you're going to get a whacking great bill, I'm afraid. The vet was asking if you've got insurance.'

Her relief was such that whacking great bills mattered not a toss. 'No, but never mind. Kate, thanks a million for looking after him. It must have been awful.'

'He wasn't a pretty sight, I must confess. We wrapped him in Paul's jumper. It's a bit of a write-off now. How's it going?'

Since Kate was still at work, it was no time for telling all. 'Fine,' Claudia lied. 'And much better now I know. Tell Paul I'll buy him a new jumper.'

'I wouldn't bother. It was manky anyway.'

After hanging up she lay on the bed, quite woozy with relief. Until the next item on the agenda hit her. Some time during the next hour Guy was going to phone about dinner.

How are you going to play it? And how are you going to dress? In that wicked little black silk camisole that shows a tantalizing hint of cleavage? Or sweetly milkmaidy in that flowery dress that's about as sexy as Enid Blyton?

In the event, it was all for naught.

She found herself gazing through sleep-fuddled eyes at the bedside clock that said 21:23.

My God, I fell asleep!. It's twenty past nine!

He hadn't phoned. She'd have woken up if he had.

What's he playing at?'

Don't ask me. Give him a ring.

No way.

Perversely feeling just as wretched as if she'd been stood up, she ordered sandwiches and coffee from room service. And after eating there was no way she could sleep. She had finished both bonkbuster and whodunnit and felt unbearably bored and restless. Opening the curtains, she gazed out at the quicksilvered sea.

Ten minutes later she was on the beach. Not a soul was there. It was warm and hushed and beautiful, with only the lap of tiny waves to keep her company. After walking for a while, she sat in the soft sand, gazing out at the sea.

Dare I go in?

Not starkers. What if somebody came?

In my bra and pants, then.

You haven't even got a towel.

Who cares?

Within seconds she had stripped off and run in. She swam about ten yards out into the warm, silky water and lay floating on her back. A little swell rocked her in a liquid cradle as she gazed at stars like diamonds on black velvet.

All her tension floated away. She swam a little further, parallel to the beach, until a sudden, colder current swirled around her legs, making her shiver. A lazy breast-stroke brought her back towards the spot in the sand where she'd left her clothes.

Only they were not alone.

Oh, Lord. What the hell is he doing here?

Looking for you, obviously. Good job you didn't go in starkers.

'Claudia!' he called.

Oh, Lord. He's going to throw a wobbly. Swimming alone at night is not the most sensible thing in the world.

That's precisely why I did it. For the illicit, naughty little thrill.

For a moment she wondered whether to play the complete bimbo – wave and giggle, 'Hi, Guysie-poos! Coming in? But she decided that might be pushing it.

Fun, though.

Never mind fun. Now you've got to get out in your bra and pants.

So what? It's no different from a bikini.

But it was different, however hard she tried to pretend it wasn't. As she waded out, squeezing the water from her hair, she thanked heaven the garments in question were not filmy white, and therefore transparent when wet, but black, and therefore not.

He was standing by her clothes, arms folded. 'Did you really think that was a good idea?'

His relatively mild tone was almost a disappointment. Having expected a grade A wobbly, she'd have liked to throw one in return. He had more or less stood her up, after all.

'This is a fine time to show up,' she said huffily, stalking up the sand.

'I'd have thought you'd have more sense,' he said as she came up. 'What if you'd got cramp?'

'For heaven's sake, you sound like my father.' Picking up her T-shirt from the sand, she used it as a towel and temporary cover, holding it to her front like blotting paper. 'I was only in for five minutes and I've never had cramp in my life. And you generally get it in cold water, after a large meal, according to tradition. Which I did not get, funnily enough, because the person I was supposed to be having dinner with didn't ring.'

'You could have rung me.'

She started pulling her T-shirt on. 'No, I couldn't, smart-ass. I was asleep.'

'So was I.'

'*What?*' The T-shirt didn't even make it over her head. It froze halfway and resumed temporary thigh-to-cleavage cover.

'I fell asleep. Crashed. Out for the count.'

Why on earth didn't I guess? I was shattered enough to crash out, and I wasn't even driving.

'Then I'm glad I didn't ring and wake you. You obviously needed it.'

'I should have set the alarm.' His voice was no longer exasperated. Its edges had softened, like bitter chocolate in the sun. 'Do you want a written apology, or shall I just grovel?'

He added that little half-smile that would have melted anybody, and she was duly melted. Or perhaps woozed would have been more accurate. 'No grovelling will be necessary,' she said lightly. 'It was a tiring day.'

'In more ways than one.'

'Hard on the feet.'

'And the patience.'

'Especially the patience.'

For several long seconds, this verbal ping-pong ceased. Only their eyes spoke in the dark.

'How's your cat?'

'Still with us. Just about.'

'I'm glad.' His voice was like that old Shetland sweater again, only someone had washed it in fabric softener.

Hers was just about steady. 'So am I.'

'I'd never have thought you'd go in. Not after all that shark talk. I'd have thought you'd run a mile.'

'You have to live dangerously now and then,' she said lightly. 'Get the adrenalin going.'

The breeze whispered over her wet skin, shivering over it, but what with her woozy central heating suddenly going full-blast, she didn't notice. It was as if the past few days had never been. They were back on the beach, in those quivering, expectant moments just before –

'I don't know about adrenalin, but it's got your goose pimples going,' he said, casting an eye over what he could see. 'Aren't you going to put your clothes on?'

'Well, of course I am. You didn't think I was going to walk back into the hotel like this?'

Well done, Claudia. Said with such brilliant nonchalance, he'll never guess how cheated you feel.

'You still shouldn't have done it,' he said, as she pulled her damp T-shirt back on. 'You should never swim on your own. Especially at night.'

He was so close, it was like torture. Whatever that wretched aftershave was that he used, it had some magic woman-woozing ingredient and ought to be banned.

'I was bored,' she said, covering her unsteadiness with irritability. 'Bored out of my mind, if you want to know. I'd slept for hours and I had nothing to read. What was I supposed to do?' She pulled on her leggings. 'How did you know I was here, anyway?'

'It was an educated guess, after you didn't answer the phone and you weren't in the coffee-shop. Since I'd more or less told you not to wander the beach at night, it followed that the beach was precisely where you'd be.' He paused. 'Have you eaten?'

'Of course I've eaten! I had a sandwich in my – Oh, my God!'

'What?'

'My room key!' She gaped down at the soft sand at her feet. 'It was on top of my clothes!'

She began a frantic visual search of the sand, but it was dark and difficult to see. Dropping to her knees, she took a closer look. 'It must be here!' But now her clothes were on, it was difficult to remember exactly where they'd been lying. What if she'd trodden it into the sand? What if *he* had, in those clomping great desert boots?

'Don't help, will you?' she said crossly. 'And can you please move your massive feet out of the way? You've probably clodhoppered it into the sand already!'

'I haven't clodhoppered it anywhere. Look.' As he bent to scoop it from the sand she saw it too, made a grab, and their hands collided.

He withdrew. As her fingers closed over the key he put a hand on her arm and yanked her to her feet.

'I'm beginning to wonder about you. Solo swims and losing keys . . .' His hand was still on her arm, but his grip had relaxed to a token. 'Maybe I should fly Mrs Pierce out to babysit the pair of you.'

Under his sardonic tone she caught an echo of something else entirely, and her Lurch organ gave a violent, painful throb. 'I should have thought you'd got quite enough stress without her too.'

'You can say that again.' His eyes were dark and shadowed, the space between them thick with tension, like the air before a thunderstorm.

If he doesn't do it now, I'll die. Oh, please, oh please, oh, please . . .

You do it. Take the initiative. It turns them on like mad when a woman makes the first move. Just reach up, touch his cheek, slide your hand to the back of his neck and . . .

'I don't know what we're hanging about here for.' He let go her arm, and dropped a not-so-light pat on her bottom. 'You might have eaten, but I haven't.'

Bastard! 'Don't – do – that!' She was so trembly with disappointment, she gave him one back in the same place, but harder. 'How do you like it?'

He paused, appearing to consider. 'I have no major objection on the grounds of its constituting offensive or politically incorrect behaviour, if that's what you're ask-ing.'

To cap it all, he was laughing at her. In that infuriating Hamilton way, of course.

He's giving you a taste of your own Thrill-Kill spray. He's showing you just how it feels.

Double bastard.

It's your own fault. You should have taken the initiative, but you dithered. She who dithers like a female wally doesn't deserve thrills.

Not a word was said until they were in the lift and he had pressed '3'.

She stared at him. 'I thought you said you hadn't eaten!'

'I haven't.'

'Then why don't you go straight to the coffee-shop?'

'I don't have time. I was sleeping for nearly three hours when I should have been working. I'll get something from room service. I'll be up till the small hours as it is. I've got an early flight to Abu Dhabi in the morning.'

'To Abu Dhabi?'

He nodded. 'It's only a quick hop.'

Idiot! How could you have thought he was thrill-killing just to pay you back? He's got more important things to do. He's not going to start anything that's going to interfere with his concentration. Particularly when he thinks you're going to make some daft remark and wriggle away after two minutes.

220

If you ask me, he's made his mind up about you. He's made up his mind that you're a silly little tease.

God, how awful.

She turned away and made a covering-up face in the mirror. 'What a sight,' she said unsteadily. Her hair was wet and bedraggled round her face. 'I look like something Portly dragged in.'

'I wouldn't go quite that far. You came out of that water like some mythical sea-nymph.'

What? Is he taking the mickey? Her eyes darted to his own, reflected in the mirror.

He was watching her watching him, a lazy, sardonic glint in his eyes. 'The kind who lures hapless men to their doom,' he added, in a mock doom-laden voice.

What did I tell you? If that's not a polite way of saying 'tease' I don't know what is.

'Well, thank you very much,' she said unsteadily, as the doors opened and they stepped out. 'But I hadn't quite realised mythical sea-nymphs do their luring in chain store undies.

Although she wasn't looking, she felt his slow, lazy glance. 'Maybe not,' he mused. 'A couple of wisps of strategically place seaweed might be more appropriate.'

In the circumstances, this conversation had gone quite far enough. 'Goodnight,' she said, as they reached his room. 'Have a good trip tomorrow. When will you be back?'

'Probably late afternoon.' His eyes flickered over her face. 'I've got some books, if you're really desperate for reading material. I usually bring a couple, but I rarely get round to reading them. I'm not sure they're quite your taste, though.'

Oh, my God, the bonkbuster. 'I read anything. Almost anything.'

'Come and take a look, then.'

She followed him in, and thought that even if she were blind she'd know instantly that this was a man's room. Like him, it smelt of clean shirts and shaving things. A towel lay on one of the beds and the cover was rumpled. She knew exactly what had happened. Just like her, he'd got back to his room tense and exhausted.

He'd had a shower and crashed out.

'Here,' he said, taking a couple of paperbacks from the bedside table. One was a Graham Greene, the other a Wilbur Smith African adventure.

'I've read this before,' she said, indicating the Graham Greene. 'But it was ages ago, and I wouldn't mind reading it again. I've never read any Wilbur Smith.'

'Take them both,' he said.

'Thanks. That's brilliant. Don't work too hard, will you?' And, before any more inane remarks escaped her lips, she turned for the still-open door.

'I'll see you tomorrow,' he said. 'Be good.'

The irony was so faint, she wasn't even sure it was there. 'You too', she said, with idiotic brightness. 'Nighty-night.'

'Goodnight.' And he shut the door behind her.

The following evening, she rang Kate again.

'Ring me back,' she said, the minute she answered. 'It costs a bomb from here, and if I don't talk to someone soon I'm going to go mad.'

It was probably going to make a heart-failure inducing entry on their itemized phone bill, but she didn't care.

'Whatever's the matter?' Kate said, two minutes later.

'Tell me how Portly is, first.'

'Doing as well as can be expected, as they say. They're "cautiously optimistic".'

'Thank the Lord for that.' She took a deep breath. 'Have you got fifteen minutes?'

It didn't take long to explain the basics, with Kate putting in the odd, 'Crumbs!' or 'You sneaky cow, why didn't you tell me?'

'I hardly slept a wink last night,' Claudia went on miserably. 'And all day I was just thinking about seeing him again and then I got back from the beach this afternoon and there was a message to say he was staying overnight in Abu Dhabi and wouldn't be back till tomorrow, and I felt like I did when I was six and my birthday party had to be cancelled because I got chicken pox. I haven't been like this since I was fifteen and had a thing about a boy down the road.'

'Hang on a minute. Paul's making tortured faces at me.' Away from the receiver she said, 'Mind your own business! Go and make a cup of coffee or something!'

'It's no use,' she said to Claudia. 'He's dying of suspenders. Can I tell him?'

'If you like.' She knew Kate would tell him anyway, the minute she'd hung up, but she didn't really mind. She liked Paul a lot. Under his jokily laid-back exterior there lurked a much shrewder brain than any casual observer would suspect. He held down the kind of City job that frequently produced ulcers along with substantial payslips, and coped with the stress by simply switching off the minute he left the office.

223

But she winced as Kate summed it up to him in her own spade-calling way. 'She's got the rampant hots for this Guy chap. He's tried it on a couple of times, but she sort of slammed the brakes on because she didn't think it'd be quite the thing since she's supposed to be looking after his horrendous superbrat of a daughter and not having the hots for her old man. And now she wishes she hadn't. Slammed the brakes on, I mean. Now she thinks *he* thinks she's a tease.'

'Christ,' said Paul. 'Sounds as if she's got herself in a right old two-and-eight.'

'He says you've got yourself in a right old state,' Kate said, into the receiver.

'Yes, I heard.' Paul was so audible, he had to be sitting right next to Kate on the sofa. 'Talk about stating the obvious.'

'She says, "talk about stating the obvious",' Kate said. 'Fat lot of use you are.'

'What am I supposed to say?' Paul sounded distinctly injured. 'Why doesn't she just tell him *why* she slammed the brakes on?'

'Because it should be obvious,' Claudia said.

After Kate had relayed this, Paul said, 'Well, maybe it isn't. If he's got the hots for her too, maybe he can't see straight. It gets us blokes like that sometimes.'

'Don't tell me about not seeing straight,' Kate said scathingly. 'Didn't you write a car off once because you were gawping at some girl in a micro skirt that showed her knickers?'

'She wasn't wearing any knickers. At least, it didn't look like it. Could have been a thong, I suppose. That's what I was trying to work out when I hit the wall.'

'Did you hear that?' Kate said into the receiver. 'Aren't they just disgusting sometimes?'

'I heard.' Claudia was beginning to wonder why on earth she'd started this conversation. It was getting her precisely nowhere.

'Did you know he had the hots for you before you went?' Kate asked.

'Kate, I hate that word! It sounds so basic!'

'Warms, then.'

Much better. Though why 'warms' should be OK and 'hots' not, she couldn't begin to fathom. 'I don't think he'd have kicked me out of bed, exactly, but I didn't think it was anything more than that.'

'And then it started warming up.'

'Yes.' She paused. 'I've got a feeling it was me doing the warming. He's one of those men who can tell a mile off when somebody fancies them, and I can't help thinking he just thought he might be in with a chance and there was no harm trying.'

'And now he thinks he's not in with a chance, so there's no point trying any more,' Kate said.

'Sort of. I'm not sure.'

'What's she saying?' Paul said. 'Tell Uncle Paul all about it, Claudia. Is he a cad and a dashed bounder who's only after one thing, as your old Granny used to say?' He launched into his Moany Old Bag voice that never failed to have them in fits. 'That's all they ever think about these days. I blame the television.'

'Will you *stop* it?' Kate giggled. 'This is *serious*!'

'Yes, dear. Sorry, dear. Tell me all about it.'

'She thinks maybe he didn't really fancy her before,' Kate explained, 'but once he realized she fancied him like mad, it sort of got him going.'

'Well, it would,' Paul said.

'And she thinks maybe he thought he was in with a chance, and that's why he tried it on.'

'He'd hardly try it on if he thought he wasn't in with a chance.'

'Paul, you're not helping!'

'OK. Let me speak to her.'

There was a scuffle as the phone changed hands. 'Sounds as if you've got yourself in a bit of a tizwoz, me dear,' he said. 'Want some advice from the enemy camp?'

'Yes, please.'

'Then play it very cool. Do your ice-maiden bit. You can do a good ice-maiden when you put your mind to it. You did a bloody good ice-maiden with that mate of mine who tried to chat you up when we went for a curry at the New Bombay.'

'That was because he'd had about ten pints of beer and kept rubbing his leg against me under the table.'

'Randy little sod! You never said!'

'He was a friend of yours. I didn't want to make a thing of it.'

'Never mind him, anyway. To be honest, I can't really tell you how to handle this bloke. I don't know him. But if you want one stark fact of life from the enemy camp . . .'

'Yes?'

'I don't want to swell your little copper head, but if pushed I'd have to say you're most blokes' idea of a cracker. And if blokes think they can pull a cracker, most of them will.'

'Bloody cheek!' With mock-injured tones, Kate grabbed the phone. 'He never tells me I'm a cracker!'

'Of course you're a cracker. Why d'you think I pulled you in the first place?'

Again, Claudia was wondering why on earth she'd started this conversation. What she'd wanted, of course, was for Kate to say, Go for it! I'm sure he's wildly in love with you already, and for Paul to say exactly the same. But how could they, when they'd never even met him?

She didn't even know how she felt herself. Was it just a case of wild chemistry? Two harmless substances that fizzed up like mad when you put them together in a test tube? If so, what would be left after the fizzing? A dirty grey mess that you'd pour down the sink?

'Sorry, hon, but I've got to go,' Kate said. 'I've got spare ribs in the oven and it smells as if they're turning into burnt offerings. Don't worry about it. If it feels right, do it. If it doesn't, go to bed early with a good book.'

As she hung up, Claudia suddenly felt so lonely she could cry. She couldn't help thinking of Kate and Paul enjoying their spare ribs with a bottle of wine, talking and laughing non-stop, as they always did. Paul was practically living there lately, and there was always muffled laughter coming from Kate's bedroom, along with other noises that she tried not to hear as she curled up alone under the duvet.

Well, not quite alone. Portly was usually curled up with her – under the duvet sometimes, if it was a specially cold night.

Being miserable in a hotel room is double miserable, she thought. *You can't even raid the fridge for comfort food.*

Since Anoushka condescended to have a drink with her later, the rest of the evening was not quite as miserable as it might have been, although conversation never rose about the superficial.

Still, she was almost pleasant. Almost like a normal human being. *And you know why that is*, Claudia thought. *Because she thinks you're not hitting it off with her father. That makes you acceptable. What if you got something going with him, and tried to carry it on after you got home?*

She went to bed with one of Guy's books and put the whole Guy question on the back burner. And there it simmered gently all night, so that by the morning it was perfectly cooked.

It was amazing how good you felt once you'd made a horrendously difficult decision. As she wandered the gift shop in the foyer, Claudia felt amazingly good about herself. She bought a local silver trinket for Kate – on Portly's behalf – and an expensively airmailed newspaper, and thought she'd read it over afternoon tea.

Leaving the shop, she walked towards the area where they served such things. And when she was halfway there she stopped. Coming from the main entrance, heading for Reception, was Guy.

Time for control-testing.

'Any messages?' he asked, pocketing his key.

'Yes, sir. One moment.'

'Hello, Guy,' she said, behind his shoulder. 'Had a good trip?'

He turned around.

It was gratifying to see just how dumbfounded he was. 'My God,' he said. 'What have you done?'

'Cut it all off.'

228

Rather dazedly he put a couple of faxes in his briefcase. 'I could do with a drink. Like to join me in the bar?'

Remember you're in control now. 'No, thanks. I was just going to have some tea.'

'OK, so we'll have tea.'

'I never thought you'd do it,' he said, as they sat down.

She shrugged. 'I just felt like a change.'

It had been the plunge of her life, taking her mind off everything else wonderfully. Having had long hair since the age of seven or eight, she had almost cried when the first copper clumps had hit the floor.

But afterwards she had felt reborn. The short, elegant cut reflected in the mirror had seemed to frame someone else's face. Someone utterly composed, utterly grown-up, and utterly in control. It was a bit late in the day at twenty-nine to start feeling properly grown up, but she did.

His eyes had never left her face. 'It suits you.'

'Thank you. May we have two teas, please?' she added to the approaching waiter.'

'Certainly, madam.'

It was amazing how cool and controlled you felt with short hair, even with a Category Four sitting only three feet away. You could sit very composedly, never having to fidget or flick your fringe back. 'How was your trip?'

'Fine. How's Anoushka been?'

'Very good. Working quite hard, but she came to the pool for a couple of hours this afternoon.' She did not add that Anoushka had given her a moment's heart failure at around two-thirty. There was no need for him to know.

When the tea arrived, she poured it very composedly. During the second cup he glanced at his watch. 'I was thinking of getting a ski in before it gets too dark. I don't suppose you'd like to join me. You'd mess your hair up.'

'That's precisely why I had it cut. So it'll be easier to manage. I'll join you, if you like.'

She was still perfectly composed when they got in the lift, even when his eyes never left her till they got out again. She was still perfectly composed as they walked along the corridor.

Outside Anoushka's room they paused. 'She said she was going to have a sleep,' she said, seeing the 'DO NOT DISTURB' sign on the door. 'She was up late last night, finishing her maths.'

'Then I'll see her later. I'll have a quick shower and knock on your door in ten minutes.'

'Fine,' she said coolly.

She changed into the jade bikini she hadn't worn yet, because it needed a tan. She had one now; it was just a dusting of gold, but it was enough. Over it she tied a matching pareo, fastening it under her arms.

It was about fifteen minutes before he knocked. He wore navy shorts and a white polo shirt, his hair still wet from the shower. 'We'll have to give ski-ing a miss.' Through the open door he nodded towards the window. 'Take a look at the sea.'

She walked to the window and looked out.

'The wind's blown up,' he said, thrusting his hands in his pockets as he came to stand beside her. 'It's getting choppy.'

He was right. Palm fronds danced in the wind, people were scuttling from the pool, and angry little white tops iced the waves.

'That's a shame,' she said.

'It happens sometimes. It can be like glass and then a hot wind comes from nowhere and whips the sea up.'

'Just like that?'

'Just like that.'

And, just like that, a hot wind from nowhere was melting her cool. A warm, wild rush of clean shirt and freshly showered Category Four was melting it like a lolly in the sun. And when he gazed down at her with all those megawatts of Greek island blue . . .

'But we could do something else.'

'Like what?' she said unsteadily.

'A windy walk on the beach? A game of cards?'

'I've got a Travel Scrabble,' she said, praying her voice wasn't wobbling right overboard. 'I'm a demon at Scrabble. I get all the triple word scores.'

A lethal little half-smile quivered his lips. 'I bet you cheat like mad.'

'I don't! Not unless my opponent cheats first. I stick by the rules.'

'The rule book rules? Or your own?'

'The rule book rules. I don't make my own.'

'Not for Scrabble, maybe.' The smile was suddenly gone, and something else had taken its place. Something far more lethal than smiles. 'I'm not so sure about other little games.'

Her heart and stomach lurched together like two drunks. 'We do make our own rules for Scrabble sometimes,' she said unsteadily. 'For the rude words version. You can use foreign swear words but only if they're really unprintable, so things like *merde* don't count, and you

231

have to prove their existence in the dictionary, but that can be awkward if it's a really juicy Greek obscenity, so we usually – '

'Claudia . . .'

The rough catch in his voice woozed her legs to jelly. 'Yes?'

'You talk too much.'

And as he put his hands on her warm, bare shoulders and drew her close, and as his mouth knocked her for six, there was only one rule that really mattered.

Before you start playing, lock the door.

CHAPTER 12

It wasn't like before. There were no tantalizing brushings, just a fierce tenderness, as if the waiting had spiced his hunger.

And not just his. After thinking and dreaming so long, *she* wasn't wasting the reality.

When they finally came up for air his voice was so rough and warm and husky that it played havoc with her heart, as well as her Lurch organ. 'Have you any idea what you've been doing to me?'

She could barely find a voice at all. 'It's nothing to what you've been doing to me.'

'It wasn't me slamming the red light on.' He drew back a fraction, brushed her cheek with his fingertips. 'Sharks and Polos and bloody Scrabble . . .'

'It's not my fault.' Her voice was wobbling right out of control. 'It's your rotten aftershave. It makes me wooze and dither till I can't think straight.'

'Then I'll sling it.'

The Greek island blue megawatts seemed to seep right into her, shivering over every nerve-ending she possessed. 'You have the most extraordinarily beautiful eyes.'

Oh, God, I'm going to dissolve. 'I bet you say that to all the girls,' she said unsteadily. 'Sister Immaculata told us all about men like – '

He silenced her with devastating effectiveness. And when they paused for breath again it wasn't her eyes he was looking at. Riffling his fingers through her cropped hair, he said, 'Why did you do it?'

Startled, she drew back a fraction. 'But I thought you said you – '

'I lied.'

As their mouths locked again, she could feel the rising tide in him. Not just in the pent-up hunger of his kiss, but in the tension of his body, in the coiled-spring shoulder muscles under her fingers.

Just like before, his hands rose slowly from her waist and came to rest within a heartbeat of her breasts. And, just like before, she wanted to scream, *Go on*! Instead she raised her arms around his neck in a silent green light.

His first touch sent an involuntary shiver through her body. With controlled, agonizing slowness he traced the lower curves, first with his thumbs, then with his fingertips.

Go on! In a silent, urgent plea, she kissed him harder, and he responded. Simultaneously his fingers moved upwards, over the thin cotton pareo and tight jade Lycra, till they found her nipples. With little circular movements he teased them with his thumbs.

Never, in all her experience of woozing, had she woozed quite like this. She felt like one of those women in the old silent films who went to pieces the minute the dashing sheikh clapped his flashing eyes on her.

I am yours, O Great One. Carry me off to your tent, tear my clothes off and ravish me.

His hand moved to the knot of the pareo between her breasts and slipped it undone. And as it fell to the floor his hands moved behind her back, to the fastening of her bikini top.

The seconds while he struggled with the clasp were a torment of anticipation. 'How does this damn thing come off?' he said, in a rough, anguished whisper.

But before she could reply, or help him, it yielded. The tight-stretched Lycra pinged back and her top joined the pareo on the floor.

'My God, the door!' With a horrified gasp, she clapped her hands over her breasts.

It wasn't gaping, only ajar, but he was there in an instant to click it shut. And just before he turned to come back, she suddenly felt self-conscious. Standing there in just her bikini bottoms with strategically clasped hands made her feel like a blushing-violet lemon. 'What if somebody had barged in?' she said unsteadily as he returned.

'They didn't.' He said it very softly, his eyes still on her face. And then he took her wrists in a firm, gentle grip and removed her hands to her sides.

Oh, heaven. If it feels like this when he's just looking, what's it going to feel like when he touches?

She soon found out.

He knew exactly how to drive her wild. He knew exactly how the lightest, finger and thumb teasing turned her nipples into exquisitely sensitive nerve centres that sent urgent, throbbing waves to that other, hidden nerve centre.

I'm going to die of ecstasy.

His mouth-to-mouth resuscitation banished the last of her 'do unto me' wooziness. As he kissed her, his hands slid below her waist to the Lycra-clad lower curves of her bottom and pulled her hard against him.

That was when she realized just what a state he was in too. The urgency that suddenly surged through her was something deep and primeval, something that had existed ever since males and females had come together under the sun.

You've found a mate and he wants you. What are you waiting for?

She kissed him back, devouring him, squirming her hips against him with an urgency that said it all. As they paused for breath he whispered into her hair, 'Claudia . . .'

His voice was low and husky, and she knew exactly what he was going to say. Not, Are you sure you want this? He could hardly be in any doubt.

'I don't have anything,' he whispered. 'Is it –?'

'It's all right,' she whispered back. 'It's fine.'

From then on she was swept along in a red mist of urgency. Everything happened in a confusion of heat and need: his mouth on her nipples, the hot line his lips traced from breasts to thighs as he slid her bikini pants to her ankles, the shudder of ecstasy as his tongue probed fleetingly between her thighs.

Then they were on the bed, her fingers frantic as she helped him get rid of his shirt. But when she groped for the fastening of his shorts he stopped her

'Don't be in such a hurry.' He took her wrists and held them, but his rough whisper only betrayed his own suppressed urgency. 'Wait a little.'

It was like asking her to wait for oxygen, but he made her. He tortured her with waiting, as his lips and tongue teased and sucked and flickered over every erogenous zone she possessed – from the side of her neck to her nipples, from her navel to the aching heat between her thighs.

She cried out, arching her back and lifting her hips in little pleading movements, until he could wait no longer either.

But even after their first moment of burning union he made her wait. 'Oh, Jesus,' he whispered, poised in quivering stillness, as if the sensation were too sweet to be borne.

She had waited too long already. Almost as soon as his stillness had given way to passion, and his first deep thrusts had driven into her, the tidal wave began, sweeping her up and up. And each time she thought it was about to break, it took her higher still.

When at last it broke, she drifted back to earth to find him covering her face with kisses. She opened her eyes and said weakly, 'Was it me, making all that noise?'

His body convulsed in a little shudder. 'Can you keep the talking for later?'

'Sorry,' she whispered, and concentrated on giving him what he'd just given her. It didn't take long, as if he'd barely been holding on.

For a little while afterwards they lay quiet, letting their heartbeats return to normal. Nestled in the crook of his arm, her head on his chest, she began to wonder what he was thinking. Was he disappointed at her lack of 'making it last' control?

He saved her agonizing any further. His arm tightened around her and he dropped a soft kiss on her hair. 'Claudia, you are something else.'

'Look who's talking.' With a little sigh, she snuggled closer. 'You should come with a health warning.'

'*Me?*' His chest quivered in silent laughter. 'Look who's talking.'

A little ripple of laughter made her quiver in return. 'I hope I was better than Scrabble anyway.'

His chest shook again. 'Better than Scrabble. A lot noisier too.'

'Sorry. I got a bit carried away.'

The way he shook again, he was beginning to feel like a series of minor earthquakes. 'That was the general idea.'

Now the heat and fever were gone, she shivered a little as they lay on top of the covers.

'You're cold,' he whispered into her hair. 'It's the air-conditioning. Lift up.'

Reaching underneath her, he whipped the bedspread down. They wriggled under it together. And slowly, as they lay in the layer of warmth, his breathing became more regular and he drifted into sleep.

She would have liked to sleep beside him, but if she did, she couldn't savour the sensation of lying close to him like this. For a long time she lay quite still, as lazy thoughts drifted into her head.

You've been and gorn and done it now.

Haven't I just? And I loved every second.

Talk about rampant things. You've never been quite that rampant before.

And she hadn't. Not with that urgency, that desperation.

Maybe it's your age. They say women reach their sexual peak in their mid-thirties, so you're still on the up. Men peak

238

*at around twenty, and from then on they're on the down. You
sort of meet in the middle.*

*If that was him on the down, I'd like to have seen him when
he was on the up.*

You just did.

A little ripple of laughter shook her body, but she
suppressed it, not wanting to wake him. Very gently
she ran her fingers over his chest, savouring his
warmth. Very gently she kissed the warm skin closest to
her lips. And as she did so he stirred, shifted a little, and
his arm tightened around her.

Ooh, how lovely. She snuggled closer still.

*How long is it since you've cuddled up to a man like this?
You're starved, and I don't just mean of nookie.*

Very gently she ran her fingers over his chest and
stomach, and there they paused delicately.

I wonder what he feels like now?

Have a tiny little feel, while he's asleep.

I can't!

Why not? He'll never know.

Gently as a whisper, her fingers stole lower. And more
gently still they touched the limp, tender thing that
seemed as fast asleep as he was.

*Soft as a little lamb's nose. Wherever did old Mother
Nature get the idea? I wonder if there were trial versions that
were ready for action all the time, and got discarded because
they got in the way?*

Very gently, she stroked it again.

'It's still there,' he murmured.

She started. 'I thought you were asleep!'

'I was.'

She propped herself up on one elbow. 'How long have you been awake?'

He opened his eyes, his mouth twitching. 'Long enough.'

'Just checking,' she said, snuggling back next to him.

With a lazy chuckle, he dropped a soft kiss on her hair. 'I'm beginning to think you are a very bad girl. God knows what your old Sister Whatsit would say.'

It suddenly struck her how different he was. How relaxed, as if all his tension had melted away.

Well, of course. What did we say about stress-busting?

'Sister Immaculata wouldn't be a bit surprised,' she sighed. 'I was always a lost cause as far as she was concerned. I'm not even a Catholic. My mother only sent me to the convent because she thought all the girls were so neat and ladylike in their little pleated skirts and berets.'

They lay silent for a little while, and then the moment she'd been dreading arrived. With a glance at the bedside clock he said, 'Jesus, look at the time.'

It was nearly seven o'clock.

'I must get moving. Go and see Anoushka.'

His voice had changed. The warm, lazy relaxation was gone and the brisk note had returned. Easing his arm from around her, he threw the covers back and got out of bed.

She could have cried. She lay watching as he pulled on his clothes and ran a smoothing hand through his tousled hair. 'Use my brush,' she said.

'Thanks.' By the time he'd applied three strokes of bristle, nobody would have known he'd just been sleeping, let alone why.

But just for a minute, before he left, the other Guy returned. He came to sit on the edge of the bed, leaned over and dropped a light kiss on her lips.   'What time do you want to eat?'

'Any time.'

'Shall I come and get you in about an hour?'

'Fine.'

'You won't fall asleep again?'

'No.' She smiled. 'Missing one dinner was quite enough.'

He bent and dropped a fleeting kiss on her forehead, and before she realized what was happening he'd whipped the bedspread down and more fleeting kisses followed. One on each nipple, and one on her navel.

'I'd better go,' he said darkly, covering her up again. 'Before I get carried away.'

The look on his face made her heart turn over.

I wish you would get carried away. I wish you could stay here and we'd get a magnum of champagne and a four-course dinner sent up and do it all over again and spend all night together and do it again in the morning. In the bath.

But she managed a little smile that said hardly any of that. 'Push off, then. Before I turn into a really bad girl and make you change your mind.'

For a moment, she thought he almost wavered. His lips twitched, his eyes glinting as they flickered over her face. 'How much badder do you get?'

'Oh, much badder,' she said airily. 'Unbelievably bad. Almost as bad as it's possible to – '

She giggled as he ripped the covers back again, but the laughter turned to shrieks as he tickled her underarms and stomach, and when she rolled over to escape he finished his attack with a little slap on her bottom.

'You rotten devil!' Stifling her giggles, she turned the right way up.

He was closer to really laughing than she'd ever seen him. 'You wicked woman. I'll sort you out later.' And with that, he left her.

She rolled into the place where he'd been sleeping and cuddled into the pillow, inhaling his scent. But the bed felt cold without him.

And slowly, as she lay there alone, her warm contentment faded a little, and thoughts she'd rather not have thought drifted into her head.

Why did you tell him it was safe? You came off the Pill months ago.

If I'd said it wasn't safe, he'd have stopped and I'd have died. Anyway, the chances of anything happening are minute. Some people try for years to have babies.

And some have them just like that. Some women only have those women who only have to look at a cream cake to put on two pounds.

Don't be ridiculous. Anyway, I'd have hated it if he'd fumbled in his pocket for a little packet. I'd have known he was only waiting his chance.

How stupid can you get? Almost as stupid as those girls who write to agony aunts asking whether you can get pregnant if you do it standing up.

Oh, shut up.

Deflated and disconsolate, she made for the shower, where hot water and pink grapefruit shower gel restored her to a more cheerful frame of mind.

I'll be seeing him in half an hour and we'll have a lovely dinner.

What if Anoushka decides to join us? She probably will, just to be awkward. It's sod's law.

Of course she won't. We'll have a lovely dinner and I'll be able to wooze as much as I like without having to worry about giving myself away. And afterwards, with a bit of luck, he'll come back up here and I'll show him just how bad I can be when I put my mind to it.

She got out, dried herself and began on her hair. It was still a shock to see it in the mirror, but oh, the bliss of short hair. Drying it only took five minutes, and it looked just as good as when she'd walked out of the hairdresser's.

What to wear was the next question. She was dying to wear the black silk camisole, but just in case Anoushka decided to join them she rejected it.

Instead she chose the flowered dress, and once she'd got it on it wasn't a bad choice. You couldn't call it sexy, exactly, but you had to admit it was ravishingly pretty in an understated way. There were no frills, but the material was lovely; cream cotton lawn smothered with pink and peach flowers, and with just enough green to flatter her eyes. The neck was just low enough to be fetching, and trimmed with heavy cream lace. With short hair it suited her much better.

She did her face with more than usual care, added a few good squirts of Amarige, and waited.

And waited.

By twenty past eight, she decided it was high time to shake off that stood-up feeling and take action. What if he'd fallen asleep again?

She dialled his number, but there was no reply.

Now what?

More browned off than anything else, she sat crossly in the armchair and turned the television on. It was all in Arabic, naturally enough, so she turned it off again.

What on earth is he doing? I'll give him five more minutes and then I'm going to the coffee-shop.

Five turned to ten. *Right, that's it.*

She grabbed her bag and made for the door. And just as she was about to open it, someone knocked.

Her, Where have you been? died on her lips. He was still in those shorts, and one look at his face told her something was amiss. 'Whatever's the matter?'

'Anoushka,' he said tersely. 'Can I come in?'

'Need you ask?' He came in and she shut the door behind him. 'What on earth —?'

'Have you given her any money?'

His blunt tone shook her. 'No!'

'Are you sure? She hasn't spun you a line about needing shampoo or whatever from the shop?'

'I haven't given her a penny! She hasn't asked!'

His tense shoulders relaxed a fraction. 'I'm sorry, but I had to ask. She's not in the hotel.'

'*What*?'

He ran tense fingers through his hair. 'The sign was still on her door when I left you, but I thought she couldn't possibly still be sleeping. She didn't answer when I knocked so I went to my room and phoned. When she didn't answer that either, I started getting worried. I thought she'd maybe slipped in the shower or something, so I phoned down and asked them to send someone with a key.'

244

'But she wasn't there?'

'No.' Thrusting his hands in his pockets, he went to the window. The curtains were still open, and for a moment he looked out before turning around.

'I looked everywhere I could think of. The coffee-shop, the pool . . . I even looked on the beach, although it's pitch-dark and still as windy as hell. Eventually I came back to her room, to see whether she'd come back while I was gone.'

'And she hadn't.'

'No.' He paused. 'I went down to Reception to see whether her key was there. She went out about three o'clock.'

'*What*? How can they know?'

'The guy on the desk remembered her because she looked pleased and excited. He asked her if she was going somewhere nice, and she said, "You bet I am."'

Claudia suddenly felt sick. She turned away, ostensibly picking up a pair of shoes from the floor.

You have to tell him, she thought, putting them in the cupboard. *You can't not tell him. It's probably nothing to worry about anyway*.

'Where the hell can she have gone with no money?' he demanded.

Unsteadily she sat on the bed. 'Guy, I think she might have gone off with someone.'

'*What*?' He started, his hands coming sharply out of his pockets. 'Who?'

'I'm not sure,' she went on hastily. 'I don't know who he is, but she was talking to somebody at the pool at lunchtime and . . .' She paused. 'He didn't look sleazy or anything, or I'd have gone and said something. They were sitting on the edge, just chatting.'

'And?'

She shrugged helplessly. 'That was it. I kept an eye on her for a while, but nothing was actually happening. I mean, she wasn't flirting terribly obviously and he wasn't smarming over her or anything, and after a while . . .'

'Yes?'

Oh, help. 'I fell asleep.'

'You fell asleep.' He did not add a caustic *Great*, but he might as well have.

She felt guilty enough already. 'It's not what you think. I dozed for about twenty minutes and when I woke up they were both gone. I ran straight up to her room, but I'd panicked for nothing. She'd . . .' *Oh, help.* 'She'd just got out of the shower.'

Exactly. And what do you do just before a date? You get in the shower.

She made a helpless, hand-spreading gesture. 'I didn't tell you because I didn't see any point. Nothing had happened. She said she was going to get on with her biology and have a sleep later.'

The silence that followed seemed to be taunting her. *You've been had*, hung in the air, along with, *My God, there's one born every minute.*

'I might have known she'd do something like this,' he muttered, pacing the room. 'No wonder she looked "pleased and excited". I'll bet she did.' He looked up. 'What did he look like?'

'Young. I didn't get much of a look, but I wouldn't say he was more than twenty.'

246

'What nationality?'

'How on earth should I know?'

'OK, but roughly? Northern European? Local?'

'He didn't look English, or anything like that. He could have been local, but it's impossible to tell when people are in swimming things. He could have been Spanish or Italian.'

He returned to the window, his back to her.

Hesitantly she came up behind him. 'Guy, I'm sure there's nothing to worry about. She was bored, she met a boy, and he's taken her out. I'm sure that's all it is.'

Rather to her surprise, his shoulders relaxed. 'I guess you're right.'

She remembered something else. 'She made quite a point of how tired she was and how she was going to crash out later. She must have thought that would cover her for an hour or two.'

'She's been gone five hours!'

'You know what it's like when you go out at that age. You tell yourself you've got to be back, and then you can't tear yourself away. You don't give a hang about getting into trouble.'

'She'll give several hangs by the time I've finished with her.'

She gave an impatient sigh. 'Guy, she's been cooped up here for days! Can you blame her if she wants to go out and have some fun?'

'Without saying a word?'

'Would you have let her go out if she'd asked?'

'Of course not. She's supposed to be grounded.'

'There you are, then. She knew you'd say no, so she didn't ask.'

'What do you expect me to say? Give her twenty *rials* and tell her to have a nice time? It's her own fault she's grounded. It's her own fault she was suspended. If she hadn't got herself suspended, she wouldn't be cooped up here in the first place!'

Under his impatient tone, she detected something else. 'Guy, I know you're worried, but I'm sure there's no need.'

'I'm not worried. I'm furious.'

She wasn't convinced. 'She's pretty streetwise. If she's been hanging round London clubs, she must be. She'll probably come sneaking back in no time, praying you haven't found out.'

This seemed to work. 'I guess so. Concocting all sorts of plausible-sounding excuses.'

'More than likely. I can remember doing exactly the same myself. Putting on a really injured tone as I told my father it wasn't *my* fault if somebody had pinched my bus money and I'd had to walk all the way home. When actually Tim Fowler had just dropped me off at the end of the road on his falling-to-bits motorbike. Which I had been absolutely forbidden to go on.'

For the first time since he'd come back, a glint returned to his eyes. 'Dear me. Even badder than I thought.'

'I did tell you,' she said unsteadily.

'I remember.' For a moment the look in his eyes told her that whatever passed for a male Lurch organ, it had just stirred rather violently. 'Were you cursing most foully when I didn't show up?'

'Not especially. Nothing about pineapples anyway.'

'Liar.' He dropped a fleeting kiss on her lips. 'I can't have you all dressed up and nowhere to go. We'll get out of

248

the hotel and go somewhere else. I'll be back in twenty minutes.'

And with a little pat on her waist, he left her.

What did I tell you about sod's law? Might have known Anoushka would put the kybosh on it.

She hasn't, yet.

Oh, no? She's taken his mind off you very nicely. He's feeling guilty now. For lusting after you when he should have been thinking about his daughter. Unless she comes back pretty damn quick, he's going to be preoccupied all evening.

Anoushka had not returned by the time they left, but he didn't seem particularly worried. 'There are burger joints in town where the kids hang out,' said Guy as they came down in the lift. 'Even a skating rink. He might have taken her there.'

He's being remarkably laid-back about it. 'She's probably having a really good time. Don't be too mad with her when she gets back, will you?'

'I'll do my best. We'll take a taxi,' he added as they stepped outside. 'I don't feel like restricting myself to half a glass of wine tonight.'

The went to a restaurant on the Corniche at Muttrah. The road ran along a curved harbour, the traffic slow with countless pedestrians trying to cross. On the sea side people wandered in the cool evening air. Shops were still open and an air of relaxed bustle pervaded.

The restaurant overlooked the sea, and the discreet service and intimate atmosphere were relaxing enough so that gradually Guy began talking about himself for once.

'We got on well when she was small,' he told Claudia as the main courses arrived. 'I'd have liked her to come to me when Anna died. It would have meant a full-time nanny but it could have been worked out. But Anna's mother couldn't bear to let her go, and as she'd just lost her daughter I could hardly press it. Besides, Anoushka was settled there. She had her friends and her school, and we thought she'd had quite enough upheaval for a seven-year-old to cope with.'

'Were you divorced?' she asked.

He shook his head. 'It was in the process. We'd left it for years. Neither of us wanted to marry anybody else and we just didn't get round to it. It was only a few months before Anna died that she told me it was time to get things moving. She'd met somebody and wanted to be free to go ahead.'

Claudia hesitated. 'What happened to her?'

'A riding accident. No hard hat.'

'How awful.'

'Yes, it was.' He looked up. 'How's your *hamoor*?'

'Lovely.' It was local fish, just grilled, with lime butter. 'Anna and Anoushka are rather alike. Wasn't it confusing?'

'Not really. Anna had always loved the name Anoushka and when she found out it was Russian and meant 'little Anna', nothing else would do.'

Through the window, the boats were still bobbing on the the sea. 'That's a dhow,' he said, following her gaze. 'You don't see so many now but they used to carry all the trade between here and India. Right down the East African coast too. Taking dates and frankincense and bringing back slaves and ivory.'

'I wonder what they take now?'

'Televisions,' he said. 'Air-conditioners and video recorders probably. I once saw a dhow in full sail coming round the coast. It looked like a Phoenician warship until I borrowed a pair of binoculars from the guy next to me and checked out the cargo.'

'What was it?'

He gave a wry grin. 'A couple of Toyotas. It rather shattered the illusion.'

Delicately she steered the conversation back. 'You must have been married very young.'

'Too young,' he said. 'I was a still a student, and in the best student tradition practically penniless. Anna was a year younger, sent to England to study. I met her in her second week, and two months later we were practically living together.'

Claudia hated herself for the little stab of jealousy that caught at her heart.

'She was different from anybody I'd ever met before,' he went on. 'She was like quicksilver. There was something elusive about her.'

She recalled that photo in his sitting room; the heart-shaped little face with huge, dark eyes, and another green stab pierced her heart.

How can you be such a bitch? The poor thing's dead!

'I suppose I was besotted,' he went on, 'but at that age marriage was the last thing I was thinking of. Marriage was something you did years later, along with mortgages and kids.'

She knew exactly what he was going to say next. 'It was a bit of a shock when we found out there was a baby on the

251

way. Anna was terrified of what her old man was going to say. He was old-fashioned about such things and she couldn't bring herself to tell her parents. She didn't put any pressure on me for us to get married, but I knew it was what she wanted. That way at least it was respectable.'

Claudia was beginning to get the picture.

'She didn't tell her parents till afterwards,' he went on. 'We went to the register office with a couple of friends and had a party in the flat. And she was so happy, I knew I'd done the right thing. It was a few weeks later that the fertilizer hit the fan. When her parents came to visit.'

He took a sip of Mouton Cadet and made a wry face. 'Her old man hit the roof. I think he'd have liked to hire a squad of heavies and have me beaten up. All he could see was a student with no money and no family money either. They weren't in the super-rich league, but they were very comfortable, and he thought I'd got her pregnant on purpose.'

'What happened?'

He raised his eyebrows. 'He wanted me right off the scene. She was going back with them, and there was going to be a quick divorce.'

'But she didn't?'

He shook his head. 'It amazed me, the way she stood up to him. I think it amazed him too. She was never stroppy, like Anoushka, but she had one hell of a stubborn streak and it came out then like never before.' He nodded towards her plate. 'Your food's going cold.'

'So's yours.'

After they'd put away a few mouthfuls, he went on, 'Her old man was a bit of an autocrat. He didn't like being stood up to, so he played his trump card. If she stayed with me, she was on her own as far as money was concerned.'

A waiter cleared the plates and Guy refilled their glasses. 'She didn't care,' he went on. 'And after the way he'd treated me, I certainly didn't want any of his money.'

'What about her mother? Didn't she like you?'

'I think she liked me well enough. At least, she didn't think I was some sort of male gold-digger, but she still thought we were both far too young.

'It was all fine at first. Anna got a part-time job in a boutique and I got a part-time job in a bar, and we managed. It was after Anoushka was born that it got difficult. I was used to being broke and burning the candle both ends and in the middle as well, but Anna wasn't. The baby exhausted her.'

'I can imagine.

'Her parents had come over when Anoushka was born and they came again six weeks later. And, naturally enough, the old man's attitude changed drastically. It was his first grandchild, and suddenly he couldn't do enough. He was even moderately civil to me. He was going to restore her allowance, with a substantial mark-up.'

'I suppose she didn't argue?'

'She couldn't. I hated accepting it, but I couldn't refuse. Things were difficult enough anyway. I was trying to study and do two part-time jobs at the same time and Anna was exhausted all the time. She'd barely got used to looking after herself, let alone a baby too. She'd never had to lift a finger at home. They'd had maids to do virtually everything. I'd had to teach her how to do the simplest things, like washing a sweater or making spaghetti bolognese.'

253

A waiter appeared with the menus. 'Desserts, sir?'

They paused to order and Guy filled their glasses again. 'If I'm boring you to death, say so.'

She could hardly say, I'm riveted. 'Not in the least.'

'We started arguing,' he went on. 'I don't think Anoushka was what they call a difficult baby, but we had our share of teething and so on, and it was usually me who got up in the night. Anna was worn out. I didn't properly realize at the time, but she was still a child herself. She wanted someone to look after her. And I did, at first. Cooked most of the meals, fussed her when she had a cold. But I had my finals looming, and what with the baby as well I just couldn't run round after her like I had before.'

Their desserts arrived, frothy concoctions of meringue and tropical fruits and cream.

'Was that why she left?' asked Claudia. 'Because she needed someone to look after her?'

'More or less. It came to a head when Anoushka was ten months old. She'd been ill – just a cold or something, but it came on top of teething and she cried all the time. Anna couldn't take it any more. She packed a bag and said she was taking the baby and going back to her parents for a rest. Just for a few weeks. And she never came back.'

She gaped at him. 'But surely you didn't just accept it?'

'I really believed it was just for a while at first. I think she did too. But when a month turned to two, and then two and a half, I got a student ticket and went to see them. And I think I knew then. Her parents doted on the baby and Anna she was like a kid again. She could go out whenever she wanted, with built-in babysitters. I just don't think she could face coming back. She didn't say as much, but I knew. She kept saying she'd come back in a week or two, but I knew she never would. We talked about it, of course, and one day she just said she was very sorry but she didn't think she loved me any more, and maybe we'd both made a mistake, and we'd be better off apart.'

His matter-of-fact tones shocked her. Until he went on, 'I was devastated at first, but gradually it dawned on me that I was missing my daughter more than my wife. It was an infatuation on both sides. It would have died of natural causes in the end anyway.'

'It's terribly sad, though, when there's a baby involved. Did you see her often?'

'As often as I could. Anna and I were never enemies, thank God. I'd always have done anything for her. We even went on holiday once in a foursome when Anoushka was five. I had a girlfriend with a little kid about the same age, Anna had an Italian boyfriend, and we all took a villa in Greece. The kids got on like a house on fire and we had a great time.'

I wouldn't have had a great time, if I'd been your girlfriend, she thought. *I'd have been watching non-stop for the rekindling of sparks.*

His mouth suddenly flickered as he gazed at her across the table. 'You've got a bit of cream on your top lip.'

'Have I? With the tip of an exploratory tongue, she licked. 'Gone?'

'No. Left a bit.'

She tried again and he shook his head, starting to laugh. Eventually he reached across with a corner of his napkin, said, 'Hold still,' and wiped it off.

And, except for a second while he did it, his eyes held hers like warm, glinting magnets.

Their plates were whisked away and the coffee arrived. 'The funny thing was,' he went on, 'Anna's parents were upset in the end that we'd split up. Once I'd passed my finals and got a job, her old man began to realize I wasn't quite such a bad bargain after all.' He gave a wry smile. 'He always gave me a shot of his best cognac after dinner anyway. And talking of cognac . . .' He beckoned to a waiter. 'Have you got a Rémy Martin?'

'Yes, sir.'

'How about you?' he asked Claudia.

'I'd love a Cointreau. No ice.'

As they sipped their coffee and talked about inconsequential things she thought how much more relaxed he'd been than she'd expected. Maybe it had done him good to talk. She guessed he didn't do it all that often.

Not once during the meal had he mentioned Anoushka's escapade, but once the bill arrived she thought she saw the beginnings of tension. After extracting a gold credit card from his wallet, he glanced at his watch.

She knew exactly what he was thinking, since the same thoughts were going through her own head.

A quarter to eleven. She must be back by now.

But what if she isn't? I'm going to be a nervous wreck until we find out.

Of course she'll be back. And then he'll do what all parents do in such circumstances. Throw a wobbly, and secretly thank God the errant child is safe.

It would almost be a relief to see him throw a really good wobbly. Far better than the alternative. If she wasn't there.

CHAPTER 13

She was expecting him to grab the first available taxi, but he seemed in no particular hurry.

They took a walk along the Corniche instead. It was still windy, the boats bobbing in the rippling water. 'They used to sew them together with rope,' he said, pointing at a traditional wooden dhow. 'And seal the gaps with mutton fat.'

'Imagine the stink!' she said, wrinkling her nose.

'Pretty ripe,' he agreed. 'Somebody made a replica a few years back, mutton fat and all, and sailed it to China. As Sinbad the sailor was supposed to have done aeons before him.'

'I thought he was just a fairytale, like Aladdin!'

'Some people think there's evidence that he was real. A sailor-adventurer from what is now Oman, who found the silk route to China. And talking of epic trips,' he went on, 'I was thinking of another before we leave.'

'Really? Where?'

'Further afield. There's a beach in the south where the turtles lay their eggs. It's a long drive, so we'd have to stay overnight – camp on the beach, if I can borrow the gear.'

A little tingle of anticipation went through her. 'How exciting! I'd love to.'

'We'll be roughing it,' he warned, touching her arm as someone hurried past. 'I can't even guarantee bushes. You might have to make do with rocks.'

She laughed. 'I don't mind.'

'Anoushka will. But it should be something to remember, even if she moans like hell at the time.'

Talking of Anoushka inevitably brought her thoughts back to other things. How could he be so laid-back about it? Maybe he was used to it. Maybe she stayed out half the night all the time in London, with people he didn't know from Adam.

At sixteen?

That's what sixteen-year-olds do, remember?. That's why they're always having rows with their parents.

Even when they finally grabbed a taxi, he didn't seem in the least wound up. And the more laid-back he seemed, the more she wanted to snap at the taxi driver to stop messing about and put his foot down.

Why did she leave her key at the desk? It was evidence that she was gone. Why didn't she just take it with her?

Maybe she thought she'd lose it.

Don't kid yourself. She intended to be back. And therefore it follows that something, or someone, has prevented her.

By the time they arrived, clammy fingers were groping at Claudia's stomach. After they'd taken their keys Guy asked, 'Is my daughter back yet? Three-oh-seven.' His voice was as casual as could be.

The man checked. 'No, sir. The key's still here.'

'Would you give me a ring when she comes in? I need a word with her before she goes to bed.'

'Certainly, sir.'

258

'Thank you.' He smiled as if he'd just confirmed a wake-up call. But he didn't say a word all the way to the lift, and once they were inside the atmosphere between them underwent a not-so-subtle change.

'I feel awful,' she said unsteadily. 'I should have realized what she was up to.'

'You're not a mind-reader.' His short tone only made her feel worse.

'I'm really sorry.'

'I said, it wasn't your fault.' His tone was shorter still, as if he'd have preferred to say, For crying out loud, will you give it a rest?

She almost wished he would say it. If he was mad, having it out would be better than undercurrents.

What d'you mean, 'if'? Of course he's mad. He's despairing at your inability to put two and two together.

He didn't say a word as they got out of the lift and walked along the corridor. Outside his door he said shortly, 'I've got work to do, so I might as well get on with it until she shows up.'

Push off, Claudia, in other words. 'Will you ring me when she gets back? I don't mind how late it is.'

'There's no point waking you if she's late.'

'I'd rather know.'

He shrugged. 'If you like.'

'Thank you for the dinner. It was lovely.'

'My pleasure.' *Now push off, will you?*

As if to drive the point home, he bent and brushed her cheek with his lips. 'Goodnight.'

It was the kind of kiss he might have given that elderly aunt from the French restaurant, and after the intimacy of the afternoon it felt like a slap in the face. 'Good-night.'

Without looking back she walked quickly to her room and threw herself on the bed, almost in tears.

Well, what did you expect? For him to ask you in to see his etchings? He blames you, whatever he says.

But the more she thought about it, the more she thought it wasn't that simple.

He blames himself too. For lusting after you while she was off with a chap who could be a cross between Bluebeard and Jack the Ripper for all he knows.

He didn't seem that worried.

Of course he's worried. Just because he's not chewing his nails doesn't mean he's not worried. If you haven't sussed it out by now, he's not the type to 'share his pain'.

She went to bed expecting to toss and fidget for hours, and fell asleep almost at once. It was half past one when she woke, and remembered straight away.

He hasn't phoned.

Maybe he didn't like to wake me.

She longed to ring him, but if he was asleep and Anoushka wasn't back he'd think it was the front desk telling him she'd just turned up.

She tossed and fidgeted till nearly three, thinking about what he'd told her in the restaurant. Obviously he'd never have got married if not for Anoushka. Not then, anyway. He'd been hardly more than a boy himself. He might have later, if they'd still felt the same.

She imagined him at twenty, trying to study late into the night. She imagined a little flat, books strewn all over the table, a cup of coffee going cold and a baby crying. She imagined him pacing up and down with a baby at his shoulder, making soothing noises. She imagined him warming bottles in the small hours as his wife slept. Had he been jealous of his friends who had had no such responsibilities? Had he wished he was like them again, able to go out for a few beers and wild-oat-sowing in the field of female students?

Had he loved that little crying baby? Or had he resented her, even subconsciously? Was it possible that even now, all these years later, she was sensing that resentment?

She dozed off again and woke with a start, knowing something had woken her. It wasn't the phone. She looked at the clock that said 5:47, and then she heard it again. A soft knocking at the door.

She was out of bed in an instant. 'Who is it?'

'Guy.'

Whatever he had been doing, it wasn't sleeping. His grey, exhausted face gave her a jolt.

'I'm sorry to wake you,' he said tersely.

'Oh, Guy.' *How could I ever have thought he wasn't worried?* 'I was only dozing. Come in.'

He was wearing only a navy tracksuit. His feet were bare, as if he'd just got out of bed and slung on the first, easiest thing he'd found. He paced to the window, one hand in his tracksuit pocket, passing the other over his unshaven face. 'She's been gone nearly fifteen hours. If she's not back soon, I'll have to phone the police.'

Feeling utterly helpless, Claudia sought desperately to reassure him. 'He really didn't look like an unpleasant type. I'm sure she wouldn't have gone off with anybody dubious. She's not stupid.'

261

'No, but she's reckless. Reckless enough to do something stupid, just to defy me. She thinks she knows it all,' he went on, his voice quickening with tension. 'If she's got herself into something she can't handle, just to defy me . . .' He thrust his hands in the tracksuit pockets, his eyes full of unspoken fears.

The images that were tormenting him were all too clear in her own brain. 'It wasn't just to defy you, Guy. She wanted some fun.'

'Fun? What kind of fun do you think he was after?' He ran a tense hand over his hair, over the back of his neck. 'You must be aware of how she looks. How she'd come across to any man. She's my daughter, for God's sake, but I can see it. She's provocative. Not because of the way she dresses or behaves; it's just something in her. And when she flirts it's fifty times worse. I've seen her in action. If she was flirting with this guy . . .'

'She wasn't. Not obviously, anyway. She wasn't giggling or being silly like girls that age do.'

'She doesn't have to.' He turned away, yanked the curtains open and stared out. 'She's never been anywhere like this before. She wouldn't realize that attitudes here are different. In a place like this, a girl who lets herself get picked up by a stranger could be seen to be asking for all she gets.'

Oh, God. She longed to put her arms around him, but in his restlessness she knew she'd probably only irritate him. The only thing that would comfort him right now was getting his daughter back.

The air-conditioning made her shiver. She was wearing only a nightie of slinky oyster satin that might have been a cement bag for all he cared.

She slipped the towelling dressing gown over it, not caring a hoot that it was a foot shorter than the nightie and looked quite daft. In the bathroom she splashed her face with cold water and dried it.

When she came back, he was still standing by the window. 'I'm sorry,' he said. 'I shouldn't be here. It's not your problem.'

'Oh, Guy.' On an impulse she went up and put her arms around him. 'I'm glad you came. I've hardly slept either.'

He did not shake her off, as she'd half expected. His body was resistant at first, as if he was afraid that sympathy would make him crack, then slowly his arms came around her in return, and he stroked her hair with fingers that were not quite as steady as they might have been.

'I feel so bloody helpless.' His voice was tense with a gritted anger that she knew was only a mask for his fears. 'I want to go and look for her, but I don't know where to start.'

What he needed more than anything was to sleep, but it was useless to say so. She'd sound like her mother and he'd probably shake her off with an impatient, How the hell can I sleep?

So what could she do? Distract him, obviously, but how? She detached herself, picked up the phone, dialled room service and ordered two hot chocolates and chicken sandwiches. 'I don't know about you,' she said, 'but when I'm worried sick the first thing I do is pick, so let's have something to pick at.'

He actually managed the ghost of a smile, but it was a pretty sick-looking ghost. 'You'll be picking on your own, I'm afraid. It's times like these when I wish I still smoked. I could murder a packet of king-size.'

The state he was in, she wasn't about to make sniffy comments. 'If you're really desperate, I expect they can send a packet up.'

'I'd smoke the whole lot. Your room wouldn't be fit to sleep in.'

'I wouldn't mind, in the circumstances.'

He shook his head. 'I've done without too long to start again now.'

She sat in one of the armchairs, trying to fight off the clammy unease round her heart. 'Guy, I'm not going to say this again, and I'm not just making soothing noises, but it's perfectly possible that she's gone somewhere with this boy and either one or the other of them has nodded off. They might have gone to a party and he's drunk too much to drive her back. There could be any number of perfectly innocent reasons why she's not back. Why don't you sit down and we'll talk about something to pass the time until she comes?'

'I guess pacing the room isn't going to do any good,' he muttered, passing a hand over his hair.

With a heavy sigh, he sank into the other chair.

He looked so exhausted, her heart went out to him. She longed to take him to bed with her, put her arms around him and cuddle him into sleep, but she knew it was the last thing he'd let her do just now. 'Tell me about when Anoushka was little. What was she like?'

A nostalgic little smile flickered his lips. 'She could be a little devil, but she could charm the daylights out of anybody. She – ' He broke off. 'I'll give Reception a ring, tell them to transfer the call here.'

He picked up the phone and said, 'I asked to be called when my daughter returned but I don't want to be disturbed. Could you please put the call through to my colleague in three-oh-nine? It's very important.' He paused. 'No, there's nothing wrong. Thank you.

'They must be wondering what the hell's going on,' he muttered, sitting down again. 'Wondering why I don't just stick a note under her door.'

'You could.'

'She'd only pretend she hadn't seen it.'

'Go on, anyway,' she said. 'About the charming little devil. Was she really naughty?'

'Now and then. She could have the mother and father of a tantrum, but I guess they all do.' He paused. 'It's funny, the things you remember. She had a book of nursery rhymes we had to go over again and again. Some of them used to upset her, especially Mother Hubbard's hungry old dog. In the end I drew a couple of bones in the cupboard and added an unauthorized verse on the end.'

'What was it?'

'I can't remember.'

Fibber. 'Try. I'll do the lead-in to jog your memory.

'Old Mother Hubbard
Went to the cupboard
To fetch her poor dog a bone
But when she got there
The cupboard was bare,
And so the poor dog had none.'

She looked at him expectantly.

With a half-embarrassed smile he continued,

265

'So she went to the shops,
And bought some pork chops,
And the dog wagged his tail and said "Yum!".'

She burst out laughing.

'Not quite Poet Laureate stuff, but it worked,' he added. 'Gave her the idea that it was all right to scribble all over books too.'

Once he'd started, he needed very little prompting. He told her about holidays by the sea where he'd taught Anoushka to swim, and, later, ski-ing holidays where she'd put him to shame at first.

The chocolate and sandwiches arrived, and despite what he'd said he put away more than she did. But still, now and then, he glanced at his watch. Claudia studiously avoided looking at the clock, but was all too aware of how the minutes were ticking by.

She wished to heaven he would sleep, if only to put him out of his misery for a while. If he'd just close his eyes . . .

Eventually, she resorted to subterfuge. 'I've just got to go to the loo.' She shut the bathroom door quietly, and sat on the edge of the bath for several minutes. Eventually she flushed the loo, ran the taps a minute and opened the door again, very quietly.

It had worked. He didn't look very comfortable, but at least he was asleep.

Very quietly she lay on the bed, not even turning off the light in case the change woke him. She glanced at the clock. It was twenty to seven.

Oh, God. Please, let her come back soon. Please, let her be all right. Let her have nothing worse than a king-size hangover.

She didn't mean to fall asleep, but keeping her drooping eyelids open became harder and harder. When the phone finally rang, she snapped awake at once. 'Yes?'

Guy was awake too, and instantly alert.

'Thank you very much,' she said, almost sick with relief. 'Yes, I'll tell him. She's on her way up,' she said to Guy. 'This minute.'

For just a second his eyes closed, and if he wasn't saying a silent prayer of thanks, he was doing something very like it. Then he was on his way to the door. 'I'm going to kill her.'

'Guy!'

It was no use. He had left the door ajar and she sat tense on the bed, waiting.

It was only a split second. 'Who the hell is that? Where have you been?'

What? She crept closer to the door. He was only just outside, and from further down the corridor she heard a tearful voice. 'Dad, *please*.'

'I'm really sorry, sir.' The voice was anxiously apologetic and could have been American. 'She didn't tell me she wasn't allowed out. We went to the yacht club. Some friends of mine were taking their boats down the coast. We'd have been back by eight last night but the weather got bad. We tried to make it but we had to turn back. The swell was too big for fifteen-foot speedboats. We all had to sleep on the beach. I'm real sorry, sir.'

There was a short pause. 'I only came up with her to explain. She knew you'd be real mad.'

How right she was. When he spoke, Guy's voice was calmer. 'Don't look like that – I'm not going to get violent.

267

It was good of you to come and explain, but you'd better make yourself scarce now.'

'I will.' The boy sounded intensely relieved. 'See you, Anoushka.'

'Bye, Sammy.'

After a few seconds' silence, in which Sammy obviously charged for the lift, thanking heaven he had escaped unthumped by an irate father, Guy said bluntly, 'Well?'

'For heaven's sake don't *start*.' Now the worst was over, Anoushka's tearful tone vanished. 'I hardly slept a wink all night and we had nothing to eat, and I'm all salty and shattered and I need a shower. And did you have to speak to him like that? His dad's a big shot in the Lebanon and he's going to Harvard business school next year!'

'I don't care if he's the Aga Khan!' Guy's voice was really boiling up, now, with grit added. 'Have you any idea how worried I've been? Do you think I've slept?'

'No, since you ask. But I could make a fair guess at what you *have* been doing, since you've just come out of you-know-who's room.'

In the moment's silence that followed, Claudia felt sick.

His voice cracked like a cold, furious whip. 'I don't care how old you are – if you're not in your room in three seconds you're going to get the first hiding of your life.'

For once there was no pert reply. Seconds later, a door banged further down the corridor.

Feeling she might actually throw up, Claudia sank trembling to the bed.

He came in, seething. 'If she carries on like this, I swear to God – '

His voice broke off as he saw Claudia's face. 'What's the matter?'

'What's the *matter*? What do you think, for crying out loud?'

His expression altered sharply as comprehension dawned. 'Claudia, it was bluff.'

She could hardly believe he'd said that. 'What d'you mean, *bluff*? She *knows*! She might have got the timing wrong, but she's got the message!'

Her voice rose with trembling tension. 'Just look at you! In bare feet and a tracksuit that looks as if you've just yanked it on in a hurry! Coming out of my room with un-designer stubble all over your face before breakfast!'

'It was bluff.' He came to sit beside her, took her gently by the shoulders. 'Believe me, you've got it all wrong. All she saw was the perfect sidetrack. This is what she always does when she's in hot water. Finds a distraction to take the pressure off. And I handed her one on a plate.'

'But she must have thought – '

'She didn't. If she thought anything, it was only that I'd come to tell you she wasn't back.'

She was not convinced. 'How can you be sure?'

'Because I know her. A damn sight better than you do. If she'd really thought there was anything between us, she'd have made some smart comment before. To me, not you.'

She wanted to believe him so badly. 'I hope you're right. If she'd thought we were at it like rabbits when she might have been – '

'Stop it.' He gave her a little shake. 'Or there'll be trouble.' Slowly, his mock stern expression changed to something else entirely.

It seemed ages since he'd looked at her like this. The glint in his eyes was a touch the worse for wear, but glinting nonetheless. 'And if you compare me to a rabbit again, there'll be even more trouble.'

'You called me a rabbit once,' she said unsteadily. 'In the Italian place, remember?'

'I remember.' More quickly than it had come, the glint faded and he released her. 'I must go. I've got a meeting.'

'You've hardly slept!'

'It can't be helped.'

'Will you see her before you go?'

He glanced at his watch. 'I don't have time. She'd never answer the door anyway.' With a finger under her chin, he brushed her lips. 'Go back to bed for a bit. I'll see you later.'

She was dreading seeing Anoushka, in case he'd been wrong after all.

She knocked on her door just after one and Anoushka opened it with a sullen expression. 'What do you want?'

'Did you have a good sleep?'

'OK.' She was still in the baggy T-shirt that passed for a nightie.

'It must have been really uncomfortable, sleeping on the beach.'

'I wouldn't have minded if I hadn't been thinking about Dad going ballistic when I got back.'

Claudia hesitated. 'He was really worried, you know.'

'Like hell.'

'He was. So was I, if you want to know.'

Anouska pushed the tangled hair back from her face, her sullen expression diluted with awkwardness. 'I only said it to shut him up. You know, about you and him. He'd have gone on and on and I was shattered. It wasn't my fault we couldn't get back. Sammy said we'd be back by eight at the latest. I'd never have got found out if the sea hadn't been so rough.'

Thank God, he was right. 'He'd have found out anyway. He was looking for you long before eight.'

'He would. He can't stand me having any fun.'

Claudia's patience began to crack. 'He was worried! He thought you'd slipped in the shower or something! He was worried sick all night!'

'I bet he was. Worried about what would happen to his precious schedule if he had to take the morning off to go and identify me in the morgue.'

Claudia was so appalled she could hardly speak. 'How can you say such a thing?'

'What do you know?' It burst out in in sudden, angry defiance. 'Why don't you just shove off and leave me alone?'

If it hadn't been for a female guest looking askance at them as she walked past, Claudia would have yelled at her right there. As it was she half pushed Anoushka inside and shut the door behind them. 'Your father was beside himself all night and you don't give a stuff, do you?' Her eyes were sparking like green Catherine wheels. 'You're a vile, selfish, unfeeling brat. How he puts up with you I'll never know! He should get a medal! He should get a bloody sainthood!'

Her words echoed round the room like a whiplash.

There was not a word. Anoushka turned away. Her shoulders crumpled and for several seconds there was silence.

It was so different from the reaction she'd expected, Claudia was suddenly uneasy. 'Are you all right?'

There was no reply. Only the gasping, indrawn breath that comes before a river of tears.

It was well over an hour later that Claudia left her. For the rest of the afternoon she waited in an agony of impatience for Guy to return.

He phoned at five. 'I'm just back and I'm shattered. I'll sleep for a couple of hours before dinner.'

A couple of hours weren't going to make much difference. 'Fine. I'll be ready when you are.'

'How's Anoushka been?'

Leave it for later. 'Exhausted. She's been sleeping most of the day.'

'I thought as much. I gave her a knock on my way up but she didn't answer.' He paused, and his voice lost its crisp-and-businesslike tone. 'How are you, after all the dramas?'

'Fine.'

'You sound a bit tense.'

'I'm fine, really.'

'Then I'll see you later. If I'm not with you by seven-thirty, give me a ring.'

'I will. Sleep well.'

He arrived all fresh and showered and looking as if he'd had at least six hours' sleep the night before. He kissed her and told her she looked great and that he'd changed his mind about her hair now he was over the shock.

'Did you see Anoushka?' she asked as they got into the lift.

272

He shook his head. 'I thought about it, but in the circumstances I thought it was better to leave it.' Something between exasperation and despair crossed his face. 'There'd only have been another row. I'd have got mad and she'd have put on that don't-give-a-damn defiance and I'd have got madder.'

She was profoundly glad he hadn't seen her. Another row would only have made matters worse.

'I put a note under her door,' he went on. 'Nothing to do with last night. I've had a couple of meetings cancelled tomorrow so I thought we might head for Turtle Beach.'

They ate in the coffee-shop, which was hardly the place for serious talk. More than once Claudia tried to broach the subject, but there was always a waiter interrupting them with menus, or somebody shrieking with laughter at the next table.

'We needn't leave till about twelve tomorrow,' he said as their coffee arrived. 'I'll have to go and pick up some equipment first. There's a guy who's been living here practically since the old Sultan was deposed. He said he'd lend us sleeping bags, cool-boxes and so on. I'll ask the hotel to knock together some food.'

'Sounds lovely,' she said brightly.

He frowned. 'Are you all right?'

'Fine.' *Why did I say that*? 'No, I'm not. I need to talk to you. About Anoushka.'

Once she'd started, it was easier. 'When I went to see her at lunchtime she said some awful things and I lost my temper. I said some awful things back.' She swallowed. 'Really horrible things. And she started crying. Really crying, I mean. And all sorts of things came out.'

'What sort of things?'

She glanced around her. 'Not here.'

His eyes were suddenly razor-sharp. 'Did something happen last night?'

'It was nothing like that! She didn't even mention last night! It was other things.'

His shoulders relaxed a fraction, but his eyes were still intensely watchful 'Something at school?'

'It's nothing like that.' Restless with impatience, she glanced around her. 'Can you please get the bill? We can't talk here.'

He beckoned to a waiter for the bill, and as soon as he'd signed it they were off.

'We'll go to the beach,' he said. 'There won't be a soul there.'

The beach was perfect. She hadn't wanted to go to either of their rooms, and the bar was too public.

Last night's wind had died completely. The sea was dark and placid, shivering in the moonlight. Once they were well away from the gardens, she sat down in the soft sand.

He sat about a foot away. 'Spit it out, then.'

She clasped her arms around her knees. 'She was in such a state. I haven't seen anyone cry like that in ages.'

For a moment or two there was silence. 'It's me, isn't it? She's thinks I didn't want her living with me.'

It rather took the wind out of her sails. 'Is it true?'

'No. And it's not that simple either.' He picked up a little stone, tossed it towards the water. 'She didn't want to come, which was natural enough. She had to leave all her friends and her school – everything familiar.'

He tossed another stone, harder. 'She's not stupid. Even at thirteen she knew I'd had to modify my lifestyle to suit her. And I had. Adapting my working hours, altering my social life . . . She thought I resented it.'

His perception rather fazed her. 'Did you?'

He glanced at her. 'I can't pretend it was a picnic, especially at first. If she'd come a year earlier it might have been different. She'd changed a lot in that year. She'd got moody, didn't want to talk . . .'

'It's called adolescence.'

'I know, and it came at the worst possible time. I knew how her mind was working. She wasn't happy, and she tried to tell herself it was my fault, because I didn't want her. That made it easier to cope with.'

Sympathy was welling in her like a warm wave. *How could I have thought he wouldn't know?*

'I told her I was happy she was with me,' he went on, 'but I could see she didn't believe me. It's as if she thought I had to say it, because I was thinking the opposite. So I stopped telling her. I bent over backwards instead. It's easy, to see with hindsight, but I was far too easy on her. I let her get away with sulking and rudeness. I thought she was pushing me on purpose, to see whether I'd snap. She wanted me to lose my temper and yell at her, just so she could prove I didn't want her.'

She could imagine it so clearly. His controlled tension, her constant pushing . . . 'She said something about a woman, some girlfriend you had at the time. She thought she broke you up.'

He shook his head impatiently. 'She didn't break us up. Not really. Camilla wasn't into kids. She didn't like it when things had to change. She didn't want days out at the kind of things kids like doing. She resented the fact that she couldn't stay the night any more. She thought I was being ridiculous when I said it wasn't on.'

A green-eyed stab went through Claudia's heart. *Did you love her?*

'We'd had a good relationship,' he went on, as if reading her thoughts. 'She was fun and intelligent and witty, but everything had to suit *her*. Her lifestyle, her career. If it didn't, she discarded it.'

'And she discarded you?'

He turned to her with a very small, rueful smile. 'More or less. I was dumped, as they say. But I didn't cry into my beer for days. We'd have come to the end of the road sooner or later anyway.'

'Anoushka thought she'd broken you up. She thought you resented her on that count too.'

'I thought as much. I tried to tell her, but she always brushed me off. Whatever I said, she always made up her mind not to believe it.'

'I can imagine.' A warm breeze fluttered the skirt around her knees. She'd have relaxed, if not for the other things in her head. While she was wondering how to put them into words, he went on.

'It gradually got easier. I won't say we got on wonderfully, but I thought she was beginning to settle. And then suddenly things got worse. I had to go away for a few days during the school holidays and Mrs Pierce's sister was sick. She had to go to her, and that left me with a problem. Anoushka was barely fifteen and I couldn't leave her on her own.'

He paused. 'Without asking me first, she arranged to stay with a schoolfriend, and I put my foot down for the first time. The girl's parents were away too, and she had older brothers and sisters I didn't care for. One of them had been cautioned for possessing cannabis. The parents didn't give a toss. I didn't want her spending three days in that kind of company. Not at that age.'

'So she went to stay with friends of yours. In the country.'

He gave her a curious glance. 'Did she tell you that?'

'How else would I know? She'd stayed there before, hadn't she? Several times.'

'She still does, now and then. I'd have asked them to have her this time, but they're having major renovations. Mike and Jenny are old college friends. They've got four kids and a rambling old house with enough animals to fill a zoo and dog hair everywhere, and nobody gives a toss about keeping anything tidy. Anoushka loved it there when she was younger. They've got a daughter a year younger and they get on like matches in a paper shop. They used to sit up in the hayloft and talk for hours.'

'She told me. She's called Louise, isn't she?'

For the first time he seemed to realize something deeper was coming. 'Claudia, what is this? If you've got something to say, will you just say it?'

She couldn't look him in the eye. 'They weren't in the hayloft. They were up in the attic, hiding from the younger ones. They had a couple of cans of cider and a packet of cigarettes and they were puffing the smoke out of the window and talking about boys. Anoushka was telling her about this friend you didn't want her to go to, and how

277

she'd "done it" with a boy in Cornwall. She started moaning to Louise about how you wouldn't let her stay there and what a complete pain you were, how you never wanted her to have any fun and how you'd never wanted her to live with you.'

She paused, bracing herself.

'And?' he said.

'And then Louise said to her, "If I tell you something, will you swear never to let on I told you?" And of course, Anoushka said, "What is it?", and Louise said, "Swear first", so Anoushka swore. And then Louise changed her mind and said she couldn't, that her mother'd kill her. And then of course Anoushka said she'd never find out, because she'd never tell.'

She couldn't look him in the eye. 'Louise told her you'd never wanted her in the first place. She told her you'd wanted her mother to have an abortion.'

CHAPTER 14

'Oh, Christ.' With a swift, jerky movement Guy rose to his feet, walked to the edge of the sea and just stood there, his hands rammed in his pockets.

How he must be feeling, she could not begin to guess. After a moment she followed. 'I told her I was sure it wasn't true. I didn't know what else to say.'

His silence seemed to say it all. Hesitantly she went on, 'I'm not making any moral judgements, Guy. If you did, it was natural enough. You were very young and – '

'I didn't!' His voice was rough, almost angry. 'I never mentioned it to Anna!' There was a long pause. 'But I thought it.'

Somehow she was only relieved. It would have been so easy for him to lie. 'Then how on earth – '

'I can imagine.' For a long time there was no sound but the lap of tiny waves on the sand. With a deep sigh, he ran a hand through his hair. 'Mike was a good friend of mine. When I told him Anna was pregnant, his first reaction was that it was a problem easily solved. Before you could say Yellow Pages he was talking about clinics. There were other friends there too, all telling me they'd chip in a tenner. They had it all worked out.'

'What did you say?'

'I don't think I said anything. I was probably still in shock.'

'But they thought that was what you wanted?'

He was still gazing out to sea. 'Of course they did. When you're nineteen, it seems the obvious solution.'

'What did you say to Anna, when she first told you?'

'Nothing, at first. I was too shocked. She was in tears. She'd known for days and been too scared to tell me. She'd forgotten to take her pills a few times, but she'd never thought, etc. etc. She was in a terrible state, worrying about what her old man would say.'

He took her arm and they walked a little further along the beach. 'I'll never forget it. It was lunchtime. I'd arranged to meet her in a café and she came out with it just like that, in the middle of the meal. We had no time to discuss anything. She'd made an appointment to see some student counsellor right afterwards. She shot off and I was left in such a daze I forgot to pay the bill. I walked out and some guy stopped me at the door. They actually called the police.'

'Oh, heavens. What happened?'

'They believed me, in the end. Made a few smart cracks about young lads who don't know what they're getting into, and let me go.

'It was that afternoon I told Mike. We were having a beer after lectures and I had to tell someone. I got back to the flat wondering what the hell we were going to do. Anna was there. She'd been to a bookshop and found some book full of photos of two-inch foetuses with their tiny little fingers. She'd been crying for hours and her face was a complete mess. She said she knew what she ought to do, but she just couldn't do it. She said it was her fault and she'd understand if I wanted out.'

For a long time neither of them spoke. Eventually he said, 'I never discussed it with any of my friends after that. I just told them she was going ahead. I know they all thought we were mad, but nobody actually said it to our faces. They probably said it all the time behind our backs. And Mike must have assumed I'd wanted something else.'

He led her away from the sea and back up to the soft sand, where they sat down again. 'Mike and Jenny were an item even then. Obviously he must have discussed it with her *ad infinitum*. He'd made his own assumptions and passed them on to her. But how the hell she could have told her daughter . . .' He turned to her, his voice rough with anger. 'Mouth-almighty woman! Louise is just a kid! How could she tell her a thing like that?'

'She didn't.'

'Then how in hell – '

'Louise overheard her mother talking to some woman friend. While Anoushka was there the time before. Saying what a shame it was about her mother, and going on to, well . . . related matters.'

'Trust her.' He ran a tense, impatient hand through his hair. 'Shooting her mouth off as usual. Don't get me wrong,' he added, 'she's not the kind of bitch who makes mischief on purpose. Jenny's well-meaning, but utterly indiscreet. She always was. She used to get drunk and say the most outrageous things.'

281

The sigh he gave was halfway between sorrow and anger. 'She'd die if she knew Louise had even heard, let alone passed it on. Just after Anoushka was born, she was pregnant with Louise. And far from going through the Yellow Pages Mike had a smirk on his face as if he was the first guy on earth to manage it. They were getting married – a big, white wedding, the works. I said to him, "You've changed your tune, haven't you?"'

He glanced down at her with a very wry expression. 'He looked sheepish and said it was different when it was your own, and the number of times they'd been careless he'd started to think he was shooting blanks. But they'd have got married anyway. You could see they clicked.'

A long silence followed. A cloud with a massive question mark on it hung over them, getting bigger every second.

'Poor kid,' he said at last. 'As if she hasn't had enough to cope with. It must have been eating away at her ever since.'

'You have to talk to her. Explain that it was all a misunderstanding.'

There was another long silence, and when he spoke again his voice was roughened with emotion. 'I wish to God I could look her in the eye and tell her truthfully that I never even thought it. But I did. And nobody will ever know how guilty I felt afterwards.'

She longed to put her arms round him, even take his hand, but she didn't. Any word or movement, she felt sure, would make him clam up.

'Until she was born, I felt very little,' he went on. 'Anna had this big lump that squirmed now and then, and I knew eventually it was going to come out and there'd be nappies and sleepless nights and a non-existent sex-life for weeks afterwards. I pretended, for Anna. But when she was born . . .'

He paused. 'I'd had this idea that it was like shelling peas. I was utterly unprepared. Anna was in agony for hours, and I've never felt so helpless in my life. I got angry with the nurses, told them for Christ's sake to give her something. Eventually they sent me out and I did the classic expectant father bit, pacing up and down. When they let me in again, it was all over. Anna was nearly asleep. She looked so white and exhausted, I felt terrible. And then the nurse produced this little bundle and said, 'Would you like to hold her?'

'She was so small, I was petrified. Her eyes were open. She was looking at me as if they weren't quite working yet and she wasn't quite sure what to make of this big ape who was obviously about to drop her . . .'

Suddenly, his crispness returned and he yanked her to her feet. 'Last night's beginning to catch up with me. Let's go.'

She was amazed that he'd got that far before normal male embarrassment overtook him. He'd never have gone the whole soppy hog like Aidan would, and said things like, *And then I found out what it means to be a father. I grew up that night, Claudia. I learnt what love really means.*

They stopped at the hotel bar for a nightcap. 'When will you talk to her?' she asked, sipping her Baileys on the rocks.

A troubled frown creased his brow. 'Talking to her's impossible at the best of times.'

'Maybe tomorrow, at Turtle Beach?' She hesitated. 'Maybe it'd be better if I don't come. If there's just the two of you . . .'

He shook his head. 'I won't go if you don't come. Turtle Beach is very isolated. If anything happened, if I broke my ankle or something daft like that, and couldn't drive, she'd be stranded.'

As they finished their drinks she could see last night was catching up with him all too easily. When he suggested another, she shook her head. 'You need your bed. Especially if we've got a long drive tomorrow.'

There was nobody else in the lift. And once the doors had closed he said, 'After the past twenty-four hours, you must be wishing you'd never come.'

He was looking right at her. The Greek-island mega-watts weren't quite as high-powered as usual, but the output was enough to bring out the flutters she'd been suppressing. 'Funny you should say that,' she said unsteadily. 'I was just thinking I'd have preferred a wet weekend in Bognor with my lowlife cousin Ryan. Only I was too polite to say so.'

Just for a moment, this was enough to banish whatever else was on his mind. The glinting spark surged back in a positively dangerous fashion. 'I am cut to the heart,' he said, very softly. 'Is there any way I can change your mind?'

He changed it with a kiss that was over nearly before it had begun. The bell went 'ping' and the doors started opening. With great presence of mind he jabbed the pool-deck button, and the lift descended again.

By the time it stopped and the doors had opened, Claudia was ready to wooze for England. A middle-aged couple were standing there. 'You are not getting out?' said the man, in an accent that could have been Dutch or German.

'No,' Guy said pleasantly. 'We overshot.'

The couple got in, the woman giving Claudia rather dubious glances.

And no wonder, she thought. *When heat like that flows through you like an intravenous drug, something has to show on the outside.*

Guy glanced down at her with a little frown. 'You're looking a bit flushed, darling. I hope it's not another dose of malaria.'

Somehow she managed not to laugh till the couple got out at the ground floor, but she shook with laughter till the bell went 'ping' again.

'You're wicked,' she giggled as they got out.

'*Me?*' He was more controlled, but still laughing. 'Something about pots and kettles comes to mind here.'

Outside his door he stopped, checked up and down for approaching eyes. When none appeared, he slid his arms around her waist and drew her close. 'I'd love you to come and tuck me in,' he said softly, brushing her cheek with his fingers, 'but I'm not in any fit state to do you justice. Besides . . .' He paused, and troubled reality returned to his eyes. 'I've got other things on my mind just now.'

'I know.' She wanted to tell him she didn't care what state he was in. She'd be quite happy just to curl up with him and go to sleep, but it was impossible to say it.

'Then I'll leave you,' she said lightly, reaching up to plant an elderly-aunt kiss on his lips. 'Recharge your batteries and be all bright and bushy-tailed in the morning.' She paused. 'I wish you'd go and say goodnight to her.'

'Did you think I wasn't going to? I either knock on her door or give her a ring every night. I usually only get a grunt in return, but I still do it.'

'Goodnight, then. Sleep well.'

She didn't sleep for ages. She lay wondering how on earth he was going to broach such a subject with a girl who clammed up even when he talked about ordinary things.

Was he lying awake, wondering exactly the same?

I wish I was lying with him.

He didn't want you there. He'd never have believed that you only wanted to sleep. He'd have thought you wanted another command performance.

His 'doing justice' remark came uncomfortably to mind.

After what you were like yesterday, practically tearing his clothes off, he probably thinks command performances are all you're after. Probably thinks you're a raging nympho.

Don't be ridiculous. If I were a raging nympho, I'd have been raging with him that first night.

Maybe he thinks you're a raging nympho who likes to pretend she isn't, for the sake of form.

She went to bed thinking of a much younger Guy. A big ape, terrified of dropping the little thing he'd created. How old must he have been? Twenty, at the most.

She rolled into the pillow, trying to find the scent he'd left the day before, but the linen had been changed and it smelt only of laundry.

With a bereft little ache in her heart, she fell asleep.

Claudia frowned at the piece of paper in her hand. 'Watch out for Table Top Mountain,' she read, 'and shortly after that, turn right at Raspberry Ripple Ridge.' She glanced at

286

Guy, bewildered. 'Are you sure this is right? It sounds like a practical joke!'

'We're going to get lost.' Anoushka's voice came from the back seat; it was practically the first time she had uttered since they'd set out. 'There's hardly even been another car for hours. We'll turn into bleached skeletons and nobody'll find us for hundreds of years.'

'We're not going to get lost,' Guy said patiently.

'But what if we do?' Under the usual bored tones was a hint of real anxiety. 'How much water have we got?'

'A dozen litres of mineral water. And enough Cola to swim in.' He glanced in the rear view mirror. 'Happy now?'

'I s'pose.'

He glanced at Claudia instead. 'It's no joke. The names are very apt, as you'll see when we get there. According to this – ' he glanced down at the tripometer '– we've got about six kilometres to go.'

It was the first time Claudia had ever been on a trip like this, where you didn't look for signposts, but counted how far you had travelled on a certain route and then watched for landmarks. The country was the most inhospitable she'd ever seen. There were no humans, no animals, no signposts. It was brown and arid without even a scrubby, goat-nibbled tree, and not so much as a six-inch oasis anywhere.

'Tired?' he asked, glancing at her. 'It's been a long old haul.'

'Not really,' she fibbed. They'd been going several hours, and now and then, after her less than wonderful night's sleep, she had felt her eyelids drooping. She had fought it, however, in case he was feeling the same. For much of the journey they had talked in low tones, because of Anoushka sleeping in the back. The conversation had been light and very general, in case she hadn't been asleep, after all.

The strain of pretending there was nothing between them was beginning to tell on her. Neither of them had said that this was what they should do in so many words, but it was an unspoken understanding.

But why the hell should we?

You know why. Even if she was a perfectly well-adjusted girl you'd pretend. Once you're home, it'll be different. Then it'll be quite legitimate for him to give you a ring and say, Doing anything on Friday night?

But what if he doesn't?

Guy brought her out of her musings. 'There's Table Top Mountain, thank God. I could murder a beer.'

It was more of a little hill, looking as if a giant had sliced its top off to make a picnic table.

A little further on there was no mistaking Raspberry Ripple Ridge either; a creamy rock face veined with pink, exactly like the ice cream.

He turned right and the Range Rover lurched as he negotiated pits and boulders, emerging on a wide beach where the waves of the Indian Ocean crashed. It was enclosed at either end by rocks, and was absolutely deserted.

Anoushka got out and gazed around her. 'So where are the turtles?'

'Patience, Anou.' Guy was already unloading things from the tailgate: borrowed picnic table and chairs, cool-boxes of food and drink.

As Claudia unfolded the chairs, he opened a cool-box. 'Here, Anou,' he said, handing her a drink, which she took without a word. To Claudia he handed another can and a plastic glass. 'Try that for size.'

It was a ready-mixed gin and tonic, wet and freezing from the ice. 'Ooh, delish,' she sighed, decanting it into the plastic glass.

He ripped the ring-pull off a can of beer. 'This isn't even going to touch the sides.'

Although he had brought folding chairs, neither of them wanted to sit after being in the car so long. 'Another half-hour and we'd have missed the turning,' he said. 'The sun's going down fast.'

Anoushka had wandered off. She was gazing at something in the soft mounds of sand twenty yards away, but suddenly she came running back. 'I just found a whole nest of baby turtles and they're all dead!'

'Show me.' He rose to his feet and followed. Claudia was a little behind, her drink still in her hand. Anoushka pointed to a little hole in the sand. 'There!'

They peered inside. Tiny, lifeless-looking bodies were just visible, crammed together with empty shells.

'They're not dead.' He put a reassuring arm around his daughter's shoulders. 'They're programmed, like a computer. They're waiting till it's dark, and then they'll make a dash for the sea.'

'How do you know? And where on earth am I supposed to go to the loo?'

'Behind a rock, Anou. There are enough of them.'

As she stomped off towards the rocks at the far end of the beach he turned to Claudia. 'I should imagine the odds on my having any sort of meaningful conversation with her tonight are about on a par with having Elvis parachute in for a beer.'

'You never know,' she said, thinking the odds on Elvis were rather more favourable.

As dusk fell they opened the second cold-box and tucked into cold chicken, beef, pitta bread and salad. Anoushka sat between them, eating more than either of them. 'I bet they *were* dead. I bet we don't see one single turtle all night.'

'I can't guarantee it,' he said, 'but last time I came we saw a lot.'

'When was that?' Claudia asked.

'Years ago, my first trip. This'll probably be the last time,' he added. 'I heard that the government's going to put these beaches off limits. There are too many people coming at the weekends. It's bound to disturb them.'

'Why did we come, then?' Anoushka demanded. 'I suppose it's all right for us to come, but not for everybody else.'

'Maybe there won't be any turtles,' he said, in a determinedly pleasant voice. 'And then we can all go back with environmentally clear consciences.'

'And then we'll have come for nothing,' she said.

'Does anybody want that last chicken drumstick, or can I have it?'

'You have it.' He frowned suddenly, scanning the sea. 'I think maybe we have action at last.'

A few yards from the edge of the surf was a small, dark head, raised, as if scanning the beach. The next wave brought it on to the sand – a huge mother turtle that began dragging herself painfully up the wet sand.

As they sat still and quiet another appeared, and then another. One by one they dragged themselves up the sloping beach. When the first had reached the dry sand, Guy said quietly, 'You can go and watch, Anou. But keep well back and be very quiet.'

For once, there was no smart remark. Anoushka slipped from her chair and went to watch as the first mother began digging a hole with her flippers.

After a while, Claudia and Guy joined her. The turtle seemed quite oblivious. When the hole was ready, she dropped eggs one by one, like wet ping-pong balls, into the nest.

The moon had come up and was shimmering over the sea. Before long there were half a dozen mother turtles on the beach. After a while, Anoushka tiptoed off to watch them.

Guy watched her go and murmured, 'She hasn't moaned once this past hour. I'll have to put it in the *Guinness Book of Records*.'

'She'll remember this for a long time,' she whispered back. 'I know I will.'

But Anoushka was calling to them, in a loud, excited whisper. 'Come and look!'

They tiptoed across the sand to where she was pointing. Out of the dry sand baby turtles were popping up like corks, their minute flippers going like clockwork as they began their frantic dash for the water.

'How do they know which way to go?' Anoushka whispered.

'I don't know,' he said. 'Maybe it's the moon, or the smell of the sea. Old Mother Nature's figured some way to let them know.'

But Anoushka was looking elsewhere. 'There's another lot! Over there!'

It was happening all around them. At intervals across the sand, babies were popping up by the dozen.

It seemed hours that they watched, and eventually Guy and Claudia retreated to the chairs. 'It makes you feel very insignificant, when you think this has been going on for thousands of years,' she said,

'Millions, probably. Mother Nature's a clever old bird.' He took another beer from the cold-box. 'Like another G and T?'

She'd already had two. 'I'll have a lemonade for now.'

It was very quiet, only the waves crashing on to the shore. Anoushka was still watching popping babies. Now and then she helped one that was heading the wrong way, or floundering as it struggled up the sandy mounds.

Gently Claudia touched Guy's arm. 'I'm going to disappear for a bit. You go to her. Talk about the baby turtles, and maybe you'll find the right moment to tell her about another little newborn baby and the big ape who was terrified of dropping her.'

Even in the dark, she suddenly saw from his face that he'd been thinking exactly the same thing. Before he could reply she stood up smartly. 'Go on,' she whispered. 'Good luck.'

'I'll need it,' he whispered, and gave her hand a fleeting squeeze. 'Maybe you could have a word with your old Sister Whatsit. Tell her I need a bit of help with a lost cause.'

'She's not lost yet. But I'll see if I can put a call through to the harp-polishing department.'

Once he'd approached Anoushka and sat beside her in the sand, Claudia looked away. She walked to the far end of the beach where they could hardly see her. She sat gazing at the waves rolling in, and up at the moon in a navy velvet sky. 'I don't whether you're up there,' she whispered, 'and I'm really sorry we used to make fun of your moustache, but if you've got a minute could you put in a word for somebody?'

It was nearly ten o'clock before she was alone with Guy again. Sitting in the sand, she was watching a mother turtle shovelling sand over her eggs with her back flippers.

Guy stole up and sat about two feet away, his arms around his knees.

'How did it go?' she asked.

'As I expected.' His voice was tired and taut. 'I thought I was getting through to her at first. At least she didn't walk off. So I carried on.' He picked up a tiny stone, tossed it towards the rocks. 'I got a bit emotional.'

'And then she walked away?'

'Not exactly.'

'What, then?'

'Don't ask.' He tossed another stone after the first. 'Let's just say it was not a resounding success.'

'Maybe something went in.'

'I doubt it.' A sardonic note entered his voice. 'Your old Sister Whatsit wants sacking. She was about as much use as, well . . . a nun at an orgy.'

She knew he was only trying to cover how hurt he felt. She longed to take his hand or put her arms around him, but for all she knew Anoushka might be watching.

293

Take his mind off it. 'I saw an animal a minute ago,' she said. 'Something cat-sized and ghostly-looking, over by the rocks.'

'It'll be a desert fox. Where there's food about, there are always predators.'

'Has she gone to bed?' she asked.

'She's taken a sleeping bag to the car. She won't sleep on the sand again, after the other night.'

After a moment he added, 'I might as well follow. I don't know about you, but I'm whacked.'

Already? How can you go to bed already? When am I ever going to get a night like this again, let alone with you?

She covered her disappointment with a little shrug. 'It was a long drive. You must be tired.'

But he didn't charge off at once. For a moment he sat silent beside her. 'I know what you're thinking.'

Do you?

'If things were different . . .' With a touch like a whisper, he traced a line with his fingertip down the inside of her arm. 'If it were just you and me . . .'

That touch electrified her absolutely. 'But it isn't.'

'No,' he said, very softly. 'I'd like to sit here with you, or go for a swim together, but I don't think it's a good idea. In the circumstances.'

'Maybe not,' she said unsteadily. 'In the circumstances.'

'I'd better go.' He turned her face towards him, brushed her lips with a rough softness that only told her how much he wanted more. Any more than a brushing, she knew, would have let the brakes off so fast they'd never have been able to find them again.

Her voice was barely steady. 'Push off, then. You don't want to find out the hard way just how bad I can be when I put my mind to it.'

For a moment she thought she'd let the brakes off after all. His eyes were warm and dark and she could almost feel him fighting himself. 'You are a very wicked woman. How am I going to sleep?'

Oh, God, this is torture. 'Count sheep,' she said unsteadily, avoiding his eye. 'Or turtles. And listen to the waves coming in.'

'Are you going to stay here?'

'Yes. For a bit.'

'You won't get any crazy ideas about going swimming on your own?'

She turned to him. 'Why? It's not dangerous, is it?'

'It's dark and it's rough.'

'Then why did you mention going in at all? Anyway; I've done it before.' *Why did you torture me with what might have been?*

'That was together.'

'And that's OK, is it?' She knew she was goading him, but she didn't care. If they had to keep the act up he should do it properly, with no shivering touches that made her ache for him. Did he think she could switch on and off like a flaming machine? 'I'm a perfectly competent swimmer. Just as competent as you are. So if you think I need a big strong man beside me just because it's a teensy bit – '

'Please don't turn this into some ridiculous feminist issue.' A tense, impatient edge had entered his voice. 'I'm not going to argue the toss about it. Just don't, that's all. Goodnight.'

With a casual pat on her shoulder, he left her.

You and your mouth! Why did you wind him up like that?

Why did he wind me up? Why did he have to put those images in my head? Swimming, for heaven's sake. Just the two of us, under the stars . . .

It wasn't as if she'd expected any wild antics in the sand. She'd known it was out of the question. She'd have been happy just to sit with him, maybe talk quietly . . .

And because he didn't trust himself I'm sitting by the Indian Ocean all on my tod.

You wound him up too. Why ever did you say that about being bad? No wonder he didn't trust himself.

She gazed miserably at the mother turtle, who was beginning to drag herself back into the water.

You don't have all these problems. Any old mate'll do, as long as he's male, and you don't give a hoot who's watching. And afterwards you don't give a hoot whether you ever see him again or not. You don't know how lucky you are.

She stayed there another half-hour, then stole on silent bare feet to their little camp. They had laid the sleeping bags about five yards apart, with Anoushka's in the middle. That was now gone, leaving a yawning gap. Guy had left a large battery lamp burning, but the moon was so bright she hardly needed it. He was lying with his face towards her, his eyes closed, but whether he was asleep or not it was impossible to tell.

She scrabbled in her bag for her toothbrush, took a bottle of mineral water from the little picnic table and tiptoed off to give her teeth some sort of brushing.

The wind was picking up and it was colder than she'd expected. Shivering a little, she took off her cotton trousers, leaving on only her T-shirt. She wriggled into her sleeping bag and lay for a few minutes, watching him.

What if he opens his eyes and catches you gawping at him? You know what he'll think.

She turned over, closed her eyes, and tried to sleep.

She awoke tired and stiff, wondering where on earth she was. The sound of waves brought her back, but there was another noise too. A faint buzzing, like swarms of angry insects.

She sat up in a dozy panic. The tide was out and the wet sand marked with what looked like tractor trails, where the last turtles had dragged themselves back into the water.

The buzzing came from Guy. Standing about ten yards away, he was applying battery-operated razor to his face and kicking at something in the sand. Then he moved a few feet and began kicking at something else.

Curious, she slipped out and went to stand beside him, pulling the T-shirt down over her hips. 'What are you doing?'

Not having seen her coming, he started, then switched the razor off. 'I hope I didn't wake you, but I'm not into designer stubble.'

He wasn't exactly bursting with the joys of morning, but it seemed that their little snap from the night before was more or less forgotten. 'How did you sleep?' he asked.

'Not very well,' she confessed. 'How about you?'

'Bloody awful.' He nodded at the sand. 'I'm burying bodies before Anoushka gets up and sees them.'

She winced, seeing a headless, flipperless little turtle at his feet. 'The fox, I suppose.'

'Probably.' He pushed it into the sand, and covered it. 'Quite a few of those tiddlers didn't make it.'

'Poor little things. You tell yourself it's nature, but you still hate it.'

'Don't look, then. Go and get some breakfast, while I continue my body-hunt.'

Almost as he said it they heard the car door slam, and Anoushka emerged in a long black T-shirt. Without so much as a glance at them, she headed for the rocks at the far end of the beach.

He glanced at Claudia. 'Let's hope she's too preoccupied with the call of nature to notice anything else.'

She wasn't. They saw her stop suddenly, gaze down at her feet.

Guy pushed his razor into Claudia's hand and walked over to his daughter.

'It's so cruel,' she half sobbed. 'The poor little thing was hardly even born.'

'It's nature, Anou. Probably a desert fox with a nestful of babies to feed.'

'It's horrible! I wish we'd never come!' She almost ran off towards the rocks.

'I give up,' he muttered, returning to Claudia. 'Let's have something to eat.'

There was orange juice and soft rolls, sliced cheese and chocolate croissants, but she could have killed for a cup of tea or coffee. Guy was tense, Anoushka silent and moody, and the atmosphere was hardly conducive to a cheerful breakfast.

But he did try. 'Coming for a swim after breakfast?' he asked his daughter. 'Before we hit the road?'

She didn't even look at him. 'There's nowhere to have a shower. I can't stand being all salty for hours until we get back.'

'Please yourself.' He turned to Claudia. 'How about you?'

It was already hot; she felt sticky and dusty already. 'I'll just tidy up first. You go in and I'll join you.'

He nodded up at the steep rocks behind them. 'Those rocks are supposed to be littered with fossils. Why don't you go up and take a look?' He directed this at his daughter.

'What would I want to look at boring fossils for?'

His controlled patience was evaporating at last. 'Oh, suit yourself. I'm going in.'

As she watched him go Claudia was suddenly so angry with Anoushka she could scream. She stood up sharply and began collecting up paper plates and plastic glasses, loading them into a rubbish bag. With sharp, furious movements, she folded the chairs and table, loaded them into the Range Rover. She could tell by her guilty expression that Anoushka knew precisely why she was furious.

Good.

She rammed empty cans back into cool-boxes and rolled up her sleeping bag tightly enough to kill it.

She had begun on Guy's when Anoushka walked off, and that made her angrier still. The wretched girl had not lifted a finger to help. Suddenly she threw down the sleeping bag and stormed after her. She had climbed up on to the rocks after all, and Claudia followed. It was not too steep, there were plenty of footholds, and at about thirty feet up it levelled into a smooth enough plateau.

Anoushka was sitting moodily, throwing pebbles on to the sand.

299

Claudia stormed up to her like an avenging angel. 'Do you actually hate him, or is this just a spoilt-brat act you're going to keep up for ever?'

Anoushka said nothing. She didn't even move. And behind sunglasses, Claudia couldn't see her eyes.

'What is wrong with you?' she demanded, standing over her inert body and feeling like slapping her. 'He tried to talk to you last night, but you wouldn't have it, would you? It was all rubbish, what Louise told you, but you don't want to know, do you? You'd rather have a reason to hate him!'

As she paused for breath a tear trickled from beneath the sunglasses, and with a trembling fingertip Anoushka wiped it away. 'I don't hate him.' Her voice was trembling even more than her fingers. 'But I just don't know how to be nice to him any more. It's as if there's a wall inside me and I can't . . .'

As her voice cracked Claudia's anger died away. Slowly she sank to the rocks beside her.

'I can't help it.' She wiped another trickling tear. 'I didn't mean to be horrible to him last night. He was telling me all this stuff about when I was really little and I know he meant it, but I got embarrassed and it just came out. I couldn't stop it.'

Her voice was cracking badly. 'I wish I'd never told you all that stuff. I wasn't that shocked when Louise told me, not really. I was old enough to realize I'd been a mistake. I know he was only young. They both were. I've got friends at school who were mistakes too. Only sometimes, when I was really miserable, I used to think about it, and – '

As her voice finally broke Claudia felt utterly helpless. She didn't know what to say that wouldn't come out wrong, or sound trite or patronizing.

'Please don't cry,' was all she managed, sliding an arm around her shoulders. 'I shouldn't have said those things.' She gave her a little squeeze. 'Why don't you come in for a swim? He'd like that. We'll go in together.'

Anoushka sniffed and shook her head. 'You go. He's waving at you.'

Claudia shaded her eyes. She had left her sunglasses in her bag and the glare was blinding. He had swum beyond the breakers. There was a big swell, lifting him gently as he trod water.

'He's waving at both of us. Come on. I'm not going unless you come too.' With a hand on her arm, she pulled Anoushka to her feet. 'I know we'll be salty, but it'll be lovely while it lasts.'

Guy had stopped waving. He had swum a little further with a powerful crawl. He stopped again, and gave another beckoning wave. Claudia waved back. 'We're coming!' she yelled, but knew he couldn't hear.

Anoushka was suddenly rigid. 'Get out!' she screamed, waving her arms frantically. 'Get out!'

Claudia stared at her, aghast. 'What on – '

'Can't you see?' She ripped off her sunglasses, handed them to her. 'Look! In the water!'

Claudia went cold.

Without the sunglasses she could never have seen. But with powerful lenses cutting out the glare she could see all too clearly.

There must have been a half a dozen of them. Dark, streamlined, stealthy shapes, circling beneath him.

'Where there's food about, there are always predators.'

This time, she knew they weren't dolphins.

CHAPTER 15

What must have gone through his mind when he finally realized why they were yelling and waving their arms so frantically she could not bear to think.

He glanced behind him, but there was nothing to see, no fins breaking the surface.

Anoushka was half sobbing beside her. 'He thinks we're joking!'

No he doesn't. Claudia's mouth was too dry to utter.

For a moment he seemed not to move. The swell lifted him as the next wave rolled to shore, and then he began a slow, easy breaststroke, as if he had all the time in the world.

Without a word they scrambled back down the rocks.

He still had some thirty yards to cover, and it seemed like an eternity. They stood together at the edge of the surf, watching.

'Why doesn't he hurry?' Anoushka's voice trembled with panicky fear.

Dear God, what must he be thinking? 'He doesn't want to thrash about. It's movement that attracts them.'

'He's going to die.' Her voice was an agony of torment. 'I was vile to him last night. I pushed him away and now he's going to die.'

'He isn't.' Gritting her teeth, Claudia tried to shut out the terrible images in her mind. 'They hardly ever attack.'

They circle, before moving in for the kill. He won't see anything. He'll hardly even have time to yell. He'll just disappear.

She refused to even think it. Other images were in her head – pictures from a ghastly book Ryan had relished as a child. He had shoved it gloatingly under her nose, hoping to send her into fits of girly horror. She had never obliged; she'd even felt a dreadful fascination for the graphic colour photos: thighs with massive chunks torn out of them, bitten-off feet recovered from the stomach of a tiger shark.

What will I do if he rolls out of the water bleeding half to death? Frantically she sought in her mind for long-ago first aid training. Arterial bleeding – find the pressure point, make a tourniquet . . .

Anoushka's face was white, her voice shaking with anguish. 'I pushed him away, and now he's going to die.'

'He isn't.' Claudia took her hand, held it so hard it hurt. 'Come on, Guy,' she urged in a desperate whisper. 'Come on. Come on.'

Please God, just let him come safely back and I'll never ask for anything again.

The last few seconds were the longest of her life. With every even stroke he made she was certain it was going to be his last. Any second he was going to yell, disappear in a thrashing of water as they stood helpless on the shore.

She wanted to close her eyes, but she couldn't betray him by looking away.

It seemed to happen in slow motion. A huge wave swelled behind him. It lifted him, rose higher, and as it broke he vanished. All she could see was a maelstrom of foam on the sand.

That was when she closed her eyes.

'Daddy!' screamed Anoushka.

When she opened her eyes again, Claudia thought she was dreaming. The wave had retreated, leaving smooth wet sand. Guy was walking towards them, his hair plastered to his head like a wet seal. 'That was a big one,' he grinned, hitching up the waistband of his shorts. 'I nearly lost my pants.'

Claudia was too sick with relief to smile. Even if she had, he wouldn't have seen it. Anoushka hurled herself at him like a missile.

If she could have spirited herself a thousand miles away, Claudia would have. Instead she walked back up to their little camp and carried on tidying up with fingers that trembled like baby sparrows.

Jesus. If I ever have to live through a scare like that again . . .

She opened the cold-box that held the drinks. The ice had melted; the remaining cans were floating in cold water. *Thank God. Two gin and tonics left.*

It was a long time before Guy and Anoushka came up. He still had his arm around her, and she was making the kind of shuddering gasps people make after they've been crying their hearts out.

'I need a tissue,' she mumbled, heading for the car.

He shot a glance at Claudia and at the drink in her hand. 'Wonderful idea,' he said drily, 'I know I'm driving, but in the circumstances . . .'

There were a couple of beers left. He ripped the ring-pull off one and came to stand beside her. His eyes and voice softened together as he gazed down at her. 'How are you feeling?'

The temptation to throw herself into his arms like Anoushka had was almost overwhelming. 'Better,' she said lightly. 'But if you give me any more nightmares like that, I'll be wanting a bonus.' She glanced down at the nearly empty can in her hand. It had seemed like a good idea at the time, but her stomach was protesting that gin on top of shock was a thoroughly bad idea.

'You must have thought all your *Jaws* nightmares were coming true.'

How he could look and sound as if he'd been doing nothing more hair-raising than water ski-ing, she could not imagine. 'Weren't you scared?'

He raised an eyebrow. 'Let's just say I've had more enjoyable swims.'

He was scared, all right.

'How many were there?' he went on.

'Enough. You'd never have seen them from the beach. It's too rough. I couldn't even see them till Anoushka gave me her sunglasses. The glare coming off the water would have hidden anything. The Loch Ness Monster could have been down there and we'd never have known.'

He raised an eyebrow. 'Just as well we didn't go swimming last night.'

Oh, my God. 'I died a trillion deaths. I've never seen anyone swim so slowly in my life.'

'How do you think I felt? Like you do when the petrol gauge is nearly on empty and you want to put your foot down and get home before it runs out.'

Remembering his calm, unhurried swim, his total lack of panic, her throat constricted.

'Still, it gets the adrenalin going.' He winked at her, raised the can to his lips. 'I kept telling myself, if I'm going to get legless, I'd rather do it with beer.'

Anoushka came back, blowing her nose noisily. 'Like a drink?' he asked. 'There are plenty left.'

'Yes, please.'

'Better now?' he added gently.

'A bit,' she mumbled, still sniffing. 'My face must be a complete mess.'

'Give it a wash, then.' He gave her a little squeeze. 'There's plenty of mineral water left.'

Anoushka opened a bottle and sluiced her face. Guy did the same, washing the salt away, before loading the boxes into the Range Rover.

In five minutes they were ready to go. 'I'm going to strip off and get into some dry shorts,' he announced. 'So if anybody's easily shocked, look the other way.' He added an almost imperceptible wink that only Claudia could see.

As they got into the car Anoushka turned to her with a half-embarrassed expression. 'I'm sure it'd take more than him stripping off to shock you.'

'Don't you believe it,' she said, covering up with a little laugh. 'I've led a very sheltered life.'

'Not that sheltered, I bet.' She was smiling now, albeit a wobbly effort. 'I got a bit hysterical, didn't I?'

She reached over the front seat, patted her shoulder. 'He's your father. You had the best excuse in the world.'

'You were so calm!'

'Not inside, I wasn't. I've never been so petrified in my life.'

'You didn't show it.'

How I didn't, heaven alone knows.

Guy got in and slammed the door. 'Right, let's hit that road.'

It was long, dusty and tiring. The wind had picked up, blowing sand across the road, and now and then he had to put his foot down or go into four-wheel drive.

Even more than on the beach, Claudia felt like a spare part. There wasn't much conversation coming from the front seats, but it was marked by a striking absence of the previous tension.

Anoushka said something about the poor mother turtles getting their flippers bitten off and he said the sharks'd probably give flippers a miss; they'd be even more leathery than Mrs Pierce's omelettes. She gave what was nearly a giggle, and said she wondered what Mrs Pierce'd say if they told her about the sharks, and he said not to bother – Mrs Pierce would only say it was nothing, that her son's best friend's uncle had actually been spat out by a great white.

Over his shoulder he added drily to Claudia that Mrs Pierce was the kind of woman who, if you told her about a friend who had some hitherto unheard-of tropical disease, would always know at least three people who'd had it twice.

'I know the type,' she smiled.

How much better it would be if he and Anoushka were alone. Maybe they'd like to get a bit soppy and talk about private things. They can't, with me here.

He continued to shoot the odd remark over his shoulder, as if to show she wasn't being excluded, but after a while she pretended to be asleep. She wished she *could* fall asleep. It would have provided a welcome escape from the gin-induced nausea in her stomach and would stop her hearing if they started talking about private things.

But they didn't. It was all light, nothing tearful or heavy, and gradually she realized why. The reconciliation was too new and fragile to stand heavy strains. They were tiptoeing gently on thin ice, feeling their way.

But what a relief it was to hear them talking at all. Maybe old Immac hadn't been quite so useless after all. Suddenly she could almost hear the scratchy old voice in her head.

'There are more ways than one of killing a cat, Claudia. And I might add that organizing half a dozen sharks at short notice was no easy matter. Still, it was worth it. Would you ever just look at them, now?'

Although the nausea had passed by the time they arrived back at the hotel, she still felt vaguely ill, in a clammy, unspecified way. Telling them she was desperate for a shower, she left Guy and Anoushka at the desk, where he was picking up a couple of faxes.

She had only been in her room two minutes when Kate rang.

'Where have you *been*? I've been trying to get you since last night!'

'Turtle-watching. How's Portly?'

'Fine. He's home and yowling for food every five minutes, but never mind him. Don't panic, there's nothing wrong, but your mother's been on the phone twice. I made up some story about you being on a Middle East sales trip. I'm not sure it worked. She said something about it being a bit odd, since you hadn't started your new job yet, and asked for a phone number. I said I'd lost it, and she said she'd ring back, and I said I still couldn't find it. I'm just telling you so we can synchronize our lies.'

'Why was she phoning? Did she say?'

'She said something about a family do they're coming over for. Your Auntie Barbara, I think.'

'Oh, hell.' Some vaguely remembered snippet of conversation came back. 'Uncle Ted's sixtieth, you see, and she's thinking of a little party, in which case we'd pop over for a long weekend. And of course she'd love to see you too, with a partner, if you've got one – I do dislike that silly word. Why can't they just say "boyfriend" like they used to? Anyway, dear, do put it in your diary, because . . .'

'I'll give her a ring,' she said. 'It'll be lovely to see them, but a do at Auntie Barbara's means Ryan, and I don't think I can stand it.'

'Just ignore him.' Kate's tone altered to its usual mischief. 'Any developments with you-know-who?'

Quite why she lied, Claudia didn't know. 'I've gone off him. He turned out to be one of those self-important prats who think they're God's gift.'

'Maybe just as well. When are you coming back?'

'Not sure yet. I'll let you know.'

After finishing with Kate, she found the code for Spain and phoned her mother, embroidering Kate's inspired lie. 'Yes, Mum, I *know* I haven't actually started yet, but my new boss thought I could do some exploratory stuff in the Gulf. There are loads of expatriates with huge tax-free salaries to spend.'

'Well, that's very nice, dear. I hope she's paying you for it.'

'Mum, since when do I work for nothing?'

'Anyway, dear,' her mother went on, 'I wanted to check that you're still free for Uncle Ted's sixtieth. It's Saturday week. We'll come over on the Friday. Will you be back by then?'

Oh, Lord. 'Oh, yes.'

'Oh, good. Only Barbara wanted to know for the rooms. Will you be bringing anybody?'

'Even if I had anybody to bring, I wouldn't. Not if Ryan's going to be there.'

A plaintive note entered her mother's voice. 'I do wish you wouldn't always have it *in* for Ryan, dear. I know he's not exactly what your father'd call *steady*, but – '

'Mother, he's a complete and utter lowlife who knows exactly how to give the opposite impression.'

'There's no need to get irritable, dear. He's got a very nice new girlfriend, according to Barbara. He's going to be bringing her. Belinda, I think her name is.'

Oh, my God. Belinda the Boobs. Must be a complete bimbo to see anything in Ryan.

'Auntie Barbara thought it'd be rather nice if you brought somebody too,' her mother went on. 'To sort of even up the numbers. But if there isn't anybody . . .'

310

'I'm very sorry, Mother.' After the kind of day she'd had, Claudia could not keep a taut edge from her voice. 'I know you'd love me to turn up with some frightfully eligible chap just so you can score points off Auntie Barbara, but – '

'Really, dear! How can you say such a thing?'

Quite easily. And underneath the hurt tone there had been more than a trace of guilt.

'Of course, your father and I'd be only too pleased if you found somebody nice, but you know perfectly well we've never said a *word*.'

'All right, Mum, all right. I'm sorry.' She put on a forced brightness. 'How are things in sunny Spain? Any juicy scandals in the bridge club? How did Dad's golf tournament go?'

It didn't work very well. Her mother's replies were tinged with a faint, huffy put-outness she couldn't quite hide. By the time she finally hung up, Claudia's vague not-feeling-well had made up its mind which direction to take. She had the beginnings of the kind of headache that would turn into a killer. And not so much as an aspirin.

She lay limp on the bed. Even going to the door when her tea arrived was a major effort, and staggering to the shower afterwards made her head pound like a pneumatic drill.

Once out of the shower, she lay on the bed again, longing for sleep that wouldn't come. There were too many things in her head.

I've upset Mum now. Why ever didn't I keep my mouth shut? And why did I lie to Kate about Guy?

You know why. So she won't feel sorry for you and make it even worse when you get back home and that bloody phone never rings.

Who says it won't?

Your intuition, that's what. Things have changed a bit, haven't they? He's got a chance to re-establish a relationship with his daughter. She's in an intensely vulnerable state, and he's sensitive enough to know it. You saw her face in the silver souk. She was jealous. She's probably been jealous of every relationship he's ever had. If he's got any sense, he's not going spread himself around for a bit. Besides . . .

She didn't like the way her thoughts were going, but they wouldn't stop.

Let's face it, it's got all the classic ingredients of a holiday fling. Exotic setting, two adults who fancy each other, and opportunity. And what happens to holiday romances once you get on the plane?

The knock at the door sounded like bombs dropping.

'Who is it?'

'Guy.'

She walked on eggshells to the door. He was all fresh, showered and smelling of shaving things. He wore a white polo shirt that made him look like an advertisement for suntan lotion.

'Oh, hi,' she said weakly, and winced as it reverberated through her head.

'Are you all right?' He frowned.

'I just had my mother on the phone and I upset her, and now I've got a stinking headache.'

'Have you taken anything?'

She shook her head, and then wished she hadn't. 'I suppose you haven't got any painkillers?'

'No. Sorry.' He gazed at her a moment. 'Anoushka and I are going for a very late lunch. Would you like –?'

'No thanks. I just want to sleep.'

'You'd feel better if you ate something. You had hardly any breakfast.'

With half a dozen navvies trying to smash her skull with hammers, she wasn't in the mood for such remarks. 'For heaven's sake, you sound like my mother!'

'All right, all right.' He held up both hands in a soothing, calm-down gesture. 'I'll go.'

He took a step forward and brushed her cheek with his lips. 'Sleep well. I'll see you later.'

And he went.

Great.

Nearly in tears, she lay gingerly back on the bed.

If that's the best he can do in the kissing-better department, I don't think much of it.

What do you expect? You spat at him like a wounded cat.

She was nearly nodding off at last when there was another knock at the door.

If it's him again, I'm going to be really nice and make up for snapping.

It was Anoushka. 'Dad bought these in the shop,' she said, handing her a packet of paracetamol. 'Are you OK?' she added anxiously.

Oh, help, do I look as if I've been crying? 'I upset my mother on the phone and now I feel awful.'

'What did you say?'

She shrugged helplessly. 'Nothing so terrible, but I was irritated and let it show. She was going on and on, you know, like mothers do . . .'

Megamouth! Why did I say that?

Anoushka raised her eyes to heaven in a 'don't tell me' manner. 'I know. Some of my friends' mothers are complete nightmares.'

Whether she'd failed to pick it up, or whether she was just covering an insensitive gaffe Claudia couldn't tell, but she was profoundly grateful.

'Tell him thank you for the paracetamol. And have a nice lunch. Maybe I'll see you at the pool later.'

'Actually, we're going sailing,' Anoushka said, rather sheepishly. 'You can come if you like, only Dad thought you'd probably prefer to keep out of the sun if you've got a headache.'

'He's right. I don't think I could stand it.'

'He said to tell you he's booked a table for eight-thirty tonight in the restaurant.' Rather awkwardly she added, 'I can't not eat with him tonight. Not after . . . well, you know.'

Claudia knew she ought to say something deep and earnest, but the girl would very likely be embarrassed. Quite apart from that, the navvies were still at it, and she was dying to get a couple of painkillers down.

'Eating with him isn't so bad,' she said, with a forced jokiness. 'I've had worse dinner companions. Not much worse, I must admit.'

Anoushka's lips curved in a sheepish little smile. 'I feel awful now. I really thought you fancied him at first.'

Oh, God. 'Heavens, no. I'm still languishing over my gorgeous Australian ex. He took off five months ago and I've been like a widow ever since.'

Looking even more sheepish, Anoushka said, 'I'd better go. Dad's waiting to eat. I hope you feel better soon.'

After she'd gone, Claudia took two paracetamol and curled up under the bedspread.

I wish he'd brought them himself.

Serves you right for being a ratty cow. What are you moaning for, anyway? It was nice of him to bother at all.

He doesn't want me going sailing with them either. He doesn't want me playing gooseberry.

Can you blame him? Would you want you playing gooseberry, if you were him?

Sniffing back a forlorn tear, she curled into a foetal position under the covers and prayed that the paracetamol would be strong enough to shift the navvies from her head.

It wasn't, quite. When she woke an hour and a half later they were still at it, but the hammering was a lot less energetic, as if they'd all been for a liquid lunch and a few of them had sloped off for a kip.

Feeling listless, and what her mother called 'muzzy', she took herself off to the pool.

A few lengths sharpened her up considerably, but not in the way she wanted. The thoughts that filled her head while she swam up and down were realistic to the point of pessimism.

I've served my purpose. I should offer to leave. She doesn't need a minder any more.

I shouldn't even eat with them tonight. I should make some excuse and let them spend the time together. Apart from anything else, it's going to kill me to sit over dinner and pretend he's just another man.

Why ever did I pretend to Anoushka that there was nothing between us? Why did I say that about Adam?

You know why. You could hardly say, Well, actually, I do fancy him like mad, and we had a wild session in bed while you were off with Sammy.

What if she repeats all that about Adam to him?

It took no imagination to realize what normal male logic would come up with. A: she's still languishing after somebody else who left her months ago. B: she's obviously possessed of a very healthy sex-drive. Add A to B and we have C: a sexually-deprived woman who hadn't needed much persuasion.

So tell him it was a fib.

How can I, unless he brings it up first? He'll think I'm angling for some hint that we're going somewhere.

It was all complicated enough to get the navvies going again.

She got out of the pool feeling depressed almost to the point of tears.

Play it by ear. If he gives the slightest hint about 'when we get home' for God's sake don't wreck it by seeming too eager. And for God's sake don't go the other way and act as if you don't really care one way or the other.

All thoughts of making excuses and leaving them alone vanished once they were in the restaurant that evening.

Now the morning's dramas were over, they needed someone else there. It had been a long time since they were easy together, and Anoushka was obviously finding it difficult to switch overnight from sulky silence to sunny smiles and chat.

As she watched her subtly from across the table Claudia could see the battle going on within her. She desperately

316

wanted to be nice but normal adolescent embarrassment prevented her. More than ever, Claudia realized how thin was the ice they were treading on. It would not take much to break it. One medium-sized row would almost take them back to square one.

Guy was patience itself, handling her as sensitively as he knew how. He did not overwhelm her with embarrassing affection, neither did he try to force her into non-stop conversation.

'How was the sailing?' Claudia asked.

'Not bad,' he said. 'Only about a force four wind, but Anoushka made a good crew.'

'I was hopeless,' she said, in half-embarrassed tones. 'I hadn't got a clue about booms and rudders and things.'

'Neither had I, when I started.'

'And I don't see why sailors can't talk plain English,' Anoushka went on. 'Why do you have to say, "Coming about"? Why can't you just say, "We're turning round"?' She said it plaintively, however, rather than in the sulky tone she'd have used before.

'Search me,' he said. 'I can remember asking my old man exactly the same thing when he first took me sailing.'

'What did he say?' Anoushka asked.

'He told me to stop asking bloody stupid questions and get my head out of the way before the boom cracked it open.' He grinned, turning to her.

She managed a small, rather awkward smile.

It was the first time he'd mentioned either parent. 'How old were you?' Claudia asked.

He shrugged. 'Eight or nine.'

'His dad left his mother when he was ten,' Anoushka put in unexpectedly. 'Ran off with another woman.'

The instant it was out, she glanced nervously at him, as if thinking she'd been indiscreet.

He did not seem in the least put out. 'Classic case of the older man running off with his secretary,' he shrugged. 'It was very hard on my mother – financially, as well as everything else. She was another classic of the era: an intelligent woman who'd been brought up to think that marriage and children were the only career she'd ever have.'

Just as Claudia was wondering whether to ask where she lived now, and equally wondering whether not to, in case he said she was dead, he went on, 'She found it very difficult getting back into the labour market. Eventually she found a job in a local hotel – the quaint, oldy-worldy type favoured by tourists.'

'Where was that?' she asked, realizing how little she knew about him.

'The Cotswolds. We were inundated with tourists in the summer. Thousands of Americans. And eventually she met a widower from Boston. At the age of twenty-six I gave my mother away at her own wedding.'

'I was there too,' Anoushka put in. 'I can still remember it. I had a lovely dress and flowers in my hair and little white ballet shoes – and I spilt orange juice down my dress at the reception and cried.'

Guy's eyes were gently amused as he turned to her. 'All the old dears were cooing over you. Until you threw up all over my trousers.'

'Oh, *Dad*.' Looking more embarrassed than ever, she applied herself to her pepper steak and fries.

Anoushka was sitting directly opposite Claudia, with Guy on his daughter's left. When they'd sat down, she'd noticed particularly how he had placed himself, so that they would not be looking into each other's eyes all the time. It had been relatively easy to pretend he was just another man. But now, as Anoushka looked determinedly at her plate, their eyes met diagonally across the table.

For several seconds they locked. And for the first time she didn't know what his were saying.

At least, she knew half of it. They were saying, *I want you* clearly enough to make her Lurch organ go into overdrive.

It was the other half she wasn't sure about. *I want you, but . . .*

That 'but' was six feet high.

He broke the contact first. 'How's that steak, Anou?'

'OK. Quite nice,' she added hastily, as if making an effort to be appreciative.

'Are you suffering from McDonalds withdrawal symptoms?'

'A bit,' she sighed. 'I keep dreaming of a Big Mac with large fries.'

His mouth twitched. 'We'll stop on the way back from the airport.'

'Promise?' She looked almost like a ten-year-old. 'I just hate aeroplane food. It all tastes the same.'

'We'll get a take-away and eat it in the cab.'

Claudia fixed her eyes on her lamb cutlets, praying nothing would show on her face. Something had just constricted inside her, something forlorn and bereft that pricked at her throat and eyelids.

A vivid picture was in her head: a taxi rank at Heathrow. He'd say, '*We can go together if you don't mind stopping at McDonalds first.*' With a ghastly, forced smile she'd say, '*No, really, I'm exhausted. I'll just go straight home.*' And he'd try not to look faintly relieved and say something like, '*Well, thanks for everything, take care,*' and she'd smile brightly and say, '*You too. Bye.*'

And somehow, she'd keep that smile glued on till they were out of sight.

CHAPTER 16

For the rest of the meal Claudia avoided Guy's eyes as if they were death rays.

What exactly had that 'but' been saying? *I want you, but that's all it is, so don't get any ideas.* Or, *I want you, but it's just not on at the moment.* Or even a bit of both. *I want you, but I'm not sure whether it's any more than that, and in the circumstances I'm not that bothered about finding out.*

By the time their coffee arrived, the strain of keeping up airy smiles and chat was a nightmare. When he suggested a liqueur, she shook her head. 'I'm ready for bed. I didn't sleep very well last night.'

'You slept this afternoon,' he pointed out.

'I'm still tired,' she fibbed.

Anoushka gave a large yawn, covering it belatedly with her hand. 'I'm shattered too.' She glanced up at Guy. 'Do you mind if I go up now?'

'I'll come with you,' said Claudia, a little too quickly.

'If you'll both wait one minute till I've signed the bill,' he said patiently, 'we can go up together.'

Until they were in the lift, she avoided his eye. She asked Anoushka whether she'd got much more schoolwork, or whether she was going to concentrate on a tan to make all her friends sick when she got home.

'I haven't got much more to do, only a bit of biology.' They were in the lift now, and hesitantly she looked up at her father. 'Sammy asked me to ring him and said we'd go out somewhere before I leave. Only I said you'd never let me because I was grounded so there wasn't any point asking.'

Metaphorically Claudia held her breath and glanced up at him. Which way would he go?

For a second his eyes said, *Don't worry, I'm not going to screw it all up now*. 'He seemed a nice enough lad. And since you got an A minus for your history essay, maybe we can forget about grounding.'

The look on Anoushka's face said clearly enough that she'd never expected this and had hardly thought it worth asking. There was no effusive show, however, no flinging of arms around necks. 'Thanks, Dad,' she mumbled awkwardly as they got out of the lift. 'I felt awful for him when he brought me back the other day. He was asking how big you were and whether you might hit him.'

As they stopped outside Anoushka's door, Guy's mouth gave a wry twitch. 'What did you say?'

'I said you weren't into violence, but you did a good line in tongue-lashing,' she confessed. 'He was expecting somebody really *old* – at least fifty – so when I said you were only thirty-seven and six foot two he was dead scared. He pretended he wasn't, but I could tell.'

'But you weren't,' he said.

She looked at the floor. 'I was,' she mumbled. 'I was having kittens. Even if . . .'

The self-reproach on Guy's face made Claudia's throat constrict. *Leave them. They need to say their goodnights alone.* 'Night, everybody,' she said brightly. 'See you tomorrow.'

Once she'd shut her door, the room began to feel like a prison cell. It was only ten o'clock, and after her siesta she knew she'd never sleep till at least midnight. Not that she'd sleep anyway, with so many uncomfortable thoughts in her head.

To take her mind off it, she gave herself a pedicure, quite unnecessarily since she'd done one just before leaving London. She spent a good hour smoothing and emery-boarding, till her feet could have graced a back page of *Vogue*.

By the time the second coat of polish was dry, she was beginning to feel tired enough to go to bed. She had just taken her make-up off when the phone rang.

Even before she picked it up, she knew it was him.

'Did I wake you?' he asked, very quietly.

'I haven't even gone to bed yet.'

'Neither have I.'

In the pause that followed, her Lurch organ stirred violently.

And very prematurely.

'I need to talk to you,' he said. 'I'll be there in two minutes.'

As she put the phone down, Claudia felt sick. In those few seconds between his first and second utterances, wildly conflicting emotions had gone through her head. Longing to see him. Tingling anticipation of what would happen when they were alone together again. And perversely . . .

You thought he was just coming for another session of what you couldn't have last night, on the beach. You thought he was just waiting till he thought Anoushka was safely asleep. You thought he knew you were just sitting here, languishing after him, and thought he might as well make the most of it. And you didn't like it.

But he hadn't been thinking any such things. She knew exactly what he wanted to talk about.

At least he had given her time to prepare herself. Time to put on a good face and pretend that sick seed of misery in her stomach wasn't there at all.

You know what Kate says. When you know he's about to dump you, dump him first.

I don't know any such thing. If anybody's going to burn boats, it's not going to be me.

Until she opened the door, she was praying she'd got it wrong.

'I'm sorry,' he said, his eyes flickering over the towelling robe and bare feet. 'Were you just going to bed?'

The apology in his tone underlined all her fears. *Act like mad. Smile.* 'I was just pottering. Come in.'

'If you'd stayed for a liqueur, we could have talked then,' he went on. 'We could go down to the bar now, but –'

'I'm not dressed. Never mind.'

How she forced such brightness into her tone she would never know. She knew exactly what he was going to say. The apologetic regret in his voice said it. His eyes said it. His entire body language said it.

They sat exactly where they had sat the night Anoushka had disappeared, in the twin armchairs.

'I know what you're going to say,' she said, in brisk,

practical tones that could have won her an Oscar. 'You're going to tell me you're not in a position to embark on a relationship.'

Please, God, let him deny it.

He didn't. A small, slow, smile touched his lips and it was no consolation to see the relief on his face at least partly tinged by regret. 'It's not a good time,' he said gently.

Oh, God, I want to die. 'I can see that. Anoushka's going to need all your attention for a bit.' Hastily she went on, 'But don't feel you have to apologize. I think you're really nice and all that, but it's no use pretending it was any more than a lovely, wild little fling. You were stressed out of your mind, and I just got carried away.'

Please, God, let him say, It wasn't just a lovely wild fling to me.

He smiled again, a small, slow, warm smile that made her want to die. 'You are the most extraordinarily honest woman I have ever met.'

If only you knew.

He paused. 'Anoushka said something about an Australian.'

Oh, God, I knew it. Tell him now. Before the last bit of boat is burnt for ever.

But while she hesitated, he went on, 'I know the feeling. I was involved with somebody in the spring, but she was posted to Singapore and I haven't see her since.'

Not in her worst nightmares had she imagined this. 'But you will see her again?'

He shook his head. 'I read enough between the lines a few months ago to realize she wanted to call it a day.'

She must be mad.

'She didn't say as much, but I could tell,' he went on. 'I gradually stopped phoning. Relationships hardly ever work at a distance, and it would probably never have worked anyway. Anoushka didn't like her much and I have to say that though Simone tried, she was always making an effort.'

But you're still languishing. Like I was over Adam, until you came along.

Or was I? Suddenly she began to wonder. Had she really been suffering all those months, even after the first pain had worn off? Or had she just been clinging to loss like a comfortable habit?

'Well, then.' She crossed her legs and put on a smile that would have fooled anybody. 'Looks like we're in the same boat. Is she French, with a name like that?'

He nodded. 'She works for an investment bank.'

She couldn't resist torturing herself. 'And there hasn't been anybody since?'

'No.' For the first time since she'd met him, a faintly awkward expression crossed his face. 'But I wouldn't want you to think . . .'

She put on the performance of her life. 'That you were just *using* me for *sex*?' she said, in mock-aghast tones. 'Lud, fetch the smelling salts. I declare I feel quite faint.'

The warm glint that came into his eyes made her heart turn over, and the way his mouth twitched in that little half-smile gave her a physical pain. If he didn't get out soon . . .

'You made me laugh,' he said gently. 'And it's a hell of a long time since I had anything to laugh about.'

I can't bear this much longer. I'm going to crack and make a fool of myself. At least let me do this with some sort of dignity.

'Well, I'm glad I earned my money.' Covering a forced yawn with her hand, she rose to her feet. 'I hate to be unsociable, but I've got to throw you out before I fall asleep.' She took his hand and pretended to pull him to his feet.

Even then he didn't go.

'I've never met anyone quite like you,' he said, touching a finger to her cheek. 'You're a one-off.'

Oh, God, please don't do that. 'Just as well,' she said brightly. 'Now, will you please let me get my beauty sleep? Otherwise . . .' She put on a mock-wicked whisper. 'Otherwise I might get carried away again and think about using *you* for sex.

The second it was out, she knew she'd gone too far – as usual. The glint faded from his eyes and a shadow replaced it. If he wasn't thinking *Many a true word spoken in jest* it was something very like it. But it wasn't her he was thinking of.

'I wasn't using you.' He said it very gently. 'I like you a lot.'

Great. 'You're not so bad yourself,' she said brightly. 'And if I don't get a chance to say it later, I do hope it all goes well with Anoushka.'

'It's not going to be easy, but we'll take it one day at a time.'

'You'll be fine, if you just give her all you've got for a few months. She must have been feeling very insecure.'

'I know. But I'd never have found out why if not for you.'

327

'Oh, rubbish. She'd have blurted it out in a row about something, you can bet. You'd have sorted it all out without me.'

'Would I?' Before she knew what had hit her, he'd brushed her lips with his own. 'I owe you one.'

Was he torturing her on purpose?

'Oh, rubbish.' As he turned to go, words tumbled out in a rush. 'Guy, you don't really need me here any more. Wouldn't it be better for both of you if I changed my ticket and left a bit early?'

He turned back, his eyes flickering over her face. 'Are you in a hurry to get away?'

'Not particularly, but . . .'

'Then I'd rather you stayed. I was planning to leave the day after tomorrow anyway and I'm going to be very tied up till then. Anoushka will need some company.'

'Then I'll work on my tan,' she said.

'Don't work too hard.' His eyes travelled over her face and neck to the pale gold legs appearing beneath her robe. 'You can over-gild the lily.' With a little pat on her waist, he left her.

It was ages since she'd indulged in the kind of thoroughly self-indulgent cry that makes your face all blotchy and hideous, but she made up for it now.

If only he'd behaved like the classic, double-standards male who thought it perfectly all right for him to have a fling, but not the other way around! If he'd been angry, even called her a slut, she could have despised him and then it would have been so much easier.

It was no surprise when Immac's crotchety old voice drifted through her misery. '*I warned you, right enough, but*

328

would you listen? You came for the wrong reasons, and now look at you.'

What would you know about it? When did you ever feel what I felt?

'*You should have exercised self-control. A man will always take what's offered. It's in his nature. But never mind that now. Maybe some good has come of it all. His daughter needs him more than you, no matter what you may be feeling now. Let that be your comfort.'*

What comfort? I'm not one of your self-sacrificing, pain-in-the-neck saints!

She almost heard an outraged sniff. '*And what have you sacrificed? Did he ever say you were more to him than a passing fancy? He did not. He likes you, right enough, but that is all.'*

Oh, shove off! You just love saying I told you so, don't you?

She almost heard another outraged sniff, a swishing habit, and then the shadow of Sister Immaculata was gone.

The last days were torture. Fearing she would give herself away, she avoided Guy as much as possible. She worked on her tan and her water ski-ing, wrote long letters to friends and swam endlessly. If nothing else she'd go back more toned than she had been in ages.

On her last morning she took a taxi to the old city of Muscat. The driver was cheerful and chatty and a good guide. He showed her the palace overlooking the sea, the twin forts of Jalali and Mirani that guarded it. Stark rocks rose from a sea as blue as the sky, forming a natural harbour.

She gazed out over the harbour wall, with the driver cheerfully puffing a cigarette beside her. 'There also British Embassy,' he said, pointing. 'British very much friends from Sultan Qaboos and Omani peoples.'

'I hope so,' she smiled.

She gazed out over the sea, thinking how different the world would look tomorrow. Grey, wintry, miserable streets, no doubt, and a grey, wintry, miserable heart to go with them.

The driver's walnut-brown brow creased under a dazzlingly white headdress. 'Sister, you look too much sad.'

How she did not dissolve there and then, Claudia would never know. Forcing a smile, she said, 'That's because I'm leaving tonight. Your country is beautiful and I'm very sad to go.'

'Then you come back, *insha'allah*.'

'Yes,' she said. '*Insha'allah*.'

The flight was tedious in the way only a long night flight can be, but it could have been worse. If they'd been crammed into Economy she might have had to endure sitting next to him, his arm brushing against her, his scent tormenting her, even his hair brushing her cheek as he slept.

He was sleeping now, just across the aisle, his face turned towards her. She could not sleep, and it was impossible to keep her eyes away.

She thought of him sleeping beside her after they'd made love. She remembered the feel of him, skin-to-skin against her, his arm around her. She remembered how delicately she'd run her fingers over his chest, trying not to wake him. She remembered the way his arm had tightened around her in his sleep, how she'd dared herself to touch his other sleeping bits and how his chest had shaken as he'd laughed.

Tears filled her eyes. She stole to the loo to recover, but not before an eagle-eyed stewardess had seen her. 'Are you all right?'

'Fine,' Claudia sniffed, with a forced smile. 'I think I'm allergic to something.'

'I've got some anti-histamine, if you want.'

If only a dose of anti-histamine could cure me. 'I'll be fine – thanks anyway.'

By the time they reached Baggage Reclaim, she was like a vertical corpse. And for the first time in her life, her suitcase was one of the first to appear.

'Let me.' With firm hands on her waist, Guy moved her aside and yanked it off.

Now it was the parting of the ways, she just wanted to get it over. 'I'll grab a taxi and go.'

With his hand still on her waist, he steered her out of the crush. 'Wait, and we'll drop you off.'

'It's out of your way. I'd rather go now.' Her voice was bright and taut with the strain of trying to conceal her feelings.

His eyes seemed troubled. 'You haven't said goodbye to Anoushka.'

She glanced over her shoulder. Anoushka had disappeared to the ladies'. 'You say it for me. I'm sure she's dying to see the back of her "minder". I'm really going to pass out if I don't get home soon.'

It was no lie, as he could see only too well. 'I'm not sure you'll make it even through Customs.'

Never in her life had she been so desperate to get away, and so desperate to stay. 'I'll be fine.'

His eyes were still troubled. 'If you must . . .' From the breast pocket of his jacket he drew a folded cheque. 'I've made a small adjustment,' he said. 'You more than earned it.'

As she unfolded it, Claudia gasped. 'Guy, I can't take this!'

His mouth lifted in the that havoc-wreaking half-smile. 'I'm not going to argue the toss about it, so don't give me any trouble.'

For the first time in days she remembered why she had come in the first place. She thought of the pale little faces at Bruin Wood, of the children who had never really realized that eggs came from chickens, or even that butterflies came from caterpillars. She threw her arms around his neck, a massive lump pricking her throat. 'Thank you, Guy. I promise you, it won't be wasted.'

'I know.' His arms came around her in return, and for a few heart-stopping moments he held her close.

It was soon over. He crisped up like an iceberg lettuce. 'Off you go, before you really do pass out.' He added a little pat on her bottom, like a full-stop. 'Thanks for everything. Take care.'

'You too.'

She didn't look back. Steering her trolley towards Customs, she could hardly see for tears. And just as she was nearly there, Anoushka grabbed her arm.

'Why didn't you wait?' As she saw Claudia's face, her expression changed dramatically. 'What's wrong?'

Wiping her eyes with trembling fingers, she managed a smile. 'Blame your father. He's been over-generous and

332

I'm a bit overcome. Anoushka, I'm so sorry, but I've got to go. I'm so tired I could die.'

She gave the startled girl a quick, tight hug. 'He needs you too. Look after him.' Without looking back, she almost ran to Customs.

The streets were not grey after all, but bathed in the crisp, brilliant sunshine you only get in winter. She composed herself in the taxi. It was still early, and Kate might not be awake yet.

The television was on when she opened the door, and Kate charged up, still in her nightie. 'You brown cow! Go away!'

'That's nice, I must say.' Now she was actually home, acting wasn't so hard. 'I suppose you're lazing about, just for a change.'

'I am not! I've got the dreaded lurgy, so don't come near me. Tonsillitis, to be precise. I had a temperature of a hundred and one yesterday.'

Although she'd wanted to be alone, to be miserable in peace, Claudia couldn't help being glad to see Kate.

Within five minutes they were flopped in front of children's television with toast and coffee.

Portly was not so pleased to see her. Still walking stiffly with a bandaged leg, he gazed at her disdainfully and turned a huffy back.

'He's put out because you weren't here in his hour of need,' Kate said.

'He's always like this when I've been away. Sulks for a day and a half and then comes for a kiss and make up.'

For half an hour, she told Kate about the hotel, the dolphins, the sharks and turtles, but left out other things.

Kate threw in the odd, 'Crumbs, what a nightmare!' and after the overseas news was over, gave her the home news. Peter the Pain actually had a *girlfriend*.

'He's never stopped smirking,' she said, making a face. 'She's not bad-looking, so heaven knows what she sees in him. Maybe she actually likes sweaty gropes.'

Suddenly changing tack, she went on, 'I hope you don't mind, but Paul's moved in. Properly, I mean.'

'Why? He's got his own flat!'

'I know, but . . .' Kate looked distinctly awkward. 'He put it on the market a couple of weeks ago, and we thought it'd take ages to sell, but a cash buyer turned up and everything went so fast . . . He's put all his stuff in storage.'

Claudia still didn't get it. 'It was a gorgeous flat! Why sell it?'

Kate shifted uncomfortably in her seat. 'The thing is, we're thinking of buying a place together. A house. And we thought it'd be easier if he sold his first, so we wouldn't get stuck in a chain. You don't mind him moving in, do you?'

'Of course not! I like him!'

'We won't be buying anything right away,' Kate went on hastily. 'I'll give you plenty of notice and everything. We want to take our time.'

It was quite daft, but Claudia felt as if her best friend was kicking her while she was down, and rubbing salt in her wounds too.

Kate gone. The thought filled her with such desolation it was a while before a more obvious thought hit her. 'If you're buying a place together, are you thinking of . . .?'

'It had crossed our minds,' Kate said sheepishly. 'Only not just yet, and no massive do. You know what my mother's like. She'd want St Paul's and at least fifty million relations. We're going to slope off to Jamaica or somewhere and get hitched on the beach with just a couple of friends. Will you be my best woman?'

'Oh, Kate. Just try to stop me.' Germs or no, she went and gave her a massive hug. 'Paul's so nice. I'm really happy for you.'

'I'm happy for me too,' Kate admitted.

It was easy then to let her eyes leak a bit without causing suspicion. Kate even joined in. 'We must be getting old,' she giggled, wiping her eyes. 'Getting all weepy and sentimental.'

If only it were just you making me weepy.

In the end she was glad of the do at Auntie Barbara's, even if Ryan had to be there. It took her mind off the aching pain inside her and it was lovely to see her parents, even if merely driving to Heathrow to pick them up touched still-gaping wounds.

Margaret Maitland wasn't even out of the airport before her eagle eye got into gear. 'You're looking a bit peaky, dear,' she said, as Claudia fed the car park machine. 'Maybe you need some vitamins.'

All I need is vitamin G. 'Mum, how can you say that? I'm brown as anything!'

'You can be brown and peaky, dear. You go a sort of pasty grey underneath.'

'Stop fussing, Mag,' said her father placidly. 'She looks fine to me.'

'I dare say she does, Richard. Men never notice these things.'

Her parents were far from peaky. Her mother looked nothing like her age. Her hair was much the same colour as her daughter's, and although it had faded it had never gone grey, and since she never lay in the sun she'd never got really lined. Her father was bronzed and fit from charging round the golf course every day.

Claudia headed for the M25, since they were going straight to Dorset. It was still sunny and crisp, the trees starkly black against a blue sky. Her mother sat in the front and did most of the talking. 'I thought you were thinking of changing your car, dear. Isn't this getting a bit past it?'

'Not really. It's only done forty-five thousand miles.'

'Still, a new one'd be nice. Maybe when you start your new job.'

'I might.' She intended to. Something shiny and nippy, with that lovely new-car smell.

'Ryan's got a lovely new car, Barbara told me.'

Oh, Lord. Here we go.

'It's not new,' said her father from the back seat. 'It's a third-hand Mercedes Sports and the young idiot'll very likely wrap it round a lamppost before he's much older.'

Thank you, Dad.

'I meant new for *him*, dear. He's very pleased with it anyway. Barbara was so glad he didn't blow too much of old Flora's legacy on something brand-new.'

'Maybe he's showing some sense at last,' said her father. 'And not before time.'

Claudia cursed as a boy racer idiot came right up behind her and flashed his lights. The centre lane was packed and there was no way she could move over.

'How lovely for Ryan, though, when she left him all that money,' her mother went on. 'Fifty-fifty between him and his father – not that Ted and Barbara need it. Ted was about the only relation Flora had got. She must have been ninety, and always very *peculiar*, according to Barbara. Too nervous to travel down, and they couldn't get up to see her very often. So, of course, when Ted got such a wandery letter from her, and Ryan was going to Scotland for a motor rally or something, they asked him to pop in and check on her.'

The boy racer flashed again, and came within about three feet of her back bumper. 'What is that prat *doing*?' Claudia muttered. 'Can't he see I can't pull over?' When a space appeared at last, the prat zoomed past. She mouthed 'Idiot!' as he went, and he stuck two fingers up.

Her father murmured something, but her mother's mind was elsewhere. 'It was right out of Ryan's way, so it was very kind of him to make the effort. Ryan mightn't be the most sensible boy in the world, but his heart's in the right place.'

A little further on, the prat was driving right up somebody else's backside. Such driving always made Claudia tense to the point of violence. 'Mother, Ryan is about as kind as Attila the Hun. He only went to see the poor old thing because he thought he'd get something out of it.'

'Of course he didn't, dear.'

'What d'you mean, *of course he didn't*? He bragged to me about it! He used to write her awful sucking-up letters just so she'd send him postal orders!'

'Old people appreciate letters, dear. Granny used to appreciate your letters very much. And I don't know what he told you, but you must have got the wrong end of the stick somewhere. They didn't even know old Flora had any money. She was one of those funny old dears who wore the same coat for fifty years – and her house was in a terrible state. No heating, not even a proper bathroom. They thought she was as poor as a church mouse. Ted sent her cheques now and then, but she never paid them in and they thought she was just too proud to accept them. And all along she'd been sitting on a tidy little nest-egg that she hadn't touched since the war.'

Claudia's Ryan-cynicism was too entrenched to be shifted. 'They must have known.'

'They didn't,' her father put in. 'Ted was dumb-founded, especially after Ryan had been there. He said the house wasn't fit to live in. All the lightbulbs had gone and she was too nervous to replace them. She wouldn't have anybody in to do anything because she was too nervous to answer the door. He spent four days there, tidying up and fixing things and putting a chain and a peephole on the door. I know what you mean about Ryan, love, but I have to say he was very good to the old girl.'

All the way to Dorset Claudia still refused to believe it. Ryan, human? It wasn't possible.

The old stone hotel where she'd spent so many holidays was not far from the sea – a pretty, chocolate-boxy place with twenty bedrooms. It had an up-market feel she'd never been conscious of before, maybe because of the restaurant, which had recently become her aunt's pride and joy. It had made a name for itself locally had even won glowing write-ups in the Sunday papers.

The car park was bigger too. She parked next to a silver Mercedes Sports with the numberplate RY 101.

Should be TOAD 101, she thought automatically, but bit it back.

Belinda was the next shock. She had expected some giggling bimbo with a massive cleavage on show, but the girl who smiled at her had smooth fair hair and a loose navy jumper covering her obvious curves.

Far too good for Ryan.

He was just the same, except that he'd cut his hair a bit. It was a bright blue jacket this time, loud enough to make her father shudder.

Many times during the evening she looked at Ryan and wondered whether she could really have got it so wrong. After dinner, while they were all having coffee in the private sitting room and Belinda was reading a magazine, he ambled up, eyeing her tan. 'Was it really a Middle East sales trip?'

'No. That was just what I told Mum.'

'What, then?' He grinned. 'A temporary posting to some randy old sod's harem?'

'Don't be ridiculous. It was quite on the level. I got the money, anyway.'

'Oh, yeah, the dosh. I was meaning to have a word with you about that.' From his inside pocket he took a cheque. 'I never paid you for those two kissograms and your sterling efforts in the office.'

'Do you think I'd forgotten? I wasn't going to let you get away with it. And it had better be the going rate, whatever that – '

Her voice broke off as she actually looked at the cheque. 'Ryan, if this is a joke . . .'

He was grinning fit to split. 'It was all a joke, Claud. The bet was a joke. I was just winding you up. I'd have given you something anyway.'

'*What*?'

'I'd have given you a cheque there and then if you hadn't risen to the bait and done your usual spark-and-twitch bit. You're so easy to wind up, you should have a key in your back.'

Her colour drained away. Had she been through all that, just because this . . . this *moron* couldn't resist a joke? Had she nearly been sick with nerves before those two kissograms, fantasized over Guy, died a million deaths thinking he was about to be torn apart by sharks, made ecstatic love with him and suffered agonies ever since, just because this grinning ape had been winding her *up*?

With everybody else in the room, a *sotto voce* hiss was all she dared produce. 'You little *toad*,' she said in a biting whisper. 'I could kill you. I hope your bloody Mercedes falls to bits, with you in it. I hope Belinda does a Bobbit and chops your willy off. I hope she chucks it in the street and a ten-ton truck runs it over before you find it!'

CHAPTER 17

She could hardly storm out and slam the door. She said, 'Night, everybody,' and smiled apologetically when her aunt said, 'Going up already?' She managed another smile when her uncle made a crack about the younger generation having no stamina, and escaped.

Room five at Weeping Ash Inn was half the size of her Muscat room but just as comfortable, in a rose-sprigged, English way.

Bloody Ryan! If only I could go home now!

It was out of the question. The do proper wasn't until the following night, and she'd never, ever be forgiven.

Twenty minutes after she'd gone up, there was a tap at the door. 'Claud, are you asleep?'

'Yes, so shove off.'

He rattled the door anyway. 'Claud, let me in.'

'Bugger off!'

'If you don't let me in, I'll go and get a pass key.' He sounded positively injured. 'I have every right to know why you want me willyless after I just gave you a sodding great cheque.'

'I've earned a sodding great cheque, after what you put me through. Now get lost!'

The old, mischievous note entered his voice. 'If you don't let me in, I'll go and tell your mum it wasn't a sales trip. I'll tell her you met some dirty old git in a London club who paid you a fortune to give him intimate massage for a week.

'And that was a wind-up too,' he grinned, when she finally opened the door. He held up a bottle of cognac. 'The old man's best. How about a truce?'

She hadn't the energy even to swear at him any more. The tears she'd been fighting ever since coming back from Muscat were winning at last.

'Christ, it's not that bad, is it?' he said.

'Worse,' she gulped, sinking to the chintzy bed.

He went to the bathroom for glasses and poured a couple of hefty shots. 'Get some of that down.'

It wasn't just the brandy that finally loosened her tongue. She needed to talk to someone so badly, even if Ryan was the last person she'd have chosen.

Through sniffs and eye-wipings, she explained. 'I didn't want to dissolve,' she gulped finally. 'What if Mum comes up?'

'She won't. They've started a rubber of bridge.'

'Won't Belinda wonder where you are?'

'She's nodded off by the fire.' For the first time since she could remember, he looked really awkward. 'I'm sorry, Claud. I thought it was all just a laugh.'

However angry she'd been before, it was quite illogical to blame him. 'It wasn't your fault.'

He refilled her glass. 'Did you sleep with him?'

She was past telling him to mind his own business. 'Only once, but I've never felt such electricity with anyone. I hope to God it was just lust, because I can't get him out of my mind.'

'You've only been back a week. I was once lusting after some girl I met in Tenerife for at least a fortnight. Can't even remember her name now.'

'You wouldn't.' She blew her nose noisily. 'Anyway, he's still languishing after that Simone cow. I know he is.'

'Sounds like it. And if he hadn't had his end away for months . . .'

'Oh, Ryan. You make it sound so sordid.'

'Just realistic, Claud.' Rather awkwardly, he put an arm round her shoulders. 'It'll wear off. Plenty more useless bastards in the sea and all that.'

It was very cold comfort. She gazed at her brandy, wondering vaguely how on earth she had come to talk to Ryan as if he were actually a normal human being.

Maybe because he is.

'Why did you wind me up like that about old Flora?'

'Couldn't resist it,' he grinned. 'If I'd told you I'd bashed her on the head and nicked the money from under her mattress you'd have believed it.'

'I never thought you were quite that bad,' she sniffed. 'A total pain, maybe, but not a murderer.'

'I'd better go,' he said. 'Just in case Belinda wakes up and thinks I've sloped off with that tasty new waitress.'

They had eaten in the hotel restaurant and the girl had given Ryan the eye more than once. 'Push off, then. You don't want her getting the wrong idea.'

'OK, I'll push.' He yawned and stretched. 'Can you believe Ma's actually given us a room with a double bed? I was gobsmacked. I thought she'd put me in my old attic

343

room for the sake of form. Let's just hope the bed doesn't creak too much.'

He didn't change. 'Keep the noise down if you're anywhere near me.'

'We'll be as quiet as copulating mice,' he grinned.

With the help of a temporary job from an agency, the days until Christmas passed more quickly than Claudia had expected. But Guy did not 'wear off'. The ache was still there, catching her at odd moments: in a traffic jam, when she heard some poignant piece of music, when she saw a pair of lovers holding hands in the street, or even in the supermarket. Many times she fought off the longing to drive past the Kensington house.

Knowing her luck, she'd see him getting into the car with another woman and wish she were dead.

As Christmas approached she agonized over a card. In the end she sent a Bruin Wood one. It wasn't very Christmassy; it showed some of the children who'd stayed a couple of years before, laughing at the camera as they sat on New Forest ponies in the sun.

It had to be addressed to both him and Anoushka, but she agonized again over what to put inside. In the end she just wrote, 'Love, Claudia'. And the very next day she got one in return. It was a charity card, for an animal charity. She guessed it had been chosen by Anoushka; it had certainly been written by her. It said, 'Lots of love, Anoushka and Guy', with two kisses. At least she knew they hadn't waited to get hers before sending their own.

Of such tiny crumbs was her comfort made.

She took the ache to Spain with her for Christmas, and spent five days covering it up; laughing and doing silly dances at the parties her parents took her to. She even flirted with a Spanish barman, just in case her mother's sixth sense was picking up any vibes.

She started her new job on the second of January, and although she loved it and had little time to think of anything else, the ache was still there.

By the end of March she'd made sales trips over much of Europe. But the ache was still there. She'd been out twice in a foursome with Kate and Paul and a friend of his with lovely eyes who'd made her laugh. But the ache was still there. She'd had dinner with a silken-tongued Italian in Florence; a Category Four who a few months ago would have made her wooze for England.

But the ache was still there.

One weekend just before Easter, when Bruin Wood was sprucing itself up for the season, she took herself off on a Saturday morning to help with the sprucing.

She wasn't really up to it; she was just getting over a stinking cold she'd picked up after sitting next to some sneezing wreck on a plane. Her nose and eyes were a trifle red, and she looked washed out, but Bruin Wood was desperate for unpaid help. All the necessary repairs had been done; it was just a case of painting and cleaning up.

The daffodils were late after a cold winter; they were still nodding fresh heads in the garden as she slapped primrose-yellow on the dining room wall. A few drops were slapping on her overalls too, but since they were only fit for the bin, she didn't care. Her hair was covered with a scarf, there were smudges of paint on her face – but who was going to see her?

With a radio playing corny old songs, she felt almost peaceful, up a ladder sloshing emulsion. When she heard someone come in over the dust-sheeted floor, she didn't even look round. 'I'll have a coffee, Julie, if you're making.'

'It's me.'

She nearly fell off the ladder. 'Anoushka! what on earth are you doing here?'

'Passing, really. We're going for lunch at some friends of Dad's and we thought we'd pop in. We never thought you'd be here, though.'

'How on earth did you know where to come?'

'It said on your Christmas card.'

So it had.

Her insides were swimming wildly. 'Well, it's a lovely surprise,' she said unsteadily. 'How are you?'

Anoushka looked as bright as a girl that age should look. 'Fine. How are you?'

'Getting over a filthy cold, so I won't kiss you. Everything OK?'

'Fine, except for that awful school. I'm leaving in the summer and going to a sixth form college instead. Dad thinks it'll suit me better. Not so many petty rules.'

Claudia she wondered what was so different about her, and decided it was her eyes. There had been a wariness in them before that she hadn't really noticed till it was gone. 'How are you getting on with him? Better?'

'We still have the odd argument, but who doesn't? He can be quite good fun sometimes. Most of my friends' dads are such boring old farts.'

346

Her stomach was suddenly full of squirming, panicky worms. *If he catches me like this, I'll die. I must at least dash for the loo and get this paint off my face, put on a bit of lip-gloss . . .*

You didn't bring any. You haven't even got anything to hide the rings under your eyes. 'Where is he?'

'Nattering to the person who let us in. Julie, I think her name is.'

Julie ran the centre. Once she knew who Guy was, and connected him with that cheque, she'd be showing him everything and thanking him for ever. If he got away inside twenty minutes, it'd be a miracle.

'How is he?' she asked brightly.

'Oh, fine. Working too hard, of course. Still, I suppose it takes his mind off other things.' With a glance over her shoulder, she lowered her voice conspiratorially 'Between you and me, I think he's languishing over some wretched woman.'

She felt sick. *That Simone cow. I hate her.* 'I know the feeling.'

'Your hunky Aussie?'

She couldn't lie any more. At least, not completely. 'He's died the death, but I remember how it felt.' She couldn't resist torturing herself. 'Have you met her?'

'Oh, yes, but ages ago. She wasn't bad. Quite attractive, if you like that sort of thing.'

With a frown, Anoushka glanced over her shoulder. 'Where *is* he? He said we couldn't stay long; we were due at Mike and Jenny's at half-twelve and I'm starving. Hold on, I'm just going to find him.'

As she darted off, Claudia panicked all over again. She waited ten seconds, and then nipped next door, where another volunteer was painting the ceiling. 'Steve, I feel really dreadful – I think it's paint fumes on top of this cold. I've got to go home. Will you clear up my paint and stuff? I've nearly finished that wall.'

He frowned at her from the ladder. 'Are you all right to drive?'

'Fine. I'll be back tomorrow if I feel better. Tell Julie I'm really sorry.'

She was out in seconds and into the shiny new Peugeot she'd indulged in. Parked right next to it was a Range Rover, just like the one they'd used in Muscat, but black.

With tears spilling onto her cheeks, she accelerated over the gravel drive and escaped.

You fool. Couldn't you have stayed, just to see him? Acted your brains out?

Like this? She glanced at her face in the rear view mirror. *With a red nose and paint on my face? Dressed like a sack of manky old King Edwards?*

It was the first sunny day for ages, and the world and his wife and kids were out. It took her ages to get home. Kate and Paul were out, househunting, and only Portly was there, running up to her with his funny little welcome-home mew.

She picked him up and buried her face in his fur. 'Oh, Portly. What am I going to do?'

He mewed again – the mew that meant, *Get into the kitchen, woman, and feed me.*

After ladling cod n' liver into a saucer, she ran a bath, lay in peach-flavoured foam, and dropped salty tears into it. *What will everybody think of me, rushing off like that? What will he think? He's not stupid. If he didn't know before, he will now.*

There was a message on the answering machine from Kate to say they were going to Paul's parents in Brighton and would stay there to eat.

Maybe just as well. If Kate had been there she'd have told her everything and had to endure sympathy as well as everything else.

She went to bed at eight-thirty with Portly, and watched the little TV that sat on her chest of drawers. And like that, with Portly nestled between her neck and her shoulder, she fell asleep.

She wasn't quite sure what woke her, but something did, some sixth sense prickling the hairs on her arms.

Somebody was in the flat.

She sat up slowly, picked up the TV remote control, turned the volume down a fraction and strained to listen.

It was unmistakable. Somebody was opening a door very quietly. Kate's door.

Adrenalin shot through her. She tiptoed from the bed, opened her wardrobe door and took out a tennis racket. It wasn't much of a weapon, but better than nothing. Clutching it tight, hardly daring to breathe, she waited behind the bedroom door. There was no bolt. There had been, but it was broken.

Her mouth dry as desert dust, she watched the door handle. It was going to be just like a horror film. Very slowly it was going to turn, and then . . .

The soft tap shook her rigid. The soft voice shook her even more. 'Claudia?'

'*Guy?*' Half rigid with shock, she yanked the door open.

His mouth gave a wry twitch. 'Your locks are hopeless.' He held up a credit card. 'A little trick I learnt in my misspent youth.'

It was all too much, and she cracked. 'Bastard! I thought I was going to be murdered in my bed!' She lifted the tennis racket but he caught her arm in mid-swipe, and as he folded her in his arms she burst into tears.

For half a minute she cried a river onto his shirt while he held her close, stroking her hair. When she'd recovered a little, he led her to the bed, where they sat. 'I rang the bell and you didn't answer,' he explained. 'I phoned three times from my mobile, and you still didn't answer.'

'I was asleep,' she sniffed. 'With the television on.'

'I thought you might be ill. Wasn't that why you left Bruin Wood?'

She couldn't look him in the eye, but he made her. Lifting her chin, he turned her face towards him. 'Or were you charging off again?'

He knows the answer to that one. He knows rather a lot of things he didn't know before.

'It was all a load of codwash, wasn't it?' he said. 'What you told me in Muscat?'

She nodded. 'I thought it was for the best. I still wasn't sure whether it was more than a massive buzz, and what with Anoushka and Simone and everything . . .'

Technically, the kiss he silenced her with wasn't the best kiss in the world. Since she was still suffering post-river gasps and shudders, they had to come up for air more often than usual, but, to Claudia, it was the kiss to end them all.

It wasn't very comfortable sitting on the edge of the bed, so as the kiss progressed they lay down.

Portly wasn't pleased at having a strange male head on his pillow; he stalked off in disgust.

'I wasn't sure either,' he said, brushing his lips against her hair. 'I wasn't sure how you felt, and since it wasn't a good time for me to start getting involved with anybody, I thought I'd let things lie and see if the buzz wore off. Only it just got worse. And as for Simone . . .'

He paused. 'It's a funny thing, but she started wearing off shortly after a nasty shock I suffered last November. I was out for dinner when a stroppy redhead barged in and accused me of fathering her child.'

She suppressed a giggle. 'What a nerve. I hope you slung her out.'

'I most certainly did, and she got even stroppier. She wasn't bad-looking, though. Lovely legs and eyes to die for. Trouble, in other words. And I had enough trouble just then, with my daughter.'

She felt warmly, woozily content. 'Anoushka looks so different. Happy.'

He chuckled. 'She wasn't after we found out you'd gone. She thought she'd shot her mouth off a bit too much and driven you away. We knew you'd be there. We'd never have called in otherwise.'

'How? Did you phone here this morning?'

He nodded. 'Your friend told me. I'd have a word with her, if I were you. I could have been anybody.'

She was probably in a hurry to get out. Late, as usual. 'You told Anoushka, didn't you?'

'I didn't have to. She knew.'

She started. '*What?*'

His arm tightened in a reassuring squeeze. 'Not everything. But she'd had a feeling. She's more perceptive than you might think. It was the odd little thing, and something you said at the airport. We were talking about the sharks the other night, and that led to you. You'd been on my mind all evening; I'd been about to ring you, so I must have shown something and she picked it up. She said, "Was there something between you two?" '

She propped herself on her elbow. 'What did you say?'

'I lied. I said no, but I liked you a lot, and she went quiet for a bit, and then she said, 'I think she likes you too.' She told me one or two things, and then she said, 'I think maybe she was pretending, because of me. Maybe she thought I'd put the kybosh on it.' We talked a bit more, and last night I rang you. Only you weren't in.'

She'd been at an Italian evening class. 'Kate never told me!'

'It wasn't Kate – unless she's got a hell of a deep voice.'

'Paul.' He'd have forgotten. They'd gone out and she'd been in bed when they'd got back.

With a sigh, she snuggled closer. 'Why did you have to pick *today*? If I hadn't looked like something out of a horror film, I'd never have charged off.'

He drew back, looked down, and tipped her face up towards him. 'I have to say you look pretty rough. Maybe I should clear off and forget all about you.'

His mouth was twitching in the way that made her heart turn over, his eyes warm with whole power-stations of Aegaean blue. 'But you smell nice.'

'It's my fuzzy peach bath stuff,' she said unsteadily.

'Is it, now.' Like a whisper, he traced a finger down her cheek. 'Just as well I didn't break in a bit earlier and catch you in the bath. On the other hand . . .'

The kiss he gave her was like honeyed cognac, bathing her in fiery sweetness that grew like a forest fire, until she knew they were at the point of no return. Although it killed her, she gently pulled away. 'Guy, I lied to you before, about it being safe. It wasn't. It still isn't.'

For a moment he gazed at her. 'You are a very bad girl,' he said softly.

'I know. But I thought you'd stop and I couldn't bear it.' She hesitated. 'Would you have?'

'Probably.' He brushed his lips against her cheek. 'And suffered for hours, wishing to God I hadn't.'

He lay on his back and drew her close.

For a minute they lay still, and then she said, 'Are you hungry? I could make you something.'

'Are *you*?'

'Yes. I couldn't be bothered to make anything earlier.'

'In that case . . .' He sat up smartly, pulled her to her feet. 'Let's go out.'

'Like *this*?' She was appalled. 'With my face like nothing on earth?'

'Then we'll get a take-away.'

Half an hour later they were on their way back with steaming bags of tandoori, eating naan bread in the car. Suddenly he pulled in to a petrol station. 'I won't be long.'

A sudden, warm flush shot through her. He wasn't filling the car up. The petrol station sold everything.

But whatever was tucked in his pocket when he came back, the only thing in his hand was a packet of mints. 'Fancy a Polo?' he grinned. 'I did have some Opal Fruits, but I've eaten them all.'

She choked on her naan bread. 'Did you want to kill me?'

His grin faded to something else. 'No,' he said very softly. 'That wasn't what I wanted.'

Her Lurch organ went wild, but it wasn't quite like before. There was urgency, but not the fierce desperation she had felt before, and it would be all the better for waiting. All the way home, all the time they were eating, the warmth was stirring in her. When they'd finished and she'd tidied the mess away, and he'd tried to help and not known where anything went, he was waiting. Leaning up against the fridge in her minute kitchen, he took her in his arms.

'What about Anoushka?' she said unsteadily. 'Is she at home all alone?'

He shook his head. 'She's staying the weekend at Mike and Jenny's.'

It was the last little obstacle swept away. Without a word, he swept her into his arms and back to the room they'd left an hour and a half before.

'And this time,' he said very softly, 'you're going to be patient. You're going to see how much better it is when you wait.'

Her Lurch organ was going frantic. 'I don't see how it could be any better than last time.'

'Then it's high time you found out,' he murmured. 'Last time was fast food. This is going to be a five-course dinner.'

It was an awful long time till they reached the coffee-and-liqueurs stage. 'Don't go home tonight, will you?' she whispered, as they snuggled up under the duvet.

'Not unless you throw me out. I don't think your previous bed partner's too pleased, though,' he added.

'Poor Portly.' He had been most put out at being chucked off the bed again. He had retired to a little chair in the corner, watched the proceedings for two minutes with sniffy disdain, and gone to sleep.

He had now woken up again. 'I don't like the way he's looking at me,' Guy said darkly. 'I'm not going to wander about starkers. He looks quite capable of taking a malevolent swipe at any moving object.'

'As if he would!' she giggled.

'I wouldn't altogether blame the poor beast. First the vet's knife and then being kicked out of bed . . . It's enough to make anybody malevolent.'

'He'll love you soon enough if you bring him a cod in butter sauce next time you come.'

'I'll bring him some Harrods' smoked salmon if he'll stop looking at me like that.'

Portly stared a little longer before deciding it was high time his left back leg had a good wash.

For a while they lay quietly. 'I've had your photo in my bag all the time,' she whispered drowsily. 'The one Anoushka gave the office. I thought it was all I was ever going to have.'

'I didn't even have a photo. I had to make do with what was in my head.'

'You were in a DJ with half a blonde next to you,' she went on. 'I gave her the scissor treatment.'

His chest gave a little shake. 'If it's the photo I'm thinking of, it was only somebody's wife.'

'I thought I'd lost it once, and I nearly went crackers.' She gave a sigh that seemed to come from her toes. 'We've been a right pair of prats, haven't we?'

His mouth lifted in the little half-smile that made her heart turn over. 'Prize prats,' he murmured, brushing her cheek with his lips. 'But I needed that time with Anoushka. Maybe it was for the best.'

'I hope she likes me,' she said unsteadily.

His mouth twitched. 'Do you know what she said?'

'What?'

'She said, "For heaven's sake, Dad, if you like her, go for it. All your other women have been such pains in the bum." If that wasn't a blessing – '

'Shh!' She sat up sharply. 'The front door!'

Kate and Paul were back.

Her bedroom light was still on, and Kate would see it under the door. She knew exactly what would happen, and it did.

'Claudia? Are you awake?'

Guy touched a finger to her lips.

'She's asleep,' came the disappointed voice from the hall. 'Do you think she'd mind if I woke her up?'

'Kate, leave her. Come to bed.'

'I don't want *bed*!'

'I do. We're celebrating, remember?'

'Get *off*!' There were muffled giggles from the hall.

In a low, lusty growl, Paul launched into his 'randy-unspecified-foreigner' voice. 'Come to bed wiz me, O pearl of Putney wiz bosoms like ze pomegranate flower only beeger. I want make luff wiz you all night long. I want you keel me wiz luff and I die happy.'

Claudia stifled an explosive giggle, and Guy's chest was shaking like an earthquake.

'Get *off*!' Kate was giggling worse than ever. 'And get that rifle out of my back!'

'Eez no rifle, O fairest one. Eez keeng-size weapon of love, for take you to paradise.'

'Go *away*!' Kate giggled. 'I'm going to wake her up. I'm dying to tell her.'

And she pushed the door open.

Claudia would have given anything for a camera to capture her face. 'Hi, Kate,' she said brightly. 'This is Guy.'

Guy behaved with perfect aplomb. 'Hello, Kate. Forgive me if I don't get up.'

Over Kate's shoulder loomed the face of Paul, looking nearly as dumbstruck as his girlfriend.

'Hi, Paul,' Claudia said, through the explosions in her stomach. 'This is Guy.'

Paul recovered himself faster than Kate. 'Hello, mate. Nice to meet you.'

Kate was still gaping.

Paul tapped her on the shoulder. 'Wake up, dopey.' Reverting to his randy-foreigner voice, he whispered, 'I seenk zey want make jig-a-jig and go paradise.'

Claudia could no longer hold back her giggles. 'We've already been. What were you dying to tell me?'

For the first time since Claudia had known her, Kate was practically lost for words. 'We found a house,' she said faintly. 'And we booked our wedding in Bermuda.'

'It's Barbados,' Paul said. 'She's not quite with it.' With a wink towards the bed, he took Kate's arm. 'Come along, dear. Time for your Horlicks.'

They just heard the finale as he shut the door behind them. 'The sneaky cow! I'm going to kill her!'

CHAPTER 18

If you actually needed an excuse to come to Barbados, Claudia thought, as she collected two rum punches from the bar, *a wedding isn't a bad one*.

The tree frogs were just beginning to tune up as she padded back through the gardens to the beach. Guy was sitting in the sand, gazing out at the placid Caribbean, where the dying sun cast liquid gold on the water.

'If Kate gets through the next two days without murdering her mother, it'll be a miracle,' she said as she sat beside him. 'They've had another row. Kate simply cannot share a room with Paul the night before the wedding. It's bad luck. She's insisting that I move in with Kate and you move in with Paul for the night.'

'Fine,' he said absently.

Not for the first time in the past few days, she gave him a searching look. She'd thought she was imagining it at first, but it had steadily got more noticeable. It had started even before they'd got on the plane – a certain preoccupation, as if something were on his mind.

Hesitantly she asked, 'Guy, are you all right?'

He turned to her with what looked horribly like a forced smile. 'Fine. Why wouldn't I be?'

That's just what I'd like to know. 'I'm really glad you came,' she said, slipping her arm through his own. 'I know it wasn't very convenient, getting away from work at the last minute . . .'

'It wasn't exactly the last minute,' he said, tossing a green baby coconut towards the water. 'I booked the flight three weeks ago. There was plenty of time to delegate.'

What is it, then? She had been overjoyed when he'd said perhaps he could manage to get away after all. Kate had booked the wedding for the last week in July, and all the other guests had made their arrangements ages before.

Kate's mother had been very put out at being deprived of a big church wedding with fourteen bridesmaids and half a ton of flowers, but had come round soon enough when Kate had said of course her parents must come too. Paul's parents could not be left out, and the rest of the party consisted of Paul's best man, Tom, and Jess, his girlfriend.

They had been there four days already, since the couple needed to be resident for six days before a licence could be granted. The hotel was on St James Beach and everything was as beautifully Barbadosish as she'd imagined.

Having Guy beside her should have been not just the icing on top, but the cream too.

Should have been.

However he tried to hide it, his tension was taking the edge off what should have been an idyllic holiday. But every time she asked what was wrong, he fobbed her off.

She knew better than to ask him again now.

The warm, fiery rum did nothing to dispel the chilly unease in her stomach. *Does he want to be alone for a while? Is he finding it a bit much, being together twenty-four hours a day?* Slipping her arm out of his, she dropped a kiss on his cheek. 'I'll go and find Kate,' she said brightly. 'See whether she's murdered her mother yet.'

'See you later.' The smile he produced put her heart through the wringer. It was wry and lop-sided – and obviously made to order.

Kate and Paul's room wasn't far back from the beach, on the ground floor of one of the little blocks that nestled in the gardens.

They were sitting on their veranda with a couple of sundowners. 'They're called Big Bamboos,' Kate said as she sat down beside them. 'I haven't a clue what's in them but the barman said they're guaranteed to blow your head off. I asked him to send one up to my mother and blow her head off before I strangle her.'

'Kate, chill out,' said Paul. 'Humour her for the sake of P and Q.'

'But she's taking over,' Kate grumbled. 'I knew she would. First she doesn't like my dress, then she's trying to tell the hotel how to do the flowers, and now she's wittering on about bad luck if you see me on the day.'

'What's it matter?' he soothed. 'I'll move in with Guy or Tom and you stay here with Claudia or Jess.'

'If I've got to have anybody, it's going to be Claudia.'

'Claudia, then. Maybe it's not such a bad idea,' he added, sipping his drink reflectively. 'We can all slope off for a stag night at the Harbour Lights and leave you girls to natter and do your nails.'

Kate groaned. 'That's all I need. A hen night with not only my mother, but my mother-in-law too . . . And if you dare get completely ratso and turn up with a raging hangover, I'll divorce you instantly.'

'I won't get ratso,' he promised. 'Not more than usual anyway. What's more, I will undertake to keep my hands off all the gorgeous women who beg me to make their day before I'm lost for ever.'

'Oh, go away,' Kate said crossly. 'Go and have a shower or something.'

With a wink at Claudia, Paul departed, singing loudly about getting married in the morning.

'It's the day after tomorrow, you idiot,' Kate yelled after him. 'And don't use all the dry towels!'

Claudia gazed out at the gardens, sipping her drink. It was dark now, and the tree frogs woe really tuning up. From somewhere in the distance came the sound of soft calypso. It would all be perfect, if only . . .

Paul had left the sliding doors a little open. He was still singing. Kate glanced behind her and sighed. 'He must really love me. What with my mother driving me round the bend I've been really ratty to the poor lamb and he's never said a word.'

'You're lucky,' Claudia said. 'Don't ever take him for granted.'

Instantly Kate picked up the unsteadiness in her tone. 'What's wrong?'

'Nothing.' She forced a smile. 'Maybe too much *Jolly Roger* rum punch this morning.'

'I kept right off the rum punch,' Kate said. 'Our breakfast waiter warned me about it.' They had all gone on the famous pirate cruise that morning; all except Kate's mother, who'd said it looked too rowdy. They had danced themselves dizzy on deck, eaten huge steaks for lunch, and laughed themselves sick when Kate had been ambushed by the pirate crew and 'forced' at cutlass-point to walk the plank.

'It was all dead corny but hilarious fun,' Kate said. 'I wouldn't have missed it for anything.'

Claudia managed a smile. 'Nor would I. Guy didn't really want to go but he had to admit it was fun afterwards. It's one of those things you have to do once, like Disneyland.'

'The music was fantastic,' Kate sighed. 'I was still dancing about four hours after we got off.' She frowned. 'Claudia, what's wrong?'

'It's Guy.' Her face crumpled. 'He's gone really quiet and odd. He's trying to cover it, but I can tell. I've seen him like this before, when we were in Muscat. Something's on his mind, and . . . and I think it's me,' she gulped. 'We've never been together so long before, not continuously. I think maybe he's beginning to wonder whether it's such a good idea. I think he's getting fed up with me.'

'Oh, rubbish,' Kate scoffed. 'He was fine this morning, on the *Jolly Roger*!'

'Yes, but that was different, with masses of other people around. It's when it's just him and me. I've just left him on the beach, gazing at the sea. He was miles away.'

'Maybe his thinking about work,' Kate soothed. 'You know what men are. Thinking somebody's going to screw something up while they're away. They all think they're indispensable.'

'If it's just that, why won't he tell me?' She gulped again. 'It's something else. I think he's going off me and he doesn't like to say.'

'Claudia, that's rubbish!'

'Will you stop saying it's rubbish? You haven't seen him.' She bit her lip, trying to stop herself breaking down altogether. 'I might have known it was too good to last. He went off that Simone when he met me. Maybe he's met somebody else and can't bring himself to tell me.'

'Oh, rubb – ' Kate checked herself. 'I'm sure he hasn't. Go back to him now and tell him you're not going away till he tells you what's wrong.

'I can't.' She wiped away another tear. 'I'm terrified to ask in case he tells me.'

For the first time Kate looked genuinely concerned. 'I'm sure you're getting worked up for nothing. For heaven's sake ask him. Put your mind at rest.'

I'm sure. Why did people always say 'I'm sure' when they were nothing of the sort? 'I'm *sure* I turned the iron off.' 'I'm *sure* I posted that letter . . .'

But, sure or not, she was beginning to wish she'd kept quiet. Kate had quite enough to put up with just before her wedding with her mother. She didn't need any worries like this to cloud her happiness. And she *was* happy, despite the minor irritations.

She forced a smile. 'I expect you're right. I always get myself worked up over nothing.'

'You always were a silly cow.'

'I know.' She drained her drink, said, 'See you at dinner, then,' and departed.

Halfway back to the beach, she turned and looked back. Kate was gone from the veranda already. Gone to tell all to Paul, no doubt. Which only proved one thing.

That however much she'd 'rubbished', Kate wasn't sure it was rubbish at all. Maybe she'd even picked something up. Maybe Paul had. Maybe they'd even discussed it already. Feeling sick, she returned to the beach, but Guy was gone.

Their room was even closer to the beach, on the first floor, with a glorious view out over the sea. He was in the shower when she got back. She called, 'Hi', and went to sit on the balcony.

From there she could hear the lap of wavelets on the shore. Tiny bats flitted about, catching insects on the wing. A gecko clung motionless to the rough coral stone wall, only a pulse in its throat showing that it was alive.

Guy seemed cheerful enough when he emerged, clad in just a towel round his waist. He had gone a gorgeous brown within twenty-four hours of arriving, and his body was as firmly muscled as ever. Once or twice she had almost wished it wasn't. It was impossible not to notice the glances of other women, and one or two were quite blatant about it, giving Claudia glances that said, *I'd pinch him if I could*. He hadn't eyed anybody up in return, but coupled with his odd, preoccupied tension it had made her horribly uneasy. For the first time in their four-month relationship, she had begun to feel insecure.

'All yours,' he said, and dropped a kiss on her hair. 'Has Kate murdered the old girl yet?'

Maybe I was worrying about nothing. 'They've signed a truce for now. But it looks as if we'll be playing musical

365

rooms tomorrow night – me in with Kate and you with Paul.' Although he was a few years older than Paul, they had become good friends, which had only added to her happiness.

'That's no problem.' He sat on the other rattan chair and put his feet up on the little coffee-table. 'Aren't you going to have a shower?'

Clad in only a black T-shirt over her bikini, Claudia was still salty from her last swim. 'In a minute.' She hesitated, then said, 'Guy, you're not worried about work, are you?'

He looked genuinely startled. 'Whatever gave you that idea?'

She hesitated again. 'You've seemed a bit, well, pre-occupied the last day or two.'

He hesitated just a moment too long. For a second, even in the dim balcony light, she could have sworn she saw a fleeting guilt in his eyes. 'Just finding it difficult to unwind,' he said, a little too easily.

'I thought so.' *Oh, how easily the lies trip off my tongue.* 'But you know what they say about Barbados. Relaxation comes with the oxygen. They've got a factory somewhere, belting it out into the atmosphere.' She rose to her feet. 'I'll go and wash this salt off and make myself all beautiful for dinner.'

His mouth gave a wry twist. 'Not too beautiful, please. That Italian guy at the next table had his eye on you last night, and I don't want to start an international incident.'

It wasn't her imagination. There was definitely something forced in his tone, as if he were making a conscious effort.

366

So she did the same. 'How do you know I didn't have my eye on him too?' she said mischievously. 'He was as dishy as the *Good Food Guide*.'

Wishing at once she hadn't said it, she came up behind his chair, slid her arms around him. 'I was only joking,' she said, kissing his hair.

'You'd better be.' He looked up and aimed a kiss at her lips. 'Now clear off to the shower before I get seriously cross.'

Biting back tears, she left him. Something was horribly wrong. He'd never been like this before, seeming almost wanting to be rid of her.

She drew the balcony curtains. The room was huge, with two double beds, and the lovely bathroom had twin basins and a shower that gushed heavenly hot water.

But when she was miserable Clauida always preferred a bath. She poured in moisturising foam and lay a while before washing her hair and soaping herself.

Not so long ago, he'd never have been sitting out on the balcony while she was in the bath. He'd have found some excuse to come in. He'd have sat on the side with a wicked glint in his eye, offering to help. And she'd have giggled and splashed him or thrown a sponge at him, soaking him so much that he'd have had to take his shirt off.

And before you could say, Where's the soap? he'd have been in there with her, giving her the most thoroughly erotic soaping of her life, followed by enough wet and wild horseplay to have them both far too shattered for dinner. They'd have slept till ten and then ordered something thoroughly self-indulgent from room service.

And now he didn't want to know.

She stood under the shower, rinsing her hair, then turned it off. She stepped out, grabbed a towel, and paused.

The door was closed. That was odd. She'd left it open at least a crack. Had he closed it while she was under the shower? And if so, why?

Hating herself for doing it, she opened it a crack, and listened.

The television was on – CNN news – but that wasn't all. He was on the phone. Holding her breath, she listened, feeling sicker by the second.

In a low, tense voice, he was saying, 'I know. I've tried to tell her, but . . .' After a pause he went on, 'I know. Of course she does. She's not stupid. Look, love, I'll try . . .'

Feeling physically sick, she closed the door as silently as she'd opened it.

She wiped the steam off the bathroom mirror and gazed at herself. Her face was barely dusted with gold, even after four days. Barbados only thirteen degrees north of the equator, and the sun was just too strong for her to lie in for more than ten minutes.

Not that she cared a damn just now. *What did you expect?* she asked her reflection miserably. *Did you really think it was going to be Happy Ever After with a man like him? Get real, Claudia. This is no fairytale. This is life – and, as we all know, life's a bitch.*

But not for anything was she going to let even a whisper show. Not for anything was she going to cast a gloom on Kate and Paul's big day. For two more days she would keep a bright, happy face on, and then it would be easy. The happy couple were going for a mini-cruise in the

Grenadines, the assorted guests were staying a few more days, and then they were all going home. Back to reality.

She dried her hair with the in-house drier and did her face in the mirror. By the time she emerged she had psyched herself up into a forced gaiety worthy of a game-show host.

Already dressed, Guy was back on the balcony with a newspaper. He had closed the sliding doors, but the curtains were open.

She drew them before getting dressed in a little jade silk top that showed just enough cleavage. Her legs weren't brown enough to flash, however, so she teamed it with a pair of cream linen trousers.

He was acting like mad, but not quite well enough. 'You look gorgeous,' he said, almost as if he meant it, and slid an arm around her waist. 'I can see I'm going to have trouble with that Italian guy tonight. It might even come to a punch-up.'

Anything you can do, I can do better . . .

'Dear me,' she said reprovingly. 'If you're going to get all horrendously possessive, I might have to think again about this relationship.'

She longed with desperation for him to say roughly, 'How can I help being possessive? Don't you know how I feel about you?'

Dream on, Claudia.

His only reply was a tense, 'I'm sorry – I didn't mean it literally. If you're ready, let's go.'

All through dinner, in the open air dining room with just a roof to keep the odd tropical shower off, she acted her brains out, laughing and talking as much as anybody.

After dinner, when she popped to the ladies', Kate joined her.

'I can see you're feeling better,' she said.

'I was just being daft,' Claudia said, with a little laugh. 'My imagination going into overdrive, as usual.'

Kate could not quite hide her relief. 'I told you it was nothing.'

You hoped it was nothing, you mean. You don't want this place turning into Heartbreak Hotel for your wedding day. 'And you were right, as usual. He's just strung-out. All this enforced relaxation is killing him.'

They had their liqueurs under the stars, sitting round a little dance floor where a steel band was playing 'Island In The Sun'.

Even Kate had mellowed. 'Just look at Mum and Dad,' she sighed fondly, as her parents took to the floor. 'Wrapped round each other like a pair of teenagers. I always thought this was such a corny song till now, but out here, with all those stars . . .' She grabbed Paul's hand. 'On your feet, O husband-to-be, and smooch me round the floor.'

Everybody was dancing except her and Guy, and Tom and his girlfriend Jess, who'd only just sat down after a couple of faster numbers.

All evening she'd tried to ignore Guy's tense preoccupation. After dinner he had been even more restless. As soon as the band had started playing, he'd dragged her on the the floor and danced with an energy that had startled her. But now, just when she was dying to drift in his arms to something so liltingly West Indian, so wonderfully sentimental, he was staring into space, restlessly tapping their room key against his thigh.

Just as she was feeling so miserable she wanted to die, the Italian appeared from nowhere. 'Please, you like to dance?'

She was just about to say, I'd love to, when Guy snapped out of his reverie. 'She's just about to dance,' he said, rather more curtly than necessary. 'With me.'

Until they were actually on the floor, she was too shocked to protest. Automatically she slid her arms round his neck as he held her round the waist, and they started drifting to the haunting music.

Eventually she found her voice. 'Guy, how could you be so rude?'

'He shouldn't muscle in on other men's women.' Holding her firmly, he steered her away from a fat couple who were about to collide with them.

Still angry with him, she stiffened. 'I am not *your* woman. I suppose that's why you wanted to pay the hotel bill? To give you property rights?'

If she hadn't been so upset in the first place she'd never have said it, and she wished instantly she hadn't. The forthcoming bill had sparked their first real argument. He had assumed he'd pay it; she'd assumed they'd go halves.

He stiffened in return. 'For God's sake, if you thought I was trying to *buy* you – '

'I didn't. I just don't want you behaving like some prehistoric fossil. It's not a crime to ask someone to dance.'

'I didn't mind him asking. What I minded was him leering at you half the night.'

'He wasn't!'

'He was.'

371

Talk about dog in the manger, she thought, nearly in tears.

The floor was packed now, as all those couples who didn't care for the more energetic stuff decided it was time to get rid of a few calories. Continually he steered her away from imminent collision.

'You can't blame him for looking,' she said, her mask discarded at last. 'The amount of attention you were paying me, he probably thought we were nothing more than fifth cousins three times removed.'

She knew at once that this had hit home. He drew back a fraction, and there was no mistaking the guilt in his eyes. But there was something else there too. *Anguish? Pain? Forgive me, for what I am about to do . . .?*

Before she could be sure, he closed his eyes and drew her close. 'I'm sorry,' he whispered into her hair. 'I'm just wound up.'

He didn't have to tell her. She could feel it. His shoulders were tense as coiled springs. She longed to melt into him, but he wouldn't melt. Suddenly desperate, she caressed his neck and shoulders, inhaling his warmth and the scent of that lethal aftershave, praying for the Guy she knew and loved to return.

For a minute or two it worked. He melted, holding her close, his breath warm on her hair as they drifted to the lilting music. Until another couple with two left feet each collided with them and shattered the magic.

'This is impossible,' he muttered, putting her from him. 'It's worse than the M25 on a bad day. Let's go for a walk on the beach.' Without waiting for a reply, he steered her through the crush with a hand on her waist, and down the path to the beach. A terrace overlooked the water; one or two couples were standing there, gazing out at the shimmering water.

He walked with quick, tense steps, and she knew with dreadful certainty that whatever was on his mind was about to come out.

Suddenly she was almost angry. Couldn't he have waited? Acted his brains out like she had all evening? Couldn't he at least have waited till after the wedding, for the sake of form?

But he said nothing until they were right away from the hotel. It was nearly dark, with only the odd lamp strung high in the feathery casuarinas that fringed the beach.

Eventually they sat in the soft sand. 'I shouldn't have said that,' he said. 'About other men's women. I don't own you.'

'You were behaving as if you did.' Her voice was tight and taut. 'I think you should apologize to him.'

'I will. If you want me to.'

'I do.'

For a long time neither of them spoke, but she knew he wanted to. She almost knew the words he was trying to form.

'As I said, I don't own you. And you don't own me, either. We're both free as air. No commitment on either side, as I'm sure you've understood from the start, being the thoroughly modern woman you are. And so you will naturally be perfectly civilized about it when I tell you . . .'

But all he said was, 'If we get through the next forty-eight hours without some sort of major drama, it won't be for want of trying.'

Like you and me busting up and you getting the first plane home? 'Like what?' she said. 'Kate and her mother seem to have settled down, and I can't see anything else spoiling it – unless one of them gets cold feet.'

'That won't happen,' he said.

'No.'

'They made up their minds months ago.'

'Exactly. They know exactly what they're doing.'

For a moment there was silence, except for the chorus of tree frogs and the lapping of tiny waves.

Claudia was very close to tears. Half of her wanted him to say it and get it over with; half of her wanted to run away before he did.

Tension hung over them like a cloud of noxious gas, and eventually she could bear it no longer. 'I'm going back,' she said, rising suddenly to her feet. 'You stay here if you want.'

Instantly he picked up the taut edge to her voice. 'You mean you'd rather be on your own?'

'I didn't say that! Why are you putting words in my mouth?' *Is that what you want to hear?*

'I wasn't!'

'You were!' She began a quick walk back to the hotel. 'You do what you want, Guy. I really couldn't care less.'

He was walking close beside her. 'And what's that supposed to mean?'

'Nothing. Except that I've got a good mind to go and find that Italian and tell him you *are* my fifth cousin three times removed. You haven't exactly been a bundle of laughs all night.'

He stopped dead in the sand. 'Claudia . . .'

'Oh, get lost,' she muttered, close to tears.

Before she had gone three paces, he caught her up. 'For crying out loud, let's not row. Not in front of all the others.'

'Who's rowing?'

His only answer was an exasperated sigh.

By the time they returned, the parents had drifted off to bed. Kate and Paul were still there, with Tom and Jess, laughing together.

They turned expectant faces. 'What have you two been up to?' Kate said mischievously.

'Just looking at the sea.' Claudia forced a huge yawn. 'I'm exhausted. Guy, can I have the key? I'm going up.'

She made a great show of giving him a goodnight kiss. 'Shall I leave the door open?'

'Don't leave it unlocked,' he said. 'I can get a spare from Reception if you're asleep.'

'OK.' With a bright smile she added, 'Night everybody. Sweet dreams,' and left them.

It was twenty minutes before Guy came, opening the door softly. 'Are you awake?' he asked, very softly.

She had turned all the lights off, but he'd opened the bathroom door a fraction and turned the light on. Even so, it was easy enough to feign sleep, breathing quietly and evenly and keeping her eyelids motionless. She felt him watching her for several seconds, and then she heard him undress and brush his teeth.

He slipped into bed beside her, but did not put his arm round her and make spoons, as he usually did. He lay on his back, and she knew perfectly well that he was staring at the walls.

He lay like that for ages, and for once she was glad she was not a mind-reader. Just as she was drifting off to sleep, she heard him say softly, 'Oh, Christ. What the hell am I going to do?' He turned towards her and finally slipped an arm around her.

Still pretending to be asleep, she wriggled it off, as if she were dreaming about something nasty getting hold of her. He retreated, turned on his other side, and then there was silence.

When she awoke at twenty past six, he was gone. She tiptoed to the sliding doors and drew the curtains back, but he wasn't on the balcony.

He had to be on the beach. The first two days, still on their English clocks which were five hours ahead, they had woken very early and walked miles down deserted beaches before breakfast.

When their breakfast came, at seven-thirty, he still wasn't back. The waiter was very cheerful, laying the table on their balcony and setting out mangoes and pancakes, bacon, coffee and toast, while hordes of tiny birds twittered up, clinging to the coral stone walls as they waited for pickings.

She ate alone. Or picked alone. And sat still as the little yellow birds finished her mango and helped themselves from the sugar bowl.

At eight-thirty there was a knock at the door.

It was a maid in a pink uniform. She had a dress on a hanger, sheathed in plastic. 'The dress you sent for pressing, dear.'

It was some full-skirted thing, not remotely like anything Claudia possessed. 'It's not mine,' she said, shaking her head. 'They must have put the wrong room number on it.'

376

Five minutes later, Guy showed up. His hair was wet, like his shorts and T-shirt.

'Where have you been?' she demanded, torn between anger and tears.

His tension was worse than ever, reminding her of a firework in the last smouldering instant before it went off. 'For a walk,' he said, running tense fingers through his hair. 'I went further than I'd thought. I grabbed a lift back with an early ski-boat, but he ran out of fuel miles away. Right down by Sandy Lane.'

Suddenly something in him seemed to snap. 'Claudia, I've got to talk to you.'

'I'm just going to have a shower.'

'I don't care. I need to talk now.' He actually grabbed her, dragged her to the bed and sat her down. 'There's something I've got to tell you. I've been trying to tell you for days, but . . .'

Oh, God. Please, not now. I can't bear it.

She had never seen him like this. He actually paced the room, running fingers through increasingly wild hair, his voice tense and anguished. 'I must have been out of my mind. It seemed like a good idea at the time, but it was taking a hell of a lot for granted – I never even asked you, for God's sake. We don't have to go through with it, I can tell them to cancel everything. And if you tell me to get lost I won't blame you – God knows what you'll be thinking after last night – I must have been mad to even think you'd want to . . .'

As his voice tailed off she gazed at him, her mind a whirl of confusion.

'To what?' she asked faintly.

CHAPTER 19

His face was a picture of almost comical despair. 'It was the most monumental piece of arrogance – I don't know what the hell came over me. I fixed everything, even down to something blue. I did everything but ask you first.'

For the first time in her life, Claudia all but fainted.

A couple of minutes later, when it had sunk in and she was in his arms and they had kissed and she had confessed her ghastly fears and they'd both laughed and cried, Planet Earth called her back.

Oh, God. How can I bear to disappoint him now?

'Guy, I want to – more than anything,' she said unsteadily. 'But I can't. Not like this. If I deprive my mother of the second biggest day of her life, she'll never, ever forgive me.'

His eyes were glinting like the waters they'd sailed the morning before – fathoms-deep Caribbean blue, with the sun on it. 'Is that your only objection?'

'Yes, but – '

'Then forget it.' He brushed her forehead with his lips. 'I have a magic wand in my back pocket.'

* * *

For the rest of the day she floated on a cloud of pink champagne bubbles, alternately laughing and crying, and frequently doing both at once.

'I just think it's the most romantic thing in the world,' sighed Jess as they lay by the pool.

Sunlight dappled the water and, overhead, lazy coconuts waved their fronds in the breeze. Somewhere a dove was cooing softly.

Only Kate and Paul had known. 'It nearly killed me, keeping quiet,' Kate said. 'Ever since we were all out for lunch at the White Swan, remember? Just after he'd decided to come after all?'

That had been barely a month ago. 'Is that where you cooked it up? At the White Swan?'

Kate nodded. 'You went off to the loo or something, and I'd had about three gins and made some daft crack about double weddings and Paul kicked me under the table and said, "For God's sake, give them a chance," and then it dawned on us both that Guy had a certain glint in his eye. He said he'd already thought of it, and I nearly went crackers, and Paul told me to shut up, and Guy said did we think he'd be able to arrange it in time, and then you came back and we all had to pretend we were talking about something else.'

Claudia's eyes widened. 'My God, so you were. The by-election result. I thought it was rather odd how you were all getting so worked up about it.'

Kate giggled. 'I thought we carried it off very well. It was partly my idea to make a surprise of it. I mean, I knew you were absolutely potty about him and he was obviously potty about you, and I told him how you just loved surprises and this'd be the surprise to end them all. In short, as they say, none of us could see so much as a teeny-weeny ant in the ointment. He would have waited till today to tell you, anyway.'

'He told me.' Claudia's throat constricted. 'He'd had it all worked out. He was going to take me for an early walk on the beach, pop the question, and then have a champagne breakfast sent up and tell me he just happened to have a couple of rings in his pocket.'

'Gosh, how romantic,' sighed Jess. 'Not that I think I'd want champagne first thing. I'm useless till I've had a cup of tea.'

Kate gave an explosive giggle, but Claudia's eyes were misting. 'Poor Guy. After he'd gone to all that trouble . . .'

'But the best-laid plans . . .' Kate sighed. 'It was all fine until about the day before we left, and then he started getting ants in his pants. Started thinking you'd have a fit. You'd think it was a bloody nerve – how dare he just presume? Etcetera, Etcetera. I kept telling him you'd be over the moon, but he wouldn't have it. As for yesterday, when you were getting all in a state . . . And if you *will* listen to phone calls . . .'

'I feel awful now.' It had been Kate, telling him for heaven's sake to just *tell* her.

'And after he'd arranged to fly your parents out and everything . . .' Kate went on.

'Never mind his mother and her husband. *And* Anoushka. No wonder he was in such a state. What if I'd said no?'

They all started laughing so helplessly that a passing waiter grinned and asked, 'Was it those Fuzzy Navels? Can I get you ladies another?'

'Better not,' Kate giggled. 'Your cocktails are all lethal, and my friend here has to meet her mother-in-law for the first time this afternoon.'

'Oh, Lord' he grinned. 'Don't fret, dear. She'll be cool. Everybody's cool when they hit Barbados. It's something in the water.'

Dreamily content, Claudia lay watching a tiny humming-bird hover on iridescent wings round a shrub with red bell-like flowers.

'What on earth did Mum and Dad say?' she wondered aloud. 'Did you speak to them first?'

'Yes, Guy thought it'd be better,' Kate said. 'Your mother was only gobsmacked for about ten seconds. He obviously scored a massive hit when you took him out to Spain for that weekend.'

He certainly had. All too vividly Claudia recalled her first minutes alone with her mother. She'd dragged her into the kitchen and whispered, 'I must say, dear, he seems very charming. Is it serious?'

'Your old man was a bit more cautious,' Kate went on, 'but between me and Guy and your mother we wore the poor man down. And I spent *hours* looking for that dress – so if you don't love it, I'll kill you. I can't think how I came to write the wrong room number on the thingy. Too many Big Bamboos, I suppose.'

Guy strolled up, in a pair of navy shorts and a white polo shirt. 'I'm just off to the airport,' he said, bending down to kiss her.

'Are you sure you don't want me to come?'

'No, you stay and relax.'

She watched him go. 'I feel awful,' she said. 'We've got to go again later, for my parents and Anoushka. He'll be in a taxi half the day.'

'Never mind,' said Kate comfortably. 'Makes them feel useful, buzzing about organizing things. We have to save our energy for looking radiant tomorrow, so our mothers can go all weepy. And, talking of mothers, I do hope you're going to like his. Not that it matters much if she lives in Boston. She'll hardly be popping in every five minutes telling you how he likes his fried eggs.'

Much to Claudia's relief, she took to Guy's mother immediately. Sarah was very much like him: tall, elegant and charming without being in the least pushy.

Her own mother barely stopped talking all the way from the airport. 'Well, dear,' she said, once she'd got her alone, 'You always said you couldn't stand boring, predictable men. I'd have preferred you to do it properly, of course, in church, but as long as you're happy.'

'But it *is* a church service, Mum, more or less. They send a vicar, and he's Church of England. They have Church of England here too, you know. And they make a lovely little wedding-thing in the gardens, all covered with flowers.'

'Oh, well. As long as I get some really lovely photos to show the bridge club.'

Kate's mother found an ally in Margaret Maitland. 'I told them they couldn't *possibly* share a room the night before,' she said flatly, over their pre-dinner drinks. 'It's terribly bad luck.'

'Quite right,' said Margaret Maitland firmly. 'I never heard of such a thing.'

'So it's worked out quite nicely,' Kate's mother went on. 'The two brides and the two grooms sharing. Mind you, I wouldn't put it past them to swap back later. I think we'll have to mount a watch, just to be on the safe side.'

'Never mind all that,' said her father. 'Let's just drink a toast to the happy couples.'

Across the table, Anoushka grinned at her. 'And to my wicked stepmother. When I think of all the awful women he could have landed me with, I suppose I should congratulate myself on a lucky escape.'

'Just a couple more, dear,' called Claudia's mother. 'Might as well finish the film.'

'Oh, *Mum*. You've taken *hundreds* of photos.'

Guy's mouth was twitching merrily. 'Humour her,' he whispered into her hair. 'After she's come all this way, a few more won't kill us.'

It was already sunset, and they were on the beach. There had been photos in the gardens, photos in the flowery wedding-bower, photos with every conceivable person – right down to the waiters and the man who drove the ski-boat, who'd popped in to wish them well. Everybody else was now partying in the garden, with oceans of rum punch and champagne.

'I must say, that dress is just lovely,' said her mother for the ninety-third time.

And it was: plain, strapless, of rustling cream silk with a full skirt that came to mid-calf. In Claudia's hair was a circlet of flowers, prepared by the hotel hairdresser.

Her only jewellery was a string of perfect, real pearls bestowed by Guy as a wedding present. His other present had been a garter of blue silk forget-me-nots, so enchantingly pretty she'd hated hiding it. Kate had accordingly demanded she flash her thigh for a quick photo, to give it its moment of glory.

Guy glanced down at her pink-tipped toes in the sand. 'I knew I'd forget something vital and screw everything up,' he said wryly. 'But you make a beautiful barefoot bride.'

Only at the last minute had they all realized that she had no shoes to go with the dress and neither did anybody else – none that fitted her.

For the umpteenth time that day, her eyes misted. 'Oh, Guy. Do you really think I care about shoes on a day like this?'

'Last one,' called her mother. 'A nice kiss in the sunset, please, with – '

'They don't need telling, dear,' said her father.

Margaret Maitland snapped her last. 'Lovely,' she sighed. 'That'll be one in the eye for Maureen Waters and her wretched daughter's wedding. Terribly fussy dress she had, however much it cost. And I can't see what's so special about a vintage Rolls. Every Tom, Dick and Harry turns up at the church in a vintage Rolls these days.'

The taxi from Heathrow took longer than she'd thought. 'I'll pay you now,' she told the driver. 'Are you sure you know what to do?'

'You've told me enough times, love.'

She checked the meter, added a mark-up and handed some notes over.

'Ta, love. Hope it's not a bomb you're giving him.'

'It's his birthday. And the anniversary of when we first met. He thinks I'm still in Amsterdam, you see. I told him I couldn't get home.'

'Hope he'll be in, then.'

'He will. I told him I'd phone at eight o'clock.'

'What if somebody else comes to the door?'

'They won't.' Mrs Pierce was at her sister's, and Anoushka was on a Spanish exchange trip.

Mrs Pierce had turned out to be not such a bad old stick after all. Her crust was thick as school-dinner pastry, but the filling was sweet enough – and if it tasted of vinegar now and then, it was usually because her corns were playing her up.

At last the taxi made it through the traffic to the street Guy had first taken her to nearly a year ago. There was no danger of him seeing them; it was dark, the curtains drawn.

She concealed herself at the side of the front door while the driver rang the bell.

'Special delivery from Amsterdam, mate,' he said, when the door finally opened.

'Good Lord.' She could hear how pleased he was. 'Should I sign for it?'

'No need, mate. Ta-ta.'

She had to be quick, before he shut the door. As the driver disappeared down the steps, she stepped smartly from her hiding place.

His face was a picture, even before she opened her coat to reveal the black satin teddy, the black stockings and suspenders. She whipped the red rose from her cleavage and handed it to him. 'Happy birthday, Guy,' she said, with only the tiniest wobble.

They were both laughing as he swept her into his arms and kicked the door shut. They were still laughing as they collapsed on the sitting room sofa.

She wriggled out of her coat and tossed it over the back of the sofa. 'It was a cream teddy last time, but you once said you'd have preferred black.'

'I remember.' He was still laughing as he scooped her up and onto his lap.

'You also said I looked like an ex-convent girl pretending to be wicked. I was most put out.'

He ran his fingers over the black stockings, to the creamy skin at their tops. 'That was before I knew how wicked you could really be.'

'But I think I'm wickeder in black,' she giggled. 'Black silk is wickeder than cream, don't you think?'

'You could be wicked in a bin-liner.' He ran his hand over her hair, and down over the back of her neck to where he knew just how to get that erogenous zone going. 'But wicked in silk is special.'

'Of course. It's your birthday.'

'But when you've been away six whole days . . .' his lips brushed her shoulder and he slipped the shoestring strap off it '. . . I think I prefer you wicked in nothing at all.'

The fire was lit and the room was very warm. The lamps were low, and the sofa plenty big enough for all sorts of activities it wasn't quite intended for.

Portly tactfully slept through it all. He was curled up on the smallest sofa, the one he now considered his own.

When their own fires had died down, they sprawled by the coal one. 'You haven't opened your present,' she said.

'I thought I just did,' he grinned, but opened the little parcel anyway. It was real caviare from Schipol Airport, something he loved.

'I've got to have it right now,' he said, giving her a kiss as he departed for the kitchen.

He returned with buttered toast and a bottle of wine and they sat and made pigs of themselves by the fire. 'I'm sorry I didn't get you a proper present,' she said, when the pot was half empty. 'At least, I've sort of ordered something, but it'll take a while to come.'

'Are you going to tell me, or is it a secret?'

'You have to guess.'

'Give me a clue, then.'

She thought. 'Each one's different.'

'Hand-made, presumably?'

She was bursting to laugh. 'Not exactly.'

'What do you mean, not exactly?'

'I mean "not exactly".' She had really got him going now. He wore that expression of maddened curiosity he adopted when the last crossword clue was eluding him.

'Give me another clue.'

She wasn't going to put him out of his misery just yet. 'You're getting a bit dense in your old age,' she teased. 'All this being wicked must be affecting your brain.'

As she'd almost known he would, he grabbed her, tickling her unmercifully until she was rolling helplessly on the rug, trying to fend off his marauding fingers. 'Stop!'

'Give me another clue, then. Before I renew my offensive.'

'You're playing dirty,' she protested through her giggles. 'I'm hardly in a position to counter-attack.' She was flat on her back on the rug, her wrists held firm as he leaned over her.

He bent down and dropped a kiss on her nose. 'Surrender, then.'

She gazed up at him. 'They come in two colours. Blue or pink. But you have to take pot luck.'

Ten minutes later he was still like the dog who'd had the Christmas turkey, bacon-wrapped sausages and all.

'What do you think Anoushka'll say?' she wondered aloud as they sat gazing into the fire.

'She'll be over the moon.'

'Are you sure?'

'Absolutely.' His arm tightened around her. 'The other day she said, "Are you and Claudia going to have any kids, or have I put you off for life?"'

She laughed. 'I expect you'd like a blue one, wouldn't you?'

'I don't care, as long as it's one or the other.'

'I think we should have a blue one, for your sake. What with me and Anoushka and Mrs Pierce, you're sadly outnumbered.'

'I've got Portly,' he grinned.

'Portly doesn't count. He's hardly a proper male, bless him.'

She glanced at the sofa, but Portly had found something more enticing than slumber. He'd sneaked up behind them and was helping himself from the caviare pot on the tray.

'You bad animal!' she scolded. 'That was your father's birthday present!'

'Leave him,' Guy soothed. 'The poor beast has few enough pleasures. And I've got an even better present to look forward to.'

'But it's an awful long wait,' she sighed. 'I'll be like St Paul's Cathedral, waddling like Jemima Puddleduck. And you'll be looking at me and wishing your present came in a less hideous wrapper.'

His mouth twitched. 'You'll be so hideous, I'll probably run off with Mrs Pierce.'

She stifled a giggle. 'I think you'd make the perfect couple. You can sit in the evenings discussing the merits of various corn plasters and moaning about all the sex on the television.'

'Don't forget everyone's ailments. Mrs Whatsit's waterworks and Mr So-and-So's embarrassing flatulence.'

She burst out laughing.

The firelight glinted in his eyes as he laced his fingers through her own, raised them to his lips, and kissed them. 'You'll be like a ship in full sail. All serene and beautiful.'

'I bet I won't.'

'You will.'

'I won't. I'll be so huge and waddly – '

Portly looked up from his caviare. Really, these humans. At it again, with that mouths-stuck-together carry-on. Why ever did they want to eat each other when there were such delicious nibbles going begging?

He'd never understand them . . .

THE EXCITING NEW NAME
IN WOMEN'S FICTION!

PLEASE HELP ME TO HELP YOU!

Dear *Scarlet* Reader,

As Editor of *Scarlet* Books I want to make sure that the books I offer you every month are up to the high standards *Scarlet* readers expect. And to do that I need to know a little more about you and your reading likes and dislikes. So please spare a few minutes to fill in the short questionnaire on the following pages and send it to me. I'll send *you* a surprise gift as a thank you!*

Looking forward to hearing from you,

Sally Cooper

Editor-in-Chief, *Scarlet*

*Offer applies only in the UK, only one offer per household.

Note: Further offers which might be of interest may be sent to you by other, carefully selected, companies. If you do not want to receive them, please write to Robinson Publishing Ltd, 7 Kensington Church Court, London W8 4SP, UK.

QUESTIONNAIRE

Please tick the appropriate boxes to indicate your answers

1 Where did you get this Scarlet title?
Bought in supermarket ☐
Bought at my local bookstore ☐ Bought at chain bookstore ☐
Bought at book exchange or used bookstore ☐
Borrowed from a friend ☐
Other (please indicate) _____

2 Did you enjoy reading it?
A lot ☐   A little ☐   Not at all ☐

3 What did you particularly like about this book?
Believable characters ☐   Easy to read ☐
Good value for money ☐   Enjoyable locations ☐
Interesting story ☐   Modern setting ☐
Other _____

4 What did you particularly dislike about this book?
_____

5 Would you buy another Scarlet book?
Yes ☐   No ☐

6 What other kinds of book do you enjoy reading?
Horror ☐   Puzzle books ☐   Historical fiction ☐
General fiction ☐   Crime/Detective ☐   Cookery ☐
Other (please indicate) _____

7 Which magazines do you enjoy reading?
1. _____
2. _____
3. _____

And now a little about you –
8 How old are you?
Under 25 ☐   25–34 ☐   35–44 ☐
45–54 ☐   55–64 ☐   over 65 ☐

cont.

9 What is your marital status?
  Single ☐   Married/living with partner ☐
  Widowed ☐   Separated/divorced ☐

10 What is your current occupation?
  Employed full-time ☐   Employed part-time ☐
  Student ☐   Housewife full-time ☐
  Unemployed ☐   Retired ☐

11 Do you have children? If so, how many and how old are they?
_____
_____

12 What is your annual household income?
  under $15,000 ☐ or £10,000 ☐
  $15–25,000 ☐ or £10–20,000 ☐
  $25–35,000 ☐ or £20–30,000 ☐
  $35–50,000 ☐ or £30–40,000 ☐
  over $50,000 ☐ or £40,000 ☐

Miss/Mrs/Ms _____
Address _____
_____
_____

Thank you for completing this questionnaire. Now tear it out – put it in an envelope and send it before 30 June, 1997, to:

Sally Cooper, Editor-in-Chief

USA/Can. address
SCARLET c/o London Bridge
85 River Rock Drive
Suite 202
Buffalo
NY 14207
USA

UK address/No stamp required
SCARLET
FREEPOST LON 3335
LONDON W8 4BR
Please use block capitals for address

WISIL/12/96

Scarlet titles coming next month:

WILD LADY   Liz Fielding
Book II of 'The Beaumont Brides' trilogy
Claudia is the actress sister of Fizz Beaumont (heroine of
WILD JUSTICE) and Gabriel MacIntyre thinks he
knows exactly what kind of woman she is . . . the kind
he despises! But Mac can't ignore the attraction between
them – particularly when Claudia's life is threatened!

DESTINIES   Maxine Barry
Book I of the 'All His Prey' duet
They say that opposites attract . . . well, Kier and Oriel are
definitely opposites. She is every inch a lady, while Kier
certainly isn't a gentleman! And while Oriel's and Kier's
story develops, the ever-present shadow of Wayne hangs
over them . . .

THE SHERRABY BRIDES   Kay Gregory
Simon Sebastian and Zack Kent are very reluctant bride-
grooms. So why is it that they can't stop thinking about
Olivia and Emma? Emma and Olivia don't need to talk to
each other about the men in their lives . . . these women
know exactly what they want . . . and how to get it!

WICKED LIAISONS   Laura Bradley
Sexily bad and dangerous to know – that's Cole Taylor!
Miranda Randolph knows she should avoid him at all costs –
until she looks into his blue, blue eyes. Miranda is different
to the other women in Cole's life and she's determined not to
let him add *her* name to those already in his little black book!